THE HIGHLANDER WHO WED ME

He gently tugged one of the glossy curls framing her face. "I wasn't nearly as careful with you as I should have been, lass. I can't tell you how sorry I am about that."

"You didn't know I was with child," she said earnestly. "So there's nothing to apologize for."

"But I knew *something* was wrong. I should have done more to help you, instead of letting you slip off to Cairndow all by yourself."

"If there is one person who should never apologize to me, it's you, Royal Kendrick. I owe you *everything*."

"You don't owe me anything, Ainsley. Truly." The *last* thing he wanted from her was the sense that all that bound her to him was obligation.

Gravely, she studied his face. He had the uncomfortable feeling she could read his mind.

"You are a very foolish man if you think that's the only reason I'm here," she said, confirming his suspicions. "I'm here because I want to be with you, not because I have to be with you."

Under her slender fingers, he could feel his heart begin to pound. "Do you think you could be more specific, Mrs. Kendrick?" Emotion had made his voice gruff. "Why are you here right now?"

A teasing smile, blessedly confident, curled up the corners of her lush mouth. "Why, for a good night kiss, of course . . ."

Books by Vanessa Kelly

MASTERING THE MARQUESS
SEX AND THE SINGLE EARL
MY FAVORITE COUNTESS
HIS MISTLETOE BRIDE

The Renegade Royals
SECRETS FOR SEDUCING A ROYAL BODYGUARD
CONFESSIONS OF A ROYAL BRIDEGROOM
HOW TO PLAN A WEDDING FOR A ROYAL SPY
HOW TO MARRY A ROYAL HIGHLANDER

The Improper Princesses
MY FAIR PRINCESS
THREE WEEKS WITH A PRINCESS
THE HIGHLANDER'S PRINCESS BRIDE

Clan Kendrick
THE HIGHLANDER WHO PROTECTED ME

Anthologies
AN INVITATION TO SIN
(with Jo Beverley, Sally MacKenzie, and Kaitlin O'Riley)

Published by Kensington Publishing Corporation

THE
Highlander Who Protected Me

VANESSA KELLY

ZEBRA BOOKS
KENSINGTON PUBLISHING CORP.
http://www.kensingtonbooks.com

ZEBRA BOOKS are published by

Kensington Publishing Corp.
119 West 40th Street
New York, NY 10018

All Kensington titles, imprints, and distributed lines are available at special quantity discounts for bulk purchases for sales promotion, premiums, fund-raising, educational, or institutional use.

Special book excerpts or customized printings can also be created to fit specific needs. For details, write or phone the office of the Kensington Sales Manager: Attn.: Sales Department. Kensington Publishing Corp., 119 West 40th Street, New York, NY 10018. Phone: 1-800-221-2647.

Zebra and the Z logo Reg. U.S. Pat. & TM Off.

First Printing: November 2018
ISBN-13: 978-1-4201-4115-3
ISBN-10: 1-4201-4115-5

eISBN-13: 978-1-4201-4116-0
eISBN-10: 1-4201-4116-3

10 9 8 7 6 5 4 3 2 1

Printed in the United States of America

To Dan, Naoko, and—of course—
Princess Abby. Long may she reign!

ACKNOWLEDGMENTS

With many thanks to my splendid agent and my equally splendid editor. I am *so* grateful for your support. And my gratitude to all the lovely folks at Kensington who do such great work and help to get my books out into the world. Thank you!

Finally, all my love to dear hubby, who makes my life so much easier. Writing books is not for the faint of heart; I couldn't do it without you!

Prologue

In the spare winter moonlight, she glowed with a beauty that lit up the corners of Royal Kendrick's battered soul. He felt alive again.

Lady Ainsley Matthews also possessed a lethal wit, one famed for sending even the most arrogant popinjay slinking off to the nearest corner. But to Royal, she was perfect, like a challenging book or complex piece of music. So perfect he'd never dared hope. He'd only dreamed—and feared, believing her notice of him was rooted in pity.

Earlier tonight, fate had placed them next to each other at dinner, a crowded affair noisy enough to give the illusion of privacy. An elderly, deaf matron had been seated to Royal's left, while Ainsley's other dinner partner was a rotund gourmand who cared only for his food. Left to their own devices, Royal and Ainsley had talked of everything and nothing, able to focus—for once—on each other.

When he'd proposed an escape from the overheated ballroom for a stroll along this quiet, dimly lit corridor, she'd said yes. Now, without hesitation, her steadfast gaze was letting him know she wanted this moment, too.

Royal wanted more than a moment. He wanted the pale, smooth skin, the shining obsidian hair, and the dark dramatic brows that framed the most impossible gaze in the world. Her eyes were the color of violets, a rich velvet-blue and so vivid he wondered they didn't cast a light of their own. Just gazing at her vibrant beauty made his heart ache even more than his leg. That was a bloody miracle, given that his damn leg had been trying to kill him ever since that appalling day at Waterloo.

Another body part ached too, and with unseemly intensity thankfully hidden by the drape of his kilt. Insanely, Royal desired the brightest diamond of the *ton* more than anything he'd ever wanted—more than a leg restored to health, more than a family resurrected from emotional ruin, more than a life untrammeled by war. His yearning for Ainsley made no damn sense, because *they* made no damn sense.

She studied him, her expression revealing an unspoken question.

"What?" he asked.

"Sir, we can sit down in that alcove if you'd like to rest your leg."

Whenever he heard Ainsley's voice, he imagined lying in a field thick with pansies that matched the color of her eyes. It muddled his brain, making it impossible to think.

Her frown deepened. "You look ready to topple over. That would be distressing for both of us, especially me if you fell in my direction."

That was pure Ainsley. Why the hell was he so smitten with the bloody woman? Some might say it was his cock, but it was more than simple physical attraction and he knew it.

"There's no need to coddle me like an infant, my lady." Not that anyone could imagine Ainsley coddling babies.

"Then please cease acting like one. Your limp is worse today, and you've gone quite pale."

He liked the fact that she paid attention to details about him. He didn't like that those details made him appear like an invalid.

You are an invalid, you idiot.

She took matters into her own hands, steering him toward an alcove with an Italianate bench. "Sit before you fall down."

Royal cast an eye down the long stretch of corridor. The hall was currently deserted, but servants or even guests could happen by at any time. Though he and Ainsley were still on the right side of propriety, sitting together in the secluded alcove, half-hidden by heavy brocaded drapes, might slide them over the line. His reputation didn't matter a tinker's damn, but hers certainly did.

When her pretty nose twitched, much like a rabbit's, it made him want to laugh.

"Mr. Kendrick, do you wish to return to the ballroom?" she asked rather tartly.

"God, no. It's mobbed with buffoons, as you pointed out a few minutes ago."

"Well, your reluctance to sit suggests that you find my company less than scintillating."

"An obviously impossible occurrence."

"Obviously. So why are you still standing?"

"Because *you're* still standing. I'm no pattern card of decorum, but I do know that ladies are supposed to sit first."

She scoffed. "You're from Scotland. You haven't the faintest idea how to behave with decorum."

"You wrong us, *Sassenach*," he said, placing a dramatic hand to his heart. "No man on earth is more courtly than a Highlander in the throes of romance."

She paused for a moment before answering. "Mr. Kendrick, are you flirting with me?"

Of course he was. Rather badly, if she needed clarification.

"If I say yes, will it get you to sit down on that confounded bench?" His leg *was* killing him, blast it.

Ainsley floated onto the seat in a graceful flutter of skirts. "You only had to ask."

"I thought I did."

"You most certainly did not."

He shook his head. "Never mind. I was somewhat confused."

"You are overcome by my presence, no doubt. Men always are, so there's no call to feel embarrassed about it."

Ainsley shifted to make room for him as he carefully sat. The bench was small, crowding them close.

"No, it's because I can't follow your convoluted mental processes," he said.

She whacked him on the arm with her fan. "Can you not even pretend to be charming? My other suitors at least have a go at it."

He managed not to grin at the notion that she considered him one of her suitors. "We both know I never pretend to be charming."

"It's rather a nice change," she said with a rueful smile. "Being surrounded by men desperate to flatter does get a bit cloying, especially since I can never tell whether it's me or my fortune they're principally after."

Her damn, great fortune stood between them like Hadrian's Wall.

Don't think about it.

"Poor Lady Ainsley," he said, returning her smile. "I shall make a point of being rude to you at least once a day, just to lighten your cruel burden."

"I don't think you need to make a point of it. You come to it quite naturally."

"And I consider it one of my best assets."

"The hostesses of London might not agree. Just ask Lady

Bassett. You managed to insult her before we even sat down to dinner."

Royal hadn't meant to offend their hostess, who seemed like a perfectly decent woman. He'd been looking around for Ainsley, and hadn't noticed that her ladyship was speaking to him.

"I did apologize," he said. "That has to count for something."

When she shrugged, a few tendrils of hair drifted down from her coiffure in silky wisps. Royal had to repress the impulse to brush them aside and set his lips to her smooth, graceful neck.

"It doesn't really matter how rude you are," she said. "Your brother is a wealthy, unmarried earl, even if he *is* a Scotsman. So if the ladies of the *ton* wish Lord Arnprior to put in an appearance, they have to put up with you, too. His lordship never goes anywhere without you, it seems."

That was true. Nick was an absolute tyrant when it came to forcing him back into society. Royal would have been happy to spend his nights at their rented town house in Mayfair, alone with a good book, but big brother had decided it was time for him to start living again. Royal had vociferously disagreed, since attending dreary parties and fending off impertinent questions about the war hardly counted as *living*. He didn't even have the consolation of being able to twirl a pretty girl around the dance floor.

It felt like he'd escaped the killing fields of Waterloo only to die of utter boredom at the hands of the *beau monde*.

Ainsley poked him again with her dratted fan. "You've gone back to scowling, and since we know you couldn't *possibly* be scowling about me, there's something else bothering you."

Her imperious attitude made him smile. "You can be incredibly annoying sometimes, my lady."

"You're describing yourself. Everything about *me* is perfect. If you weren't such a thickhead, you'd realize that."

Oh, how he realized it. If there was a more beautiful, self-assured girl in London, he had yet to meet her. Ainsley's family pampered her like a princess, and her suitors slavered over her like witless fools. Thankfully, she rarely took herself seriously, and took her legion of beaus even less so. Her odd combination of arrogance and wry self-awareness gave her a confidence he found enormously appealing.

"I have no doubt you could wave your hand and split the Thames, like Moses parted the Red Sea," he said.

She wrinkled her nose. "Thank you, but I'd rather walk on top of it. Then I won't have to see all the nasty things lying at the bottom."

He started to laugh but ended up biting off a curse when a muscle in his thigh picked that moment to spasm painfully.

"Your leg *is* bothering you," she said with a concerned frown. "We should go back to the ballroom. I'm sure this corridor is too cold for you."

Royal forced a smile past his gritted teeth. "Are you cold? Because you're the one who should be shivering in that silly gown."

She was wearing an absolute frippery of a dress, with tiny cap sleeves ready to slip from her shoulders with the slightest encouragement. Her gauzy skirts were the height of fashion, but it was an insane outfit for the dead of winter.

"I never get cold. You, however, are still recovering your health and should not be loitering in drafty hallways. I don't know why I let you talk me into coming out here in the first place."

When she started to stand, Royal wrapped a hand around her wrist and gently pulled her back down. "As I recall, you were the one who talked *me* into leaving the ballroom."

"Nonsense. And there's no call to manhandle me, sir," she said, sounding a trifle breathless.

"You call that manhandling?" he said, surprised.

"I do. Clearly, you do not know your own strength."

Actually, he did, though most days he felt like a pale reflection of his former self. If he turned sideways he feared he might even disappear.

"Then I sincerely beg your apology," he said.

"Fiddlesticks. You're not sorry at all."

"When you grow up with six brothers, you tend to skip over the social niceties and the apologies."

"Especially when you're Highlanders, I imagine. My maternal grandmother was born in Inveraray, and she was forever talking about the wild men of her clan."

Royal perked up. "No wonder I'm smitten with you. You're part Scot, and from my part of the country, too."

She looked slightly taken aback by his honesty but flashed a mocking smile. "I'm only one-quarter Scot, and I try to conceal the fact. Granny Baynes was wonderful, though. She told the most outrageously tall tales."

"Scots are prone to dramatic license, especially when it comes to family history. But my brothers and I certainly had our share of adventures growing up."

She shifted to face him more directly, brushing her delightfully plump thigh against his good leg. His leg, and other parts of him, approved.

"Did you often get into trouble, Mr. Kendrick?"

"On a regular basis. I remember an incident involving the local parish priest and the communion wine that probably earned us a decade in purgatory." He let out a rueful laugh. "I don't know how my mother put up with us. We were a great handful, to say the least."

"It sounds like you had tremendous fun," she said in a wistful tone.

"We did."

Until their parents died, and everything went catastrophically wrong. He shifted on the hard bench, wincing at the ugly memories.

Ainsley cast him a worried glance. "Are you sure you're not catching a chill?"

Bloody hell. Next, she'd be asking if he needed a flannel waistcoat and a hot toddy.

"Lass, I grew up in a drafty old castle in the Highlands. Trust me when I say you don't know the meaning of cold."

Her nose twitched again, a clear sign of irritation. "There's no need for you to get snappish."

"And there's no need for you to pity me."

They glowered at each other for a few moments before she jabbed a finger at his chest.

"One. I do not pity you." She jabbed two fingers. "Two, you are obviously in pain, as any dimwit could tell, and I am *far* from being a dimwit. I suspect you could be suffering the torments of hell and you'd still insist you were fine."

"I've already suffered the torments of hell. Once you've done it, everything else seems tame by comparison."

"And three," she added, "I have no wish to be held responsible for a relapse. Your brother would probably murder me with his dirk or some other equally horrifying Scottish weaponry."

He mustered a smile that might look more like a grimace. "I'll sign an ironclad waiver absolving you of responsibility if I do relapse."

She eyed him in silence.

"Really, there's nothing to worry about," he said in a softer tone.

"It's not that, precisely," she said.

"Then what, precisely?"

"It *does* hurt a great deal, does it not? Even though you pretend the opposite."

"Yes," he said reluctantly.

"Worse than usual, too. I can tell."

That startled him. "How?"

Even when the pain clawed at him like a thousand demons, he schooled his expression and forced a consistent gait. The new exercises were helping in that regard. Nick had finally found a doctor who seemed to know his business, unlike the other high-priced quacks they'd seen since their arrival in London. The first physician had morosely shaken his head and recommended a stout cane and a lifetime of laudanum. The second had actually had the nerve to suggest Royal's leg be amputated.

That particular appointment had not ended well.

"Because when your pain is worse, you go white around the lips," Ainsley said. "And your right eyelid often twitches."

Royal gaped at her. He knew he often turned pale as a ghoul when his pain was particularly bad, so that was no surprise, but noticing the tic in his eyelid? No one had ever picked up on that except for his grandfather. Not even Nick, who watched him like a bloody hawk.

She shook her head. "The fact that you never complain is amazing to me."

"There's little point in complaining, since it won't change anything," he said gruffly.

Ainsley slowly unfurled her fan to study a painted scene of nymphs cavorting amongst a ruin. "You never boast about it, either," she said in a thoughtful tone. "Most men would. After all, you're a legitimate war hero."

"Only a bloody coxcomb would boast about something that all but killed him."

She shot him an irritated glance. "I'm not talking about your injury, you booby. I'm talking about the sacrifices you made for your country."

He snorted. "Sacrifices that got me and all the other poor

fools nothing but pain and suffering. When you're bleeding out on the battlefield, it doesn't matter one damn bit what you're fighting for. English or French, the blood runs the same red."

He'd seen rivers of the stuff, including his own, leaching into the dirt and mud. It had rained the night before that last battle, and Royal could still feel himself sinking into the horrendous, foul-smelling muck. Too weak to even turn himself over, he'd almost drowned in a shallow ditch before an infantryman had dragged him away to the temporary shelter of a British line.

Ainsley stared at the opposite wall. "This was a mistake," she said in a flat tone.

His heart cramped, but he managed a sardonic smile. "I realize that penniless, crippled soldiers are not in your usual style."

She shot him a resentful look. "You can be remarkably unpleasant at times, Mr. Kendrick."

"So I've been told." And he hated himself for it, hated that anger and sarcasm seemed the only defenses left to him, other than despair.

She clambered to her feet. "Do you need help getting up?" she asked, half turning away from him.

"I'm not helpless," he gritted out as he pushed himself to stand. "You've done your duty by the poor invalid, my lady. You can return to your friends with a clear conscience, knowing you've accomplished one good deed for the evening."

Ainsley flinched, looking set to flee to the refuge of the glittering lights and laughter of the ballroom. It was certainly what she should do, what part of him wanted her to do. Then the inevitable rejection would finally be over, and he could get on with the business of forgetting how much he adored her.

Instead, she squared her shoulders like a grenadier, and

Royal braced for the cutting words that would surely flow from her beautiful lips. God knew he'd earned them.

But when he saw the tears in her eyes, glittering like star sapphires, his heart blackened with shame.

"You've got it so wrong," she choked out. "I don't pity you. I admire you."

A startled laugh somehow escaped his tight throat. "Why, for God's sake? I'm an ill-tempered fool without a shred of courtesy. You should find a vase and smash it over my thick skull."

She shook her head so hard her curls bounced. "You don't hide from your pain, but you don't make a show of it, either. You just . . . live with it, as if it doesn't matter. I don't think I could ever be that brave."

Oh, it mattered. Pain was now the cornerstone of his life. But as for living with it, what choice did he have? Nick had defied his superior officers and risked his own life and career to save Royal from certain death. Because his brother and the rest of the family needed him, Royal would bloody well keep on surviving for their sakes.

How could Ainsley ever understand that? And why did she even care?

"My lady, I don't know what you want from me," he said.

She swallowed before answering. "I . . . I like you, that's all. If you can say that to me, why can't I do the same?"

He shook his head, afraid to even think what she meant.

"Besides, I'm trying to be nice," she added, sounding rather surly. Inexplicably, that tone eased the tightness in his chest. "I *can* be nice, you know, despite what people say about me. And I choose to be nice to you, specifically, you dreadful man."

As he took a step closer, Ainsley held her ground, meeting his gaze with one both defiant and curiously vulnerable.

And Lady Ainsley Matthews was never vulnerable.

He gently rested a hand on her ridiculous poof of a sleeve. Royal longed to touch the smooth, bare skin just beyond the frill of lace and silk, but he didn't yet dare. They barely knew each other, and yet the connection between them was battering through his rib cage, forging a path straight to his heart.

When she didn't pull away from his touch, he found his voice. "I don't need you to be nice to me, either."

She stared up at him, her violet, wide-eyed gaze shimmering with vulnerability and longing. Longing for him? It seemed impossible.

"What does that mean?" she whispered.

He left the safety of her sleeve, brushing across her soft skin to cup the back of her neck.

"This," he whispered as he lowered his head to her parted lips.

He sank into a cloud, into a soft whisper of passion with the promise of more to come. Though their lips barely touched, their breaths became one, a press of silken heat between one heartbeat and the next.

Those heartbeats were enough to know he was forever changed, no matter what happened next.

Drawing in a steadying breath, he reluctantly let his hand drop away, straightening to put some room between them. It was still much too close for propriety's sake, since her breasts—God, those magnificent breasts—all but brushed the front of his coat.

Ainsley breathed out a little sigh that he *swore* was one of regret, then her eyelids fluttered open. He waited for her to speak—or haul off and slap him—but she simply gave him a dreamy, sweet smile. It was so unlike her that he was tempted to laugh. Or collapse from the joy and astonishment flooding through him.

He was struggling to find a safe path through the emotional earthquake. "Lady Ainsley, shouldn't you apologize for taking advantage of me? I am quite shocked, I must say."

She blinked, the smile fading as her expression turned blank.

He was a moron of the first order to make a joke of their first kiss—a confounded, stupid joke.

Then she giggled, a charming ripple that drifted around him like butterflies on a summer breeze. Everything about her was magical. She transformed the air he breathed and made him dizzy.

She playfully tapped him on the shoulder. "Mr. Kendrick, if you think—"

"What the devil is going on here?" blared an aggrieved voice from behind them.

Ainsley jerked away, the backs of her knees connecting solidly with the bench. Royal shot out an arm to steady her, but his damn leg chose that exact moment to buckle and he staggered. She slapped her hands on his chest, bracing him against a humiliating tumble.

"Are you all right?" she gasped.

"Yes," he ground out. He glanced at the tall man charging at them like a boar with a spear in its rump. "Who the hell is that?"

"The Marquess of Cringlewood," she said in a tight voice.

"Never heard of him."

She shot him a grim look. "You're about to hear quite a lot, I fear. And please, Mr. Kendrick, let me do the talking."

Ainsley stepped forward, as if to protect him. While Royal would have liked nothing better than to pull her behind *him* for safekeeping, his energies were directed toward staying on his blasted feet.

"My lord, what a surprise," she said as their intruder stalked up to them. "I didn't expect to see you back in town so soon."

Her cool, well-bred elegance acted like a shield. Still, Royal could read her tension by the hike of her shoulders.

He could feel it, too. If he wasn't mistaken, Ainsley was more than embarrassed. She was downright nervous.

"Lady Ainsley, what are you doing out here?" Cringlewood demanded, glowering like a stage villain. "And who the devil is this person?"

Royal finally took Ainsley by the arm as he moved up by her side. She all but jumped out of her shoes.

"Remove your hand, you cad," Cringlewood hissed.

Royal repressed the impulse to roll his eyes at the man's absurd theatrics.

"My lord, there is no cause for alarm," Ainsley said, pulling her arm away. "Mr. Kendrick simply offered to escort me out to the hall for some cooler air. The atmosphere in the ballroom was stifling."

The marquess still eyed her with heavy disapproval. "Without a chaperone? I cannot imagine your parents would be pleased to see you wandering about unprotected. Nor, might I add, am I."

Royal gave him a smile that was mostly teeth. "Her ladyship is not unprotected. She's with me."

Cringlewood ignored him. "Your mamma is waiting for you, Ainsley. She's grown concerned by your absence."

So, the aristocratic blighter was on a first name basis with her. That was a painful revelation, especially since he was tall, handsome, and dressed with an expensive elegance that Royal could never hope to match. Even worse, he was evidently hale in all limbs.

When Ainsley sighed and gave a resigned nod, Royal frowned. She never catered to any man but her father, the Earl of Aldridge.

He laid a gentle hand on her arm. She glanced up at him, startled, but then gave a tiny shake of the head, as if to warn him.

But warn him of what?

"My lady, perhaps you might formally introduce me to your friend," Royal said. "He seems such a charming gentleman."

Consternation flashed across her features before her control reasserted itself.

"Of course. Mr. Kendrick, it is my pleasure to introduce you to the Marquess of Cringlewood." She gave the marquess a bland smile. "Mr. Kendrick is the brother of the Earl of Arnprior."

The man barely managed a nod before holding out an imperious arm to Ainsley.

Bloody ponce. Even his name was ridiculous.

"Delighted, I'm sure," Royal said. "And now that we've got the niceties out of the way, I'm happy to return you to the ballroom, Lady Ainsley." He lifted an eyebrow at the marquess. "Your assistance is no longer required, sir."

Cringlewood's nostrils actually flared. The man really did have a promising career on the stage if he ever decided to give up life as an aristocratic idiot.

"That won't be necessary, Mr. Kendrick," Ainsley quickly replied. "I'm more than happy to return to the ballroom with Lord Cringlewood."

Despite the words, she looked anything but happy. In fact, she looked all but ready to break out in hives from a severe bout of nerves.

"Are you sure?" Royal asked quietly. "If you're uncomfortable with him, I'll escort you to your mother."

Cringlewood immediately adopted another outraged expression. "Since Lady Ainsley is to be my wife, she obviously does not feel uncomfortable with me."

The floor tilted under Royal's feet. He must even have staggered a bit, because Ainsley put a hand under his elbow.

"Be careful," she said.

"Is it true?" he asked.

"Of course it's true," the marquess snapped. "We're to be married by the end of the Season, as anyone with a brain in this town surely knows."

"You get ahead of yourself, my lord," Ainsley said coldly. "There has been no formal announcement, as you are well aware."

Something in Royal's chest seemed to explode. He almost thought to look down and see a gaping hole where his heart had been.

He took a step away from her that felt like a retreat back into darkness.

"So, you are betrothed." He forced a little bow. "Allow me to offer my congratulations."

She shook her head. "It's not what you think. I mean . . ." She cast the marquess a frustrated glance as her voice trailed into silence.

"I demand to know what's going on here," Cringlewood said angrily.

After Ainsley maintained a tense silence, Royal shrugged. "I'm sorry to say, my lord, that your fiancée is a determined flirt who enjoys leading unsuspecting fools to their doom. As anyone with a brain in this town surely knows."

She gasped, but he refused to spare her a glance as he limped away as quickly as his blasted leg could carry him.

Chapter One

Castle Kinglas, Scotland
April 1817

Clearly, not even his brother's library could provide safe haven.

With a sigh, Royal glanced up from his book when his sister-in-law marched into the room. Though the former Victoria Knight was now Countess of Arnprior, and wife to the chief of Clan Kendrick, she was still very much a governess in spirit and looked ready to box his ears.

He raised a polite eyebrow. "Is there something I can do for you, my lady?"

She arched an eloquent brow in return. Perhaps they could conduct this sure-to-be-unpleasant discussion entirely through facial expressions.

No such luck, he thought, when Victoria raised an imperious finger.

"Indeed, there is. I want you to stop moping about the castle. You've been doing it all winter, and it's become ridiculous."

She was never one to mince words or shy away from an

unpleasant task. And now that she'd sorted out his brothers, she'd clearly made Royal her special project.

"I'm not moping. I'm reading a very good book."

Victoria glanced down at the leather-bound volume, then plucked it from his hand and turned it right side up.

Royal winced. "I was just giving my eyes a rest."

"Of course you were," she said dryly.

He'd barely glanced at the blasted thing, a history of the Punic Wars he'd ordered last month. After starting it with a fair degree of enthusiasm, he'd quickly lost interest. Today, he'd read only a few pages before his attention had wandered to the windswept vista of craggy peaks hulking over the loch behind Kinglas. Not even the dramatic beauty of the Highlands had the power to soothe him—not like it once had.

He supposed he could go fishing, which he normally enjoyed, but that hardly seemed worth the effort.

"At least join us for a cup of tea," Victoria said in a coaxing voice, switching tactics. "Taffy made her special seedcakes for you. She said you barely touched your breakfast. Or your lunch, for that matter."

He glanced over to see a generous tea service set up on the low table in front of the library's fireplace. He hadn't even noticed the footman lug the damn thing in.

His sister-in-law's understanding gaze—along with the fact that Taffy, the castle's housekeeper, thought he needed coddling—triggered an irrational spurt of irritation.

"I'm not one of your pupils, Victoria. Don't try to manage me with promises of treats."

"True. My students invariably displayed better manners."

"She's got you there, old fellow," said Nick from behind the ledgers stacked on his desk. "You *have* been moping about. More than usual, that is. It's time you do something about it."

When Nick and Victoria exchanged furtive glances, Royal had to repress a groan. Clearly, they'd planned this little ambush.

He put his book aside and glared at his older brother with predictably no effect. The Earl of Arnprior was well used to his obstreperous siblings, since he'd all but raised them after the death of their parents. Although the most generous of men, Nick was the proverbial unmovable object when it came to deciding his family's best interests. And once he made a decision, it all but required an Act of Parliament to change it.

"I repeat, I am *not* moping," Royal said. "And don't you have enough to worry about without fretting over me like a granny with gout?"

As usual, Nick was buried under the mountain of work that came with managing the estate, not to mention a large and sometimes fractious Highland clan. Any normal man would founder under the load, but he never failed to rise to the challenge. And now that he'd married Victoria, Nick had finally found the richly deserved happiness so long denied him.

Royal couldn't help feeling envious of having a loving wife *and* a sense of purpose—the feeling that one's life mattered. A compelling reason to wake up in the morning had been lacking in his life for a long time.

Nick had once relied quite heavily on Royal's support for everything from running the estate to managing the younger lads. But Victoria now appropriately filled that role, as well as still tutoring Kade, the youngest Kendrick. The boy had struggled for years with ill health, but under Victoria's loving care, he grew stronger by the day.

Aye, she was a blessing, was the new Countess of Arnprior, though not entirely for Royal. His sister-in-law was as bad as her lord when it came to wanting to repair the broken things around Castle Kinglas, including him.

"And you needn't regard me as if I'm falling into a decline," Royal said to her. "I'm perfectly fine. Better than ever, in fact."

Instead of contradicting that obvious load of bollocks,

Victoria smiled. "Of course you are, dear. But I would feel better if you had something to eat."

She held out a hand.

Sighing, he took it, because today he did need help getting to his feet. The pain was always worse in blustery, damp weather. Some days Royal feared he was losing ground with his recovery. Though he faithfully followed the regime of rest and exercise prescribed by the London sawbones, his pain somehow seemed linked to the heaviness in his heart.

"Need help?" Nick asked.

"I'm not a cripple," Royal gritted out, even as he struggled to stand.

"And you know I'm stronger than I look," Victoria said to her husband.

"Aye. Skinny but strong as an ox," Nick said with a grin.

"If that's the sort of compliment you employed to woo the poor girl, it's a wonder Victoria ever married you," Royal said as he found his footing.

Victoria laughed. "That's what my grandfather used to say when I was a young girl hanging about the stables of his coaching inn. I loved helping with the horses."

"He was right," said Royal. "For such a wee *Sassenach*, you're quite hardy."

"I have to be to survive a houseful of wild Highlanders," she cheerfully replied, watching Royal carefully to make sure he wouldn't topple over. "I know. I'm an old mother hen."

When his gaze strayed to the decanters of whisky behind his brother's desk, she waggled a finger. "Tea and something to eat first, Royal."

"Old mother hen is an understatement." He patted her on the shoulder. "You do realize you cannot fix everything, no matter how hard you try."

"I know, and it's just about *killing* me." When he started to laugh, she jabbed him in the arm. "But don't think I'm giving up, either."

"Thank you for the warning."

Nick joined them at the tea table, dropping a quick kiss on his wife's head after she took her seat. "I think we're being a bit hard on you," he said. "You've done a splendid job organizing the family and estate papers, and we all know they were in . . . quite the state."

"*Catastrophic disarray* is the phrase you were searching for," Royal said.

"Don't let Angus hear you. He all but flayed me alive when I took the job from him and gave it to you."

"So I heard. My ears are still ringing."

Nick laughed. "Aside from the fact that Angus is a disaster when it comes to paperwork, the old fellow's getting on in years. He's earned his rest."

"I hope to God you didn't tell him so," Royal said. Their grandfather would be devastated if he thought they were putting him out to pasture.

"Since my instincts for self-preservation are quite good, I did not," Nick replied.

When Nick and Royal were away during the war, Angus had managed affairs at Kinglas, watching over the younger Kendricks and serving as estate steward. He'd done his best, but with mixed results. The old fellow had an abiding mistrust of modernity—which to him meant anything after the last Stuart monarch.

"Angus did mention that you did a passable job organizing the papers," Victoria said as she poured them each a cup of tea. "Which from him is high praise, indeed."

"Seriously," Nick said, "I can't thank you enough for taking that on. I know it was gruesome."

Royal shrugged and reached for a seedcake. "I was happy to do so."

Oddly enough, that had turned out to be true. His big brother had dragooned him into taking on the job, determined to get Royal "off his arse."

"You need to accept that your military days are over," Nick had said, adopting his most lordly manner. "It's time to figure out what you wish to do with your life and then simply get on with it."

The problem was, Royal *still* didn't have a clue what he wanted to do.

All he seemed to be good for was mooning over Ainsley Matthews and wondering what might have happened between them if he hadn't been stupid enough to abduct her back in January. He'd kidnapped her with the best of intentions, determined to save her from an arranged marriage she was trying to avoid. Of course, he would have gained the only woman who'd ever made him feel truly alive, but that was beside the point. He'd done it for *her*, and any benefits accruing to him would have been merely accidental.

Still, he knew that reasoning was utterly insane. Ainsley hadn't wanted to marry him only slightly less fervently than she hadn't wanted to marry the Marquess of Cringlewood. She'd made that clear in language so caustic it was a wonder he hadn't been reduced to a pile of smoldering ash.

After Ainsley departed for her great-aunt's manor house a few hours north of Kinglas, Royal had descended into an even gloomier mood alleviated only by drastic amounts of whisky. Fed up, Nick had finally shoved him into the dusty old estate office and ordered him to work. And wonder of wonders, reading through the history of his family and clan had been absorbing. Putting those records in order, watching the ancient story unfold over the centuries, had given Royal a renewed appreciation for his heritage. The proud Kendricks had fought hard for their rightful place in the history of Scotland, and their story was worth remembering.

For a while, the Kendrick sense of pride had even rubbed off on him.

"For all the good it'll do me now," Royal muttered into his teacup.

"What's that?" Nick asked.

Royal waved off the question. "As I said, I was happy to help, especially since it put an end to your incessant nagging."

His brother adopted an air of mild offense. "I never nag anyone. I simply pass on a suggestion now and again."

Victoria choked on her tea.

Nick gently patted her on the back. "Are you all right, sweetheart?"

"Just a little something in my throat," she said as she exchanged amused glances with Royal. Though the Earl of Arnprior always had everyone's best interest in mind, whether the rest of the family agreed with his determination of *best interest* was another matter.

Victoria put down her teacup. "The fact remains that unless we intend to start Royal on the laundry lists, his task has been completed."

"I suppose that's why you've taken up brooding again," Nick said. "Nothing else to occupy your mind."

Except for the debacle with Ainsley was the clear implication.

"You make it sound as though I've made a hobby out of it," Royal said.

"You rather have, dear," Victoria said.

"And you're bloody good at it," Nick wryly added.

Royal mentally winced. "Everyone's got to be good at something."

"You're good at many things," Victoria said. "Besides brooding," she added when Royal lifted a pointed eyebrow.

"Yes," Nick said with an encouraging smile. "You were a fine scholar before your soldiering days. And you've always been the best in the family when it comes to fencing, riding, and training horses. You managed some horses no one else could get near."

"You forgot I was also the best sword dancer in the county," Royal responded dryly. "But my leg prevents me from taking up that mantle again, or training horses for a living. And since I have no intention of burying myself in a library for the foreseeable future, a life of scholarship is out, too."

When Nick and Victoria exchanged another worried look, he sighed. "I'm sorry. I know you're only trying to help. It's just that . . ."

"You were forced to give up soldiering, which you excelled at," his sister-in-law said. "Believe me, I understand. When I stood accused of murder last year, I was deathly afraid I'd never be able to teach again."

Before she married Nick, Victoria had planned to open her own seminary for young ladies.

"Do you miss teaching?" Royal couldn't help asking.

"Sometimes I do, although I'm fortunate I can still tutor Kade." She flashed her husband a quick smile. "But I found something else to love even more than teaching."

Like her, Royal thought he'd found something new to love—something more important than even his military career. Too bad he'd been wrong about that, too.

Nick raised Victoria's hand to his lips. "Perhaps we'll have a schoolroom full of Kendrick children you can teach someday," he murmured.

She blushed and gave him a shy smile.

"Would you like me to leave the room?" Royal asked politely.

Victoria wrinkled her nose. "Too much?"

"You are rather making me lose my appetite."

She laughed. "Point taken. Let's get back to you."

"On second thought, I think I'd rather see you two act like romantic idiots," Royal said.

"We can do that anytime," Nick said. "Besides, we've been avoiding a discussion of your situation for too long."

Royal eyed his brother with distaste. "You are incredibly annoying."

"If so, it's for your own good. Now, given that you did such a splendid job with my paperwork, I have a suggestion to make."

"Just one?"

Nick, as usual, didn't rise to the bait. "Since we've now uncovered your talent for organization, you should consider working with Logan. You know he'd be thrilled to have your help."

Logan, the second oldest brother, had recently returned to Scotland after years of self-imposed exile in Canada. And now he was rich, owning a successful company trading in fur and timber. Logan was setting up an office and warehouse in Glasgow and had offered a job to any family member who wanted one. Royal had briefly pondered accepting the offer before deciding he'd rather put a bullet through his good leg than spend the rest of his life touting up columns in a dusty warehouse.

"I have no intention of becoming a glorified clerk," he said. "Besides, I'm not much of a city man. After a few weeks in Glasgow, I'm ready to crawl out of my skin."

That feeling had intensified after coming home from the war. The noise, the crowded streets, the bustle and hurry . . . sometimes he could almost imagine the buildings closing in on him.

"You don't seem particularly enamored with the country these days, either," Nick pointed out.

Royal simply lifted his shoulders in another vague shrug.

Victoria studied him over the rim of her teacup. "Have you heard from Lady Ainsley recently?"

Royal had been about to take another seedcake, but he put down his plate and cautiously regarded his sister-in-law. "No. Why do you ask?"

"Since Glasgow is apparently not to your liking, it might be nice if you made a trip to Cairndow to visit her. The poor girl has been cooped up in that small village for the entire winter with only her great-aunt for company. I'm sure she'd love to see you."

Royal and Nick stared at her as if she'd lost her mind.

"What's wrong with making a little visit?" she asked. "After all, it's less than a day's ride from Kinglas. In fact, I'm quite surprised none of us thought of the idea until now."

"One generally waits for an invitation first," Royal said sarcastically.

"She'd probably shoot you if you showed up at her door unannounced," Nick commented. "You didn't exactly part on the best of terms."

"It wasn't that bad," Royal muttered. Yes, she'd still been furious with him about the failed elopement, but she'd also given him an astonishing, bone-crushing hug before shoving him away and stomping out to her carriage.

"And she *has* written to you over the winter," Victoria pointed out.

Nick glanced at Royal, clearly surprised. "Really? With the exception of Victoria and Kade, she made it clear she thought the rest of us were idiots. Especially you."

"*Chuckleheaded nincompoop* was her exact description for me," Royal said.

"Then, why—"

The door opened and his grandfather stomped in, sparing Royal the need to explain Ainsley's erratic conduct. He wasn't really sure why she'd written to him, except that she'd sounded rather lonely and bored. But her tone had also made it clear she harbored a lingering irritation with all things Kendrick.

"Ye all look as queer as Dick's hatband," Angus said as he joined them at the tea table. "What's afoot?"

"My dear wife has just suggested that Royal visit Lady Ainsley Matthews as a cure for his melancholy," Nick said.

Their grandfather's bushy eyebrows bristled like agitated tomcats. "What? That bloody woman can tear the hide off a man just by lookin' at him—that's if she doesn't stab the puir lad first."

"She's not that bad," Royal said, irritated by his grandfather's somewhat accurate assessment.

"Indeed not," Victoria added. "Lady Ainsley is a lovely girl."

"She's a looker, I'll grant ye," Angus said. "But have ye forgotten her behavior on the elopement? Because I have not." He directed his scowl at Royal. "Her high and mightiness treated us like muck on her boot heel."

"Of course I remember. I was there, wasn't I?"

It was *all* etched in Royal's mind with hideous clarity. In addition to Ainsley, his grandfather, and his idiot twin brothers, Royal had been dealing with two other young ladies from Glasgow whom the twins had been courting for several weeks. The lasses had initially been enthusiastic elopement participants.

Ainsley, however, had not been willing, and Royal had completely misread her. After he scooped her up that fateful night and dumped her into his carriage, she'd exploded in a fury of thrashing arms and legs, all but unmanning him. Fortunately, her foot had landed on his bad thigh instead of an even worse spot. Royal had practically passed out from the pain, but at least it had brought her up short.

Once he'd recovered himself, he'd explained the plan to a still furious Ainsley. She had then surprised him by declining his offer to return to Glasgow, saying she'd rather be ruined forever than marry the Marquess of Cringlewood. An aborted elopement with Royal, she'd decided, would be enough to generate the sort of scandal necessary to ruin her reputation and convince Cringlewood to leave her alone.

She'd then spent the rest of the trip north ordering his family about like a bunch of lazy servants and fighting almost constantly with Angus.

"One can hardly blame her for being angry," Royal said. "After all, I did kidnap her."

"And then subjected her to three horrible days caring for a castle full of sick people," Victoria replied in a humorous tone. "It's a miracle she didn't shove you off the battlements as repayment."

On top of everything else, one of the twins had slipped off the coach step and broken a leg on the way to Kinglas. After their arrival home, half the family and staff had promptly come down with a severe cold, pitching the entire household into chaos. Nick and Victoria, who'd followed the elopers in hot pursuit, had ably managed the crisis with assistance from Royal and—surprisingly—Ainsley, who'd turned out to be a rather competent nurse.

"Angus, even you must admit Lady Ainsley acquitted herself well under the circumstances," Victoria said.

"I'll give ye that," the old man grudgingly acknowledged. "The lass did better than I expected. But I still say she's a *Sassenach* harridan, and our Royal shouldna have anything to do with the likes of her."

Victoria shook her head. "I'm concerned about her. She said a few things while she was here that quite worried me. I regret I didn't have the opportunity to follow up on them."

"You were too busy getting arrested for murder," Royal said, "so I think you can be excused for the oversight."

Nick frowned. "The less said about that incident, the better. I will not have anyone upsetting my wife with reminders of that exceedingly unpleasant time."

"Yes, dear," Victoria said in soothing tones, patting his arm. "Although everything did turn out for the best, so all's well that ends well."

Nick's mouth quirked up. "Now you're just managing me, love."

"She manages all of us, in case you haven't noticed," Royal said. "Which is a good thing, since we cause more trouble than we're worth."

"Speak for yourself," Angus said in a lofty tone. "I'm a paragon compared to the lot of ye."

"If you're a paragon, then I'm Robert the Bruce," Royal said. "And I do believe I left my crown in the drawing room. Will you fetch it for me, Grandda?"

Angus bristled with indignation. "Now, see here, laddie—"

Nick interrupted the impending Angus Eruption. "We've wandered some distance from the original topic of Royal's future. He cannot spend his time moping around Kinglas. He needs to find something useful to do with his life."

"Well, I'll not be thankin' ye to give him any more of *my* work," the old man said. "Ye'll not be puttin' me out to pasture just yet."

Their grandfather was understandably touchy, on the lookout for any hint that he wasn't contributing to the family's well-being or was in any way a burden. Royal knew exactly how he felt.

"It's just that Royal seems at loose ends," Victoria explained. "We're trying to decide how best to address the situation."

"And do I actually get a say?" Royal asked sardonically. They ignored him.

"Running aboot after that stuck-up English miss is the last thing he should be doin'," Angus said. "Besides, I doubt she'd even see him."

Royal thought about Ainsley's last letter to him a few weeks ago, the one where she'd sounded . . . sad. "Actually, I'm not sure she'd mind a visit."

Nick put down his teacup and stood. "You'll make your

own decision, of course. But I would be grateful if you would at least consider working for Logan."

"And ye'll no be turnin' the lad into a glorified clerk, either," Angus objected. "He'll be stayin' right here at Kinglas, where he belongs."

His grandfather meant where he could keep an eye on him, since he constantly feared Royal might suffer a relapse of some sort or the other.

"It'll be fine, Grandda," Royal said. "Don't fash yourself."

"Of course I get fashed," Angus said gruffly. "After all, ye almost died fightin' for the stupid English."

"Ahem," Victoria said loudly.

Nick clamped a hand on the old man's shoulder. "Come along, Grandda. I want to take a look at the south wall of the stables. It might even need rebuilding, and I'd like your opinion."

"Of course, lad," Angus said, instantly diverted. "I've been thinkin' the same myself."

"Then let's get to it." Nick started to propel Angus toward the door.

"Laddie, don't be makin' any plans without talkin' to me first," the old man called to Royal before he disappeared.

"Thank God," Victoria said with a sigh. "I do love the old fellow, but sometimes he can be such a trial."

"But you manage him exceedingly well."

"As much as Angus *can* be managed. I admit that sometimes I'm tempted to clobber him with his own bagpipes."

When Royal laughed, Victoria gave him a relieved smile. "The discussion was getting rather fraught, wasn't it? I'm sorry we made such a fuss. I know you hate it."

"A fuss is entirely unnecessary, I assure you. I'm perfectly well."

A moment later, his youngest brother came rushing into the library.

"Nick just told me Taffy made seedcakes," Kade said as he plopped down next to Victoria on the settee. "Oh, good. You saved me some." He promptly crammed one into his mouth.

"Dear, there's no need to wolf it down," Victoria said, handing the lad a plate and a serviette. "Remember your manners."

Royal leaned over and ruffled his brother's hair. "If you're not careful, someone will mistake you for one of the twins."

"Taffy hardly *ever* makes seedcakes, so you can't blame me. And Graeme and Grant aren't nearly as bad-mannered as they used to be," Kade said around a mouthful.

"Swallow before talking, please," Victoria admonished.

"The twins have become marginally civilized thanks to you, Victoria," Royal said. "We were all barbarians until you came along."

"Oh, you weren't that bad," Victoria said.

"Oh, yes, we were."

She grinned. "All right, the twins and Angus were quite appalling at first, and you were only slightly less objectionable. I still have nightmares about my first days at Kinglas. Kade, though, was perfect from the outset."

The boy leaned affectionately against her shoulder, throwing Royal a smug glance that made him laugh. It was grand to see Kade doing so well after years of ill health and suffering.

"What were you talking about when I came in?" Kade asked, reaching for another cake.

Victoria hesitated, eyeing Royal. He shrugged.

"We were discussing whether your brother might like to visit Lady Ainsley," she said.

Kade fastened an earnest gaze on Royal. "So, why don't you?"

Royal waggled a hand. "I'm not entirely sure she'd want to see me."

"She would," Kade said before biting into his seedcake.

"You're sure about that, are you?" Royal asked dryly.

After swallowing another enormous bite, his brother nodded. "I think Lady Ainsley likes you. A lot."

Royal ignored the jolt to his heart. "She certainly liked to scold me."

Kade shook his head. "She didn't mean it. It was just her way of dealing with you. Sometimes you can be quite gruff, you know. So she pushes back."

"Kade's opinion makes a great deal of sense," Victoria said.

Royal thought so too. Although only fifteen, Kade had a perception that was beyond his years and probably greater than the rest of the Kendrick males put together.

"Besides," the boy added, "I like her, because Lady Ainsley always says exactly what she means. Adults usually don't."

"She's honest, I'll give you that," Royal said.

"Regardless of your rather fraught past with Lady Ainsley," Victoria said, "I agree with Kade. She might have trouble admitting it, but I'm sure the girl is very fond of you."

He'd been sure of that at one point too, and look where it had got him.

"Maybe," he said in a neutral tone.

"If nothing else, she's your friend," Victoria said. "And I have the feeling she could use a friend right now."

"Even one of us blasted Kendricks?"

"One Kendrick in particular," she said firmly.

He finally allowed himself to seriously consider the idea. Seeing Ainsley again would be a challenge. They were often like two comets colliding, generating a good deal of heat, noise, and smoke. They also tended to leave a pile of rubble in their wake, which was not pleasant for anyone who happened to be within the blast range.

More to the point, Royal couldn't figure out what she wanted from him. More than once she'd come to him, as if needing comfort and protection, but then she'd pushed him away and claimed she never wanted to see him again. The confounded girl was as mysterious as the bloody Sphinx.

Then again, she *had* written to him three times this winter, hadn't she?

Victoria's gaze was astute. "You will never know how she feels unless you ask her directly."

"She'll probably demonstrate her feelings by smashing a vase over my head."

"That is a distinct possibility, I admit," said Victoria. "But whether she is worth the risk is a question only you can answer."

"Lady A has my vote," said Kade, "despite what anyone else says about her. She's a corker, if you ask me."

Clearly, a second Kendrick male had fallen under the spell of Ainsley Matthews's considerable charms. And since the lad *was* probably the smartest of them all . . .

"As it so happens, little brother, I agree with you." Royal hauled himself to his feet, a surge of unfamiliar energy coursing through his body. "Now, if you'll excuse me, I must pack a bag for my trip."

"Oh, good," Kade said, reaching for the tea tray. "More cake for me."

Chapter Two

Royal pulled up his horse outside the half-open iron gates fronting the drive to Underhill Manor. The gates would have been imposing were they not almost rusting out of the brick walls that marked the boundaries of the secluded estate. The gatehouse was equally neglected. Its sagging appearance, with cobwebs stretching over the door, signaled that no one had been in residence for some time.

Lady Margaret Baird, Ainsley's eccentric great-aunt, was apparently as unwelcoming as her reputation suggested.

The journey to Cairndow had been a slog. Normally an easy, half-day ride, the deplorably bad roads had forced him to slow Demetrius to a walk any number of times. Bad enough to have a lame rider, a lame horse as well would have been completely ridiculous.

Royal had made a quick stop at the local tavern where he'd watered his horse, downed a tankard of ale, and quizzed the publican for information about Lady Margaret. The fellow had been remarkably closemouthed, grouchily offering that her ladyship minded her own business—as did everyone else who knew what was what.

An odd statement, since gossip was the lifeblood of small Highland villages, especially when it came to the lords and ladies who exerted so much influence over the lives of the locals. Whether the fellow was simply loyal, bad-tempered, or indifferent was difficult to gauge, and no one else in the tavern had seemed inclined to talk to a stranger.

He nudged Demetrius forward. "Come along, old son. With a little luck, there'll be oats at the end of this drive and maybe even a warm stall if we're lucky."

His roan's snort sounded as skeptical as he felt. If the rest of the estate was as run-down as the gatehouse, they might end up foraging in the woods for their supper. He found it ever harder to imagine Ainsley willingly spending a week, much less the winter, in so remote and gloomy a spot. Even the rutted drive had a sad air, surrounded as it was by dense woods of beech and elm, the underbrush thick and tangled around their trunks.

The fact that Ainsley *had* come willingly was not in doubt. Despite her vociferous complaints that her father had exiled her to the Highlands for refusing to marry Cringle-wood, Royal had sensed relief on her part. She'd been so eager to leave Glasgow she'd fled almost as if a wolf pack was snapping at her heels. When Royal asked her to explain the hasty departure, she'd responded by telling him to mind his own confounded business.

Typical Ainsley.

Demetrius shied when two red squirrels darted across the leaf-strewn path in front of him. Royal brought the horse quickly under control.

"Pay attention, you idiot," he muttered to himself.

There would be plenty of time to ponder Ainsley's odd behavior when he arrived at Underhill. Then again, it was still quite possible she'd refuse to see him, or her eccentric aunt would throw him out on his ear.

He ignored those possibilities as he rounded a bend in the road and crested a small rise. Beyond the woods lay a large pasture, dotted with sheep and shaggy ponies, all amicably grazing. The drive meandered down a gentle incline to curve past hedges and some spectacular azaleas in fulsome bloom. Clumps of daffodils lined the road, lending an additional note of spring cheer to the landscape.

Beyond the hedges and the surprising splashes of color rose Underhill Manor, a large house that would have dominated the landscape if not for the presence of the loch behind it and the craggy hills on the other side. It was a typical Scottish landscape of water, mountain, and sky, one he'd loved his entire life. Sublimely spare and harshly beautiful, it seemed the last sort of place one would find a sought-after diamond of the British *ton*.

Royal's heart skipped a few beats in anticipation of soon encountering that highly polished gem, but he chose to ignore it. He was here to see a friend and possibly lift his own black mood. If there were anything that could kick him out of his frustrating mental state, it was the sharp side of Ainsley's tongue.

He set the roan to trotting and made his way down the hill. For all the neglect he'd seen up to this point, the areas surrounding the house presented a better picture. The fences along the pasture were in good repair, the hedges trimmed, and the sheep looked champion—fat and healthy even after a long winter. Around the ewes gamboled a fair number of lambs, and the ponies, obviously work animals, looked sturdy and well cared for under their coats.

Lady Margaret might not give a damn about some appearances, but it was clear she cared about what truly mattered. The pasturelands appeared well managed, and the livestock were in peak condition.

Whatever else was going on, Ainsley was not languishing away in eccentric poverty.

Royal tucked his head against a stiff breeze off the loch and urged the big horse into a canter. A few minutes later, he rode through a gap in the low stonewalls that surrounded the manor's immediate grounds and into the courtyard that fronted the house. Bringing Demetrius to a halt before the front door, he glanced around the eerily deserted space with a frown. The unease that had dogged him in the woods returned full force.

Underhill was a typical seventeenth-century manor house, sturdy and dour. It had uneven rooflines with crow-stepped gables, crenellated walkways connecting two wings to the main tower house, and a number of fanciful-looking corner turrets. The stone had gone smoky with age, and the diamond-paned windows were dark, drapes grimly pulled against the day. If he didn't know better, he would have assumed the house empty.

Incongruously, the front door was a bright, cheerful blue, a welcoming note in the otherwise lonely aspect. The only signs of life were the weeds growing up from the gravel and a pair of dippers flitting from turret to turret.

When no footman emerged to take his horse, Royal sighed. He swung his bad leg up over the saddle, grimacing as he made a sliding dismount, putting most of his weight onto his good leg. Thankfully, Demetrius was used to his awkward antics by now, so he did little but shake his bridle, impatient for watering and a feed.

Royal patted his neck. "I know, old fellow, we'll get you squared away soon enough."

Noting the absence of posts to tie up his horse, he dropped the reins to the ground. Demetrius was too well behaved to bolt.

He stalked up to the door and knocked, then peered up at the windows on the first floor. Several long seconds passed before a curtain twitched at one of the windows. He waited another few minutes, then once more thudded his fist on the blasted door. This time, he heard the faint echo of his knock.

Unfortunately, it failed to produce any additional proof of life.

He rubbed his forehead. Were Ainsley and her aunt no longer in residence? Was it possible she'd returned to London? She'd said in her last letter that she wouldn't travel south before June, but she could be impulsive that way, and it was possible she'd decided to defy her father's orders and return home early.

Or maybe she'd even changed her mind about Cringlewood and decided to marry the blighter. That seemed unlikely, given her apparent animosity toward the marquess. But she wouldn't be the first woman to change her mind about a man, especially one who was rich, titled, and handsome.

And able-bodied.

Royal closed his eyes and pulled in a few deep breaths, trying to ease the tight feeling in his chest at the thought of Ainsley as another man's wife. A loud whicker brought him back to himself, and he turned to find Demetrius regarding him with what he swore was equine sympathy.

"I hear you," he said, returning to pick up the reins. "I'll never find out the truth if I keep standing about like a pinhead. Let's see if anyone's around back."

They walked around the west-facing wing to find a well-maintained set of stables and two smaller outbuildings. There was also a large kitchen garden, tidily kept and showing evidence of spring planting. Beyond the boxes of vegetables and herbs were ornamental gardens and a lawn that ran down to the loch. The flower garden and the lawns, however, looked poorly tended. In fact, some of the sheep had wandered over from the pasture and were calmly wreaking havoc in the flowerbeds. Royal couldn't help wincing at the wreckage. Perhaps Lady Margaret had been forced to economize, spending only on those things that supported the estate.

Or perhaps she was as barmy as everyone said and didn't give a damn about appearances.

One of the stable's double doors opened and out clomped a stooped-shouldered man dressed in breeches and a smock. His boots were so deplorable it was as if he'd been mucking out the Augean stables. He looked seventy if he was a day but stomped over with a fair degree of energy, even if the scowl on his face suggested he suffered from the rheumatics.

"Here, now. Who are ye to be sneakin' aboot like a cutpurse?" he barked. "Her ladyship weren't expectin' no visitors. Be on yer way, or I'll be forced to fetch me pistol and have at ye."

Since there was no pistol in sight, it wasn't much of a threat. But Royal gave the old fellow full marks for effort. "Your precautions, while laudable, are entirely unnecessary. While I may not be expected, I'm sure Lady Margaret will see me."

"Then why didn't ye say that?"

"I just did," Royal said.

"Bloody nob with yer breaktooth words," the old man muttered. "I doubt her ladyship will be wantin' to see the likes of you."

At least she was home. "I'm a friend of Lady Ainsley Matthews, who *is* expecting me."

It was an out and out lie, but he had no intention of leaving until he was sure she was safe. His instincts were now practically screaming at him.

His wizened nemesis gaped at him. "Ye know Lady Ainsley is here?"

Royal frowned. "Of course I do. It's not exactly a secret, is it?"

"Who are ye, if ye don't mind me askin'?"

"Royal Kendrick. I've ridden up from Castle Kinglas to call on Lady Ainsley and her aunt."

The old man snorted. "One of the Kendrick lads, eh? That explains it."

Royal wasn't sure exactly what it explained, but he suspected that the twins' wild reputation might have made it to this little corner of the Highlands. Still, he fancied that his interrogator's hostility abated a jot.

"And who do I have the privilege of addressing?" Royal asked with exaggerated politeness.

"Darrow, stable master and coachman to her ladyship. And groom," he added in a disgruntled tone. "When young Willy is off on errands."

Lady Margaret must be verging on destitution if she could only employ one decrepit coachman and one groom.

Darrow's expression suddenly switched to one of professional interest. "That's a fine piece of horseflesh ye have there."

"He is, and I would be most grateful if you could see to his needs. If you're up to it," he added a moment later. "If not, I can do it."

"Of course I'm up to it," the old man snapped. "I'm no in the grave yet. Will ye be stayin' the night?"

Royal pulled off his hat and scrubbed his head. "I have no idea. I've yet to talk to anyone in the house."

"Why the bloody hell not?"

"Because no one the bloody hell answered the door when I knocked."

"Och, that'll be Hector, for ye. Useless," Darrow said. "All right, I'll see to this laddie's needs and get him settled."

"Thank you." Royal patted Demetrius. "I'll come check on you in a bit, good boy."

The horse nickered and then docilely went off with the old man, who handled the animal with practiced ease.

"By the way, how do I get into the house?" he called after Darrow.

The coachman pointed past one of the outbuildings. "Go ye to the kitchen and knock. Mrs. Campbell or Betty will let ye in and fetch her ladyship. If ye try the front door again, ye'll be waitin' all bloody day for Hector."

Clearly, Lady Margaret had a servant problem. Royal found it hard to believe that Ainsley would put up with the likes of the mysterious Hector.

The kitchen was easy enough to find, since several large windows were opened to catch the breeze, and the smell of apple pie and baking bread wafted out in delicious waves. Lady Margaret might preside over a madhouse, but it appeared that Bedlam had a competent cook.

Since the door stood wide open, Royal ducked his head under the lintel and took the few steps down to the flagstone floor. A middle-aged woman, her brown hair tidy under a neat cap, was slicing potatoes at a wooden table in the middle of the old-fashioned but well-organized kitchen. She quietly sang an old Highland ballad that Royal's mother used to sing, although she broke off when a clattering noise erupted from a door on the other side of the long, low-ceiling room.

"Och, Betty," she exclaimed. "Ye'll not be dropping any more of the crockery, I hope. Not after ye broke my best mixing bowl, just last week."

"Never fear, Mum," answered a cheery voice. "Just puttin' the trays away."

A moment later, a young woman emerged, wiping her hands on her apron. "I was . . ." She pulled up short when she saw Royal. "Mum, who's that?"

The cook spun around. "Excuse me, sir, but how did ye get in here?" Then she winced before trying for a smile. "I mean, how can I help ye?"

Royal doffed his hat. "I'm sorry if I startled you, ma'am.

I've come to see Lady Margaret. When I knocked on the front door, no one answered."

The women exchanged a glance. "Hector," they said simultaneously.

"Indisposed *again*, the daft fool," Mrs. Campbell muttered.

Indisposed, no doubt, imbibing a wee too many drams of whisky.

"I beg yer pardon, sir. Willy has gone into the village on an errand," she said apologetically, "else he would have answered it."

Betty, a bonny girl with a pretty smile and flaming red hair, gave Royal a flirtatious wink. "Or I would have, if I'd heard ye. Ye can be sure I would have answered."

"Er, thank you," Royal said.

"None of that, lass," her mother said with heavy disapproval. "He's a gentleman, dinna ye ken? Not one of yer flirts down at the tavern."

"Sorry, Mum," her daughter said, not sounding the least bit sorry.

"Is Lady Margaret at home?" Royal asked with some exasperation.

"And is her ladyship expectin' ye?" Mrs. Campbell asked a mite warily.

"Not entirely," he hedged. "But Lady Ainsley will not be surprised to see me. We're good friends."

The cook eyed him, clearly dubious.

Royal gave her a coaxing smile. "Perhaps you could tell Lady Margaret or Lady Ainsley that Royal Kendrick has ridden up from Castle Kinglas. I apologize for appearing so abruptly, but my brother, the Earl of Arnprior, asked me to convey his greetings."

As might be expected, invoking Nick's title tipped the scales in his favor.

"Betty, take Mr. Kendrick straight up to the front parlor," said the cook. "Then see if Lady Margaret is available."

"Aye, Mum."

"Take him *straight* to the parlor," the cook reiterated.

Betty rolled her eyes, but nodded.

Royal followed her through a swinging door, then up shallow steps and into a narrow corridor running toward the front of the house. They emerged into the entrance hall, a handsome, somber space with stone floors and paneled walls covered with large, ornately framed portraits of pre-sumably Lady Margaret's ancestors. He could swear they were eyeballing him with the same suspicious regard he'd encountered from the servants.

None of it made any sense.

Betty opened a door off the hall. "Please wait in here, sir."

He limped past her into the room. "Thank you. And if Lady Ain—"

"I think Lady Margaret is takin' a nap," the girl inter-rupted. "I'll pop up and check."

"Could you please tell her I'd like to see her as soon as possible?" he asked, grasping the fraying ends of his temper.

"If she's awake, I'll do just that." She flashed him a cheeky grin before smartly shutting the door.

Royal muttered a few curses to relieve his spleen, then made his way to a red velvet chaise by the fireplace. If only he'd thought to ask Betty to fetch some tea—or, better yet, whisky, since the long day had taken a toll.

Easing down onto the settee, he looked around the spa-cious and well-appointed drawing room. With expensive, rather old-fashioned furnishings, good carpets, and splendid silk drapes swagged back with extravagant gold cords, it was obviously for formal use. Still, despite its splendor, there was an air of rather sad, faded gentility. A thin layer of dust coated the furniture and no fire was laid in the grate, sug-gesting little use.

After ten minutes, his leg stopped aching quite so fiercely, so he got up to inspect the fine landscape over the fireplace and the excellent collection of Meissen porcelain in a pair of glass-fronted cabinets. That took up perhaps ten minutes, after which he returned to the settee. After an equal amount of time, all spent straining his ears to detect any signs of life in the hall, he decided enough was enough.

Mentally cursing eccentric old ladies and young stubborn ones, he stalked out to the entrance hall. Only the dust motes were stirring, dancing in the bolts of sunlight coming in the narrow windows set high in the wall. Two corridors led off from the central space, one back to the kitchen and the other likely to more drawing rooms and the dining room.

That meant he should head for the spiral staircase at the back of the hall and the family rooms on the upper floors. He just hoped he didn't have to search the entire bloody house to find Ainsley. God knows what he might stumble into. A mad monk locked in the cellars wouldn't surprise him in the least.

When he reached the top of the stairs, a long hall ran straight to the back of the house. As he followed it, a thick carpet runner muffled his footsteps. Royal could usually move as quietly as any man raised to hunt and track in the Highlands, but his limp was more pronounced after the long ride. Bad enough to be skulking about like a common criminal, worse to sound like a peg-legged pirate while doing so.

The first door he came to was open, so he stuck his head in.

And almost fell flat on his face.

Sitting on a chaise by the bay window, her slippered feet resting on a stack of pillows and a book propped up on her belly, was an exceedingly pregnant Lady Ainsley Matthews.

* * *

Ainsley grimaced at another sharp twinge in the vicinity of her tailbone. The pains in her lower back had been worse the last few days. It was certainly discouraging, since both the midwife *and* the doctor claimed she had at least another three weeks before the little acrobat in her tummy was ready to make an appearance. Spending that much time in monumental discomfort was a daunting prospect, especially because it also meant another month of ceaseless worry. Her brain—like her body—felt sluggish and thick, refusing to do what she needed it to do.

Come up with an answer to her growing—literally—dilemma.

She sighed and rubbed her enormous stomach both to comfort herself and the baby, who was often kicking like a stubborn donkey. Sometimes she thought the poor mite could even be rebelling at its fate—a monster for a father, and a mother foolish enough to let such a man into her life in the first place.

Ainsley knew that if she didn't exercise a great deal of brains and caution, she and her child would find themselves forever yoked to a man who didn't possess a shred of decency or compassion in his cold, black heart.

She needed a solution, and she needed it fast.

At least she had Aunt Margaret in her corner. No one else could have protected her as fiercely as the elderly woman who had taken her in without hesitation, throwing herself wholeheartedly into the ruse. So far, they'd pulled it off, too. But for the doctor and the midwife, no one outside this household knew Ainsley was pregnant. Certainly, her own family had never guessed, still thinking she'd come north into unwilling exile.

While there *had* been a potentially permanent solution to her problem, the handsome and immensely irritating Scotsman who'd unknowingly thrown her a lifeline deserved better than the horrific scandal Ainsley would drag in her wake. Royal Kendrick had been through enough without her further torching his life like a Guy Fawkes effigy.

Sighing, she once more propped her book on her stomach and tried to focus on the page. It was quite a dreadful book, but she'd run out of reading material last week and had been forced to raid Aunt Margaret's library. Sadly, her aunt's taste tended to run to turgid philosophical tracts and bad translations of Latin poetry.

A quiet footstep sounded in the hall. She felt rather than saw someone pause in the doorway and heard a choked exclamation. Frowning, she glanced up, and what little brain she had left scattered like a flock of frightened starlings. Gazing back at her were the same green-glass eyes she'd been so vividly recalling only a few moments ago. That riveting gaze was now taking in her gigantic belly with ever growing astonishment.

Royal looked as tall, broad-shouldered, and handsome as ever. Many a susceptible girl had all but swooned when he came into a ballroom, imagining him to be a sensitive and romantic poet, with his brooding manner and extraordinary malachite eyes. His limp only added to the image, as did the dramatic Highland garb he wore to such effect.

The idiotic misses had been wrong, at least about the romantic, sensitive part. Royal was as blunt and bad-tempered as Ainsley.

At the moment, though, it wasn't his looks or his manners that were stealing her breath. It was the horrifying realization that her secret was finally out.

When her head started to swim, she had to force herself to start taking in slow, deep breaths.

Don't panic.

Royal was clearly stunned, which meant he hadn't known

about her condition. So now she just had to persuade him to keep his Scottish mouth shut.

"What are you doing here?" she blurted out.

He shook himself, almost like a retriever coming in from the rain. "I was checking to see if anyone actually lived in this benighted house. I found only the cook and her, er, charming daughter."

Ainsley couldn't help scowling. Betty was a very pretty girl, who was also not as big as a house.

"I suppose Betty flirted with you, didn't she?" Then she mentally winced. Who the blasted man flirted with hardly mattered under the circumstances.

Royal stared at her for another excruciatingly long moment. Then he flashed a smile so warm and charming she went lightheaded again.

"You know I don't flirt," he said. Then he tilted his head, as if considering. The late afternoon sunlight caught the red in his burnished mahogany hair, making it glow like fire. "Except with you."

Her heart skipped a beat. She ignored it, since her pulse was often a tad erratic these days.

"I repeat, sir," she said firmly. "What are you doing here?"

"I should think it obvious. I've come to see you."

He crossed the room to join her, his limp pronounced.

"Eating for two, I see," he said, inspecting the generous tea service of sandwiches and cakes. "I hope you don't mind sharing. I thought I would starve to death waiting in vain for your aunt to appear."

"Ah, so you thought you'd explore on your own. That was brassy of you."

When he sat down next to her, Ainsley tried to shift over to give him some room. Royal Kendrick was a big man, and given her present state it would be a miracle if the old chaise didn't collapse under their combined weight.

"You don't have to move," he said. "There's plenty of room for both of us."

They were all but thigh-to-thigh.

She was reminded that Royal had very nice thighs, indeed. "You're quite squishing me. You're ridiculously big."

"Not as big as you," he said as he reached for a teacake.

She glared at him. "Thank you for reminding me what an imbecile you are."

"I'm teasing, lass," he said after he swallowed the teacake in one gulp. "You're as lovely as always. But I'm sure you know that."

When his gaze flickered over her body with evident appreciation, she couldn't help gaping at him. How could a man find her attractive when her figure resembled the Prince Regent's rotund bulk?

"Although your present condition does explain a few things," he added.

Oh, God. Whatever must he think of her? This had to be the most embarrassing moment of her life.

"Royal, I—"

He plucked the book from her lap and lifted an eyebrow. "Spinoza? Really?"

"I was trying to lull myself into a doze."

"That would do it."

After placing the book on the table, he reached for the teapot and replenished her cup. "Here, have some more tea. I suspect my sudden appearance has given you a shock, although no doubt a welcome one."

She eyed him, not trusting his cheerful mood. "You're sure of that, are you?"

"Without a doubt. We always get along so splendidly."

"Perhaps, when we're not trying to kill each other."

"Drink." He handed her the cup.

After a few sips, which did seem to steady her, she

put down her cup and adopted a stern expression. "Mr. Kendrick—"

"Mr. Kendrick? Pet, I think we're beyond such formalities, especially under the present circumstances."

"Mr. Kendrick," she repeated firmly, "I do not want you to take this the wrong way—"

He flashed a roguish grin. "You're sure of that, are you?"

She contemplated stabbing him with the cake knife.

He took in her glare. "All right, I promise I won't tease anymore."

"A promise you will no doubt break within the next ten minutes."

"Ainsley, it's just so bloody good to see you that I couldn't help myself."

He *was* studying her with obvious pleasure, which she found rather perplexing. "Royal, what are you doing here? Now is not the most convenient time for visitors."

"Yes, but I had no way of knowing that."

"You know very well that you shouldn't just pop in on people without warning. Nothing in my letters suggested for a moment that you should."

It had been a mistake to write to him, but she'd been bored, lonely, and afraid of what lay before her. While Royal often drove her into a mental frenzy, he also made her feel safe, as odd as it seemed. Sending those letters had eased her anxiety, as if setting words to page would somehow protect her and the baby from harm.

"Victoria was worried about you, so she suggested I ride up here and see if you were all right." His shrug was apologetic. "It seemed like a sensible suggestion at the time."

Her heart stuttered as she pressed a quick hand to her belly. "Do you think Victoria knows about this?"

"No, pet. She simply sensed something was wrong. Nothing specific."

"Thank God." Then she mustered a scowl. "Apparently, it

didn't occur to you to give me some notice before charging north on your noble steed."

He weighed his reply. Or perhaps he was simply pondering what to eat next, since he reached across her for a meringue.

"It occurred to me. But you might have told me not to come," he said before swallowing the tart whole.

"Will you *please* stop shoveling food into your mouth? It's like watching a vulture attack a carcass."

He smiled. "You're one to talk."

"I'm allowed, you brute. I'm eating for two."

"I recall that you liked to eat even before you got in your present condition."

For some ridiculous reason, his comment stung more than it should have. "If you're going to be insulting, please leave now."

He looked startled that she took his banter so seriously. "Ainsley, I like that you don't pretend to be something you're not. Society girls pick at their food, and they must spend a good part of their life on the verge of starvation. You're far too intelligent for that nonsense."

She managed a weak smile. Really, it was ridiculous to fight about something as inconsequential as her eating habits when her carefully constructed ruse was crumbling to bits.

"And you *should* have something to eat," he added, placing some sandwiches on her plate. "You need to keep up your strength."

He seemed perfectly sincere. Even when they argued, she always knew Royal worried about her more than himself.

In fact, no one had ever worried about her quite like he did, not even her own family. When he abandoned her after that horrible incident in London, she'd felt astonishingly bereft. Yes, she'd behaved badly by not telling him about Cringlewood, but he'd never given her the chance to explain.

When she tried, sending him an apologetic note two days after that disastrous dinner party, he and Lord Arnprior had already departed for Scotland.

Ainsley had done her best to forget Royal Kendrick after that, knowing that her future did not lie with an impecunious younger son from the Highlands. Only when they met again in Glasgow this past Christmas had they been able to reestablish a tentative sort of friendship.

She took a bite of cucumber sandwich, mostly to please him. The baby now took up so much room she felt like her stomach was crowding into her throat.

Royal studied her. "How are you, sweetheart? Really?"

She forced a wobbly smile, resisting the foolish urge to start bawling. "I'm perfectly well."

He lifted a skeptical eyebrow. "Try again."

She put down her plate with a sigh. "All right. If you must know, I feel perfectly wretched."

And she wasn't just talking about her aching back, or her swollen feet, or how hard it was to get a decent night's sleep. Her life was a disaster, and she had no idea how to repair the damage.

"I take it that the Marquess of Cringlewood is responsible for your present condition."

She blinked in dismay that he would take so blunt a tack. Then again, *blunt* was Royal Kendrick's middle name.

"I wouldn't have expected anything else," he added as she stewed in silence. "I'm just a bit surprised that it happened in the first place."

Meaning no decent girl would allow something like this to happen. Or, if she did, she would have the good sense to marry the man responsible.

"You aren't the only one," she muttered.

He frowned. "What do you mean by that?"

She grimaced. "I cannot imagine what you must think of me."

Even though he'd done a very good job of hiding it, he had to be disgusted with her. It made her sick to her stomach to know she'd lost his good opinion.

And it wasn't even your fault.

But how could she tell him that? Men always blamed women, even good men like Royal Kendrick. Ainsley wouldn't hold it against him if he did, because her own naïve foolishness had walked her right into the situation in the first place. No one had forced her to go off with Leonard that afternoon, nor had she tried to stop him—at least not at first.

By the time she had, it had been too late to do anything but try to manage the stunning and terrible consequences. Because everyone, from her father on down, would have held *her* responsible, as unfair as that was. They would have said that *she* was the guardian of her virtue, not the man she was supposed to marry. Some might even say she was lucky Leonard still wanted to marry her, given that she was no longer a virgin.

Well, *they* could say whatever they wanted, because Ainsley would never let any man treat her like that again, even if it meant spending the rest of her life in a dreary hole in Scotland. She would join a convent before she allowed Leonard to touch her again or get anywhere near her child.

She jumped a bit as Royal's long fingers wrapped around hers in a comforting hold. She gripped him rather desperately, feeling like a lost child as she stared into his warm gaze.

Apparently, he wasn't disgusted with her, after all. She sniffled, horrified to find herself blinking back tears.

"Och, tears from Lady Ainsley?" he gently teased. "Does she have a heart, after all?"

"You're a lout," she said, trying to scowl. As usual, he understood she hated feeling vulnerable. "And my tears have nothing to do with you. Breeding tends to make one feel mawkish."

"I'm not judging you, lass, especially not for wanting to avoid marriage with Cringlewood, which I presume is the reason you're hiding in this backwater. The man's an intolerable ass. Why you let him come near you in the first place is the bloody mystery."

Annoyed, she tried to yank her hand away. "It wasn't really my choice."

When his fingers tightened, she mentally cursed at her slip.

"Are you saying he forced himself on you?" he asked in a voice that had gone soft and rather terrifying.

Damn, damn, damn.

"That's not what I meant," she said, finally able to extract her hand. The *last* thing she needed was a knight errant. Knowing Royal, he would ride straight to London and challenge Leonard to a duel. Then the cat would be truly out of the bag.

"What *did* you mean?"

"I . . . nothing."

His incredulous gaze dropped to her belly. "Nothing?"

She bit her lip in frustration. Pregnancy had turned her brain to mush. "It was a misunderstanding. Between his lordship and me."

"That is one hell of a misunderstanding."

"Don't you think I know that? I'm the one with the cannonball in my stomach."

Royal shook his head, clearly perturbed. "If the marquess finds out about this . . ."

"I'll be forced to marry him. Which is why he can *never* find out."

He made a visible effort to collect himself. "Ainsley, I don't wish to offend you—"

"Too late, I'm afraid," she interrupted.

"And you know I'll support you in any way I can," he

continued. "But Cringlewood is the father of your child. When he does find out you kept this from him—"

She jabbed a finger into his cravat. "You don't know a blasted thing about it, Royal Kendrick. I do *not* want that man anywhere near me, or my child. He's utterly selfish and mean-spirited, and would make my life a misery. I refuse to marry him."

Troubled, he searched her face. Ainsley's heart all but lodged in her throat, praying he would accept her vague explanation.

He wrapped his hand around her finger. "I would never betray you, lass. I promise. Word of a Kendrick."

Relief swept through her, leaving her feeling limp and washed out. "Thank you," she whispered.

Then his gaze narrowed. "But if that bastard hurt you, he won't get away with it. I won't let him."

She again yanked her hand away. "Leave it alone, Royal. Please."

"Ainsley, I'm not—"

A thumping out in the hall interrupted them.

Thank God.

"Splendid. That must be Aunt Margaret," Ainsley said with idiotic false cheer.

A moment later, her great-aunt stomped in, her polished walnut cane thudding emphatically on the floorboards. She stopped in the middle of the room, a startling sight in her extravagantly trimmed purple gown, matching turban, and glossily buckled heels that had ceased to be in style years ago. With her pince-nez firmly in place, she was the very picture of decrepit ferocity as she glowered at Royal.

Aunt Margaret did enjoy making an entrance.

"Ainsley, have you gone mad? Why are you receiving visitors in your state?"

"It wasn't by choice, I assure you," Ainsley said dryly.

Royal hauled himself to his feet, regarding Lady Margaret

with something akin to astonishment. Ainsley understood exactly how he felt.

Lady Margaret Baird was the daughter of an earl and the granddaughter of a duchess. She was both wealthy and well connected, and could live however she chose—which in her case meant taking the occasional lover and dressing like an Eastern pasha in wildly colored silk banyans and matching headgear. In her later years, it had also meant an increasingly reclusive lifestyle, tucked away on her estate in this quiet corner of the Highlands.

"Then what the devil are you doing up here, young man?" Aunt Margaret demanded. "Why didn't you wait in the drawing room until I arrived?"

"I did," Royal said. "After a considerable time, I assumed everyone had forgotten I was there."

"I was taking a nap," the old woman said.

"Well, that explains it," Royal said with polite sarcasm.

"It actually does," Ainsley said. Her aunt's afternoon nap was sacrosanct. No one dared interrupt it unless the house was burning down, and possibly not even then.

"I take it you know my niece," Aunt Margaret said.

Royal nodded. "We're friends."

"And who are you? For some reason, Betty couldn't remember your name."

"She was too busy flirting to commit it to memory," Ainsley couldn't help saying.

Her aunt ran a practiced eye over Royal's figure. "Can't really blame the gel for that, I suppose. He *is* a fine-looking specimen."

Ainsley glanced at Royal's expression and had to swallow a chuckle.

"This is Royal Kendrick, Aunt," she managed. "Lord Arnprior's brother."

"So, you're one of the Kendrick boys, are you?" She

glanced at Ainsley. "I *did* fancy his brother, at one point. A lovely, braw laddie. We got along splendidly, as I recall."

Royal looked appalled. "Ah, do you mean the earl?"

"Lord, no. He's a handsome fellow but much too starched-up for my tastes. I meant the next one down. Logan, I believe was his name. Such lovely shoulders." She winked at Ainsley. "Not to mention the rest of him."

"Good God," Royal muttered.

"Well, enough reminiscing of days gone by," Aunt Margaret said, once more looking severe. "You're here now, Mr. Royal Kendrick, and I suppose we'll just have to deal with you."

"It's all right," Ainsley said. "I'll take care of him."

"What you will do is take a nap. *I* will have a little chat with Mr. Royal, and find out exactly why he's here."

Ainsley's heart jumped as if the baby had just elbowed it. "Oh, he's just visiting—"

"I will be happy to speak to her ladyship," Royal said firmly.

When Ainsley started to protest, her aunt threw her a sharp look and gave a tiny shake of her head.

There was no arguing with the old girl once she'd made up her mind. Besides, what choice did she have? Aunt Margaret had so far guarded her secrets with canny loyalty. Ainsley had to trust she would know how to throw Royal off the scent.

"If you're such a good friend, help the gel up," her aunt said. "Can't do it on her own anymore. Sometimes we forget about her, and then she has to spend all afternoon stuck on the chaise."

"She's joking," Ainsley explained, when Royal looked outraged. Still, she couldn't help blushing to the roots of her hair. Her aunt was the *most* embarrassing person, if also the kindest.

Royal hooked a hand under her arm, easily hoisting her off the chaise. When Ainsley staggered, he carefully supported her until she was steady.

"Sorry," she said. "My balance isn't very good these days."

"Your center of gravity is off," he said with a faint smile. "Considerably."

She stuck out her tongue at him, which only made him laugh.

As he helped her to the door, he bent his head to murmur in her ear. "By the way, I intend to have a very frank discussion with your aunt about this situation."

"You will not," she hissed. "It's none of your business."

"Och, don't fash yourself, lass," he said, teasing her in a heavy brogue. "Ye ken I'm on yer side."

She didn't doubt it, but the truth was the last thing she could—or would—ever tell him.

Chapter Three

When Royal entered the parlor after dinner, Lady Margaret leveled a scowl at him from her perch by the fireplace.

"Your visit is monstrously ill timed, sir," she complained again. "We've gone to exhausting lengths to protect my niece's privacy, and now you've upended everything." The old gal snorted. "Just like a Kendrick. Always causing trouble."

"Not me," he protested. "I'm the good Kendrick."

"Ha," said Lady Margaret.

"Ha," Ainsley echoed from the chaise, her teacup resting on her belly.

Still in the same gown she'd worn this afternoon, she'd kicked off her shoes and propped her swollen feet on a stack of pillows. Although never a high stickler in terms of behavior, Ainsley had always been fanatical about her appearance. She'd never looked anything less than perfect, down to the last button and bow. The fact that she wouldn't bother to change her dress for dinner, and that she casually displayed her stocking feet in front of a man, told Royal volumes about her state of mind.

To him, she would always be spectacular, no matter what she wore. If anything, pregnancy had enhanced her beauty, turning her into a lush goddess of impending motherhood.

Yet it was clear she was in a great deal of discomfort, and he couldn't help but be worried. She'd all but winced her way through dinner, constantly shifting in her chair and barely touching her food.

Royal hated seeing her so wan and forlorn, and he had to repress the overwhelming impulse to gather her into his arms and rock her like a fretful child. Acting on that instinct, however, might earn him a dainty fist to the jaw. Like him, Ainsley hated coddling.

She hadn't minded a wee bit of coddling this afternoon, before they started talking about Cringlewood, but then she'd turned into a harridan. She'd been angry with him for wanting an explanation. Also, if he didn't miss his mark, she'd been panicked, and that made him even more determined to get to the bottom of the mystery. If the marquess *had* harmed her in any way, Royal would see to it that the bastard faced the consequences.

For now, though, he had to do what was best for Ainsley, which meant soothing rather than upsetting her. Lady Margaret had made that abundantly clear during their chat this afternoon—a chat that had quickly turned into a high-handed lecture. She'd dodged all his questions about Cringlewood, making it clear that the marquess was none of his business.

Royal had no intention of giving up on the matter. But retribution, if required, would obviously have to wait.

"Again, my lady, I beg your pardon for surprising you," Royal said as he lowered himself into the matching club chair next to Lady Margaret. "But I would *again* like to point out that none of this is my fault. How was I to know I would be walking into so dramatic a situation? No sane person could have expected this."

"You know, I should just have the footman throw you out on your ear and be done with it," Ainsley said tartly.

"You'd have to find him first," Royal said.

Hector had finally surfaced for dinner. The lone footman

was at least sixty years old, wore an elaborately curled wig, and dressed in black and gold livery that had obviously seen better days. He was also, as Lady Margaret had explained, quite deaf and so rarely heard the bell. After depositing a number of plates on the sideboard, he'd disappeared for the rest of the meal. Royal had served their food, since Lady Margaret couldn't be expected to do so and Ainsley could barely get out of her chair.

Lady Margaret's gaze drifted thoughtfully over him. "I do believe you'd make a rather good footman, Mr. Kendrick. You've got a grand set of shoulders and lovely leg muscles." She waggled her wiry gray brows at him. "I'd quite like to see you in livery."

Ainsley smothered a laugh. "Have some tea, Royal. You look about to choke."

As he poured a cup, Lady Margaret went back to glaring at him. "But don't think your considerable manly attributes excuse the impropriety of your sudden appearance on my doorstep. My niece is correct. We should have Hector evict you, forthwith."

Royal simply gave Lady Margaret a bland smile and handed her a teacup.

"I was only joking, Aunt," Ainsley said. "Since he's here now, he might as well be of some use."

"I'm happy to help in any way I can," he said after getting himself a cup. "Even serving as footman when necessary."

He took a sip. It was a splendid gunpowder tea, expertly brewed. Lady Margaret was eccentric, but she didn't stint on comfort. Dinner had been excellent, the wine French and expensive, and the after-dinner port top-notch. He'd had ample opportunity to enjoy it too, since Lady Margaret had insisted he remain at the dining table in solitary splendor for a half hour while the ladies repaired to the drawing room to await the tea service.

If not for the pressing nature of Ainsley's situation, he would have found the entire episode irritatingly comical.

There'd been nothing comical about her behavior last January in Glasgow. Her changeable, even erratic emotions now finally made perfect sense. It was clear to him that much of her conduct had been generated by fear of scandal and fear of what Cringlewood would do if he discovered her pregnancy.

Lady Margaret finally gave over her tetchy mood. "I know my household must seem rather ridiculous to you, Mr. Kendrick, but there is a method to our madness."

"Not ridiculous or mad in the least, my lady," he said. "Just a wee bit unusual."

"'Ridiculous' does rather fit the bill," Ainsley said, struggling to reach for the teapot.

"Here, let me," Royal said, jumping up too quickly for his protesting thigh.

Ainsley frowned. "Be careful of your leg. I'm sure your ride today wasn't good for it."

"My leg is fine, pet," he said as he prepared her cup.

"I *am* going to hire you," Lady Margaret said with approval. "After all, there's nothing like a handsome footman in livery to cheer up the ladies, eh? That's why I hired Hector all those years ago." She winked at Ainsley. "It wasn't for his skill in polishing the silver, I assure you."

Ainsley pressed a finger to her lips. Royal couldn't tell if she was amused or horrified.

"Sadly, my lady, I must draw the line at prancing about in livery," he said, trying not to think about who exactly polished what, back in Hector's better days.

"Ah, well," said Lady Margaret, "I suppose you wouldn't look any better in livery than you do in that kilt, so I'll just have to be grateful for small favors."

Royal made a mental note to avoid spending any time alone with the old girl.

"Speaking of additional help," he said, determined to change the subject, "I'm assuming you have such a small staff in order to protect Ainsley's privacy. You've pulled it off exceedingly well. I heard not a word of gossip in the village, and I did ask questions."

"And I am determined to keep it that way. Do you understand?" Lady Margaret asked.

"You have my word that Ainsley's secret is safe with me."

"I'm glad to hear it," she replied. "I'd be most distressed to order Hector to shoot you and toss your body into the loch."

The notion of Hector lurking about with an old flintlock was rather alarming. "I don't imagine my family would be too happy about it either."

"She's joking," Ainsley said. "But it hasn't been easy. Not for any of us."

"Did you let some of the servants go? Surely, you're not always this short staffed."

Ainsley shrugged. "Yes, we are, actually. Betty, Cook, and Hector take care of the house, and there's old Ben and Willy in the stables. Others come in from the village as needed."

"Could never abide legions of servants tromping around my house," the old woman said. "Or guests, for that matter. All they do is eat their fool heads off, natter like idiots, and cause a great deal of fuss and bother."

Royal arched an eyebrow at Ainsley. "Underhill Manor seems perfect for your needs."

"Thank God," she said. "I would have been sunk without Aunt Margaret and Underhill to safeguard me from . . . well, you know."

Whenever Royal thought of the marquess, he wanted to punch something—preferably Cringlewood's rotten face.

"I wondered why you wouldn't stay in Glasgow for Nick

and Victoria's wedding celebration," he said. "It seemed odd at the time."

"I wanted to be there," she said. "But I was beginning to gain too much weight."

He'd noticed she was plumper as soon as he first laid eyes on her in the Glasgow Assembly Rooms in December. She'd carried it well—and still carried it well—but he'd had no idea of the cause. No one had, except possibly Victoria, and she'd never breathed a word.

"When did you know you were . . ." He waved a vague hand in the direction of her stomach.

Ainsley blushed. "Well, um . . ."

Lady Margaret rolled her eyes. "It is beyond me why the young people today are so missish. When I was young, we didn't mince words on such matters. Ainsley became pregnant at the end of August."

Again, it all made perfect sense. "Which means you could give birth at any time."

"Not according to the physician," Ainsley said with a sigh. "He thinks another three weeks, at least."

"Good Lord, you're as big as a house," Royal said. "Ah, what I mean is—"

"I know what you mean," she groused. "It seems impossible that I could get any bigger."

"Dr. MacTavish is an imbecile," Lady Margaret said. "I feel sure you'll go into labor within the next few days."

Alarm spiked in Royal's gut. "The physician is an imbecile? Then why the hell are you letting him anywhere near Ainsley?"

"Dr. MacTavish is actually very good," Ainsley said. She put her teacup on the low table between them and wriggled her body around until she could put her feet on the floor. "He's been attending to Lady Margaret for years."

"And ordering me around for years," she grumbled.

"Telling me not to drink whisky *or* take snuff. He's more of an old woman than I am."

"Most importantly, he's discreet," Ainsley said. "He's very loyal to my aunt and has sworn to keep my secret."

"That's *not* the most important thing," Royal said. "The most important thing is that you have a physician who knows what he's doing. You should not be endangering yourself in any way, Ainsley."

"I'll be in more danger if my secret gets out."

"Christ in Heaven, are you saying your reputation is more important than your life?"

She let out an exasperated sigh. "You don't need to fuss about this, really."

"Someone has to," he snapped. "You're as pale as a ghost and you're obviously in pain. I'm writing to Nick tomorrow and having him send our doctor up to see you."

When panic flared in her beautiful gaze, he got a bit of a shock. Ainsley looked terrified, and nothing had ever terrified her before.

"Dr. MacTavish is perfectly capable of attending my niece's delivery," Lady Margaret said, reversing course. "Lord knows he's delivered enough squalling brats over the years, and Ainsley is perfectly healthy. I'm sure there won't be an issue."

"But—"

"The village midwife is taking care of me too," Ainsley said. "She's very experienced."

He couldn't help but worry. Childbirth was a dangerous time for a woman, as he well knew. His own mother had died bringing Kade into the world, and her traumatic death had wrought devastation on his family. If anything happened to Ainsley . . .

"Royal, please," she said in a tight voice. "Let it go."

He moved to join her on the chaise. She stared up at him,

her violet gaze wide and pleading. She was frightened and it was obvious it had nothing to do with her impending labor.

When he took her hand, her palm was damp. "All right, sweetheart. I'll let it alone, but only if you promise me that the doctor and midwife really are competent."

She sagged forward with relief. "Yes, I promise they are."

"There is no need for foolish heroics. I have the matter quite in hand," Lady Margaret said, making a huffy noise. "I know how to take care of my own niece, sir."

"I apologize, my lady," Royal said. "I didn't mean to offend."

"As if you care about offending people," Ainsley said. She took up a napkin from the tea tray and blotted her cheeks and forehead.

Royal eyed her. She'd recovered her equanimity, but she was perspiring and looked utterly worn out.

She gave him a wan smile. "I'm a little overheated. The midwife says it's completely normal at this stage."

"I'll take your word for it," he said with a reassuring smile. "So, the midwife is to be trusted to keep the secret as well?"

"Mrs. Peters wouldn't be allowed near Ainsley otherwise," Lady Margaret said.

Taking in her stern countenance, Royal could believe it. Still . . .

"Tell me how you've been managing these last few months. After all, people *do* know you're visiting your aunt. Don't they wonder why you've gone into seclusion?"

Ainsley shot her aunt a disgusted look. "Aunt Margaret has told everyone I'm suffering from melancholy and occasionally even fall into bouts of hysteria. Dr. MacTavish has recommended total seclusion and complete bedrest."

When Lady Margaret flashed him a smug grin, Royal had to chuckle. Ainsley was not a woman prone to hysterics.

"I'm glad you both find it so amusing," Ainsley grumbled. "Because I'll never live it down."

"Better than Cringlewood finding out your secret," Lady Margaret replied.

Royal's amusement suffered a quick death. Ainsley refused to meet his eye, but he could sense anxiety curling within her like a tangled skein of yarn.

"Yes, about that," he said.

When the clock on the mantelpiece chimed, Lady Margaret looked surprised.

"Heavens, look at the time," she said. "I must be off to bed." It was only nine o'clock, but her attitude suggested they'd been carousing for hours. "Now, where did I leave my confounded cane?"

Royal fetched it from under her chair, and then gave her a hand to rise.

"How nice to have a brawny fellow around the house," she said. "If I were twenty years younger, I wouldn't mind looking under *your* kilt, my lad. Poor Hector is rather long in the tooth for that sort of thing."

"And if you were twenty years younger, I might let you," he replied with a grin.

"Ugh. You're both going to make me ill," Ainsley said.

"Fah, my dear," her aunt said. "I know *exactly* what you're thinking about this handsome young buck. Not that you can do anything about it in your condition."

"Too bad, that," Royal said with an exaggerated sigh.

Ainsley stared at them with patent disbelief.

Her aunt laughed. "We're just teasing, child. Now, do you want me to ring for Betty? She can help you to bed."

"What's the point?" Ainsley said in a grumpy tone. "It's not like I'll be able to sleep."

"I'll keep her company, my lady," Royal said. "When she's ready to go up, I'll ring for the maid."

The old woman looked dubious. "Well, I suppose I can

leave the two of you alone. Despite our jesting, you can hardly get up to mischief in her current state."

I'd be willing to give it a try, though.

Royal squashed the unseemly thought. "She'll be as safe with me as if I were a vestal virgin."

"For God's sake," Ainsley said. "Do you really suppose . . . oh, never mind. It doesn't even bear thinking about. Please go to bed, Aunt Margaret. I'll be up shortly."

"See that you are, my dear. You need your rest."

After her ladyship thumped out, Royal joined Ainsley on the chaise. She wriggled over to make more room for him.

"Are you sure you don't want me to ring for Betty?" he asked. "You're looking rather worn out."

"You try carrying all this extra weight and see how you feel."

"Gruesome, I imagine."

"Especially when the little blighter makes a habit out of drumming its heels on various parts of my insides." She grimaced. "Quite vigorously, I might add."

"Must be a boy," Royal said. "No girl would dare to be so ill-tempered."

She managed a rueful smile. "I'm sorry to be so ill-tempered, myself. You don't deserve to catch the brunt of it."

"You know I don't mind. And I mean it when I say I'll do whatever I can to help you."

She regarded him with a slight frown. "Yes, I do know."

"I admit to quite enjoying your aunt's company. She's almost as entertaining as Angus."

"Please, do not remind me of your grandfather. He should count himself lucky that I didn't murder him during that stupid elopement."

Royal grinned. "He feels the same about you—not that you had to spend much time with him that day. You were spared that much at least, unlike the twins and their hapless victims."

"That's because I refused to allow him into our carriage,"

Ainsley said. "The Kendrick family should be exceedingly grateful to me, because it's the only reason your grandfather is still alive."

After kidnapping Ainsley from a ball, they'd traveled north in two coaches. The lass had made a point of ripping into Angus, berating him over the stupidity of his plan and then ordering the old fellow into the other carriage. Royal and Ainsley had made the rest of the trip alone. Once she'd unburdened her spleen to him, they'd barely exchanged another word until they arrived at Kinglas.

He took her hand and held it in his lap. "I'm sorry if I made things worse for you. That certainly wasn't my intent."

She glanced up, her eyes wide. "Why do you think you made things worse?"

"Because I almost ruined your reputation with our benighted scheme."

"Your grandfather's benighted scheme, you mean. I know you and your brothers were simply witless participants," she said dryly. "But please remember that I didn't ask you to return me to Glasgow. I was quite happy to travel north to Kinglas, once I thought about it."

"You didn't seem happy. You were furious with me for days."

"Recall that I was several months pregnant at the time and not feeling my best."

"Yes, I'm sorry about that, too. It was unfortunate that I put you in so awkward a position." If he *had* known of her predicament, Royal would have done his best to convince her to marry him. It wouldn't have solved all her problems, but at least he could have protected her.

"Under the circumstances, I certainly couldn't marry you," she said. "That would have been horribly unfair to you."

He wanted to disagree, but there was little point.

She withdrew her hand from his loose grip. "I had no intention of marrying Lord Cringlewood, either. I hoped that participating in such a scandalous affair would ruin my reputation, making me entirely unsuitable for marriage to the marquess or anyone else that mattered."

When he flinched, Ainsley sighed. "Sorry, that didn't come out right. I didn't mean you."

"Yes, you did."

She wrinkled her nose, looking adorably rueful. "I couldn't marry you, Royal. I couldn't marry anyone."

"It doesn't matter. As it turns out, your reputation was spared by Nick and Victoria riding to the rescue."

His brother and Victoria had followed in hot pursuit, surmounting all the obstacles that Angus had placed in their path—including an avalanche triggered by his blasted bagpipes.

"Yes, all your hard work was for naught," she gently mocked.

"It was a stupid plan, and I'm well aware that I should have discussed it with you first."

"Or at least made some attempt at courtship before abducting me," she joked. "That's generally how it works."

"What did you think I was doing all those weeks in Glasgow, you daft woman?"

"If reading me lectures is your idea of courtship, no wonder you're still a bachelor."

And would forever remain one, as long as Ainsley Matthews refused to marry him.

"Whether I'm leg-shackled or not is hardly of relevance," he said. "What *is* relevant is finding a solution to your problem, and quickly."

She winced and tried to arch her back again. "Thank you for that entirely unnecessary reminder. Believe me, I am acutely aware of the moment of reckoning hurtling my way."

"Again, what can I do to help?"

"Aside from causing Lord Cringlewood to meet with an unfortunate accident?"

Royal clenched a fist against his thigh. "I wish you would tell me what he did to you."

"Why, so you can kill him with a clear conscience?" she asked with more grim humor.

"Ainsley—"

She waved a hand. "It doesn't matter anymore."

"It matters a hell of a lot. The man's the father of your child, and you're moving mountains to keep that information away from him. Any sane person would want to know why."

She threw him a warning glance. "Any sane person should mind his own business."

"Too bad I'm more than a bit demented, then."

"No, you're just incredibly annoying."

"I work very hard at it, so I'm glad you noticed."

She huffed out a laugh but seemed to be considering how much to tell him. Royal forced himself to be patient, not one of his virtues.

"The Marquess of Cringlewood is not a good man," she finally said. "By the time I came to that conclusion, it was too late. But I simply cannot marry him."

"Not even to give your child the rightful privileges and protections of a father?" he cautiously probed.

"Not even then." She met his gaze, steadfast and determined. "And believe me when I say I have fully considered the consequences of my actions."

He did believe her. Though Ainsley was imperious, she was not impetuous. "And you're obviously convinced your parents would not support you in this decision."

Her laugh was bitter. "My father would drag me to the altar and perform the marriage himself, if need be. This is the only way, Royal. I've thought it through very carefully."

He shoved an exasperated hand back through his hair. "Not carefully enough, if you ask me. What the hell are you going to do once the baby is born?"

"Again, that is none of your business."

It was as he thought. She didn't have a plan for that part yet. *Here goes nothing.*

"Then I suppose you'd better marry me, after all," he said firmly.

She all but rolled off the chaise.

After Royal hauled her back into position, she glared at him. "You *must* stop asking me to marry you."

"Why?"

"You couldn't possibly wish to marry me under these circumstances, and you know it. You're just being noble and self-sacrificing."

"It wouldn't be much of a sacrifice." He was encouraged that she hadn't refused him outright.

"If you're after my money, you can give it up. My father would disown me if I married you."

"I don't give a damn about your money." He'd take her wearing only the gown on her back.

He'd take her out of the gown, too.

She shook her head. "Royal, you are exceedingly generous, but you know we'd kill each other within a week."

"Oh, I can think of worse ways to go."

Ainsley gaped at him. "Are you blind? I look like I swallowed a cannonball. Two cannonballs."

"True, but your bosom has gone from splendid to spectacular. I'm thinking of building a monument to honor your décolletage."

For a few moments, she looked like she didn't know whether to be amused or appalled.

She chose to be appalled. "That is the most disgusting thing I've ever heard. I refuse to sit here and be insulted."

"That was definitely not an insult, Ainsley."

She made a show of getting up, flopping about for a bit

before subsiding with a ferocious scowl. "A gentleman would have helped me up."

"When did you get the idea that I was a gentleman? Certainly not from anything I ever did."

She let out a grudging laugh. "True enough."

He took her hand again. "Ainsley, I meant it when I said I would do anything to help you, including marriage."

She peered at their joined hands, as if they presented her with some sort of problem. "Thank you, Royal. I'm afraid it wouldn't help, though. For one thing, it would simply generate too much gossip."

He ignored the hollow drop of his stomach. He'd known she would refuse him, but he had to try. "Then what can I do to help?"

"I—" She broke off, and then slid him a sideways look so calculating it raised the hairs on his neck.

"What?" he warily asked.

She suddenly sat bolt upright. "Something," she said in a tight voice.

"Could you be more specific?"

She pulled her hand free and clutched her belly. "Something that shouldn't be happening for another three weeks."

Royal stared at her with slowly dawning dismay. "You mean . . ."

"Yes, you'd better fetch my aunt," she gasped. "In fact, you'd better fetch everyone."

Chapter Four

Ainsley leaned on Royal's arm as they inched along the upstairs hall outside her bedroom. Three hours had passed since her water broke and her labor had only slowly advanced. She thought of her bed with longing, but the midwife had suggested she keep moving to speed the baby's entrance into the world.

Of course, the redoubtable Mrs. Peters was currently down in the kitchen, having a nice cup of tea with Cook, not stumbling about the halls. So far, midwifing had certainly not taken much work on her part.

Aunt Margaret had popped out for a bit in a flannel wrapper and an enormous frilly nightcap. After hearing from Mrs. Peters that Ainsley still had hours to go, she had departed for bed, after instructing Royal to keep an eye on things. Amazingly enough, he'd been more than willing to do so, and had even instructed Betty to get some sleep, knowing her assistance would be required later.

In the meantime, there wasn't much for Ainsley to do except walk, curse during the occasional bout of contractions, and beat her brains against her skull. She'd been hoping for a few more weeks to sort out her baby's future, but time had caught up with her.

Royal had been supporting her with quiet concern as she wandered about the halls or tried to find a comfortable seat to take a bit of a rest. His limp was particularly bad tonight. In fact, he was probably in almost as much pain as she was, although he'd never admit it or ever complain. When Ainsley thought about all he'd been through, about the physical and emotional pain he'd endured, her troubles seemed easier to bear.

"Stoic, that's what you are," she muttered.

He bent his head. "What's that?"

She managed a smile. "Nothing."

At the end of the hall, they paused by a window overlooking the gardens. A light rain obscured the dark landscape in a ghostly mist. It was eerily quiet, with only the sounds of the occasional tap of the rain on the windowpanes or the creaking of the old house around them.

Ainsley leaned a hand against the wall, blowing out a breath as a cramp pummeled her lower back. Like all the others, though, this contraction quickly faded, allowing her to straighten up with a sigh.

"All right, love?" Royal murmured.

In the light thrown by the branch of candles on the end table, she saw weariness mark his handsome features. Shadows played under his high cheekbones, and worry or pain, or both, carved lines around his mouth.

"You needn't do this if your leg is bothering you too much," she said. "I'm fine."

He rolled his eyes. "You're in labor. That is far from fine."

"It's a perfectly natural process, as both the doctor and midwife have made clear. With tedious frequency, I might add."

Both Dr. MacTavish and Mrs. Peters were typical nononsense Scots. They'd refused to let her indulge in any fears about the birthing process or engage in lengthy discussion about it. At the time, she'd been grateful for their practical approach. Now, however, she had to admit to being rather terrified, and wished she knew more about what exactly was going to happen next.

"Of course it is," he said in a soothing tone. "There's absolutely nothing to worry about."

"You needn't humor me. I'm not a moron, Royal Kendrick. I know perfectly well the sorts of complications that can arise during birth."

Like dying.

A starkly grim expression contorted his features for a moment. Then he mustered a smile. "I wouldn't dream of calling you a moron. You'd stab me."

She stared at him for a moment, trying to read his mood. Then she remembered that his mother had died in childbirth.

"I'm the moron," she sighed. "Royal, I'm so sorry. This must be a very unpleasant experience for you, given what happened to your poor mother."

He tucked her hand in his arm and got her walking again. "Nonsense. There's nowhere else I'd rather be than with you right now."

She suspected it was the simple truth, and it was miraculous considering what he'd had to put up with since arriving on their doorstep. He'd barely blinked at any of it, though, not even when her water broke in the middle of his marriage proposal. That had possibly been the most mortifying experience in her life, although there'd been quite a string of them lately.

When she'd started to blither out an apology, aghast at the gush of liquid between her legs, Royal had remained calm and hauled himself to his feet.

"Trust me," he'd said as he grabbed a lap blanket from Aunt Margaret's chair. "I've been knee deep in blood and guts more than once. This is nothing."

He'd then wrapped the blanket around her, swept her up into his arms, and carried her off to her bedroom. Though Ainsley had felt the hitch in his step, he'd never faltered. By any measure, Royal Kendrick was a strong, impressive man. He had to be, since lugging her off without dropping her was a herculean feat.

"Still, I'm sure you can't like this," Ainsley said as they slowly made their way back down the softly lit hall. "God knows *I* don't like it."

"I've never been part of a groaning party before," he mused. "It's an experience."

The term was vaguely familiar. "What's a groaning party?"

"Och, it's when the local women gather to help a mother in labor. They clean and cook and assist with the birth. They take care of anything that needs taking care of—including the men, who are regarded as entirely useless in these situations."

"You deserve honorary admission, certainly. You've been exceedingly useful so far." She squeezed his arm. "I'm very grateful that you're here, Royal. Truly. I don't know how to thank you."

"You don't owe me anything, Ainsley. I hate like hell that you've had to go through this by yourself. Your mother and friends should be here to support you."

"I had Aunt Margaret, and now you're here. That's more than enough, as far as I'm concerned. I have no desire to parade my stupidity before the rest of my family and friends."

"You were *not* stupid. Simply naïve."

"That's one way to look at it." She'd certainly been naïve in trusting Leonard, although that wasn't entirely her fault. Her family had been pushing her into his arms for months.

"The fault lies with the bastard who took advantage of you," Royal said grimly. "And with your family. It's insane that you can't depend on them for support."

For someone like him, whose family displayed legendary loyalty to one another, it must indeed seem insane. Despite the many troubles the Kendricks had suffered over the years, she couldn't help but admire and envy their closeness.

"It's pathetic, I'll admit," she said as she came to a halt. "But I simply cannot take the chance that Cringlewood will get wind of this."

Leaning against the wall, she focused on breathing through the contraction that clawed its way through her body. Royal put his arm around her back to support her.

"Do you want to sit now?" he asked.

She squeezed her eyes shut and shook her head, still waiting for the nauseating wave to pass. When it finally did, she straightened up and glanced at the bracket clock on the demilune table.

Hell and damnation.

It was twelve minutes since the last contraction, the same as it had been for *ages*.

"I need to get this blasted baby out of me," she said. "Let's keep walking."

"Are you sure?"

"Yes. What were we saying?"

It helped to keep talking. As long as she had Royal by her side, speaking quietly in that lovely, low brogue of his, she felt she'd be able to manage whatever the rest of the night would bring.

"I was going to ask you why you couldn't tell Victoria. You know she is entirely trustworthy. She could have come here and supported you when you needed it most."

"True, but then she would have told her husband."

"So? Nick would never betray you either."

In Ainsley's experience, men tended to stick together, especially noblemen. It might very well be that Lord Arnprior, a stickler for duty and honor, would believe that Leonard had both the right and the responsibility to care for the child he had fathered. Certainly, the law would see it that way.

The law can go to blazes.

"Sorry, but I can't take the chance. Aunt Margaret is the only person I can trust."

When Royal flashed her an ironic look, she waggled a hand. "And you, of course, Royal. I do trust you."

"I should hope so, if for no other reason that I didn't run screaming into the night when your water broke. That was quite a moment."

She grimaced. "Stop. I was utterly mortified."

He gave her a lopsided grin. "I'm teasing. It's impossible to embarrass me, pet."

That was true. Ainsley had publicly insulted him more than once, and Royal had invariably laughed. Then he'd proceeded to insult her right back, never holding her words against her.

Leonard, however, took every slight—real and imagined—and stored it away in his massive vault of anger and resentment.

She stopped again, digging her nails into Royal's arm as she rode out another wave of pain. This one pulled every muscle in her torso into an unforgiving, unbearable knot that left her gasping and hunched over. When she could finally straighten up, she realized she'd all but dug holes in Royal's sleeve.

"Sorry," she gritted out.

He'd pulled out his pocket watch, frowning at it. "That contraction was quite a bit closer than the others. You sit down while I go fetch the midwife."

Mrs. Peters had said she'd feel an overwhelming urge to push when it was time. Ainsley certainly had an overwhelming urge, and it was to down a brandy to help with the pain. But push? So far, that instinct eluded her.

"Not close enough, I'm afraid," she said as she pushed straggles of hair off her brow. "And it still feels better to walk, believe it or not."

He gave a tight nod. "Whatever you wish."

"You're the one who should have a rest. Why don't you fetch Betty? She can walk with me."

He shot her a look. "Daft girl. I'm fine."

She sighed. "I don't know how you do it."

"What?"

"Bear the constant pain. Much more of this, and I'd be ready to shoot myself. And yet you manage it on a daily basis."

"It's nothing remotely like labor, I'm sure."

"Still . . ."

"I admit it can be bad some days."

"So, how *do* you keep from going utterly mad with it?" she asked, as much from curiosity as the need to distract herself.

"Whisky helps."

"Ha. Stop pretending you're a drunk."

"No, but I have drunk myself into oblivion on more than one occasion."

"When the pain got to be too much, I'm sure."

He frowned down, looking at the faded carpet runner, as if the floral pattern was a puzzle. "I don't think it was the physical pain so much as how I felt about . . . everything."

"You mean the war?"

"That and the aftermath," he said in a somber tone. "The impact the injury had on my life."

She thought she understood that very well. In the weeks after her rape, unable to find rest or a decent night's sleep, Ainsley had resorted to laudanum drops. Unfortunately, those had produced nightmares, and too much wine gave her a headache.

"Did the doctors ever give you drugs?" she asked.

"In the beginning. They were afraid I'd destroy my leg completely if I kept thrashing about." He looked a bit embarrassed. "I was quite out of my mind with fever for a while, acting like a damn fool. The drugs were to knock me out, and they worked."

Suddenly, she found herself blinking away tears. The idea that he almost died and that she would never have known him seemed too horrible to contemplate.

He tipped her chin up. "There's no need to get mawkish, pet." His brogue was soft and deep. "All is well now."

"I just hate thinking about what happened to you," she said gruffly.

His warm hand slid over to cup her cheek in a loving touch that soothed the grief in her heart. Grief for innocence lost and for a future that would never be.

"I survived, lass, when so many did not. And I have a family that loves and supports me, no matter what." His lips tilted up in a wry smile. "Even if they are pains in my arse. *No moping about* should be the Kendrick motto. They nagged me back to life, I tell you."

"I wish I had a family who cared for me that much," she said wistfully.

His expression sobered. "You asked how I put up with the pain. I do it for them. My family is worth whatever paltry sacrifice I have to make."

Just like my baby is worth any sacrifice I have to make, she thought.

"Now, what are you going to do with this wee babe?" Royal asked, as if reading her mental processes. "And no putting me off this time."

"I . . . I don't know. Aunt Margaret has offered to take the child, but that's no permanent answer. She's too old. Besides, someone would probably figure out where the babe came from, which would mean—"

"Cringlewood would eventually hear of it," he said grimly.

"It's just so wretchedly complicated. I don't know what to do."

Royal took her hand. "I do. You should marry me and let me be father to your babe."

As she stared into his earnest gaze, Ainsley could feel the need building inside her to finally say yes. It was almost as powerful as the wave of pain currently gathering at the base of her spine. But saying yes to Royal would mean giving up everything she'd ever known for an uncertain future—and still with no guarantee her baby would be safe from its father. The mistakes of her life would come back to haunt Royal as well as herself, possibly even destroying them. He, of all people, did not deserve such a fate.

"I wish I could marry you, Royal," she said, blinking hard. "Truly, I do. But there are too many complications."

Leonard could very well deduce the reasons behind their marriage and raise a terrific scandal—perhaps even take legal action against her or Royal. Ainsley's entire family would reject her, with potentially disastrous results.

Her former betrothed and her father could lay utter waste to her life. And then what would happen to her poor baby?

"Lass, I'm very good at complicated," Royal said. "I can handle it."

She shook her head. "I wish I was as brave as you, but I'm not. I need to find a haven for my baby, and then return to London and get on with whatever sort of life I can rebuild from this mess. Certainly a life that keeps my secrets buried. That would be the best thing for all of us."

He grimaced. "It's a hell of a thing to give up a child, Ainsley. I don't know if you would ever get over it."

At his words, a wave of pain swept through her, more terrible than anything her body could fashion. It was like her heart was being ripped from her chest.

"I know, but it must be done," she said. "As long as Cringlewood doesn't know I birthed his child, the baby will be safe." That had to be the *only* thing that mattered.

When he looked ready to argue, she clutched his hand. "*Please*, Royal. Please do this for me."

She saw his warring emotions in the green fire of his gaze.

Eventually, he gave a tight nod. "All right, lass. Whatever you need."

"Thank you. I'm so—" She broke off, startled by a notion that darted into her head.

Good Lord. Could it really be that simple?

"What's wrong?" he asked.

How could she ask such a thing? It was so clear, and yet so monumental. "Oh, God," she gasped as the pain slammed through her. It was epically worse than anything she'd felt up to this point.

And suddenly she wanted to push more than she wanted to breathe.

She dug her fingers into his arm. "You need to get Mrs. Peters. The baby is coming."

"Well, it's about time." With an easy sweep, he lifted her into his arms and started for her bedroom.

Ainsley wanted to fuss about his leg but she was too busy trying not to shriek at the top of her lungs.

Just as they reached her door, Betty appeared at the top of the stairs.

"Lord, sir, is everything all right?" the maid cried.

"Lady Ainsley is ready to have her baby," Royal said in a calm voice. "Please fetch Mrs. Peters and your mother."

"Yes, sir." In a flurry of skirts, Betty pelted back downstairs.

Royal shouldered open the bedroom door and carried Ainsley to the bed, gently depositing her on the coverlet. She flopped back, panting, as the debilitating pain gradually receded.

"That was awful," she managed, breathing heavily.

He stroked back the damp tangle of hair on her forehead. The gesture was so tender that Ainsley almost burst into tears.

Stop it. You never cry.

"Everything will be over very soon," he said.

"I'm afraid of dying, Royal," she whispered.

He frowned. "Ainsley, you are *not* going to die. You will come through this with flying colors." He went nose to nose with her. "I won't have it any other way."

She swallowed against the hard lump in her throat. "I—I'll try."

"Ainsley Matthews, you are the most stubborn, arrogant woman God ever put on this blessed earth," he said. "It is inconceivable that you would allow anything to go wrong."

Oh, yes. Until last summer, she'd been arrogant enough to believe that nothing truly bad could ever happen to her. Life since had taught her otherwise.

Royal pressed a soft kiss to her forehead. "Do you hear, love? Everything is going to be all right, I promise."

She curled her fingers into his cravat, demolishing it. "Promise you won't leave."

"Of course not. I'll be close by the entire time," he said in a voice gruff with emotion.

Mrs. Peters bustled into the room, followed by Betty.

"Now, what's all this?" the midwife said. "Betty here said young miss fainted, and had to be carried to her bed."

Annoyed, Ainsley struggled up to a sitting position, Royal helping her. "I never faint. Mr. Kendrick was simply overly cautious."

"That's what I get for trying to be gallant," he teased.

"Well, that's grand," said Mrs. Peters. "But it's time for the fine gentleman to leave the ladies to their business." She nodded at Royal. "Cook is bringing tea up to the parlor for ye."

"I'll be waiting in the hall," he replied in a tone that brooked no opposition, then gave Ainsley's hand a little squeeze.

"Suit yerself, but it may be some time, ye ken."

Ainsley groaned. "Oh, God." Then she bit down on her lip as another wave of pain came rushing toward her.

When Royal started to reluctantly pull away, she grabbed his arm. "Promise me that you'll take care of my baby if anything happens to me," she gritted out.

He blinked. "Uh, what?"

"If I die, you must take my baby. Keep it safe."

The midwife patted her shoulder. "Och, ye'll not be dyin' tonight, my lady. Ye be as strong as a nanny goat, not to mention quite broad in the beam. I ken the wee one will slip right out of ye."

Ainsley stared at the woman in disbelief, then glared at Royal, who was trying not to laugh.

"Beautifully broad in the beam," he choked out.

"Bugger—" She couldn't finish because the contraction hit full force. Grabbing his cravat, she yanked him down so they were again nose to nose.

"Promise you'll take care of my baby." Ainsley needed him to do this, and she needed him to agree to it *now*, before the pain obliterated her ability to think straight.

He covered her hand with his. "Yes, all right, love."

"Say it."

He stared down at her, his gaze troubled. "I promise. I will take care of your baby. You have my word, no matter what."

Ainsley fell back with relief. Whatever happened next, she could face it. Her baby would be safe.

"Away with ye, sir," Mrs. Peters ordered, flapping her hands at Royal.

"I'm going," he said reluctantly.

Ainsley suspected he'd rather stay with her, and part of her desperately wished him to. But that would be scandalous and ultimately embarrassing when she started shrieking like a bloody fishwife.

Which would be happening any moment now.

"Do *not* let anything happen to her," Royal added in a firm tone to the midwife as he backed out of the room.

"Men," Mrs. Peters said, after the door shut behind him. "A bloody nuisance at a time like this."

"Only guid for one thing," Betty said, giving the midwife a saucy wink.

In Ainsley's case, there'd been nothing good about it at all.

"Mind yer tongue, lass," the midwife said sharply. Then she smiled at Ainsley. "Now, my lady, let's have a look. If ye're ready, we'll move ye to the birthin' stool."

Ainsley peered at the uncomfortable looking contraption by the fireplace and took a deep breath. "All right, Mrs. Peters. Do your worst."

When the next contraction hit, she realized that the worst was just getting started.

Chapter Five

Royal caught sight of Lady Margaret thumping down the hall to Ainsley's room as he came up the stairs from breakfast. Her ladyship had slept through her niece's ordeal. He admired her insouciance, since he'd been a nervous wreck for most of the night, although he'd done his best to hide that from Ainsley.

Fortunately, the lass had safely delivered her child shortly before dawn. She'd done it with a stoicism that left him in awe. Hovering just outside the bedroom door, straining his ears, Royal had heard very little aside from a few curses and one shriek just at the end. He'd been tempted to charge into the room at that point, as if he could somehow protect her.

A few minutes later, Betty had popped out with the happy news. After thanking her, Royal had sunk down to the floor and buried his face in his hands, sucking in deep breaths and trying to calm his racing heart. The maid had patted him kindly on the head, as if he were a frightened puppy. It had made him feel like an even bigger idiot.

If anything had happened to Ainsley, Royal truly hadn't known what he'd do.

The midwife had refused to let him see her, leaving him

no choice but to retreat to his own bed. After a few hours of fitful dozing, he'd finally given up any real attempt to sleep, knowing he wouldn't rest until he saw Ainsley.

"Lady Margaret," he called out. "A word, if you please."

"There's no cause to rush," the old woman said as he joined her. "You'll strain that leg of yours, and I'll not be responsible for sending you home a cripple. Lord Arnprior would be most displeased."

"I doubt it could get much worse, so no worries there."

"Ainsley told me you spent most of the night walking with her or lugging her about." She waggled her eyebrows. "And we both know she's no frail little miss. I shouldn't wonder if you're feeling it this morning."

He was, but he had no intention of admitting it. "I'm fine."

"You look a wreck. Worse than my niece."

"I'll get some rest later," he said dryly. All in all, his leg seemed of little import, given the questions now facing them.

"How is Ainsley?" he asked. "Is Dr. MacTavish satisfied she's recovering as she should?"

The physician had arrived only an hour ago, and through the window of the dining room, Royal had just spotted the man departing in his phaeton. He'd taken the quick visit as a good sign.

"He was most pleased with her condition. Despite being pampered all her life, my niece is an exceedingly strong young woman. That's the Scot in her. She's just like her grandmother, in that respect. My dear sister, God rest her soul."

"I'm relieved to hear it. And the babe?"

"Small but perfectly healthy." She heaved a sigh. "She is a blessing, of course."

Royal understood her conflicted emotions. Now that there was an actual bairn to deal with, decisions must be made.

"Lady Margaret, I know it's awkward, since I'm not family—"

"Ainsley doesn't seem to agree," she interrupted. "Apparently, she asked *you* to take the babe if anything went wrong."

Royal frowned. "No, she asked me to make sure the baby was taken care of. I was happy to agree."

Lady Margaret narrowed her rheumy gaze on him. "That's not what she told me."

Clearly, the old woman had misunderstood. "Well, thank God no such action is necessary, but it does raise the issue of what happens next. Ainsley suggested last night that plans had not, er, been finalized."

The old woman snorted. "I've been trying to get the lass to make a decision for weeks."

"She told me you'd offered to raise the baby."

"Yes, but we both know that's no good solution. I'm practically at death's doorstep."

Lady Margaret then sighed and thumped over to a high-backed chair, sinking into it. With such a forceful presence, it was easy to forget she'd passed her eightieth year some time ago. But now she looked frail and much too old to deal with so fraught a problem.

"Surely not," he said gently. "But I agree a longer-term solution must be found. And I suspect you've given it some thought."

She stacked her wrinkled hands on the knob of her cane and thoughtfully met his gaze. "There is a family I think will do quite well. They're distant relations and members of our clan, so they're loyal and very respectable. They own a tidy farm some hours north, so it's ideal in that respect, quite out of the way. I, of course, would make financial arrangements and monitor the situation for as long as I could."

Most would find that a more than suitable arrangement for the illegitimate child of an aristocrat, since it was rare for by-blows to be raised within their own families. They were generally—and quietly—placed somewhere in the countryside. That would certainly be the expected solution for a girl in Ainsley's situation.

"Then why does Ainsley not agree?" Royal asked.

"She thinks it too precarious a situation for the child. Especially since I am a decrepit fossil with one foot in the grave."

"Did she actually say that?"

"What do you think?"

He smiled, sure of the answer. "I have to say, I do see her point. You won't be around forever, and it would be dangerous if Ainsley maintained contact with the family."

"It would be fatal. She would have no peace of mind. Most importantly, she must leave no trail for Cringlewood to follow. I will not have either my niece or her baby put in danger of discovery by that man."

For the last twenty-four hours, Royal had been suppressing his questions and his anger about the marquess, but he was done with that. "What the *hell* did the bastard do to her?"

Lady Margaret snorted. "You may be able to intimidate the average *ton* dandy with that glower, Royal Kendrick, but it is wasted on me. Ainsley knows what she is about. If you are indeed her friend, you will support her, not question her."

"Of course I'm her friend," he snapped.

"Then leave it alone. Nothing good can come of drawing attention to her situation, I assure you."

Royal blew out a frustrated sigh and crossed his arms. "So, that's it. She gives the baby away and returns to London, as if nothing ever happened."

"That is exactly it. If this situation can be managed, she is still young enough—and rich enough—to attract an excellent match. Although her other suitors are not as wealthy or as influential as Cringlewood, most would certainly make better husbands."

While Royal's heart rebelled at the notion of the lass wedded to another man, Lady Margaret's reasoning was sound. If Ainsley could overcome the trauma of giving away her child, she could return to the former life that had suited her so well.

"But for some reason, she will not agree to the plan," he said.

"No," she said. "Which is unfortunate. Ainsley is already growing attached to the babe. We'd hoped to have the wet nurse on the premises when she went into labor, so the child could have been removed right away. But the blasted woman won't arrive until late tomorrow."

When she started to rise, he helped her up.

"Thank you," she said. "Now, make yourself useful. Go in and see how the girl does."

"You've already seen her?"

"Before the doctor came." She suddenly flashed him a sly grin. "Besides, she'd much rather see you than me."

He narrowed his gaze, suspicious. "You're up to something, aren't you?"

She cackled. "I'll be in the morning room. Come see me when you're done."

After she tromped away, Royal quietly tapped on the door. A moment later Betty opened it.

"Good morning, Betty." He smiled when the girl stifled a yawn. "I take it you didn't get much sleep last night, either."

She flashed him a charming set of dimples. "Aye, my bed is callin' to me. I'll be snugglin' in for a nice, wee nap as soon as I can."

Ainsley, propped up in bed writing at a small lap desk, glanced up. "That will be all, Betty. You can go downstairs and get your breakfast."

The girl looked dubious. "Are ye sure, my lady? Mam

said it wasn't proper that I left ye alone with Mr. Kendrick last night. There not bein' a proper chaperone, and all, after her ladyship retired."

Ainsley stared at the girl with disbelief. "I assure you, Mr. Kendrick and I will not be getting up to any frolics. Besides, you are the last person one can imagine serving as an effective chaperone."

"Happens you're right, my lady. Mam says I'm a terrible flirt," Betty cheerfully replied.

"Your mother is a perceptive woman," Ainsley said.

Royal choked down a laugh that largely stemmed from the enormous relief flooding through his veins. Clearly in fine fettle, his sweet lass looked unexpectedly robust and so, so beautiful, even after what she'd just been through.

"We'll be sure to ring if we need anything," he said to Betty.

The maid flashed him another saucy smile. "Aye, sir, if ye need anything. *Anything.*"

Including a frolic, apparently.

"That girl is positively indefatigable," Royal said after the door closed behind her.

"You mean incorrigible," Ainsley replied. "Not that I truly blame her. There's not been a man under the age of sixty in this house for two months. She's only got poor Willy to flirt with, and he's only sixteen."

"I'm enjoying being the decorous one, for once," he said, as he strolled over to the bed.

The massive four-poster was ornately antique and, like the rest of the furniture, was from a time when clan fought clan and life in the Highlands was dramatic and wild. The setting was perfect for Ainsley, who might have been a Scottish princess come to lord it over her loyal subjects.

Like me.

She gave him a wry smile. "Everyone in my aunt's

household is so ridiculous that your dreadful manners pale in comparison."

When he burst into laughter, she cast a quick glance at the cradle by the fireplace.

"Sorry," he said softly. "I take it the little mite is sleeping."

"After I fed her, she went right to sleep. I must say, she's a very good baby, so far."

Royal grinned. "She was only born six hours ago, lass. I'm not sure if that's quite enough time to make a determination."

Ainsley's chin went up in that imperious little tilt he loved. "I'm her mother, so I should know."

"I stand corrected." He leaned against the bedpost, enjoying the sight of her.

She was garbed in a white dressing gown lavishly trimmed with lace, and her ebony-silk hair was piled into a simple knot on the top of her head. With her pink-cheeked complexion and her clear violet gaze, Ainsley looked so lovely it was hard to believe that mere hours ago she'd been doubled over with pain, thin-lipped and sweating her way through each painful contraction.

"And you're really all right?" he asked softly.

"Healthy as a heifer, according to Dr. MacTavish," she said. "He made a point of telling me that my anatomy was exceedingly well designed for the task at hand, if you can believe it."

"'Broad in the beam' was the exact phrase, I believe."

She crinkled her nose. "How rude of you to remember."

"You know us Scots. Blunt to a fault."

"Appallingly so." She tilted her head to study him. "Are *you* all right?"

"Of course. Why do you ask?"

"You look exhausted. Like you've been worrying yourself half to death."

He rubbed a finger along an old gouge in the bedpost. "Something like that, I suppose."

"You were thinking about your mamma," she said softly. "I'm sorry. This must have been difficult for you."

It had been a difficult night, truth be told, worrying that the same dire fate might befall Ainsley. "I won't deny to feeling a wee bit of concern, especially when the midwife booted me from the room. I would rather have stayed with you."

"Count yourself lucky you didn't. The whole process is gruesome and rather scary."

"That's exactly why I wanted to stay with you."

When she silently held out a hand, Royal came to the bed. As he curled his hand around her dainty fingers, emotion choked up his throat. It was from the old sorrow over the loss of his mother, of course, but even more so from the profound gratitude that Ainsley and the baby were alive and healthy.

"Royal, I can't thank you enough for being here," she said in a gruff little voice. "I don't know what I would have done without you."

"I was happy to be here, lass. You know I would do anything for you."

Their gazes locked for a long moment, and something stark and even grief-stricken lurked in the violet depths of her eyes. It made his heart clench, as if something precious was slipping away.

Then Ainsley shook off whatever it was. "I doubt Hector would have been able to pick me up. I still consider it a miracle that even someone as strong as you didn't drop me."

"Och, ye're as light as a feather," he teased.

"You're positive you didn't hurt your leg?"

"I'm positive. Even if I had, it would have been worth it."

She flashed him another wry smile before withdrawing her hand. "You're quite insane, sir, but I am most grateful."

"I'm just glad you and the babe are healthy." He frowned. "She is healthy, isn't she?"

"She certainly is. She's a bit small, but perfectly fit. Dr. MacTavish said he's rarely seen a baby as alert as she is," Ainsley said proudly.

Royal bit back a chuckle. He'd seen his share of newborn infants over the years. They always looked rather dazed to him, as if astonished and slightly embarrassed by their helpless state.

"Then she obviously takes after her mother," he said.

Her gaze dimmed. "I hope so. I'd hate for her to take after her father in any way."

"She'll be just like you," he said firmly.

"Would you like to see her?" she asked.

"As long as you're sure I won't wake her."

"She seems to be a champion sleeper. She'll be fine if you're quiet."

Royal tiptoed over to the cradle. Inside, the wee baby girl was dressed in a white smock and covered with a soft wool blanket. Although small, as Ainsley had said, she was plump and healthy-looking, with pink cheeks and a profusion of dark curls. She was sound asleep, one little hand curled under her chin.

"She's perfect, isn't she?" said her mother.

"She is that." He glanced over his shoulder. "You're not swaddling her?"

"The midwife suggested it, but the doctor and I disagreed." She grinned. "Dr. MacTavish and Mrs. Peters had quite the set-to about it. I was forced to intervene."

"Good. It's a barbaric custom, tying the wee mites up like a parcel."

She studied him. "You must know quite a bit about babies, having all those younger brothers. I keep forgetting that."

"Especially Kade," he said, turning back to the cradle. "After our mother died, I spent a lot of time with him."

With the exception of Nick, who'd been forced to take charge of things, the entire family had fallen apart in the aftermath. Their father had been too wrenched with grief to even look at his newborn son. But as wrecked as he'd been too, Royal had known his mother had loved Kade with all her heart. She'd even told Royal to take care of his brother, just before she'd died. It had been his last promise to her, a solemn vow that was nothing like the silly promises rambunctious boys made to their mothers, ones meant to be broken.

"I even snuck in and slept by Kade's cradle," he said, smiling at the memory at how foolish he'd been. "Needless to say, the nursemaids had something to say about that."

"You know, despite your bests efforts to convince the world otherwise, you're really a very nice man."

He threw her a glance of mock astonishment. "Perhaps I should get the doctor back in here? I'm sure you're suffering from a fever."

She narrowed her gaze. "To quote your grandfather, bugger you."

"Tsk, tsk. Such language in front of a baby."

A chuckle was her only reply.

He gazed down at the slumbering infant and couldn't hold back a smile. She was a pretty little lass and looking at her made the world seem like a better place. Carefully, he reached in and touched her wee fist.

"Have you given her a name yet?"

When silence met his query, he turned to look at Ainsley, who was staring down at her lap.

Royal frowned. "What's wrong?"

"I . . . I haven't named her yet," she said, finally meeting his gaze.

"Why not?"

"I didn't think I had the right. After all, I'm not going to raise her. What if the people who take her hate the name?"

"Then they can change it," he said. "But she's *your* daughter, and she'll always be your daughter. You have the right to give her a name."

"No, I don't," she said in a quiet voice that held legions of sorrow.

"Ainsley," he said, taking a step forward.

She blew out a breath, as if annoyed with herself. "There's no need to fuss, Royal. I'm perfectly f . . . fine."

That little wobble in her voice all but killed him. "Oh, my sweet lass," he said, starting for the bed.

She held up a hand. "Would you please bring her to me? I'm sure she must be hungry."

Her abrupt tone brought him up short. Ainsley hated feeling vulnerable, and the glint in her eyes signaled a clear warning. But as much as Royal knew anything, he knew she needed comforting at the moment.

She forestalled him by shaking her head. "Please, Royal. I just want my baby, for as long as I can have her."

He turned back to the cradle. He'd sacrifice anything for Ainsley—walk through the torments of hell to love her. But she didn't want him. And what she did want—or need—he could never give her.

Staring blindly down at the infant, he wrestled himself under control. This wasn't about him. It would never be about him, when it came to Ainsley. All he could do, as her aunt suggested, was be her friend. That would have to be enough.

"Royal?" Her voice was tentative. "Are you all right?"

"I'm fine," he said, throwing a smile over his shoulder. "Just trying to remember how to do this."

"Very carefully."

He huffed out a chuckle and reached down to slide his hands under the blankets.

As soon as he touched the wee lass, her eyes popped

open. Her gaze wide, the baby stared up at him. Royal felt a jolt in the center of his chest. Her eyes were a deep velvety-blue, and the color of violets.

Exactly like her mother's.

He had to swallow hard before he could speak. "Well, there you are, little lady. Would you like to see your mamma?"

When she flapped her tiny arms, as if answering him, his heart thudded again. "You're a bonny lass, aren't you? All right, here we go." He gently picked her up.

"Make sure you support her head," Ainsley said.

"Yes, my lady," he replied with an amused snort. He was damn sure he'd held a lot more babies in his life than she had.

"You needn't be so smug, Royal Kendrick," she said as he carried the baby to her. "I know you have miles more experience than I. But I *am* trying."

"You're doing splendidly." He gently deposited the baby in her arms.

He couldn't help staring at the beautiful picture they made. Her face soft and vulnerable, Ainsley smiled down at her daughter, oblivious to everything but her. The wee mite peered back, her focus locked on her mamma's face. They were an absolutely perfect pair, and never had Royal wanted to be a part of something more in his life.

But never had he felt more shut out, as if an unbreakable wall was between him and the only thing that mattered.

Suddenly feeling like a voyeur, he wandered over to the window, fiercely concentrating on the untrimmed rhododendrons in the garden below. The grounds were quite beautiful and would make a magnificent frame for the dignified old manor house if someone paid more attention to them.

He spent a few minutes mentally trimming bushes and reordering paths to his satisfaction before glancing back over his shoulder. Ainsley was watching him with an expression he couldn't decipher.

"Do you want me to go so you can feed her?" he asked.

She smiled. "No, I want you to come sit with us."

Oh, he recognized that smile. His lovely lady was scheming. "What are you up to now, lass?"

She patted the bed. "Come sit. I'm sure your leg needs a rest."

He scoffed. "You're the one who just had a baby. You should have the rest, not me."

"As you would say, I'm fine." She patted the bed again, this time more firmly. "Please, sit."

He eased down on the side of the bed, being careful not to jostle her. "Don't blame me if your aunt comes in and kicks up a fuss because we're in bed together."

"Because no doubt we'd be engaging in frolics," she said with heavy sarcasm.

"What else would we be doing in bed?"

"Idiot. Here, take the baby. You can't do anything outrageous as long as you're holding on to her."

Surprised that she would relinquish her, Royal arranged the baby in the crook of his arm.

"You really are good with infants, aren't you?" Ainsley said.

"All right, that's at least two compliments from you in the last ten minutes. What's afoot, lass?"

"Really? I can be nice too, you know."

"No, you can't, so you might as well just spit it out. What is it you want?"

"You are so awful," she said.

He simply raised his eyebrows.

"Oh, very well," she said. "I suppose there's no point in trying to soften you up, especially since what I have to ask is so enormous."

In the back of his mind, a faint warning bell sounded. "Then you'd better just get it out."

She sucked in a deep breath, as if for courage, pushing her lovely breasts against the lacy trim of her dressing gown.

"I want you to take my baby," she said. "And stop staring at my chest."

He jerked his gaze up. "What . . . what did you just say?" He stared at her, his brain scrambling to make sense of her words.

"I want you to take my baby."

Good God. She was serious. Even though she calmly regarded him, he could feel the tension pouring off her in waves.

"You don't mean, permanently, do you?" he asked.

"Of course I mean permanently, you dolt." She closed her eyes for a moment, collecting herself. When she opened them, she grimaced an apology. "I'm making a hash of it, I know. It's because I'm so nervous."

Royal forced himself not to overreact. "It's all right, love. I'm just trying to understand. Why would you think it a good idea to give the baby to me, especially since your aunt already found a suitable family?"

She touched her babe's cheek with a gentle fingertip. "I can't bear the idea of her going to strangers. I suppose that's stupid, since that's how these situations are typically handled. But I simply *cannot* do it." Her desperate gaze begged him to understand.

"It's not stupid at all," he said. "But surely you can trust your aunt to have this right."

She made a helpless gesture. "I don't know. I've never met them, and I can never meet them if I want to keep her safe. If Cringlewood ever found out, he would use the baby against me. He would force me to marry him, and that I cannot abide."

"Ainsley, I would gladly take care of that bastard, if you'd let me." And he would enjoy every moment of it.

"You would only make things worse."

"But—"

"Please don't argue with me about that," she said firmly. "And stop upsetting the baby."

He glanced down. The mite had once more fallen into slumber, her mouth sagging open as she made little baby snores.

Ainsley gave him another sheepish smile. "I told you she was a good sleeper."

"So you did." He thought for a few seconds, and then nodded. "All right. I will respect your privacy on this particular issue—for now."

She went back to looking huffy. "You don't really have a choice."

"I do if I'm to take your baby."

She froze for several long seconds. "Does that mean you'll actually do it?"

Dammit. He'd walked right into that one. "I'm still trying to understand why you're asking me, of all people."

"Because you're my friend, Royal, my true friend. I haven't got many of them. And I trust you to keep my secrets." She pressed a hand to his shoulder, leaning forward a bit. "I trust *you* to keep her safe."

The intensity of her gaze robbed him of breath. He wanted to believe she had no idea what she was asking of him, but that was nonsense. Ainsley knew exactly what she was doing. She always did.

"All right, you trust me. But how can you think I could possibly take care of an infant? I'm hardly in a position to support myself, much less a child."

"But you wouldn't have to do it alone, would you?" she argued. "You'd have your entire family to help, especially

Victoria. I can't think of a better family to protect and raise her than the Kendricks."

He stared, incredulous. "But I thought you hated most of my family."

"Well, I do hate your grandfather," she admitted. "But the rest are quite nice."

"Even the twins?"

"They'll probably be all right once they get older." She hesitated for a moment. "Probably. But the rest of you are quite splendid."

Royal felt like he'd been run over by a herd of wild boar. "And you're willing to have your baby raised in Scotland?"

"Better than in England on Cringlewood's estates," she said, her voice taking on a bitter tinge. "I know she will be safe at Castle Kinglas, as safe as she could be anywhere on earth. And since the Kendricks rarely travel south of the border, any possible connection to me will quickly fade."

It took a moment for the full weight of her words to sink in. When it did, he felt the blow through his entire body.

Ainsley abruptly withdrew her hand, her gaze sliding sideways. "It does mean, of course, that we can never see each other again. It would be too great a risk."

When he cursed under his breath, she faltered. "Or . . . or at least not for a long time. It's the only way to keep me safe, Royal. To keep my baby safe."

"You mean keep your blasted reputation safe." When she flinched, he mentally cursed himself. "I'm sorry. I had no right to say that."

She shook her head. "No, you have every right. And I do want to protect my reputation, which is admittedly selfish of me, but it's more than that. The only true way to protect my baby is to pretend that I never gave birth to her."

"I understand."

He did, too. But it did nothing to patch the hole in the middle of his chest.

"I'm so dreadfully sorry," she said quietly. "I have no right to ask this of you. If it's too much . . ."

Royal knew he was the one being selfish. After all, he'd promised Ainsley countless times that he would do anything to help, anything to protect her. That had to mean a willingness to take on any sacrifice or pain, any responsibility, even one this enormous. If not, the promise had meant nothing.

"Of course you should ask me," he said, "and I'm honored you did."

She ducked her head. "Thank you," she whispered. "You're incredibly kind."

He didn't feel kind. He felt like cursing the heavens, raging at the injustice of it all—for him, for Ainsley, and for the innocent babe.

Looking down at the bundle in his arms, he studied the sweet, slumbering child. Something both terrible and wonderful stirred in his chest, filling the dark hole just a wee bit.

"So, I'm to walk into Kinglas with this little lass and say what, exactly?"

Ainsley's head jerked up, her eyes going wide. "Does that mean you'll do it?" She sounded breathless.

He gazed at the woman he adored—the woman he was losing all over again, and this time forever. "Aye, lass. I'll take your daughter, and I'll cherish her like my own."

Chapter Six

Ainsley stood in the shelter of the staircase, watching the bustle in the entrance hall. Today Royal would take her baby away. From this day forward, Ainsley would have no say in her daughter's life.

She glanced at the darling bundle in her arms. Her daughter, asleep as usual, was wrapped against the gusting breeze off the loch, a soft knit cap on her little head and a cashmere blanket softly swaddling her. Royal had sent an express to his brother, requesting Arnprior's coach. Along with the wet nurse, he and the baby would make the journey to Kinglas in safety and comfort, guarded by the earl's grooms.

But Ainsley still worried. Her daughter was but four days old and shouldn't even be out of her mamma's arms, much less taking a carriage journey. But escaping as soon as possible to avoid discovery was paramount.

She sucked in a harsh breath to stem the tears. Not only was she losing her child, she was losing Royal and all they might have been to each other. He was the only man she'd ever thought she could love.

"I'm so sorry," she whispered to her daughter. "It's my fault. I should have been smarter and braver."

No matter how hard she pummeled her brain, she could see no path forward but this one.

Her daughter stirred, her rosebud mouth gaping open in an endearing yawn. Her eyelids fluttering open, her deep blue glaze unfocused and soft with sleep, she stared up at Ainsley for several long seconds, then snuffled a bit as her eyelids drifted back down. Soon, her breathing evened out and she slumbered once more.

"Oh, you are the *best* baby." Ainsley couldn't hold back a watery laugh. "It's a miracle how splendid you are."

No matter what, she would *never* regret bringing this blessed child into the world.

"Now, lass, what are you up to over here in the corner?"

She glanced up, mustering a smile for Royal. His voice was gruff and his brogue strong—a sure signal his emotions were running high.

"Please tell me you've finally come up with a name for my daughter. She cannot leave here without one." She'd left that decision up to him, but he'd been annoying reluctantly to make a choice.

He'd also been avoiding her the last few days, only coming to see her to discuss specific details of their plan. While he was always polite and kind, it was obvious he wanted to spend as little time in her company as possible. Even though she understood the reasons why, his subtle rejection stung like a swarm of bees.

Ainsley understood that he was struggling with a complex stew of emotions—including sorrow and anger—so she couldn't blame him for staying away. After all, she was all but gutted by what she was feeling. There was also a great deal to be done before they left, and the responsibility for all that fell on him.

Royal placed a hand on the baby's head. His touch was so gentle that it made Ainsley's throat go tight. Whenever he'd come to see her, he'd made a point of holding the baby, pacing slowly back and forth with her in his arms as he and Ainsley thrashed out tricky logistics.

"I want the lass to get used to me, and to know I'll always be there for her," he'd explained.

He'd always be there for the baby, but not her. After he'd left the room, Ainsley had buried her face in a pillow and bawled like a child.

Royal smiled. "Ah, yes, the name. I think I've finally got it."

"Do you hear that, my girl?" she said, gazing down at her daughter. "You're finally going to get a name."

"I think we should call her Tira," he said.

She glanced up, startled. "Isn't that your mother's name?"

"Aye. It's a good one, don't you think?"

"That's . . . that's very special," she stammered. "Are you sure?"

"She's a special lass, so she needs a special name. My mother would have loved her, just like *her* mamma loves her."

Ainsley could practically hear the cracks sundering her heart. "Royal, I don't know what to say," she whispered.

He briefly cupped her cheek, his palm rough and warm on her skin. "I know, lass. It's a hard—"

"Sir, I'm right sorry, but I need a word," interrupted one of the grooms, coming up to them.

Royal cast an annoyed glance over his shoulder. "I'll be there in a moment."

"Sorry," he said to Ainsley.

"It's fine. I'll just wait here until you're ready."

He stepped back and ran an assessing gaze over her figure. "Are you sure you should be standing here on the stone floor? Shouldn't you still be resting?"

"I'm fine, and if I have to stay in bed another moment, I'll shoot myself."

Besides, once Royal and the baby left, she would probably crawl into bed and spend the next three weeks crying her eyes out.

"Well, we can't have that," he said with a quick flash of a smile. "It won't be much longer, but make sure you and Tira stay out of the draft."

The lump in her throat became a boulder at the sound of her daughter's name. It was a beautiful name. His *mother's* name.

"You may not have noticed, but there's a roaring fire less than ten feet away from me," she said tartly, trying to cover up her distress. "I'm practically expiring from the heat."

Royal gestured to Hector, who lurked behind an old suit of armor in the corner, doing his best to avoid any work, as usual. "Bring her ladyship a chair," he ordered before striding off to speak with his groom.

Sighing dramatically, Hector lugged over one of the ladder-back chairs that flanked the front door. Ainsley thanked him and sank down, grateful to be off her feet. She might be sick of lying abed, but her back ached and her legs still felt a bit wobbly. Royal would notice that, of course, and worry even more that she was overexerting herself.

Soon she wouldn't have him to worry about her, ever again.

She sat quietly, watching as he conferred with his coachman and supervised the grooms who were loading the last bit of luggage. As usual, he managed everything with a natural sense of command.

"That young man is certainly impressive," Aunt Margaret said as she joined Ainsley. "I confess I will miss him."

"You'll miss the fact that he's so handsome."

Her aunt gave her a sharp look. "You finally realized that, did you?"

"Aunt Margaret, I always realized it."

"Then more fool you for not acting on it. Kendrick would

have made a better husband than all those frippery Londoners who hang about your skirts."

Ainsley was well aware of that, which was rather adding insult to injury at this point. "It's water under the bridge now."

Her aunt glanced at the baby. "Did you name her yet?"

"Yes, Tira, after Royal's mother." She leaned down and kissed her baby's forehead. "Do you hear that, darling? You have the most splendid name."

Aunt Margaret sighed. "You've spent too much time with her, Ainsley. It's not good for you."

She had to swallow before answering. "I know it was stupid. I don't know how I'm going to say good-bye. It feels impossible."

To lose either Tira or Royal. Ainsley had thought that grief for her daughter would push everything else to the side, so it shocked her how much she was going to miss him. She'd come to realize that her heart was much bigger than she'd ever thought, which meant there was that much more to break.

Her aunt rested a gentle hand on Ainsley's shoulder. "You will say good-bye because you know it is the right thing to do. You and this child both deserve a good life, a happy life. Thanks to Royal Kendrick, your baby will have one. As for yourself . . . that is up to you, my dear."

"As long as Tira is safe, that's enough for me." It would have to be enough, because Ainsley knew she would never be truly happy. How could she be, with most of her heart forever left behind at Castle Kinglas?

"Things will get better, I promise," her aunt said. "Someday you will find a good man to marry, and you will bear more children."

Ainsley looked into her baby's face, trying to memorize every sweet curve and line. "I don't want to get married. I only want to be with her."

"Fah, now you're talking nonsense. You were born to

marry a great man, my dear, and to take your rightful place in society."

She cast her aunt an exasperated glance. "Like you did?"

Aunt Margaret waved a hand. "That's entirely different. I was too independent to be married. Besides, I never found anyone who inspired me to even consider fidelity to one man, much less the wedded state."

Ainsley shifted, wincing slightly with pain. "Considering what I just went through a few days ago, a life of celibacy sounds fairly appealing at the moment."

"Now, what would be the fun in that?" her aunt said.

Ainsley shook her head in disbelief. If she never had sex again, she would count herself lucky. In her case, the act of creating a baby had been a great deal more distressing than actually having the baby.

Stays creaking, her aunt bent down to look her in the eye. "Ainsley, you had a terrible experience with a villain, and I'm more sorry for that than I can say. But it needn't be that way with a man, I assure you. In fact, it *shouldn't* be that way."

"It's not something I can think about right now," Ainsley said, sighing.

Her aunt straightened up. "I would like to murder Cringlewood with my bare hands. Slowly and very, very painfully."

"Get in line behind me," Ainsley said.

Royal came back inside, his open greatcoat swinging around the top of his tall, polished boots.

"The carriage is loaded," he said. "I'm very sorry, but we must be underway."

"Where is the wet nurse?" asked Lady Margaret.

"Already in the carriage," Royal said. "I'll bring Tira out to her as soon as Ainsley says good-bye."

Ainsley's arms tightened around her daughter. Mrs. Monroe was a kind and experienced woman who'd already had three children and had been highly recommended by Dr. MacTavish. While Ainsley knew she should be grateful they'd be able to secure her services, she'd barely been able to bring herself to look at the woman. Knowing that a stranger would be nursing her child made her feel as hollow and as a dried-up, weed-covered well.

"Then I will make my farewell, Mr. Kendrick," Aunt Margaret said, extending a hand. "My niece and I can never properly express our gratitude to you or to your family."

Royal bowed over her hand. "I'm honored that I was able to be of service, ma'am. Please know that I will always do whatever I can to help you and your niece."

"My regards to your brother and his countess," Aunt Margaret said with a nod, before moving away.

Royal looked down at Ainsley, somber ghosts lurking in the back of his gaze. "I'm sorry, lass. I'd give anything not to have to do this to you."

Ainsley braced herself to carry it through. "No, you're rescuing us. My aunt is right. I can never possibly repay you."

"There is no need," he said. "Just know that I will always be at your service. Always."

His quiet words were a solemn vow, one she knew he would never break. He was a good man and he loved her. And stupid, stupid woman that she was, she'd lost her only chance to love him back.

"You're doing the best possible thing for me you could ever do," she said. "Here, take Tira now."

He reached down and carefully gathered the baby up. Cradling Tira securely in one arm, he then helped Ainsley stand.

She gazed at her daughter, so secure in his strong embrace, and felt tears begin to spill.

"Och, don't cry, love," he murmured, resting his gloved hand against her cheek. "You'll kill me if you do."

Ainsley had to resist the impulse to wrap her arms around

them and keep them with her forever—her baby and the man who would rightly be her father.

Instead, she blinked several times and mustered a smile. "No, I won't cry anymore, I promise."

"Tira will be fine, you may be sure of it. And I'll send a message as soon as we reach home."

She let out a shaky sigh. Since it was less than a day's travel to Castle Kinglas, she would receive word from him by sometime tomorrow. "Thank you. I appreciate that."

He nodded. "I'll write every few days to let you know how she does."

"That would be wonderful. I'll be staying with Aunt Margaret for another month. After that I'll be returning to London." She rested a hand on her baby's chest and made herself say the words. "Once I return home, though, you can't write to me anymore. It wouldn't be safe."

Ainsley no longer trusted her father. He was on Cringlewood's side and would take any advantage in pressuring her into marrying him. She wouldn't put it past him to go through her letters or even intercept them.

Royal's expression turned hard. "Are you in danger? Because if you are, I'm not letting you return to London. And I don't give a damn about the bloody scandal."

"No, I'll be fine," she assured him. "I meant that it's not safe for the baby's sake. If anyone were to find out . . ."

He still didn't look happy but gave a reluctant nod. "Then you and Victoria can write to each other. You're friends, so no one would think twice about that."

That made sense. They'd already agreed that Royal would tell Victoria and Lord Arnprior the truth. To be able to hear regularly that Tira was safe and well felt like an enormous and undeserved gift.

"Yes, that would work," she said with a grateful smile. "Please tell her to be careful what she says, though."

"I will."

She kept her hand on Tira's chest as she stared up into Royal's starkly handsome face. Though she should say her good-byes and step away, she felt inextricably bound to him, intimately connected by the child he held in his arm. In a very real way, they were now family.

"I wish we could have spent more time together," she whispered. "I've barely seen you these last few days."

He closed his eyes and let out a weary sigh. When he opened them again, her heart throbbed at the pain in them.

"I'm sorry, lass, but I couldn't. It hurt too much."

"You were angry with me. I understand."

His shook his head. "Never at you. At circumstances. At life."

"I know exactly how you feel." The words shredded her throat.

"I wish I could make it better for you," he said, his brogue low and rough.

"You already did."

Suddenly, she was flooded with a fierce, overwhelming gratitude for him, one that burned clear into her soul. She knew in that moment that she would kill for Royal Kendrick. She would give up her own life for him, just as she would for Tira. After her daughter, no one would ever mean as much as Royal did.

One hand still resting on her daughter's little body, Ainsley curled the other around his neck and tugged him down to meet her lips.

Their mouths met in a soft fusion of sorrow and love. It was as sweet and tender as the kiss they'd shared all those months ago in London. This one spoke of a thousand broken promises, but also an invisible bond that would hold them for a lifetime, even if they never saw each other again.

He retreated first, reluctant but clearly determined. "It's time, love."

She blinked the tears from her eyes, gathering herself for the final good-bye.

"Good-bye, my darling," she whispered, stroking her daughter's kitten-soft cheek. Tira snuffled in her sleep, turning her face with instinctive trust into Ainsley's palm. The sweet pain of it ripped her soul to pieces.

"Be a good girl for your papa," she choked out.

"I will always love her, Ainsley," Royal said. "All the Kendricks will love and protect her."

She bent and pressed a last kiss to Tira's forehead, breathing in her daughter's soft, milky scent, one she would never forget. Then she somehow forced herself to step back, even though every muscle in her body shrieked in rebellion. The hole in her heart became a chasm.

Be strong, for Tira.

She drew herself up and met his gaze. "Be happy, Royal Kendrick. For my baby's sake and for yours."

"Is that an order, my lady?"

"It is."

He forced a smile that fractured at the edges. "And the same to you, lass. Be happy, for all our sakes."

Thankfully, she was spared the need to reply when he turned and strode across the hall, his tall figure quickly disappearing in a dazzle of sunlight through the open doors. The sun hadn't shone for days, and now it streamed into the hall like a benediction.

Her aunt moved to her side and wrapped an arm around her shoulders. "The child will have a good life with the Kendricks, my brave girl. And now *you* can have a real chance at happiness, too. You'll see. It'll get better, I promise."

Ainsley nodded, even though she knew she would never be truly happy again.

* * *

As the carriage pulled into the courtyard of Castle Kinglas, Royal took off his hat and rubbed his throbbing head. Never had he been happier to arrive home and more terrified at the same time. He couldn't begin to imagine how he could pull this demented plan off.

He leaned across and touched the arm of the wet nurse, dozing on the opposite bench. "We've arrived, Mrs. Monroe."

She came instantly awake, peering into the basket on the seat next to her.

"Tira is still asleep," Royal said.

"Thank the Lord. I thought the poor bairn would never go down."

Ten minutes after they departed from Underhill Manor, Tira had startled from her slumber. She'd taken one look at her surroundings and started wailing. She'd more or less kept it up for the entire journey, despite their best efforts to soothe her. Mrs. Monroe, who was obviously a competent and experienced nurse, had done her best, rocking her and quietly singing old lullabies for hours on end.

Only when Tira was feeding did she stop crying, and even then not for long. It felt like she was protesting the absence of her mother, her distress growing stronger with each mile that separated them.

Royal had never felt more helpless in his life, and he hated himself for what he'd done.

He'd torn a family asunder and ripped out his own heart at the same time. Like Ainsley, he'd racked his brain for a better solution and, like her, had come back to this one every time. For both mother and daughter, *this* was the best way to keep them safe. That's what his head told him, although his heart disagreed.

Tira had finally fallen into a deep slumber a half hour ago. Royal prayed it would hold until they got her inside and settled under their housekeeper's competent care. Taffy had helped to raise all the Kendrick brothers and had soothed many a fractious baby over the years. Thank God because the responsibility was monumental, and would require the cooperation of his entire family.

When the door to the carriage opened, Royal held up a warning hand. The groom nodded and let down the steps as quietly as he could. Royal got out and then turned to take the baby from Mrs. Monroe.

She lifted Tira from the basket and carefully handed her over. The baby's cheeks were flushed and her eyelashes still damp from the last bout of tears, but she appeared deeply asleep—probably from exhaustion, poor mite. Royal felt like he'd walked from Cairndow, and no doubt Mrs. Monroe was even more pulled about.

"I'll take her if you wish, sir," she whispered.

He shook his head. "No, I'm fine. I'm going to send you off with our housekeeper to have some dinner and get settled. You must be tired."

A sturdy, comfortable sort of woman in her late thirties, Mrs. Monroe gave him a cheerful smile. "Och, no. I've raised three bairns of my own, so I'm well used to fussy babies."

That was obviously true, since she'd handled Tira in a gentle, competent manner. Mrs. Monroe was the wife of a tenant farmer and had served as wet nurse to other aristocratic ladies. Lady Margaret was no doubt paying her a generous fee, but it was well worth it to secure the services of a good woman willing to be away from her own family for at least three months.

Just as important, Mrs. Monroe could be trusted to keep Ainsley's secret.

He led her toward the door of the main tower house. "Well, I've got her now, and she seems inclined to sleep. So I suggest you take the chance to have some dinner. I'll bring her up after you're settled in the nursery."

"Aye, Mr. Kendrick."

The door opened before they reached it and Andrew, the youngest footman, hurried out. He took one look at the bundle in Royal's arms and all but tripped over his feet.

"Um, is that a baby, Mr. Royal?" His gaze darted back and forth between Tira and Mrs. Monroe.

"Obviously, Andrew. Now, see to the bags," Royal said. "Taffy will explain the new arrangements to the staff in a bit."

"Aye, sir," Andrew said, clearly expiring with curiosity.

Royal mentally sighed, bracing himself for the scene he must now enact for the sake of the servants.

"You've got the story straight, Mrs. Monroe?" he murmured, pausing at the stone porch that sheltered the front door.

She nodded. "Never fear, sir. I'll be protectin' the babe's secret, ye can be sure."

"You have my thanks."

Taffy appeared in the doorway, her wrinkled features softening in a kind smile. She was approaching seventy, but her gaunt, neatly garbed figure was as upright and strong as ever.

"Mr. Royal, it's good to see ye," she said. "All the arrangements have been made. At least as well as I was able to with so little detail," she pointedly added.

His letter to Victoria had of necessity been sparse on information. He'd simply asked for the carriage to be sent to Cairndow and instructed the Kinglas nursery to be prepared to receive a newborn baby.

"Thank you. Is Lady Arnprior about?"

"I've sent a footman to fetch the laird and my lady." She peered at the bundle in Royal's arms. "Aye, that's a wee bairn. I was a mite doubtful of her ladyship's instructions, but I see she had the right of it."

Might as well get on with it. "This is my daughter. Her

mother is not a reliable person, so the bairn will stay with us at Kinglas."

He winced at the crash behind him. Andrew had dropped Mrs. Monroe's trunk.

The housekeeper raised a skeptical eyebrow. "Is that so? Now, that's a sad situation, if I ever heard one."

Royal gave her an apologetic smile. Taffy had always been able to tell when he was lying. But she was loyal to the family and the clan, and would stick to whatever tale he chose to tell.

Her glance flicked to Mrs. Monroe, who was quietly waiting.

"And this is Mrs. Monroe," he said. "My daughter's wet nurse. If you could get her settled, I would be—"

"Royal, what the hell is going on here?" his oldest brother barked from the back of the hall.

Nick strode toward him, looking thunderous. Victoria scurried along in his wake, trying to catch up with him.

"You really brought a baby here," Nick said when he reached them. "I could hardly believe my eyes when I read that nonsensical message you sent."

"Yes, and if you wake her, I'll have to murder you," Royal said in a low voice. The baby had stirred at the commotion but thankfully, still slumbered.

"I'll take Mrs. Monroe to the kitchen," Taffy said. "And then send tea up to the drawing room."

"The library is warmer," said Angus, popping up seemingly out of nowhere. "Don't want the wee one catchin' a chill, now."

Royal frowned. "Where did you come from? And where are the blasted dogs?"

Angus was invariably followed about by a pack of Skye terriers. His grandfather's darlings, they were badly behaved and yappy. Royal had every intention of keeping them as far from Tira as possible.

"I locked them in the stables." Angus leaned in to peer at the baby. "They won't be disturbin' the bairn."

"Oh, she's beautiful," said Victoria, crowding close behind Angus to look at the baby. "Can I hold her?"

For the life of him, Royal couldn't help gazing at Tira with pride. Victoria was right—she *was* beautiful. And she was now his, to love and cherish. She would be the only child he would ever have, and was all the more precious for it. She might not be his by blood, but she would be his daughter by every other measure that mattered.

"In a bit," he said, smiling at his sister-in-law. "She just fell asleep, and I don't want to jog her awake."

Victoria wrinkled her nose. "Spoilsport. I do think, however—"

"And *I* think someone had better explain himself," Nick said, thankfully keeping his voice down. "What are you doing with a newborn infant, Royal? Or do I even want to know?"

Royal calmly met his brother's gaze. "She's my daughter."

His comment was met by stunned silence. Nick's imperious features went completely blank for several long seconds before his brows snapped together in a monumental scowl. Stormy weather was definitely blowing in.

Royal glanced over to the central staircase where Andrew and Robert, the other footman, were taking a great deal of time to organize the luggage. The Kinglas servants were devoted to the family, but except for Taffy, they tended to be a rare pack of gossips. In this case, that served his purpose. The more word got around that Tira was his natural daughter, the better.

"Your daughter," Nick blankly repeated.

Royal nodded.

"Now, don't overreact, my lord," Victoria said to her husband.

Nick stared at her in disbelief before his flinty gaze snapped back to Royal. "Who, may I ask, is the mother?"

"You don't know her."

"Tell me anyway," Nick said.

"She's a barmaid from Inveraray. Obviously, the lass was not in any position to raise a child, so I offered to take her." He glanced down at the sleeping babe in his arms. "How could I not?"

Nick scoffed. "Inveraray. That doesn't make any sense. Nine months ago, you could barely sit a horse."

"I took a carriage up north for a week or so, remember? Visiting friends?"

"But you don't have any friends up—"

Victoria clamped a hand on her husband's arm. "Perhaps we should repair to the library for this discussion."

"Aye," said Angus, who'd leaned in even closer and was making ridiculous faces at Tira. "Don't want the bairn to catch a chill out here in the hall."

"Grandda, she can't see you making faces," Royal said, torn between amusement and exasperation.

"I fancy she was peeking out at me, dinna ye ken?" He wriggled his fingers at the obviously still-sleeping infant.

"You're taking this exceedingly well," Nick said to Angus in an irritated voice. "Did you know about this?"

Their grandfather simply rolled his eyes.

"To the library," Victoria said, giving her husband a little shove.

She herded Nick and Angus ahead of her, who started arguing with each other. Shaking her head, she dropped back to join Royal.

"Are you all right, dear?" she asked quietly. "You look exhausted."

"It's been a trying few days," he admitted. "I've not had much sleep."

"How is your leg holding up?"

"It's fine," he answered automatically before he realized

it was true. He'd barely thought about the leg, nor had it bothered him very much. He'd simply had too many other things to worry about.

"How is Ainsley?" Victoria asked.

Clearly, his sister-in-law wasn't fooled by his Banbury tale. "As well as can be expected." He wasn't yet ready to talk about Ainsley. "Where is Kade?"

"Upstairs. I gave him a new piece of music to work with, so he'll be up there for hours."

"Good. I need to figure out what to say to him about all of this."

"The truth might be the best, at some point."

He eyed her as they followed their quarreling relatives down the hall. "And here I thought I was so clever in my letter."

"You were suitably vague, I assure you, as you can tell by your brother's mystified response. I take it you didn't know until you arrived at Underhill Manor?"

"To say I was surprised would be an understatement."

"Well, you seemed to have recovered quite quickly, if your little companion is any indication." Victoria touched his arm to stop him before he followed the others into the library. "Are you sure about this, Royal? Really sure?"

He sighed. "Far from it, to be honest. But I have to do it for Ainsley and the baby. I'm afraid that their safety depends on it."

She looked startled for a moment, but then nodded. "Then we will do whatever is necessary to help."

"You'll convince Nick?"

"No, dear, you will," she said before preceding him into the library.

Nick was already behind his desk, looking stern and every bit the laird. He'd spent the last few years doing his utmost to reform his scapegrace brothers, keeping scandal at bay, and this would certainly throw a fair spanner in the works. Royal couldn't blame him for being annoyed.

Victoria went to stand behind her earl, while Angus sat in one of the club chairs in front of the desk. Carefully, Royal took the other club chair, wincing when the frame loudly creaked under his weight.

"I'll hold the bairn, if ye like," said the old man. "Ye're looking a bit puggled, lad, and ye don't want to be droppin' her when Nick starts yellin'."

"Nicholas will not be yelling at anyone," Victoria said firmly.

"No, he won't," Royal said, "because that would wake up the baby."

"I promise I will not yell," Nick said. "Besides, Angus is always a great deal noisier than I am. *He'll* wake the baby, not me."

"Och, I'll do nae such thing," Angus said. "But I'd still like to hold her."

Royal had forgotten how much his grandfather loved babies. "You can hold her later, Grandda. I promise."

"No one is holding anyone until you tell us what the damn hell is going on, Royal," Nick said.

"Language, dear," Victoria said. "There's a child present."

When Nick shook his head with exasperation, Royal almost chuckled.

Almost. Given his exhaustion and the black mood that had once again descended on him, he couldn't help wondering if he'd ever muster a laugh again.

When the wee mite in his arms finally stirred, he glanced down. Tira cracked a huge baby yawn and her eyelids fluttered open. She stared blearily up at Royal for several seconds, calm as anything, before drifting back into sleep.

It took him a moment to realize he was smiling at her like a totty-headed fool.

"What's her name, laddie?" Angus asked.

He looked up to meet his grandfather's gaze. "Tira."

Angus blinked in surprise. "Ye named her after *my* daughter?"

"Yes." Royal had no intention of backing down on this. He'd meant it when he told Ainsley that her baby deserved a special name, and he'd seen how touched she'd been by the gesture. "Why wouldn't I name my daughter after *my* mother?"

Angus narrowed his eyes, as if trying to decide whether to take offense. Then he glanced down at the baby again, and his rheumy gaze softened. "Aye, well, it's a grand way to honor yer dear mother, and that's a fact."

Royal breathed out a sigh. "Thank you, Grandda. It did seem like the right decision."

"I'm glad there was at least one decision that seemed right to you," Nick said. "Now, can we please try to focus on what's important?"

"Which is?" Royal asked.

Nick closed his eyes and pressed a finger to the center of his brow. Probably counting to ten.

"I think your brother would like to know what your plans are for Tira," Victoria said.

Nick opened his eyes. "Yes, but first I would like *very* much to know who the mother really is. As far as I can remember—and I have an excellent memory—you were not cavorting with barmaids in Inveraray nine months ago. You were in Glasgow, with me. We went down to get Kade settled for his school term, remember?"

Royal grimaced. "Oh, blast. I'd forgotten that." He'd deliberately chosen Inveraray because it was fairly remote, and curious folk would be much less likely to ferret out the more dubious elements of the story.

"Who is the real mother of this child?" Nick demanded.

"Darling, you really cannot guess?" Victoria asked with exaggerated patience.

"Obviously not," he gritted out.

"It's Lady Ainsley, dinna ye ken," Angus said. "Who else?"

Nick stared at Angus, clearly dumbstruck, before looking at Royal. "Lady Ainsley Matthews."

"Correct," said Royal.

"Good God, then why the bloody hell don't you marry her, if that's the case," his brother snapped. "For heaven's sake, Royal. I never expected this of you. I feared the twins might one day do something this stupid and irresponsible . . ." He trailed off, frowning. "Wait, that doesn't make any sense either."

Royal waited for him to come to the inevitable conclusion.

"Lady Ainsley didn't arrive in Glasgow until December," Nick said. "Which means . . ."

"Which means you've arrived at the wrong conclusion," Victoria finished for him. "It's all right, my love. It's been a surprise for all of us."

He shot her a narrow-eyed look. "You figured it out."

"She's obviously smarter than you are," said Royal. "As is Grandda."

"I don't think you can entirely blame me for misunderstanding," Nick said. "This is not exactly an everyday occurrence, even around here."

Angus tsked. "Ye were thinkin' the worst about the lad, and he didna deserve it."

Nick sighed. "I did, and I'm sorry for it, Royal. I should have known better. But why that little charade out in the hall?"

"Royal is trying to protect Lady Ainsley, of course," Victoria said.

"And the baby," Royal added. "It's imperative that no one find out about her parentage. This seemed the best way to do it."

His brother's eyebrows shot up. "By ruining your reputation? That is rather a drastic solution. Why isn't Lady Ainsley's family dealing with this?"

"With the exception of Lady Margaret, her family doesn't know she was with child. They believe she was sent north as punishment for disobeying her father."

"Because Ainsley's father wanted her to marry Lord Cringlewood, and she refused," Victoria explained to Nick.

"I take it that Cringlewood is the baby's father?" Nick frowned. "If that's the case, why didn't she marry him? They were all but engaged some months ago, as I recall."

"She developed an acute dislike for his lordship," Victoria said. "I asked her about it once. The only thing she would say was that she would rather join a convent than be forced to marry him."

"Cringlewood has proven himself to be unworthy of her," Royal said tersely. "She refuses to have anything to do with him, and will not allow the baby to be used as a means of manipulating her into marriage."

"Did he force himself on her?" Nick asked quietly.

Royal was torn between fury at the marquess and the desire to protect Ainsley's privacy. "I don't know. But be assured that Ainsley has her reasons, and they are sound."

Victoria and Angus exchanged troubled glances, but held their peace.

Nick studied him with thoughtful regard, but Royal stood his ground, refusing to make additional explanations. The story was Ainsley's to tell, not his.

"All right," his brother finally said, "I accept that. Why not marry you, then? It's the perfect solution, if you ask me."

"Because no one would believe for a second that the baby was mine. And once Cringlewood found out, that would be the end of it."

"But you'd be married," Nick argued, "so what would it matter? Surely she knows we would protect her."

"Sadly, I failed to convince her of that." Royal stared

at his brother, willing him to drop this unpleasant line of unquestioning.

Victoria sighed. "Royal, I'm so sorry."

He gave a small shrug, as if it didn't matter.

"I'm sorry for the lass," Angus said, "but she's a fool to reject ye, lad."

"Thank you, Grandda."

The old man leaned over to carefully touch the baby's head. "Ye did get the wee lassie, and she seems grand."

Royal gazed down at the slumbering innocent in his arms. "Aye," he said softly. Grand, just like her mother.

"So, you offered to be the hero and take this child on as your own," Nick said. "Regardless of the scandal that's sure to result, and the black mark it will give our family."

Royal gave him an apologetic grimace, knowing full well how much the Laird of Arnprior hated scandal. "I know it's a lot to ask, old man, but I hope I can count on your support."

His brother again studied him in silence.

"Of course he supports you," Victoria said, poking Nick in the shoulder.

He cast her a sharp glance before looking back at Royal. "You're absolutely sure you need to do this?"

"I am."

"All right, then," he said with a nod. "I'll do whatever I can to support you and keep Lady Ainsley's secret. We all will."

"It won't be easy, Nick," Royal said, relieved but wanting to be sure. "It could get ugly. The denizens of Glasgow might even snub us."

"Horrors," Victoria murmured with a gleam of amusement.

Nick raised a lordly eyebrow. "Nobody snubs a Kendrick, and that includes my brother *and* my niece."

Royal had to struggle with his emotions for a moment

before he could answer. "Thank you, Nick. You cannot know what this means to me."

"I will always have your back, laddie," his brother said quietly. "Always."

Victoria gave her husband a resounding kiss. "You are truly the most splendid man, my lord. Thank you."

"Was there ever a doubt? Of course we'll support ye, lad," Angus said firmly. "That's what clan and family does. And now that we've got that sorted, how about lettin' me hold the wee bairn? After all, she *is* my first great-grandchild."

As if startled by the notion of joining a rambunctious Highland clan, Tira came fully awake. She screwed up her face, preparing to howl.

"Here," Royal said, carefully handing her over to Angus. "She's all yours, Grandda. By the way, I think she might need changing, too."

Chapter Seven

Glasgow
September 1817

"That's enough for today, laddie," Logan said as he strolled into Royal's office. "You're working yourself to the bone, and I won't have you falling ill on my watch."

His half-brother still talked to Royal like he was a boy. Logan was seven years older and also a giant of a man, so he supposed most men must seem like boys to him.

"You're worse than Victoria," Royal said. "Fussing like an old woman."

"I'm under strict orders from her ladyship *not* to let you overwork."

"Frightened of a wee lass like Victoria, are you?"

"She may be wee, but she's mighty. I'd rather face a pack of hungry wolves than Victoria in a snit." Logan settled into the chair fronting Royal's desk. The wood protested under the weight of his large frame.

"True enough," Royal said. "When Victoria works up a good scold, the only thing a man can do is surrender."

"We both know she's usually right," Logan said as he

flipped shut a ledger on Royal's desk. "There's no need for all these long hours, my boy. Truly."

"I am a bit tired, I'll admit," Royal said, rubbing his eyes. "But we need to get the rest of the warehouse inventoried before the next shipment arrives from Halifax."

Logan shrugged. "Just say the word, and I'll hire another clerk to help you."

"No need. I'm almost finished with the current goods, anyway."

After all his steadfast refusals to work at Kendrick Shipping and Trade, Royal had discovered that he did have a talent for organizing and numbers. It made him the perfect man to help his brother set up the Scottish branch of the business. Royal and Tira were now settled with Logan in the family mansion in Glasgow, and had been for the last three months. It was not the life he'd ever thought to have, but he was finding a sense of purpose and even peace in it.

"I'm sure Tira misses you," Logan said. "You should go home earlier."

"She's more likely to miss Angus," Royal said dryly. "Or the blasted dogs."

Tira was the real reason he'd moved to Glasgow and taken up work with his brother. Her entry into his life had been a cataclysm that required major adjustments—and planning for the future. Royal had never expected to be a father, much less a sole parent, but he'd come to love Tira more than he'd ever thought possible. She was his daughter, and he'd do anything to protect her, no matter the sacrifice.

Logan nodded. "Angus is devoted to the wee lass, I'll give you that. It reminds me of the way he was with you, when you were a babe."

Since Tira's arrival, Angus had taken on the role of great-grandfather with enthusiasm and renewed energy. He'd insisted on moving to Glasgow with them, even though it meant giving up his duties as Nick's estate steward.

"I know ye'll be missin' my help," he'd told Nick. "But I canna be lettin' them go off to that bloody city without me to look after them."

"I completely understand, Grandda," Nick had said, trying to muster a convincing show of disappointment. "I don't know what I'll do without you, though."

Royal had all but spit out his mouthful of whisky.

"Besides," Angus had added, shooting him a dirty look, "ye'll be needin' me to help ye handle the gossip over ye and Tira."

The news that Royal Kendrick was raising his illegitimate daughter within the bosom of his family had created the scandal of the summer in Glasgow. Rather than hiding Tira away, the family had conducted themselves *as bold as brass*, in the opinion of the gossips. But since the powerful Earl of Arnprior had made clear his full support for Royal, the worst of the scandal had dissipated fairly quickly. Logan had also been enormously helpful. Whenever there was even a hint of a mean-spirited remark, Logan issued a thinly veiled threat, which invariably put the fear of God into the offending party.

The brazen display they'd planned left little room for speculation about Tira's mother, and most of the gossip had swirled around Royal. But since Logan and Royal tended to keep to themselves, working at the office during the day and spending evenings quietly at home, even that was minimal. Angus and the nursemaid could now take Tira for her daily walks in the park and barely anyone took notice.

Life was finally settling into an orderly and peaceful routine, with Ainsley's secret safe. The Kendricks, it appeared, had pulled it off. Royal might not be deliriously happy with his new life, and there would always be an empty spot in his heart that only Ainsley could fill, but he was content.

Contentment felt rather like a miracle, and was more than he deserved.

Royal corked his ink bottle. "It's not surprising that Angus is so devoted to her. After all, he loves to feel both useful and to order people about. Fortunately, Tira is much too young to realize how irritating he can be."

"I think she loves the old goat as much as he loves her," Logan said.

"True," Royal said. "She smiled at him before anyone else, including me."

"It was probably just gas."

"Please tell me you didn't say that to him."

"I did, and I thought he was going to run me through with a dirk," Logan said with a grin. "He even read me a grand lecture on how his wee great-granddaughter is the smartest child ever born."

"And I'm a lucky man to have such a grand family," Royal said.

Logan shook his head. "If anyone deserves our support, it's you. You've saved us from ourselves any number of times. Nick and I would have killed each other without your intercession."

It wasn't a figure of speech or an exaggeration. Nick's first wife had died a tragic death, leaving him with a little son. Wee Cameron had been the light of all their lives. Tragically, when he was only four, he'd slipped into a river and drowned while fishing with his uncles. Going in after the boy, Logan had almost perished in a brave but futile rescue attempt.

In his terrible grief, Nick had blamed Logan for his son's death, and they'd all but murdered each other in a brutal fight. Royal had managed to separate them, but the damage had been done. Nick had exiled Logan, ordering him never to set foot on Arnprior lands again. Knowing his two older brothers needed time apart, Royal had convinced Logan to follow his laird's orders.

What the family had assumed would be a separation of only a few months had turned into seven long years of exile in Canada for Logan. Only recently had Nick seen his way past the old grief and anger. With Victoria's help, he'd finally been able to forgive Logan and welcome his return to the clan.

"Thank God those days are behind us," Royal said. "We were apart for far too long, and we're grateful that you're home."

His brother rubbed a hand through his thick black hair. "I might have to be going away again."

"Really?"

"I'm afraid I'll have to return to Canada for a while. There are a number of issues that need to be dealt with in the Halifax office. They're not pressing at this point, but will be eventually."

"I thought you'd found a good manager to handle things on that end?"

"I thought so too," Logan said, "until I discovered he was skimming profits from my timber trade. Not huge amounts, but enough that I finally noticed."

"The bastard. But can't you find someone trustworthy to take up the position, and send him over in your stead?"

"Easier said than done. I'll advertise, but it's entirely possible I'll have to go back, sort things out, and find someone over there." He shrugged. "Not everyone would be prepared to uproot his life and move to Canada, or even Halifax. It's a splendid country, but life can be rugged."

Royal pondered the notion for a few moments. "I would."

"You would what?"

"Be willing to move to Halifax to manage your offices. Me and Tira, of course, when she's a bit older and can manage a sea voyage."

Logan gaped at him. "Laddie, you truly have no idea what you're talking about."

Royal didn't, and the thought had more or less popped out of his mouth. But it had immediately made a certain sense. As well as things had worked out with Tira, there was always the risk of discovery here. Taking her so far away would remove that risk.

But there was more to the appeal of Canada than that, and he knew it. There was a special kind of loneliness here in Glasgow. Every time he turned a corner or walked into a shop, he half expected to see Ainsley. The sensation had even dogged him at Kinglas. It was a gentle, sorrowful haunting that Royal suspected might never go away, because he was convinced he'd never love anyone but Ainsley. For Tira's sake and for his own sake, it might be better to leave all those memories behind and start over abroad.

"In Canada, we could start over," he said. "For Tira, it would certainly be better. She'd be out of reach of anyone who could threaten her safety."

Logan scowled. "No one is going to threaten her safety. Not while Nick and I have anything to say about it."

"Logan, we can tell ourselves that all we want, but if Tira's true identity is ever discovered, we would have no legal standing to keep her." He glanced out to the hall and lowered his voice. "Cringlewood *is* her father, after all. And if he took her from us . . ."

"He could use her as leverage against Ainsley," Logan said. "Yes, I know that. What I don't understand is why the idiot is so obsessed with the bloody woman. Surely he can find another pretty girl to wed. There must be plenty who would be thrilled to become a marchioness."

If there was one thing Royal understood, it was Cringlewood's obsession with Ainsley. But unlike the vile marquess, he wanted what was best for her, and what was best for her was up to Ainsley alone to decide.

"The man's an arrogant bastard who thinks he can buy or claim whatever he wants. I'm sure he sees Ainsley's refusal as an insult that his pride cannot bear. She's also a considerable heiress, which is no doubt an added incentive."

Logan shook his head in disgust. "And her family is obviously no help. What kind of father tries to force his daughter to marry a *Sassenach* bastard like Cringlewood?"

"Another *Sassenach* bastard," Royal said dryly. "Lord

Aldridge has promoted this marriage for years, as have other members of both families."

"I still think she was a fool not to marry you as soon as she birthed the child. She couldn't have asked for a better husband."

"Maybe, but Cringlewood and Ainsley's family would likely have figured out almost immediately that this mysterious baby was hers. They can count backward from nine. Add in her months-long seclusion, and it wouldn't take a genius to arrive at the correct conclusion."

"It all sounds positively gothic," Logan said. "And stupid. You would have protected the lass. We *all* would have protected her."

Like the rest of the family, Logan couldn't understand why Ainsley hadn't been willing to take the risk and marry Royal, especially if it meant being able to keep her daughter. In fact, they thought her a fool for not doing so.

But Ainsley was terrified of Cringlewood, and her need to keep Tira safe from him trumped every other consideration. That was something Royal both understood and accepted.

"She made the decision she felt was best for her and for Tira," he said. "I have to respect that."

Logan grimaced with sympathy. "I'm that sorry, lad. I know how you feel about her. I only wish . . ."

"Thank you," Royal said, cutting him off. There was no point in dwelling on what might have been. "But let's get back to your problem. It's worth thinking about having me take on the job in Halifax, Logan. I'm sure I could manage it."

"I'm sure you could too." Then Logan hesitated, his expression turning troubled. "It's not easy raising a child on one's own, especially without family to support you."

Something in his brother's tone seemed off. "I'm sure we'd manage."

Logan rolled his lips inward, and then shook his head.

Royal recognized those signs. His brother wanted to tell him something but wasn't sure if he should.

"Whatever it is, you should just get it out," he gently prompted.

His brother expelled a weary sigh. "I've got a son, Royal."

"Um, you do?"

"His mother died a few months after his birth," Logan quickly added. "It was . . . difficult. Her parents moved in with me to help, thank God. I would have been lost without them."

Astounded, Royal could do nothing but gape at him.

Logan's mouth tipped up in a wry smile. "Close your trap, little brother. You'll be catching a grand big fly if you don't."

"Were you and the lass married?" Royal finally managed to ask.

Logan scowled. "Of course. Unfortunately, we only had a few years together before she died."

"I'm truly sorry for that," Royal said quietly. "But why the hell wouldn't you tell any of us? You could have written to me, or to Angus."

"It was . . . complicated."

"How complicated can it be to tell your family you have a wife?" Royal asked with exasperation.

When Logan arched an ironic eyebrow, he was forced to concede the point. Apparently, the Kendricks only did complicated when it came to women and marriage—or not marrying them.

"Well, you can tell me about her now," Royal said. "Who was she?"

Leaning forward, Logan braced his forearms on his thighs and stared at the floor. "Her name was Marguerite Pisnet. Her father was a trapper, and he was one of my first employees—although he quickly became much more than that. It was largely due to Joseph that I was able to establish myself so quickly. He knew everyone in the fur trade east of Montreal." He glanced up with a quick smile. "Joseph was smart as hell and as honest a man as you'd ever want to meet."

"He sounds just the sort of man you'd want for a father-in-law. And if *you* married his daughter, I'm sure she was splendid too."

Logan sat up and stared absently at the lone window in Royal's office, one with a view over the bustling commercial street. There were ghosts in his stark, blue gaze, and Royal's heart ached to know that his brother had encountered yet more sorrow in his troubled life.

"Marguerite was a bonny lass with a kind and gentle heart," Logan said. "I never once heard her say a mean word about anyone. I didn't deserve her, but the lass decided she loved me, and there was no talking her out of it."

Royal's throat went tight at the quiet sorrow in his brother's voice. After a fraught moment, he forced a smile. "I'll wager she was pretty, too. She had to be, if you married her."

As he'd hoped, Logan huffed out a grudging laugh. They both knew Logan had always had an eye for the ladies and they'd eyed him right back. "I'll have no cheek from you, lad, or you'll find your arse flying out through that window."

"You always did get the prettiest ones, you lucky bastard," Royal said with a grin. "So, what else can you tell me about her? With a name like Marguerite Pisnet, she was obviously French."

The French had settled quite a bit of Lower Canada before the English arrived to complicate things.

"Not really," Logan said tersely.

Royal frowned. "She's English, then?"

"No."

"Logan, do you want me to guess some more?"

His brother threw him a challenging gaze. "Marguerite was Mi'kmaq."

"I don't know what that means," Royal said slowly.

"The Mi'kmaq are the native inhabitants of that part of Canada."

Royal blinked. "Oh, I see. Why does she have a French name, then?"

"There was a great deal of intermarriage between the French settlers and the Mi'kmaq. Many of the natives converted to Catholicism, as well. Marguerite's father is half French, or Acadian, more properly, and there's an Acadian grandmother on the maternal side, too. The Acadians were the French who permanently settled the region."

That he did know. "They were then driven out by the English in the wars of the last century, were they not?"

"Indeed, although Marguerite's family never left. They stayed in Nova Scotia and mostly survived off fishing and trapping, although they also had a small farm. I met her father shortly after I arrived, and he almost immediately came to work for me."

"I see." Royal cocked an enquiring eyebrow. "And did you really think we would hold it against you that you married someone of native blood?"

Logan lifted his shoulders in a diffident shrug.

"Don't be such an idiot," Royal said. "We're Highlanders. To the English, *we're* the savages. They treated us like that for centuries, as you recall. We would have understood your situation better than anyone."

His brother spread his hands in apology. "I know I should have written and told you. But you'll recall that the Kendricks were a complete disaster at that point. Nick was barely functioning after little Cam's death, and then you both took up your commissions and went off to war. I could have written to Angus, but he was trying to hold everything together at Kinglas. Then, when it finally made sense to let you know I was married and had just had a son, Marguerite fell ill."

"I'm sorry, old man," Royal said. "What was it?"

A brief spasm flexed his brother's features. "Smallpox."

"Bloody hell."

"Aye, that's the phrase for it," Logan said grimly. "It was a small mercy she went quickly. But I was left with a three-month-old babe and not a clue how to manage any of it."

"Not to mention you were grieving." Coming after Cam's death only a few years prior, it must have been a horrible blow. "I'm so sorry, Logan. I wish I had known."

His brother waved a hand, obviously uncomfortable with all the emotion. "Don't fash yourself, lad. You had your own problems to deal with."

"But your son avoided the illness, I take it."

Logan's eyes lit up. "Aye, Joseph is a strong and healthy boy, thank God."

"Ah, I have a nephew named Joseph. That's capital," Royal said.

"Joseph Logan Kendrick. We named him after my wife's father."

"And you."

Logan gave him a sheepish smile. "Marguerite insisted."

"It's a splendid name, and I'm sure he's a splendid boy."

"He is." Logan fell silent for a few seconds. "I miss him more than I can say."

"He's with his grandparents, I take it?"

"Yes. They moved into my house in Halifax after Marguerite died. Joseph was helping me manage the business, while Marie—my mother-in-law—took care of my son. But Joseph had a stroke last year and can no longer manage the work."

"I see why things are so complicated, but that still doesn't explain why you didn't tell us as soon as you returned home,"

Royal said, giving him a stern look. "You know we would all support you."

"Even Nick?"

"Why the hell wouldn't he? The two of you reconciled months ago."

Logan stared down at the floor again. "Because I still have my son, and he doesn't."

Ah, hell.

"How old is the lad?"

"He's four."

The same age as Cam when he had drowned. Complicated, indeed.

"I'm not saying it won't bring up some difficult feelings for Nick," Royal said. "But he *has* forgiven you. Even more importantly, he's forgiven himself. Cam's death was a tragic accident, and he knows that now. And Nick is happy thanks to Victoria. He wants you to be happy too."

Logan eyed him dubiously.

"You need to trust him," Royal insisted. "He's your brother, as well as your laird and chieftain. Nick will be royally pissed if you keep this from him much longer, as will everyone else." He lifted a significant eyebrow. "Just imagine how Victoria will react."

Logan winced. "I know. I'm trying to figure out the best way to tell them. If you could keep this under your hat a bit longer, I would be grateful."

Royal mentally sighed. Apparently, he was the keeper of secrets. "Of course. And if you want me to be there when you tell Nick, just say the word."

"Thank you, but I'm mostly depending on Victoria to keep him from killing me."

"He'll only kill you if you don't tell him."

"I'll do it soon, I promise."

Royal nodded. "What are your plans for Joseph? Surely he should be with his father, here."

Logan scrubbed a hand over his head. "I didn't want to uproot him if I wasn't going to stay."

"But you *are* going to stay, are you not?"

"I'd like to."

"Then you should bring him here to live with you, Logan. How can you not want that?"

His brother shot him a dirty look. "I do want that. It's just that he's so close to his grandmother. She's been everything to him."

Royal studied him. "That's not the only reason, is it?"

"No," Logan admitted. "I'm afraid of what he might face here, as an outsider. There's a powerful lot of hatred in the world, Royal, and I don't want my boy growing up with that. It's hard enough back in Canada, but at least his family is there. His people are there. It's the only life he's ever known."

"Yet he has a family in Scotland who would also love and be there for him. Never doubt that."

"Thank you, lad," his brother said with a grateful smile. "I will think on it, I promise. Now, get yourself home. Your daughter is waiting for you."

Royal stood and retrieved his hat from the bookcase behind his desk. "You're not coming?"

"I'll walk out with you, but I promised to meet with my banker at the Tontine Coffee House on the way home."

"We'll wait dinner for you, then."

After locking up the offices, they headed out and parted ways at the top of the street. Though Royal could have taken a hackney to Kendrick House, it felt good to stretch his legs after so many hours behind a desk. Still, he couldn't deny that he liked earning an income again, especially the generous one his brother insisted he take. While Nick would always provide for the family's needs, Royal was happy knowing he could support Tira and put money aside for her future.

A short time later, he turned into a quiet street lined with distinguished houses, most of which had been built by the Tobacco Lords of the previous century. Kendrick House, which stood in the middle of the block across from a small garden square, served as home for various members of the family, although right now only Royal, Logan, and Angus were in residence. Braden, the second youngest Kendrick, had recently moved to Edinburgh to study medicine.

As much as Royal missed Braden, given how accident-prone the Kendricks were, having a physician in the family would certainly come in handy.

"Good evening, Mr. Royal," said the footman who responded to his knock. "There's a visitor to see you, sir. In the front drawing room."

"Thank you, Will." Royal handed over his hat and gloves. "Who—"

"Hsst, get up here, lad," came a loud whisper from above them.

Royal glanced up to see Angus at the top of the stairs. His two favorite terriers were sitting at his feet and Tira was propped on his shoulder.

"Grandda, what are you doing?"

"Hush," Angus said. "Just get up here."

Royal glanced at Will, who'd adopted a studiously bland expression, and headed up the staircase. Angus waited impatiently, jiggling Tira.

"I hope she hasn't just eaten," Royal said. "You'll jog her dinner right out of her."

"Och, she's fine," Angus said.

Royal smoothed a hand over his daughter's jet-black hair. "Hello, darling. Papa is very happy to see you."

Tira, half-asleep, gave Royal the smile that never failed

to turn him into mush. Then she yawned and rubbed her chubby cheek against her grandfather's coat.

"You look ready for bed, little one," Royal said, patting her back. He glanced at Angus. "Why is she still up?"

"Never mind that," the old man said. "We've got a problem."

One of the terriers let out an anxious little yip as if to underscore his master's concern.

"This mysterious visitor, you mean?"

"It's that blasted *Sasse*—"

The sound of a door opening and a quick footfall below in the hall cut him off.

"Hell and damnation," Angus muttered with a scowl. "Ye're in for it now, laddie."

Royal turned around and almost toppled down the stairs.

Ainsley stood at the base of the staircase, garbed in an elegant walking dress and holding a lace-trimmed parasol. She'd regained her splendid figure, and looked as extravagantly beautiful as he'd ever seen her.

She also wore an expression that threatened mayhem.

"Good evening, Mr. Kendrick," she said in a freezing tone. "If you and Mr. MacDonald are finished lurking about on the stairs, perhaps you might find your manners and come down here. I do believe we have some pressing business to discuss."

After he got his brain working again, Royal noticed that Ainsley wasn't looking at him. Her gaze was glued to Tira. Her determined expression told him that his world was about to come crashing down around his ears.

Again.

Chapter Eight

Ainsley resisted the urge to dash up the staircase and snatch Tira into her arms. Her bones ached with the need to hold her daughter and feel the warmth of that small, lovely body against her chest. The emotion of the moment all but choked her.

Of course, Angus would probably boot her down the stairs if she got that close. He glowered at her and clutched the baby tightly, as if he were protecting her from a pack of snarling hellhounds. Even the stupid, scruffy dogs looked ready to pelt down and attack the English intruder.

"Please bring Tira back to the nursery," Royal said to his grandfather.

Ainsley swallowed a protest. Upsetting Royal more than she already had would only put him on the defensive. She needed him almost as much as she needed her baby. Needed him to trust and support her more than ever.

Angus nodded. "Do ye want me to join ye for this little palaver after I do that?"

"I think not," Royal said in a voice dry as dust. "I'll send Will up if I need you."

Ainsley thanked God. The old fellow positively loathed her and would do anything he could to keep her away from

Royal. The idea of explaining everything in front of even one other person made her stomach churn. Bad enough to confess her failings to Royal, but to expose herself to anyone else would be unbearable.

Royal ruffled Tira's glossy black curls with affection. "Off with your Grandda, lass," he said as she waved her chubby little fists at him. "I'll see you soon."

After another troubled glance at Ainsley, the old man turned and headed down the hall. She craned to try to see Tira's face again, but Angus disappeared before she could get a good look.

Soon you'll see her all you want. Be patient.

Royal came slowly down the stairs, halting a step from the bottom and looming over her. Of course, he was doing it on purpose, just to make a point. It was silly, though. He was so tall he threw her in shadow even when standing flat on the ground. Royal Kendrick had made her feel uncomfortable and perplexed and a thousand other difficult emotions, but he would never intimidate her.

Because he would never hurt her, at least not by choice.

They cautiously studied each other, like strangers trying to identify enemy or friend. Ainsley gazed into his extraordinary green-glass eyes and had the oddest sensation that she was falling *up* into them. It made her head swim, and she was tempted to grab the bannister to steady herself.

Yet, despite the fraught moment, it was *so* good to see him that she had to blink hard against a rush of tears.

Royal's carefully blank expression became a frown. "Are you all right?"

Rather than succumb to an embarrassing bout of hysterics, she took refuge in a display of bad temper.

"I've been waiting *forever* for you to arrive." She directed a glare at the gangly footman, who was doing his best to look invisible. "*William* stuck me in the drawing room, where I've been kicking up my heels for the better part of an hour."

She switched her glare to Royal. "By myself."

He threw a startled look at the footman, who grimaced in apology. "We sent a lad around with a note, sir. He must have missed you."

"Apparently," Royal said. "Did anyone think to bring Lady Ainsley refreshments?"

"Lady Ainsley has not had so much as a cup of tea," she butted in. "And I'm utterly starving."

She wasn't, really. But she had to kick up a fuss about something or she'd fall apart. The last five days had been a mad dash north all while praying that Cringlewood or her father wasn't following. She had arrived in Glasgow only this morning, exhausted, anxious, and desperate to see Tira.

But she could only see her daughter if Royal agreed. Either that or if she did something incredibly stupid, like announce to the world that she was Tira's mother. Since that was not an option, she had to gain Royal's support for her desperate plan.

"We can't have you fainting from hunger," Royal said, sounding faintly amused. "Will, bring tea into the study, and make sure Cook includes some scones and plum cake, if she's got any."

"Aye, sir. She made a fresh cake just this afternoon," William said, scuttling backward toward the service door.

Royal took her elbow and steered her toward the back of the house. "I apologize. Angus was obviously being difficult. If I'd known you were here, I would have come home straightaway."

"You'd think I was going to give Tira the plague from the way he acted. I was all but ready to storm the nursery."

His hand briefly tightened. "Hush, my lady. Wait till we have a little privacy."

She took hold of herself, searching for a measure of

control. His unruffled demeanor was having an alarming effect on her nerves. She wasn't used to Royal maintaining the cooler head. He seemed different, more mature and reserved than she remembered.

It made him even more attractive, and he was already *fatally* attractive.

Then again, his control might signal that his feelings for her had faded away. She sensed he wasn't happy to see her, something so distressing it sent her mind into a tizzy. Ainsley had counted on Royal still wanting her, still loving her. In fact, it had never crossed her mind that he wouldn't.

And aren't you the arrogant one, my girl?

Perhaps he'd even concluded that she was a woman of low morals, after all. If so, she could hardly blame him. Whatever the extenuating circumstances—most of which he didn't know—she'd been with another man and then had not even the brains to marry him.

He gently pulled her to a halt outside the study door. Ducking a bit, he gave her a swift perusal.

"Stop it," he said.

"Stop what?"

"Whatever is going on inside your pretty head. I can practically hear the bloody wheels spinning away."

She blinked. "I, uh—"

He tipped her chin up even as he cast a glance down the hall. Then he pressed a swift kiss to her lips. It was firm, decisive, and scattered every thought in her head. She was forced to curl a hand into his coat to keep from staggering.

"Whatever it is, we'll figure it out," he said when he pulled back. His voice held a deliciously rough note that made her shiver. "You've worked yourself into a stew, and we've barely exchanged two words."

"I'm just t . . . tired," she stammered. "And how dare you kiss me like that, here in the hall," she belatedly added, even though she felt weak with relief. Apparently, he still cared for her after all.

He flashed his rogue's grin. "Would it be all right if I kissed you in the study?"

Ainsley had to clear her throat before she could answer. "Certainly not. That would be most inappropriate."

Dignity and self-assurance felt like a distant memory, thanks to the disaster her life had become.

"I suppose you're right," Royal said as he ushered her through the door. "Angus, for one, would be horrified to see us acting with such reckless abandon."

She was tempted to stick her tongue out as she swept past him.

He led her to a pair of needlepointed wing chairs in front of the fireplace. Even though it was August, a small fire burned in the grate. It had been an unusually cool summer, especially up north. Glasgow felt damp and dreary, so she sank down gratefully and let the warmth wash over her.

Still, it wasn't London. For the moment, at least, she was safe.

Time to get on with it.

She straightened her shoulders and primly folded her hands in her lap. "Speaking of your grandfather, my dear sir," she started in a disapproving voice.

He interrupted her as he took the other chair. "Ainsley, you look like you have a pole up your—"

"Royal Kendrick!"

"Spine," he finished with a smile. "You needn't be so formal, pet. Now, since you seem a tad worn around the edges, why don't you sit back and relax? We'll have tea first, and then we can talk."

"I arrived in Glasgow this morning after almost a week on the road. I'm allowed to look a little worn out, aren't I?" With everything she'd been through these last weeks, it was a miracle she didn't look a complete hag.

"Ainsley, you look as beautiful as always. But you do have shadows under your eyes, and you're paler than usual."

She was slightly mollified by his concern but refused to be distracted. "As I was going to say, I was quite disconcerted to see Angus carting my daughter about in so casual a fashion. Surely you should have a nursemaid taking care of her, not a, er . . . elderly man."

Thankfully, she managed to stop herself from calling his grandfather a disgusting old reprobate. The gleam in Royal's eyes suggested he had a good idea what she'd been about to say.

"Angus is better with Tira than the nursemaids are. He certainly spends as much time with the lass as they do."

"I don't believe it."

"Believe it," he said with a wry smile. "You needn't worry about Angus. He's devoted to Tira, and she adores him."

"Good God."

"Don't forget that Angus helped raise us after my mother died, especially the younger lads."

"And look how well that turned out," she said tartly. The twins, Graeme and Grant, were two of the most appalling young men Ainsley had ever met.

"You mean the twins. But they're much better than they used to be. And you must admit that Braden and Kade are exceedingly nice, despite their youth."

"That's true," she admitted. "But I refuse to believe the twins are anything less than horrible. And you, Royal Kendrick, are your grandfather's favorite and you're absolutely dreadful."

His smile slid into something so warm and lovely that Ainsley suddenly felt a bit overheated.

"You don't seem to mind," he said.

"Don't flatter yourself. And why are those dreadful little dogs at Kendrick House instead of up at the castle? Please don't tell me that they're allowed in the nursery."

"They sleep there, actually. Under Tira's crib."

When she stared at him with unalloyed horror, Royal burst into laughter.

"Don't fash yourself, lass," he managed to gasp out. "The terriers are as devoted to her as everyone else, and they make splendid guard dogs. They don't let anyone they don't know within ten feet of her. If she so much as drops her rattle, they raise a fuss until someone picks it up for her."

"Oh, Lord. My daughter is being raised by wild animals and even wilder Highlanders."

"Your daughter is being raised by a family utterly smitten with her," Royal said gently. "And she's thriving."

She closed her eyes for a moment. "Truly? I couldn't see her well enough to tell."

"She's the happiest, healthiest, and chubbiest baby that ever lived. I promise."

Ainsley's anxious heart finally began to settle. These months away from her daughter had been torture, even with the regular if obscurely worded reports from Victoria.

"I'd like to see her, please," she whispered.

Royal frowned, looking wary again. "Ainsley, I—" He broke off at the tap on the door. "Enter."

William carefully balanced a large tray loaded with a teapot, cups, and several small plates of cakes and scones. Irrationally annoyed by such a display of bounty after having been left to stew for an hour by herself, Ainsley couldn't help scowling at him.

When the footman caught her look, his eyes widened with alarm. The tray wobbled, and a plate of scones slid toward the edge.

Royal jumped up and steadied the tray in time. "Put it on the desk, lad. I'll serve her ladyship."

"Aye, sir," William said with evident relief. He lowered

the tray too hard, causing the cups to rattle, and beat a hasty retreat.

"Still terrifying the servants, I see," Royal said.

"Good. I thought I might be losing my touch."

When he lifted an incredulous eyebrow, she wrinkled her nose. "Well, he did stick me in that room and leave me there. That wasn't very nice."

"I expect Angus told him to do it."

"Ridiculous," she said, exasperated. "Your grandfather treats me like I'm some sort of horrible interloper. A villain."

He handed her a cup of tea, prepared with lots of sugar and a bit of milk, just as she preferred. Then he propped a shoulder against a corner of the mantel, looking down at her with thoughtful regard. "The truth is, Angus is afraid of you."

She frowned. "Why? He's never been nervous around me before. Quite the opposite."

On more than one occasion, she and the old man had gotten into screaming matches that all but rattled the timbers at Kinglas.

"He's afraid you're going to try to take Tira away from us," Royal said.

Ainsley stared at him in shock.

"I confess I'm concerned too," he said with an attempt at a casual shrug. "I hear not a word from you for months, then you suddenly appear on my doorstep." His malachite gaze all but drilled into her. "It wouldn't be an unreasonable assumption to worry that you're here to take her away from us."

"I would never do that," she snapped, anger getting the better of her. "But may I remind you that no one has more right to her than I do."

"Except her father."

She flinched, spilling tea into the saucer.

"Dammit." Royal grimaced. "I'm sorry. That was unforgiveable of me."

"Yes, it was." She clamped her lips shut, too upset to say more.

When he rubbed the corner of his eye, guilt flashed through her. His eyelid must be twitching, something that only happened when he was particularly upset or in pain. She was making a complete hash of things but couldn't seem to control her emotions.

"It's just that it would kill us to lose Tira," he said. "She's my daughter now, lass. Do you understand?"

Ainsley fought for her composure. "Of course I do. And I know this is the best place for Tira, truly. I'm more grateful to you than I can ever say."

When he simply studied her in silence, she took a sip of tea to mask her sense of shame. That he could think her so cruel . . . then again, when had she done anything but bring trouble into his life? She supposed she couldn't blame him for his continued mistrust.

Ainsley rested her cup on her knee. "I mean it, Royal. I would never take her away from you."

He breathed out a quiet sigh of relief. "Thank you for that reassurance, especially for my grandfather's sake. He and the dogs would probably throw themselves from the highest tower at Kinglas if they lost her."

Oh, blast. Royal was trying to make a joke, for her sake, which made her feel like an idiot for blundering in so clumsily, trampling over everyone's feelings. One of these days, she would learn to think of others before she thought of herself.

"You do realize that's rather an incentive," she said, trying for the same light tone. "Royal, I know I'm a rather selfish person, but I'm not a monster."

"Sweetheart, of course I don't think you're a monster," he protested.

"But you do think I'm selfish, and you're not wrong. I *am* selfish, but not when it comes to Tira."

He came down on one knee before her. Taking her teacup, he placed it on the round table between the chairs.

"I wasn't finished with that," she said weakly as he took her hands. He started to strip the kid gloves from her fingers.

When he finally wriggled one off, he frowned. "Why is your hand so bloody cold?"

He stripped the other one off and began gently rubbing her hands. "Dammit, Ainsley, one of these days you've got to start taking better care of yourself."

She didn't know whether to laugh or burst into tears. He'd always scolded her when he worried. Only when she thought she'd never see him again had she realized how much she'd miss it.

"I've spent the last five days in a damp coach and even damper inns," she said. "It's a miracle I'm not dead or covered in mold."

"You didn't travel alone, did you?"

"No, I brought my maid with me."

He looked aghast. "That's it? Not even a footman?"

"I was traveling incognito, Royal. Besides, if you saw my maid, you wouldn't worry. She's a veritable Amazon and even meaner than your grandfather."

That was why she'd hired the woman after returning to London. While a bit rough about the edges, Forde was strong, competent, and loyal to the bone. Ainsley had fired her last maid when she found her going through her correspondence. The girl had refused to say who'd put her up to it, but it had to be Cringlewood.

"Is she here with you today?" he asked.

"Of course not." She trusted Forde, but not with this. Not yet, anyway. She didn't trust anybody when it came to Tira, except the Kendricks.

Royal adopted a stern expression. "You know it's not appropriate for you to be calling at a gentleman's residence by yourself."

"Good God, of all people to be lecturing me. When did you turn into such an old biddy?"

"You gave me the responsibility for saving your reputation, or have you forgotten that salient point?"

She rolled her eyes. "Nobody knows I'm here. And please get up off the floor. You look ridiculous, and you'll hurt your leg."

"My leg is fine."

"Splendid, but I'm worried you're about to start spouting lines from *Romeo and Juliet*. Or *Hamlet*, which would be even worse."

He snorted. "Please. *Macbeth* or nothing, in this household."

"With me playing all three witches, no doubt."

"You and Angus could trade off." He briefly pressed her hands and rose to his feet with an easy, masculine grace. He really seemed healthier than she'd ever seen him.

And he was so very, very handsome.

He went to the tea service and filled a plate, stacking it high with scones and cake before bringing it back to her.

"Where are you staying? And if it's at a coaching inn or hotel, I will murder you on the spot," he said a moment later as he poured himself a cup of tea.

Because she'd just taken a huge bite of the most delicious plum cake she'd ever tasted, she couldn't stick out her tongue at him.

"I'm staying at Breadie Manor, for the moment," she managed after she swallowed.

"Really? I didn't know Alec and Edie were in town," he said, settling into the other chair.

Alec Gilbride, heir to the Earl of Riddick, normally resided at his grandfather's castle north of Glasgow. But the family also owned Breadie Manor, a lovely mansion on the outskirts of the city. She'd stayed there last Christmas while visiting with Alec and his wife, Edie, who was a chum from Ainsley's school days.

"They're not," she said, "but they'll be coming down to the city in a few days. My visit was, er, a bit of a surprise."

Ainsley had only written to her friend once she was safely away from London. Edie had barely had time to notify the servants of Ainsley's impending arrival at Breadie Manor.

"They know about Tira?" Royal asked.

She lifted an eyebrow. "You didn't tell them?"

As well as being a good friend to the Kendricks, Alec Gilbride was also Victoria's cousin. Both were the illegitimate offspring of royalty. In Victoria's case, her father was the Prince Regent himself. The cousins were close, so she'd rather expected Victoria to eventually confide in Alec. It was embarrassing, but Ainsley knew the Gilbrides could be trusted to keep her secret.

Royal shook his head. "Victoria and I felt it was not right to share that information without your permission. Not even with Alec and Edie."

"That was very kind of you, but I'm sure Edie knows. That's why I thought you might have told them."

"Why do you think she knows?"

"Because Edie is always talking about you in her letters, extolling your virtues as a father." She flashed him a rueful smile. "Believe me, I never had to write to Victoria to find out how things were going. Edie made a point of filling me in on the Kendrick family on a regular basis—and on you, in particular. You are now a veritable paragon in her eyes, unable to do wrong."

Those letters from Edie and Victoria had been a lifeline, but they'd been painful, too. Each one had driven a nail into her heart as she read about the daughter lost to her, seemingly forever.

He scoffed. "I'm hardly a paragon, I assure you."

Ainsley pressed a dramatic hand to her heart. "I am deeply shocked to hear that."

When his gaze flickered down to her chest, warming with appreciation, she hastily grabbed her teacup and took a sip. Still, she couldn't help feeling a teensy bit pleased that his attraction to her apparently hadn't faded.

"I do try to be a good father, though," he said after a moment. "Not that it's difficult. Tira is so easy to love."

"I . . . I hope you'll let me see her. I promise I won't make any trouble, and I'll be very careful not to reveal anything."

His smile faded. "All right, but you need to tell me why, Ainsley. I need to know why you've changed your mind about this. You were so adamant that you have no contact with her—or me, for that matter."

She put down her teacup. "I'm in trouble, Royal. Tira and I both need your help, now more than ever."

He instantly put down his cup and leaned forward, frowning. "You know I will do what I can to help you. What sort of trouble are you talking about?"

She took a deep breath and then leapt into the unknown. "I need you to marry me, and I need you to do it as soon as you can."

Chapter Nine

If Royal had just taken a mouthful of tea, he probably would have spit it all over her pretty gown. He had the feeling his eyes were bugging out of his skull as he stared at her beautiful, tense features.

Ainsley's image had haunted his sleep for months. But even those dreams—nightmares, in a way, since he always woke to bitter reality—had started to fade. He'd begun to accept that she would never be his and was finally making his peace with it.

Now here she was, upending his life yet again.

"Ainsley, did you really just ask me to marry you?"

Her pale cheeks threw up red flares. "Are you now troubled with hearing problems? That would be unfortunate, given your other afflictions."

Royal pinched his nose. This was the Ainsley he knew, the living definition of chaos. She'd blown up his life more times than he could count. But she'd also given him back his life, and at the precise moment when he thought he had nothing to live for. She'd dragged him back from the brink in a fury of white-hot emotion he would never forget.

She'd also given him Tira, the best gift of all.

And now she wanted to marry him. After everything they'd been through, it was utterly, wonderfully absurd.

"What's wrong?" she asked, her brow suddenly wrinkling with concern. "Are you trying not to sneeze?" Then she sighed. "Oh, blast, are you growing sick on top of everything else? That's just perfect."

Royal couldn't help it. He burst into laughter so hard it made his gut ache before he managed to bring himself under control. Then he caught her indignant expression and went off into another round of guffaws.

"If you don't stop this instant, I will brain you with that fire iron," she threatened, pointing to the hearth tools.

He wiped his eyes. "We wouldn't have much of a discussion after that, I imagine. And I'd have another disability to contend with."

Ainsley drew herself up straight, looking immensely offended. God, he'd missed her imperious snits. Even if she boxed his ears, it would be worth it.

Aye, he was still in a bad way when it came to Lady Ainsley Matthews.

But as much as he loved the mother, there was now the daughter to consider. Whatever crack-brained idea Ainsley had come up with, it would be his responsibility to make sure it didn't harm Tira or her in any way.

"If you're going to be ridiculous," she said in frosty tones, "I'll leave and come back when you're capable of sensible conversation."

Ah. Royal heard a hint of vulnerability and even a wee bit of shame behind that infamous dignity of hers.

He never wanted her to feel ashamed. Not with him.

When she made to stand, he wrapped a hand around her wrist. "I'm sorry, sweetheart. I didn't mean to offend you. You simply surprised me."

She huffed a bit. "You were very rude. It's not easy for a

woman to make an offer of marriage, you know. It's not the done thing."

He smiled at her. "And when have we ever done the done thing?"

She twisted her mouth sideways for a moment before letting go of her outrage. "Never, I suppose. We always seem to do everything backward."

"It makes life more interesting, doesn't it?"

She eyed him, as if uncertain of his mood. "I meant it, though."

"Meant that you need my help, or meant your rather exciting marriage proposal?"

"Both."

"Then we need something stronger than tea for this discussion," he said, standing up. "A sherry, perhaps?"

She wrinkled her pretty nose. "I don't think sherry will quite do it. Do you have brandy?"

"Of course."

The angry flush in her cheeks had faded, leaving her pale and weary looking. And although she tried to hide it, she was shivering. Ainsley had always been a robust girl, not one of your Dresden misses. But now that he'd gotten over the shock of seeing her, Royal noted that she'd lost a great deal of weight—more than the baby weight. Though her figure still possessed exceedingly delightful curves, she seemed almost fragile.

He stirred the fire and added some coal, which earned him a grateful smile. Then he crossed to the drinks trolley to pour a whisky for him and a brandy for her. Clearly, they both needed a bit of liquid courage to smooth the tricky conversation ahead.

After handing Ainsley her glass, he pulled his chair around so they could face each other. He needed to look into her amazing violet eyes while they thrashed this out. Needed to sense her emotion. And he wanted to be close to her. To breathe in her enticing, jasmine-scented perfume, to see the faint blush that colored her pale skin when her emotions ran high.

Whatever else would come of this day, she was with him now. He would cherish the moment he thought he'd never have again.

They sat knee to knee while she sipped her brandy. He was pleased to see some color returning to her cheeks.

"I'm sorry I was mean to you," she said. "But you rather deserved it."

"I did. But there's very little you can say to me that would truly insult me, Ainsley."

"It's one of the things I most like about you," she confessed. "It's quite nice not to have to worry about someone taking offense at everything I say."

"Certainly not offended, but curious. Sweetheart, why the change of heart? I've asked you to marry me more times than I can count, and you always refused me."

"I know," she said with a sigh. "I must seem ridiculous."

"Charmingly so, naturally. But I take it your proposal has more to do with the trouble you mentioned than a sudden discovery of an undying passion for me."

He spoke lightly, since he didn't want to embarrass her. But only an idiot would think Ainsley had spent the last four months pining for him.

Too bad his stupid heart was hoping, in fact, that she had.

Ainsley put down her glass and took his hand, threading her fingers through his. Everything inside him came to life at her touch, like a parched garden reviving with a spring shower. He wrapped that little hand up in both of his.

"Royal, surely you know I'm exceedingly fond of you," she said earnestly. "What we felt for each other in London, when we first met, well . . . I didn't fake that, despite what appearances might have suggested."

"I know," he said gruffly.

"I care for you very much—more than any man, in fact. So, please don't think I'm taking any of this lightly or trying to take advantage of your kind feelings for me."

He smiled at her tepid description of his emotions. "You can take advantage of me as much as you want, lass."

Amusement gleamed in her eyes for a moment before she sobered. "I've changed my mind because I'm in serious trouble. Marrying you would be the best solution to my problem."

"Which is?"

She withdrew her hand and curled it tensely in her lap. "It's twofold, but the most pressing one is that Cringlewood has threatened to expose me if I do not agree to marry him by the end of the month. He will let it be known that I slept with him and then refused his offer to marry."

"God," Royal muttered, disgusted. "He really is a complete bastard."

"I assure you he would take great delight in humiliating me if I refused."

"Why don't you just call him a liar to his face? It's his word against yours. It's not like you and your family aren't wealthy and well regarded, too."

"Royal, you do understand how the world works, do you not? Women *always* take the blame in these sorts of situations. Always."

"I understand that such is *usually* the case. But you've never chased after men or acted in any way to damage your reputation. The opposite, in fact."

"You mean I have no bones about humiliating men if they annoy me?" She sighed. "That is unfortunately true, and it means I have more than my share of detractors. Cringlewood will be clever about it too. He won't come right out with it. Instead, he'll start a whisper campaign, putting out nasty little rumors that will slowly but thoroughly destroy my reputation."

He grimaced at the ugly but all-too-real scenario. "Yes, I see, and it's appalling. Yet, though I don't mean to make light of it, surely the damage would only be temporary. Tira is safe with me, and your parents won't throw you out in the street. The scandal would eventually fade and you could once again return to your old life."

He didn't want to lose her again, but he needed to make sure, for all their sakes, that she truly wanted this marriage.

"Royal, you have no idea what you're talking about," she said tartly. "My family and I would be utterly humiliated. I would be forced to retire permanently to some out-of-the-way village. My friends would shun me and my family would hate me. I did *not* go through all the trouble of concealing my pregnancy to spend the rest of my life in exile because of what that vile man did to me. *He* was the one who wronged *me*."

By the time she finished, fury shimmered in the air around her. Her sense of frustrated rage filled Royal with a deep foreboding.

He took her hands again. They were shaking, so he gently squeezed them. "Ainsley, please tell me the truth. Did he force himself on you?"

When she flinched, and her gaze slid away, his stomach twisted into a thousand knots.

"Love, I would never judge you," he said. "But I need to know what happened. I need to know how to . . . to manage this."

And how to manage her. Because it now seemed clear that Ainsley had been grievously wounded.

When she finally returned his gaze, it was both defiant and vulnerable. "Yes, he forced me."

Royal closed his eyes against the blinding rush of dark emotion. For her sake, he'd wanted to believe that such had not been the case, that Cringlewood hadn't physically harmed her. But now her stark admission ripped through his heart like an exploding shell.

He opened his eyes. "I am going to London, and I'm going to beat the living shite out of him."

"No, you are not," she said firmly.

"He hurt you, and he needs to be punished." Royal should have trusted his bloody instincts and done that long ago. Instead, he'd allowed the bastard to get away with the worst act a man could perpetrate against a woman.

"Believe me, that wouldn't improve the situation."

"Ainsley, no man should be allowed to get away with that," he said, his frustration building. "I can deal with him, I assure you."

She visibly struggled to wrestle her emotions under control. "Cringlewood doesn't see it that way. He thinks he did nothing wrong. Your charging in will only make things worse."

He forced himself to concentrate on her, instead of his own terrible anger. "Can you explain how he could possibly think that?"

When she pulled away and sat back in her chair, he had to resist the urge to snatch her into his arms, keeping her forever safe. But coddling was not what she wanted. She needed to do this her way, and he needed to somehow find the patience to support her.

"You must understand that everyone assumed that Cringlewood and I would be married," she said. "As you know, he'd been courting me for some time before I met you."

"Yes. I remember."

"You probably also remember that he was proprietorial, even when he had no right to be." Her lips tightened for a moment. "My parents encouraged him in that, I'm sorry to say, and I didn't do enough to discourage it. It seemed an excellent match that both families favored. Leonard is wealthy and powerful, and my mother was thrilled with the notion of her daughter becoming a marchioness."

"Such is the way of the *ton*."

"Disgusting, isn't it?"

"You didn't always think so, did you?" he asked gently.

She sighed. "No, and although my feelings for him were tepid, I didn't dislike him. I had to marry someone, after all. Why not a family friend I'd known for years?"

"A handsome, rich, and titled friend," Royal said. "What else could any young maiden ask for?"

"Perhaps a personality that didn't resemble a slimy toad."

He chuckled, since she had obviously intended him to. "He fails on that account."

"The marquess hid his loathsome nature fairly well, I'll give him that." She shrugged. "Then again, I'm not a pattern card of a demure docility, am I?"

"I consider that one of your greatest charms. So, the families were promoting the match, and you more or less went along with it—mostly from inertia, it seems."

"Yes, that's exactly right. When it came down to it, I suppose I didn't truly wish to marry anyone. But that, of course, was not an option."

The most brilliant catch on the marriage mart had been expected to make a brilliant marriage that further elevated her family's status. Dwindling into spinsterhood would have been considered abject failure.

"So, Cringlewood was the obvious man." He raised an eyebrow. "Although I suspect I threw a temporary spanner in the works, didn't I?"

Her smile was rueful. "You did. The aftermath of that incident was not pretty."

"I'm sorry. I was an idiot to behave so badly."

"It's because you're a man. You can't help it."

"Thank you," he said with a faint smile. "But Cringlewood still wished to marry you?"

"Yes, eventually he forgave me," she said dryly. "Although for a while I truly didn't care, since he was acting like such a prig."

He frowned. "Then why didn't it end there?"

"Papa convinced me that his lordship's reaction stemmed from jealousy, resulting from his great affection for me. Fool that I was, I suppose I believed him. Papa was eager to begin discussion of the marriage settlements and Mamma was itching to forge even stronger connections with Cringlewood's mother and other relatives. So we agreed to visit their family seat in Hampshire for three weeks in order for me to acquaint myself with the estate and for the necessary financial discussions to commence."

The process seemed so damn cold-blooded. "It's like you were a prize going to the highest bidder."

"A prize heifer," she said with quiet bitterness.

"Ainsley—"

She shook her head. "In any event, it went well for the first few days. The marquess was charming to my parents and paid me a great deal of attention. It was all proceeding better than I expected, so I agreed to go for a walk with him one afternoon, just the two of us. It was *so* stupid of me," she muttered.

"Perhaps not, considering you were all but engaged," he said, hating that she would blame herself.

"But I knew what he wanted, you see. And I went along because I was curious. I wanted . . . to see if I would like it."

It took Royal a moment to answer. "You obviously had doubts."

"Yes. We'd barely even kissed."

Royal couldn't help remembering *their* first kiss. It had been fleeting but memorable, and her response had never been in doubt.

"None of that is unreasonable," he said. "After all, you

were considering spending your life with the man. It's quite sensible, when you think about it."

She gave him a tentative smile. "I thought so." Then her mouth puckered up in a grimace. "But he used it against me. When I asked him to stop, he told me to stop playing the innocent. He said I wanted exactly what he did."

Anger crashed through Royal, swift and hot. His hands ached with the need to wrap them around Cringlewood's throat.

Someday. Soon.

Royal forced himself to focus on Ainsley, who was composed but very pale. This wasn't about him. It was about her, and how he could help her. "You don't have to tell me anything else, lass. I understand."

"No, I need you to know what happened. And I'm almost finished, anyway."

"Do you mind if I hold your hand while you tell me?" he quietly asked. "Please say no, if you don't."

She seemed startled for a moment, but then nodded. "I would like that very much."

When her slender fingers were secured within his, she continued in a tone akin to a grim but steady march. "He took me to a gazebo by the lake, some distance from the manor. It was all right, at first, but after a while I told him I wasn't comfortable and I wanted to return to the house. When he wouldn't stop, I had to give him a shove." Her smile briefly flashed. "A hard one."

His gut twisted with both dismay and admiration. She was so damn brave, fighting off a predator so much bigger and stronger than she. "What did he do then?"

She paused for a moment. "He backhanded me. Quite forcefully."

The world seemed to tilt on its axis, and Royal had to struggle for a few seconds to get it back to the proper angle.

But nothing would ever be truly right until Cringlewood was punished for what he'd done to her.

"I'm sorry, Ainsley. I'm so goddamned sorry."

"I know." She cleared her throat. "Anyway, it was over rather quickly after that. He pushed me down onto the daybed and . . . and did it. It was horrible, of course, but I was so stunned I could barely react. It seemed unreal, somehow." Frowning, she stared down at their joined hands. "I remember listening to the birds. They were madly tweeting away, and the sun was shining through the leaves and the lake was glittering like diamonds. It was a perfect summer day. How could something so ugly be happening when the world was so beautiful?"

Royal felt like he was dying inside. "I'd kill him for you, if I could."

Someday I will.

She actually flashed a wry smile. "Oh, you'd have to wait in line behind me and Aunt Margaret. We've come up with several gruesome scenarios. I suppose it makes me an awful person for finding comfort in the notion."

"It makes you the smartest, bravest lass I've ever met."

Her smile disappeared like a will-o'-the-wisp. "Not so smart that I went off with him in the first place. I suppose in his mind, I gave him permission."

"Cringlewood is a right bastard who deserves a bullet through the brain," Royal gritted out. "The fault was entirely his, not yours."

"My mother didn't think so."

"You told your mother?"

"Yes. Afterward, Cringlewood helped me straighten my clothes, and then he escorted me back to the house, as if everything was fine. He talked about plans for our wedding and how happy he was that matters were finally settled."

"He thought he'd taken away your choice in the matter."

Her gaze skated off to the small coal fire. "Yes."

She was holding something back. It unsettled him, but he decided not to press her.

"As soon as I cleaned up . . ." She paused, her lips pressed into a distressed line. All he could do was hold her hand and wait.

"As soon as I changed, I went to see my mother," she finally went on. "She was shocked, naturally, and dismayed by his lordship's behavior. But she found my behavior equally distressing. As far as she was concerned, we were both at fault."

Royal couldn't imagine *his* mother ever saying anything like that to a daughter. "I didn't realize her ladyship was such a fool."

"She's not a fool, but she's old-fashioned and very much a high stickler. So she was utterly horrified I would even think to refuse marriage, after what happened. As far as Mamma was concerned, I had no choice but to go through with it."

"Aye, but you were too smart to accept such nonsense."

That earned him a rueful but genuine smile. "My mother told me I was completely mad. She also made me swear not to tell my father."

"Because he would be furious with Cringlewood?"

"No, because he would be furious with *me* for complicating matters. Papa would no doubt feel obligated to reprimand Cringlewood for behaving so poorly, which would be awkward. Mamma was terrified he would then refuse to marry me if Papa made a fuss."

"That's it? Your father would simply deliver a reprimand?" Royal asked in disbelief.

She nodded.

"Good God. Your entire family must either be mad or criminally stupid."

"Both, probably. As you can imagine, I left for London almost immediately. Papa was livid about that, of course, and believed whatever *stupid fight* we'd had shouldn't matter. He continued to press for the engagement, and I continued to refuse." She shrugged. "There was no point in telling him the truth, since he would simply agree with my mother."

"Did you see Cringlewood after that?"

"Just once. I told him that I would never marry him, and that he should direct his attentions elsewhere. He was quite . . . taken aback, for lack of a better term."

Royal's stomach clenched. "Did he hurt you again?"

"No. I suppose he was too surprised. That's when Papa decided to send me into exile in Scotland."

"You maneuvered him into that, I imagine."

"I may have said something to the effect that I'd rather bury myself in the Highlands than marry Cringlewood. Papa couldn't believe I meant such a thing, so he decided to test my resolve."

"That was clever thinking on your part."

"Thank you." Her smile faded. "What I hadn't counted on was Cringlewood's persistence."

"What the hell is wrong with the man? Why continue to pursue an unwilling woman?"

"For my fortune, probably, although he does seem quite obsessed with me," she said, glancing away.

Again, he got the odd sense that she was holding something back.

When she met his gaze, it was again steadfast and determined. "Whatever the reason, I know he won't give up. That's why I need you to marry me . . . before he utterly destroys my life."

Chapter Ten

Instead of responding to her terse plea, Royal frowned at their joined hands, his thumb absently gliding over her skin. Ainsley was too uncomfortable with the silence to enjoy the sensation.

"Are you all right?" she finally asked.

It had been horribly difficult and embarrassing to tell him the ugly story. She certainly wouldn't blame him for being embarrassed, too.

He glanced up. "I'm just trying to grasp the implications of all this. It's rather complicated."

Oh, blast. That sounded like a dodge. Or, perhaps—

"Royal, are . . . are you involved with someone else?" she asked, trying not to sound as appalled as she felt.

He scoffed. "Ainsley, between trying to be a good father and dealing with the demands of Logan's business, I'm run ragged. The fair maidens of Glasgow are not my priority."

"I wouldn't blame you if you were," she said. "It's not as if you ever thought you'd see me again."

Instead of answering, he reached up and tugged on the bow under her chin. "Why are you still wearing this blasted hat?" He untied her bonnet and tossed it in the general direction of a chair by the fireplace. It hit the edge of the seat and tumbled to the floor.

"That's a new hat," she protested. "And it was *quite* expensive." She'd made a point of going on a buying spree before she left London. God only knew when she'd have access to her funds again, if ever.

Royal tipped her chin up. "Lass, you are completely daft if you think I would waste my time capering after other women. If you don't know that by now, you're not as smart as I thought."

"You're not exactly the sort to caper at the best of times," she said, trying to make a joke.

Better to joke than to cry. Most days, her mood was so flat that she wondered if anything short of an explosion could jolt her back to life. But after glimpsing Tira and sharing her misfortunes with Royal, a tide wall had been breached. Her emotions were surging with an intensity that almost overwhelmed her.

His smile was tender as he stroked a thumb across her cheek. "No capering with this leg."

"I'm sorry if I made you uncomfortable," she said after a few moments of fraught silence. "It's such an ugly story."

He leaned in, so close she could see gold flecks in his green gaze. "My only discomfort was on your behalf, love. Never think I blame you for anything."

She had to repress the impulse to kiss him, because the thought of kissing any man, even Royal, still made her a little nervous. "Sir, you're making my eyes cross."

"Imp." He dropped a kiss on the tip of her nose before sitting back. "I mean it, Ainsley. You can't blame yourself for what Cringlewood did. The bastard should be drawn and quartered."

"I'm very grateful for your support, truly. I also know the immensity of what I'm asking of you. I've caused so much trouble for you these past few years, and it's hideous of me to try to take advantage of you again."

His smile turned rueful. "Any number of times I have wished for nothing more than for you to take advantage of me."

Her heart sank. "But no longer?"

He hesitated a fraction too long. "As I said, it's a complicated situation."

Ainsley swallowed her stark sense of dismay. She refused to make him feel guilty, not after everything he'd done for her. For Tira's sake, she *would* do the right thing.

"I understand, and I'm sure I'll manage somehow. If . . . if you'll just let me spend a little time with my daughter before I leave Glasgow, I'd be immensely grateful. I promise I won't make any trouble."

His brows snapped together. "What the hell are you talking about?"

"You obviously don't want to marry me. I'm trying to say that I understand and I'll manage," she replied with what she thought was commendable patience.

"Ainsley, I never said I wouldn't marry you."

Her heart kicked out a hard thump. "Then you will?"

When he hesitated again, she almost shrieked in frustration. "Royal, will you *please* just tell me exactly what you do mean?"

He grimaced. "Sorry. It's not you. I'm worried about what this will mean for Tira."

She'd thought endlessly about that too, in the dark reaches of the night. "Are you afraid I won't be a fit mother? Because you must know I would never hurt her."

"Don't be daft. I know how much you love her. But that's the point. How do we continue protecting Tira from Cringlewood if you're in her life?"

"I don't think that's a concern anymore. It's been five

months, and simply *everyone* believes Tira is your daughter. Your family did a splendid job in that respect."

Ainsley felt quite confident in that regard. There'd not been a speck of gossip about her long absence from London. Some might not understand her reasons for jilting Cringlewood, but her friends thought her long exile in Scotland punishment enough.

"Unfortunately, people might make the connection once they see you together," Royal said. "Tira looks exactly like you."

"She's just a baby."

"One who has your coloring, including your eyes."

"All right, but I don't think that's an insurmountable obstacle. People generally believe what they're led to believe, and they all clearly believe Tira is a Kendrick. Several of your brothers have dark hair and blue eyes, so we can say she takes after them."

Royal's only reply was a grunt.

"It's not like we ever have to visit London," she pressed, "and hardly anyone I know comes to Scotland, including my family."

Not that anyone in her family would ever talk to her again.

"Ainsley, you do remember that you hate Scotland, don't you?" he asked. "Are you really prepared to spend the rest of your life here, as the wife of a common younger son?"

Royal didn't believe she could give up her pampered existence, but he was wrong. "I'm sure I'll adjust."

When he hauled himself up and walked over to replenish his glass, Ainsley marshaled patience. Given everything he knew about her, including that she'd given up her daughter partly to return to her old life, his caution was entirely understandable.

When he again propped a shoulder against the mantel, she sensed he was putting distance between them.

"Ainsley, you've spent your life in the lap of luxury. I'm

not a rich man, by any means, nor is Glasgow the most exciting city in the world."

"What good did that pampered life do for me?" she challenged. "It couldn't keep me safe, or even give me the freedom to make my own choices. If anything, the fact that I'm an heiress has made my life more complicated."

He pondered that for a few moments. "I don't wish to pry, but I'm not sure what the arrangements are regarding your fortune." He held up a hand before she could reply. "And I don't give a confounded hang about your money. It won't affect my decision."

She smiled at him. "I know, and I don't mind telling you. I'll be worth fifteen thousand pounds a year if I marry an acceptable suitor. Papa will also gift me with a prime hunting box from his grandmother, along with a portion of my maternal grandmother's jewels."

"What if you marry someone not acceptable?"

"Then my father will ensure that I receive not a shilling."

She was rather proud of how unconcerned she sounded, even though she felt sick even saying the horrifying words. But she'd been repeating them in her head for weeks now, so she would get used to it. The idea of being poor and dependent was daunting. But if she had to be dependent on anyone, she would choose Royal in a heartbeat.

He shook his head. "I always thought your father doted on you."

"So did I," she said dryly.

"That's bloody awful." He hesitated. "You're truly sure about this? Because you must know it won't be easy to give up everything you're used to, including your family."

Ainsley stood and joined him by the fireplace. She placed a hand flat on his chest and met his cautious gaze.

"Royal, I only desire two things. First, I want to be safe from Cringlewood. Even more importantly, I want to be with my daughter. These five months away from her . . ."

Her throat went tight, forcing her to pause for a moment. "It's just about killed me."

He covered her hand. "I knew you would miss her, of course, but I thought you'd be able to move on with your life, knowing she was safe with us."

"I tried, I truly did." Her voice cracked. "But I simply cannot go on without—"

He pressed a kiss to her brow. "You don't have to say more. I understand completely."

"I'm sorry," she choked out. "It's shameless the way I'm using you—asking you to agree to a sham marriage just so I can be with my daughter. I can't imagine what you must think of me."

She was so wrapped up in her bout of self-pity that it took several moments to realize he'd turned into a block of stone. "What's wrong?"

"You said 'sham marriage'?"

Ainsley grimaced. "Oh, blast. I didn't mean . . . Royal, you must know how fond I am of you."

"Thank you. I think."

"Sorry," she said. "I suppose that rather sounded like I was talking about my pet pug, didn't it?"

He frowned. "Do you have a pet pug?"

"Heavens, no."

"Good, because the terriers would tear it apart."

"Oh, I forgot about them," she said.

"In any case, this isn't about the dogs. It's about how you feel about *me*. If we have any chance of making a marriage work—"

"Does that mean you'll do it?" She clutched his hand with both of hers.

When he flushed under his tan, she realized she'd placed his hand firmly against her breast. With a weak smile, she let go and began awkwardly fussing with the collar of her gown.

Royal looked regretful. Then he cleared his throat and got

rather brisk. "I will never abandon you, Ainsley, but I would be grateful to know how you actually feel about me, as a husband, that is."

She struggled to find the words to explain, desperate not to hurt him. "You must understand that most days I don't even know how I feel about *myself*. I'm a mess, if you want to know the truth."

"You're too hard on yourself, sweetheart," he said softly.

"Perhaps. But there are some things I do know. I know that I love my daughter and I want to be with her. And I know that I trust you and feel safe with you. You're the only person in my life who makes me feel that way. When I'm with you, it's like I'm myself again. Although perhaps not quite as selfish and pigheaded," she finished ruefully.

"You were never really selfish, love. Just a little spoiled."

"But certainly pigheaded."

"That's why we're so well matched," he said in a light tone. Even though they were over the heavy bit, he was still trying to clear the way for her. And that was so like him too.

She pressed her fingers into the fine wool of his coat. "Royal, I know I'm a bad bargain, but please believe me when I say there's no one else I would rather be with than you. You are the best man I've ever met. After all, I gave you the most precious thing in my life. Would I have done so if I didn't believe in you?"

"I suppose not," he said gruffly.

"I didn't ask you to love and protect Tira because it was convenient for me. I did it because it was the only thing in my life that made sense."

"You honored me in doing so. But you must be sure about marriage, Ainsley. Once you make this decision, there is no going back."

"I've done little else these last five months but think about you and Tira, and how much I want to be with you. Both of you," she emphasized. "Truly, I'd swear an oath to that effect, if it would help. Surely there must be some demented Highland ceremony where we would cut our wrists, mingle our blood, and then twirl around half-naked in the moonlight."

His lips twitched. "Well, I'd very much like to see you dancing half-naked in the moonlight."

"It would only work if we both did it."

"As intriguing as it sounds, I'm no dancer, so we'll have to be satisfied with a simple church wedding."

Her insides jumped. "So, you'll do it?"

"Aye."

While her legs went shaky with relief, she somehow managed to muster a scowl. "Royal Kendrick, I just poured my heart out, and all you can do is say aye?"

"Ainsley, I've been nursing a hopeless passion for you—with the emphasis on hopeless—for well on two years, and now we're finally to be wed. If I get any more emotional, I'll have to ring for smelling salts."

She choked out a laugh. "As your grandfather would say, you are a complete jinglebrains."

As usual, when feeling emotional they both took refuge in silly jests and mild—or not so mild—insults. It was easier that way, and sometimes safer.

"You're stuck with me now." He steered her back to her chair, plucking up her brandy glass. "Here, you look like you could use this."

She took a sip, relishing the reviving jolt. Royal settled into his chair, watching her with quiet intensity.

"Now that we've got everything sorted out, may I see Tira?" she asked.

"Of course, although I do think we have a few more things to sort out."

She cocked an eyebrow.

"For one, when do we get married?" he asked.

"Well, it's Scotland, so we can just pop off and find the nearest blacksmith, can't we?"

"As charmingly quaint as that would be, I would advise waiting a few weeks. That will give my family a chance to gather and will allow us time to plan a proper church wedding and celebration."

"I don't need any of that. I want to get married immediately." She leaned forward, her anxiety sparking again. "We can't afford to wait, Royal."

He took her hand. "I promise I won't let anyone hurt you or Tira."

"But—"

"No, lass. Running off will only look suspicious and raise more questions. I've only just got past the scandal of bringing my by-blow into the house. Marrying you in such a slipshod fashion will only generate more gossip."

Ainsley chewed on her lower lip, feeing mulish and afraid.

"You're not alone in this anymore," he said. "You've got me and the rest of my family. We'll protect you."

She wrinkled her nose. "I've been dealing with this on my own for so long. It's hard to give up control."

"You're not giving up control. You're just letting me help you."

Help. She'd wanted that for so long, and now she finally had it. It felt both odd and miraculous. "All right, I'll defer to you on that. Is there anything else to discuss?"

He considered for a moment. "I think that's enough for now."

Ainsley breathed a sigh of relief. She felt exhausted and battered by her emotions.

"I know you're rather impatient to see your daughter," he said with a smile.

"*Rather* would be putting it mildly."

He rose and headed for the door. "I'll have Angus fetch her right away."

"Oh dear, must he?" Angus was the last person she wanted to deal with, especially while finally meeting her daughter again.

"He'll insist, I'm afraid."

"Then can we delay telling him that we're to be married, at least for today?"

He threw her a surprised glance over his shoulder.

"You know he'll be furious about it," she said, "and I'd like to focus on Tira, if I may."

He nodded. "Of course."

She flashed him a grateful smile.

When he opened the door, Angus all but fell into the room.

"Hear anything interesting, Grandda?" Royal asked sardonically.

"Not a bloody word," the old man groused. "Ye both mumble too much."

"We'll talk later," Royal said. "For now, I'd like you to bring Tira down."

Angus gaped at him, thunderstruck. "Doon here? To see *her*?"

"Yes."

"But the wee lass is nappin'," he protested. "And, besides, I dinna ken—"

"Now, Grandda," Royal ordered, gently shoving him out of the room.

Ainsley stood up. "This is going to be a disaster, isn't it?" She couldn't help wringing her hands. "Angus is going to try to ruin everything."

"No need to worry, love. He's devoted to Tira. He'll only want the best for her, and that means her mamma."

Ainsley was quite sure Angus would not consider that the best thing for Tira.

She began pacing the room. Thankfully, Royal didn't urge her to sit or attempt to calm her with silly platitudes. He simply watched her, radiating waves of quiet reassurance.

The biggest miracle of all was about to happen. She'd finally have everything she'd fought so diligently to achieve—her daughter, and a husband strong enough and devoted enough to protect them both.

And yet she'd never been more terrified in her life.

A few minutes later, Angus walked in, cradling the baby wrapped in a plaid blanket. Royal took Tira and came over to Ainsley, who stood frozen like a lump in front of the fireplace.

"Here's your daughter," he murmured. "And she's a bonny lass, just like her mother."

She had to blink furiously as she gazed at the sleeping baby in his arms. Tira had the sweetest, chubbiest cheeks, a wealth of glossy black hair, and the most adorable nose Ainsley had ever seen. In short, she was the most beautiful baby who'd ever lived.

"Would you like to hold her?"

Ainsley hardly dared breathe. "May I?"

Angus popped up behind Royal's shoulder. "Best not. The lassie's always a wee bit cranky if ye startle her out of a nap."

"It'll be fine, Angus," Royal said.

Ainsley couldn't help flashing the old man a smug grin. He scowled and uttered a few choice words under his breath.

"I certainly hope you never talk like that around Tira," she said.

"She's used to it," Royal dryly said. "Here, take her."

Carefully, he eased the babe into her embrace. Ainsley held the soft weight in her arms, amazed at how big her daughter had grown.

Angus sidled around to stand close to her. "Make sure ye support her neck, or she'll be floppin' about like a fish."

Ainsley huffed but followed his instructions. While

Angus might be a horrible old man, he clearly knew his way around babies.

"That's it," Royal said. "You're a natural."

Ainsley flashed him a grin. "I was very good with her when she was a newborn, if you recall."

Although Tira was still asleep, her face was now screwed up in a frown, as if something troubled her. Perhaps it was the blanket, which had twisted a bit under her chin. Ainsley jiggled her more securely in her arm and tried to rearrange the soft wool wrap.

Tira's eyes suddenly flew open, and Ainsley found herself staring into a deep violet gaze that matched her own. It was a sleepy gaze, certainly, but a mirror image of hers nonetheless.

It was astounding and utterly wonderful.

The baby contemplated her with an indecisive air, as if waiting for something to happen.

"Hello, darling," Ainsley whispered. "Remember me? Remember your mamma?"

Tira's eyes popped even wider for a moment. Then she screwed up her face, opened her little mouth, and began to screech. Out in the hall, the dogs began to yowl in mournful solidarity, creating an unholy din.

Ainsley winced. "I suppose she doesn't remember me, after all."

"Welcome to motherhood, lass," Angus said with a snort. "I hope ye're ready for it."

Chapter Eleven

Ainsley eyed the wicker contraption she and Victoria were pulling along the smooth path. "Are you sure this is safe?"

"Oh, yes. Angus spent a great deal of time working on it. He saw an illustration of a children's cart in a gazette and worked very hard to improve on the design."

"But those carts are generally for older children. And they are usually pulled by dogs, not people, are they not?"

"Angus originally thought the dogs could pull this," Victoria said wryly, "but Royal put his foot down. Could you imagine the terriers careening around the park with poor Tira in tow?"

"The mind reels."

Still, the little carriage seemed quite sturdy. Angus had mounted a wicker bassinet on a base that resembled a small pushcart. Lined with blankets, the bassinet served as a comfortable cocoon for Tira to venture out into the world—or at least as far as around the garden square in front of Kendrick House.

"The pull handles were a good addition," Ainsley admitted. "But we must look rather ridiculous."

They'd received more than a few startled glances from the nannies and nursemaids who were quite sensibly carrying their charges or helping the toddlers walk. Or perhaps they were simply agog at the sight of aristocratic ladies trundling a cart around the square, especially when one of those ladies happened to be the Countess of Arnprior.

"It's splendid exercise," Victoria said. "I hate being cooped up in the house all day."

"Yes, splendid." Ainsley tried to ignore the perspiration trickling down her spine. "Let's muck out the stables next."

Victoria laughed. "Poor Ainsley. But you must agree this outing worked on Tira."

"Thank God." Ainsley twisted a bit to peer into the carriage. "She's *finally* asleep."

After a week of rainy weather, today's sunshine had prompted this much-needed stroll. Nicholas and Victoria had arrived in Glasgow a few days ago, and the commotion of their arrival—and the surprise over Ainsley and Royal's engagement—was only now settling down. Victoria was clearly eager for a private chat, and Ainsley was just as eager to escape from a household full of loud and opinionated Kendrick males.

Spending quiet time with Tira was a bonus. As grateful as Ainsley was to Royal, she couldn't get past the notion that he and the other Kendrick men were constantly judging her fitness as a mother and finding her lacking. Naturally, Angus was the worst, offering a stream of comments that detailed the failings of English women in general and Ainsley in particular. Unfortunately, the old man's assessment tended to be more accurate than not, and today was another case in point.

Tira had started fussing as soon as they left the house. By the time they reached the park she'd worked up a full head of steam. Ainsley had done her best to soothe her until finally admitting defeat and handing her over to Victoria. After the countess had rocked Tira through the worst of the storm, they'd wheeled her around the small park and the motion of the cart finally lulled her to sleep.

It had been another monumentally discouraging episode. At least only Victoria had been witness to Ainsley's inability to comfort her own child.

"I don't suppose we dare sit on that bench," she said. "If we stop moving, she might wake up."

Victoria peeked under the light throw draped over the top of the bassinet. "I think she'll sleep for a while. She's exhausted from all that crying."

Ainsley sighed. "Whenever I get close it's like a bell goes off in her head. Even the dogs have taken to hiding when I come to visit, and you know how they usually stick to Tira's side."

"She's teething, dearest," Victoria said. "That's why she's so fussy. It's not you, I promise."

When Ainsley gave her a look, her friend wrinkled her nose. "Well, maybe it's you just a wee bit, but only because Tira doesn't know you yet. And it doesn't help that there's been a great deal of commotion at the house."

"But it's been over a week since I arrived. And she positively *hated* the doll I bought for her," she added rather inanely, referring to the very pretty and very expensive doll she now held in her free hand. "It's like I'm cursed, or the blasted doll is."

Ainsley had put it in the carriage, hoping to divert her daughter from her tears. Tira had wailed like a banshee until the doll was hastily removed.

"I'm her mother. She *should* know me." When she waved the doll in frustration, the wretched thing's starched cambric bonnet fell off and landed in a mud puddle.

"Hell and damnation," she muttered as she bent to retrieve it. She jammed it back onto the doll's head, even though it was now a sodden mess.

"Babies don't think rationally," Victoria said. "They're much like men in that respect."

Ainsley gave her a rueful smile. "I know I'm acting like

a bigger baby than Tira. At least she expresses her dissatis-
faction with a good, healthy cry. I spend most of my days
whining and driving everyone crazy."

"Dearest, you've been through a traumatic time. You have
every right to be frustrated and worried. And you're still exhausted, I'm sure."

"I shouldn't be, since Edie and Alec spoil me to bits."

Even though she spent most days at Kendrick House,
Ainsley returned every night to the Gilbrides' manor on the
outskirts of the city. She would have preferred to stay close
to Tira, but Royal insisted on strict propriety so as to tamp
down the burgeoning gossip.

"But it's never easy to live a lie, is it?" Victoria said with
a shrewd glance. "Even when the lie is necessary."

"No, and I'm living with more than one at the moment."

She'd piled up so many it was hard to keep them straight.
There were the out-and-out fabrications, and then there were
the lies of omission—the truths she didn't dare tell anyone,
even Royal. In some ways, those were the worst.

They wheeled the carriage to a bench underneath a sheltering oak. The genteel, quiet square was almost deserted,
with only a few nursemaids and their charges, along with a
footman hurrying through on an errand. After carefully ma-
neuvering the carriage into the shade, Ainsley and Victoria
sank gratefully onto the bench.

"At least all the lying is keeping me safe," Ainsley said.
"That's some consolation."

"The Kendricks will keep you safe, even Angus. Never
doubt that."

"I have to admit the old fellow has surprised me in that
regard, although I know it's truly about Tira." She sighed.
"It's mind-boggling how good he is with her."

Any baby in her right mind should prefer her doting
mother to a grumpy Highlander who looked and acted like
he'd escaped from a lunatic asylum.

"Angus is better with Tira than anyone, including her nursemaids," Victoria said. "It's rather endearing, when you think about it."

"I try very hard *not* to think about it," Ainsley replied.

"He's a trial, I know. It took me weeks to bring him around, but I eventually managed it."

"That's because you're a miracle worker and a saint. I, unfortunately, am neither."

"The trick is to understand that everything Angus does, no matter how bizarre, is out of loyalty to family and clan."

"Emphasis on *bizarre*," Ainsley said, forcing a smile.

Victoria saw through her halfhearted jest. "Do you want me to talk to him?"

"I don't know why I even care. It's not as if Angus is trying to prevent Royal from marrying me. It's . . . it's just that I know how much he dislikes me." She forced another pitiful excuse for a smile. "I'm usually the one with her nose stuck up in the air. I suppose it's only fitting that I finally get a taste of my own medicine."

Victoria warmly pressed her hand. "It's not personal with Angus."

"I must say, it feels rather personal when he makes a point of detailing all my failings, especially when Royal isn't about."

"You must realize that Angus is acting so hideously only because he's afraid of you."

She frowned. "Really? Does he think I'll change my mind and take Tira away? Because I'd never do that."

"No, it's Royal he worries about." Victoria hesitated for a moment. "Angus is afraid you'll hurt him again. Royal was something of a wreck after the last time."

Ainsley mentally grimaced. She'd been so focused on Tira and worrying about her own fate that she'd not focused much on her betrothed's state of mind. Nor had she and Royal spent any time alone this last week. He was either busy with work or there were other Kendricks lurking about, making private conversation impossible.

She was beginning to suspect he was avoiding her. For a man who'd once sworn undying devotion, Royal hadn't so much as tried to steal a kiss or make the slightest romantic overture. Perhaps he felt the same fears as his family.

"I suppose I shouldn't be surprised that the family thinks that way. Royal and I did fight like barbarians on more than one occasion." She threw Victoria a smile. "I suspect Angus isn't the only one who worries what will happen once I have Royal in my evil clutches."

"My husband worries about everyone, so you'll have to get used to that. As for the twins, I'd say their feelings about you could best be described as terrified."

"I was quite hard on them during that blasted elopement, wasn't I?"

"Grant said he was afraid you were going to steal a pistol from one of the grooms and shoot him and Graeme."

"I actually threatened to do just that." Though it seemed almost comical now, it hadn't been one of her better moments.

"The twins will come around, I promise. And Logan and Kade certainly like you, so they're no problem."

Ainsley scoffed. "Logan Kendrick likes anything that's female and well proportioned, so I don't put much stock in his approval. Kade, however, is a genuinely nice boy. I haven't a clue why he likes me so much."

"He's at a rather impressionable age. So, let's just say you made *quite* the impression on him," Victoria said with a twinkle.

"Too bad the others aren't equally impressionable."

"Dearest, it truly only matters what Royal thinks."

Ainsley raised a hand in frustration. "But I don't *know* what he's thinking. I can usually tell, but these days he's like a cypher."

"One generally has to be quite firm before Royal will admit that something is bothering him."

"It's not what I was expecting, to tell you the truth," Ainsley said. "Even when we fought, we always seemed to understand each other." It was as if they were somehow connected beyond words, although it sounded too silly to voice such a thought.

"I think he's nervous. That's why he's being so careful with you."

"But he's never been nervous before, Victoria. Royal and I are *always* stepping on each other's toes. It's what we do."

"But now you have a daughter to worry about. That's bound to affect your relationship."

"Not for the better, apparently. I'm not sure he trusts me anymore."

While Victoria frowned, apparently thinking about that observation, Ainsley took the opportunity to peek into the carriage. It was as much to check on her daughter as to cover up her embarrassment. Discovering that Tira slept soundly, she had no choice but to meet her friend's sympathetic gaze.

"Are you afraid Royal no longer has feelings for you?" Victoria asked.

That was precisely her fear. While their marriage might never be conventional, she'd hoped to create a satisfying, affectionate relationship with Royal and a loving family life for Tira. It was depressing to contemplate that he might only have agreed to marry her out of some dreary sense of duty. All she wanted was a bit of love, for both their sakes.

You're a sentimental fool.

"It doesn't matter," Ainsley replied. "All that matters is that Tira is happy and I get to be with her."

Victoria rolled her eyes. "Royal adores you as much as ever, you goose."

"He's got a funny way of showing it, since he's acting like I've got some horrid disease."

"I suspect his behavior stems from an excess of emotion rather than a lack of it."

"What exactly does that mean?"

"His feelings for you are, shall we say, robust," Victoria explained. "Physically as well as emotionally."

Ainsley's cheeks grew warm. "He didn't tell you that, did he?"

"God, no. He'd shoot himself if he knew we were having this conversation. But it's obvious to me that he would be delighted to get you alone and, er . . ."

"Have his way with me."

"Indeed."

Ainsley fussed with the lace trim on the doll's dress, trying to sort through the confusing emotions roiling through her.

"And how do *you* feel about Royal in that regard?" Victoria prompted.

"I'm not sure. Sometimes I quite desperately want him to kiss me, and . . . and do other things. But then at other times . . ."

"At other times, it frightens you," Victoria finished.

"Yes. Whenever memories of what Cringlewood did rush back in a horribly vivid wave, the idea of anyone touching me seems impossible." She held the wretched doll in a death grip. "It's awful, and I can't seem to control when it happens."

Victoria gently pried Ainsley's fingers off the doll. "Here, give me that poor thing before you break it."

"What difference would it make?" she groused. "Tira hates it."

"No, she doesn't. Besides, it's your first gift to her, which makes it special."

Ainsley gave her a weak smile. "I'm being an idiot, aren't I?"

"You are not," Victoria said firmly. "It's quite a natural

reaction, as I know from my own experience. And your trauma was far greater than mine. Royal is worried about the effects of your assault, and is therefore treading carefully."

Ainsley shook her head, disgusted with herself. "Oh, good Lord. He's afraid to touch me because of what Cringlewood did to me. Why did I not see that?"

Because you never think about anyone but yourself.

She slammed the door on that accusatory voice, one that sounded remarkably like her father's. That person wasn't her anymore—not since Tira had come into her life.

"I'm sure Royal is afraid of provoking some hurtful emotions for you," Victoria said. "He's sensitive that way because of his own experience. After Waterloo, nightmares haunted him for months, according to Nicholas."

"Nightmares caused by the injury? But he never says anything about that. The man's a complete stoic."

Her friend cast her a surprised glance. "You do know that he was left unattended on the battlefield for hours after he was wounded? People thought him already dead. It was quite a harrowing situation until Nicholas finally found him."

Ainsley gaped at her, horrified.

Victoria winced. "Oh, I thought Royal must have told you."

"No, but you certainly can."

"Well. I think it would be best if you discuss it directly with him."

"That's not fair. He'll never tell me, at this rate."

"He will when he's ready. I only raised the issue to explain his behavior. His experience has taught him that wounds to the psyche often require more time to heal than wounds to the body."

Ainsley shook her head. "Well, there's one thing that's obvious."

"What's that?"

"My betrothed and I are quite a mess, so we're perfectly

matched. Although these days, Royal is less of a disaster than I am, which is annoying. I'm not used to being so chicken-hearted."

"Please don't be so hard on yourself," Victoria said. "You reacted to a terrible assault with true strength of character. I'm in awe of how capably you managed the whole thing."

"Up to a point, I suppose. I've still got the awful Cringle-wood to deal with." She poked her friend in the shoulder. "And I don't mean to sound envious, but at least you got to kill your attacker."

Victoria let out a strangled laugh. "Good God, you're as bad as Angus."

"He approved of your killing the evil *Sassenach*, didn't he? Maybe I should tell Angus what happened to me and see if I can persuade him to murder the vile marquess."

"No one is murdering anyone," Victoria said firmly. "Besides, you forget that *accidentally* killing my assailant put me in a terrible position. I was arrested and then later almost murdered myself. That's certainly not what I would call good fortune."

"It turned out all right in the end, though. The Kendrick brothers saved you, you were cleared of any charges, and you married the Earl of Arnprior. Well done."

Victoria looked incredulous. "I repeat, that almost got me killed in the process."

Ainsley flapped a hand. "I know, I know. But at least you defended yourself, Victoria. You *fought back*."

"Ah. That's what's troubling you. You didn't fight back."

Ainsley looked down at her lap, unable to meet her friend's sympathetic gaze. It looked too much like one of pity, and she was so tired of feeling pitiable.

"I froze," she admitted. "And I *hate* that I did. It was like my mind and body went blank." Like a stupid, frightened rabbit.

Victoria took her hand. "You were stunned, dearest.

Shock is a natural reaction to a horrible event that is taking place."

Ainsley slid her a sideways glance. "But *you* pushed past the shock."

"I'd been warned, so I was partly prepared. And don't forget I was raised in a coaching inn and taught to defend myself. Young ladies of the *ton* are generally not, unfortunately."

"We're only taught to embroider handkerchiefs, look pretty, and bat our eyelashes at idiot men," Ainsley said bitterly. "Women like me are utterly useless when it comes to taking care of ourselves."

After the attack, she'd stumbled up to her room, and rage had consumed her like a terrible fire, turning her body inside out. As she'd emptied her stomach in the chamber pot, she'd thought about finding a gun and killing the bastard. Doing something—*anything*—that might assuage the awful sense of violation.

"It was a terrible betrayal," Victoria said, "and by a man you should have been able to trust above all others. You could not have anticipated it."

"I never really trusted him, you know. I should have realized what he was capable of, and I'm still angry that I didn't."

"Nonsense. Your anger should *only* be directed at Cringlewood and at your family for not protecting you. So no more talk of blaming yourself, Ainsley Matthews. Are we clear?"

She smiled. "You are an excellent friend, Lady Arnprior. I don't think I deserve you."

Victoria gave her a quick hug. "You certainly do, just like you deserve Royal. But you must talk to him about what's bothering you. You'll never sort this out if you don't."

"Talking is a bit of a challenge, when all I see is his backside exiting whichever room I happen to be in."

Victoria laughed. "Ainsley, you have never let Royal get

away with anything, so don't start now. Lock him in a room if you have to, but make him talk."

"You're right, of course. I've let this go on for too long. It's time he and I talk about how we truly feel about each other. How we're going to make this marriage work."

Despite that it was less than two weeks until they would be man and wife, they'd yet to discuss the details, including what they expected of each other in the bedroom. That particular topic hovered over them like an anxious ghost.

"Excellent, and I think you're going to get your chance sooner rather than later." Victoria nodded toward the opposite side of the park. "I see your betrothed coming to join us right now."

Chapter Twelve

When Ainsley first spotted him, her face lit up with unguarded pleasure. Then her smile faded into the polite wariness Royal had come to expect. Each time he saw that mental barrier slam into place he wanted to put his fist through a wall or, better yet, the bloody Marquess of Cringlewood's face. Someday, he would punish the bastard for damaging her bright spirit.

"Are you listening to me?" Kade asked.

Royal refocused on his brother, walking beside him. "Of course, and I agree with you."

"So, you *do* think it's a good idea for Angus to go along on your wedding trip. He'll be so pleased to know you approve."

Royal halted in the middle of path and grabbed Kade by the shoulder. "Please tell me this is a joke. If not, I'm a dead man."

"Of course I'm joking. I was just making the point that you weren't listening."

He lightly cuffed his little brother's arm. "Rascal. All right, I plead guilty. I was distracted, and I beg your apology."

"Apology accepted. I was simply saying that I'm happy

you're going to marry Lady Ainsley. She's quite jolly in her own way, and I think she'll be good for you."

"If by jolly you mean ruthlessly sarcastic," Royal said.

Kade laughed. "She's also smart and quite the prettiest lady I've ever seen. Don't tell Victoria I said that, because she's very pretty, too."

"It will be our secret. And it so happens I'm in complete agreement."

"You're good for her too, Royal," Kade said, turning serious. "She needs someone to look after her. Someone who will protect her from whatever is scaring her."

He mentally blinked. They'd been so careful to hide the full truth about Ainsley and Tira from everyone but Nick, Victoria, and Logan. Even Angus didn't know many of the details, especially those concerning the rape.

"Scaring her? What do you mean?"

Kade made an impatient sound. "I'm not a child anymore. I know exactly what's going on."

"And what do you think you've figured out?"

"She's Tira's mother. It's hard to miss it, given the eyes. Plus, you did go visit Lady Ainsley and then mysteriously returned with a baby."

Royal placed both hands on his brother's shoulders. "We can never acknowledge the truth to anyone. Do you understand?"

"I won't say anything outside the family, I promise. But I'm old enough to know these things. And to help."

"I didn't intentionally cut you out, laddie. I didn't tell Braden or the twins, either."

"I hate to tell you, but they've figured it out too."

Alarm spiked in Royal's gut. Braden could be trusted, but the twins tended to blurt out any thought that came into their heads.

"They won't say anything either," Kade said. "We all want to protect Tira."

"Ainsley needs protection too. It's important, Kade,"

Royal said sternly. "We all have to pretend that Tira is *my* daughter, or things will go south very quickly."

His brother immediately looked contrite. "I'm sorry. I only want to help, and I . . . I just wanted you and Lady Ainsley to know that."

"You have helped enormously by accepting her with such kindness."

Kade waved a hand. "It's easy to like her."

"Tell that to your grandfather."

"You just leave Grandda to me," Kade said stoutly. "I'll bring him around."

Royal smiled. "Good luck with that. But please keep this discussion between us, and always remember that Tira is my daughter. Because in every way that matters, she is."

"I know she is." Kade's voice cracked in the endearing way of a boy his age. "I would do *anything* to protect Tira, even if it meant sacrificing myself for her."

That promise wasn't just youthful bravado on his brother's part. Despite his sensitive nature, the lad possessed more heart and courage than any of them.

Royal gave him a brief hug and got him moving again. "I'm hoping the only sacrifice you'll have to make is hearing Angus complain when Ainsley and I move out of Kendrick House."

"You know he won't like that you're taking Tira away. He dotes on her."

"It can't be helped. If Grandda and Ainsley were to live in the same house, there's no telling what will happen."

"It would be like living with two of the Four Horsemen of the Apocalypse," Kade said in a droll voice.

"Except not as restful."

They were still laughing when they joined the ladies.

"Care to share the joke?" Ainsley asked.

"Can't," Royal said, winking at her. "Not for a lady's ears."

Victoria narrowed her eyes. "Royal Kendrick, if you've been sharing naughty stories with your little brother . . ."

"He wasn't," Kade said, throwing Royal a mischievous grin. "Actually, we were discussing Lady Ainsley and Grandda. We were saying they're rather like—"

"And how are the ladies today?" Royal hastily interrupted. "Well, I hope?"

Ainsley was not to be deterred. "I am the soul of courtesy to your grandfather. I cannot be held responsible for the actions of a deranged Highlander."

"I hope you didn't tell him that," Royal said.

"She did," Kade replied. "I heard her."

"Good God." Royal wavered between exasperation and amusement.

"In my defense, it was not until he called me a spoiled *Sassenach*," Ainsley pointed out.

"Also true," said Victoria. "I was forced to separate the combatants."

"That was actually a bit disappointing," Kade said. "I was enjoying the fireworks."

Ainsley poked him in the shoulder. "Don't think I didn't hear you chortling behind your hand, young man."

"I'm thankful I missed that particular encounter," Royal said.

"I'm sure there will be more such episodes for you to witness," Ainsley said. "If you deign to grace us with your presence."

He had to repress a wince. He *had* been carefully avoiding her and equally hoping she wouldn't notice. "I apologize if you think I've been neglecting you."

"Oh, I don't *think* it, if that's what you're wondering," she said.

"Tira is beginning to stir," Victoria said, tactfully redirecting the conversation. She smiled at Royal. "She must have heard your voice."

He bent to look into the carriage. Tira's eyes were still closed, but she'd kicked off her blanket and was squirming a bit.

"She'll be awake soon," he said. "She's probably hungry."

"We'd better go back, then," Ainsley said, instantly sounding concerned. "She might cry if she gets too hungry."

The poor lass always seemed to take her daughter's tears personally. Royal thought them more a sign of teething, and of bad timing, to a certain extent. Tira had reached the stage where she didn't like strangers. To her, Ainsley was a stranger.

"The nursemaid assured me that Tira consumed an exceedingly hearty breakfast this morning," Victoria said. "And a snack just before we fetched her."

Ainsley checked the watch pinned to her waist. "Still, it's almost lunchtime. It won't do to let her fret."

Royal glanced into the carriage again. Tira had stuck her thumb in her mouth. With her eyes now at half-mast, she looked the picture of drowsy contentment.

"You're the one who's fretting, love," he said. "Tira is fine."

A faint blush colored Ainsley's cheeks, but whether from his endearment or his teasing he didn't know. Despite her jab about being ignored, she was rather skittish with him. They were a pair they were, since he was skittish too. In fact, he was bloody terrified of hurting her by saying the wrong thing.

"I know. I'm a complete fussbudget," Ainsley ruefully said. "But I had no idea babies were so complicated."

"They're not, really." Royal reached into the carriage and gently hoisted Tira into his arms. She snuffled around her thumb, and then nestled against his chest. "They simply want food, love, and a warm place to sleep. Not necessarily in that order."

Kade smiled at him. "You would know, since you practically raised me. Although I doubt you changed my dirty clouts."

"You'd be wrong," Royal said, "because I certainly did."

Ainsley scoffed. "That cannot be true."

"It's not an experience one forgets," he said.

"Didn't your father hire proper nursemaids?" she asked.

"Of course he did. It's just that . . . well, never mind." It was not a topic he wished to discuss.

"He used to sneak into the nursery at night and take me back to his room," Kade explained. "Nick said the first time it happened, the household went crazy looking for me. Finally, they found me cuddled up in Royal's bed, happy as a grig."

"On top of that, you changed his nappies, too?" Ainsley's tone suggested she thought him dicked in the knob for doing so.

"What else was I supposed to do? Babies do need their clouts changed on a regular basis."

"I'd wager the nursemaids weren't happy about you raiding the nursery," Victoria said with amusement. "They disapprove of disruptions in their fiefdoms."

"They were less than keen, I'll tell you that," Royal said, shaking his head at the memory. "I got more than one scold for doing it."

And several hard whacks from the senior nursemaid when no one was looking. Still nothing had stopped him from carting Kade off to his room.

Ainsley was obviously perplexed. "But *why* did you do it?"

He started to give an awkward shrug but realized he might disturb Tira. "He wasn't any trouble, if that's what you're thinking."

"He was afraid I was lonely," Kade said. "We'd lost our mother, you see. Royal worried that I would feel all alone, even though I was just a babe and too young to know the loss."

Royal blinked, startled. His little brother knew the story, of course. It was one of the family jokes—a rambunctious eight-year-old playing nursemaid to a squalling infant. He had never told anyone why he did it, but he wasn't surprised Kade would see to the heart of it.

The lad always did.

"What an *excellent* brother you are, Royal Kendrick," Victoria said, rubbing a gloved fingertip under one eye.

"Victoria, for God's sake do not start bawling," Royal said as he gently rocked the baby.

"My brothers certainly never did anything like that," Ainsley said quietly. "I suspect they never set foot in my nursery, much less cared whether I was happy or sad—at least until I was much older."

And, Royal suspected, probably not even then from the sounds of it.

Kade grimaced in sympathy. "That's very sad."

"You were lucky to have such a nice family," she told the boy with a smile.

If she thought Kade or any of the brothers were lucky, with all the bad fortune they'd suffered over the years, it made Royal wonder what her childhood had truly been like.

"No one could have asked for a kinder, more generous family," Kade said. "Royal especially takes the cake, even though all my brothers are splendid."

"When we're not all getting into trouble and driving Nick crazy, that is." Royal was well aware he'd been anything but kind the last few years. Monumental pain in the arse to his long-suffering family was a better description. "Ainsley, why don't you take the baby," he suggested, uncomfortable with the conversation. "She's gone back to sleep, so I'm sure she won't fuss."

Ainsley shook her head. "It took forever to get her to stop crying when I held her before."

"It wasn't that bad," Victoria protested.

"Yes, it was."

"You're trying too hard, love," Royal said. "Just relax."

Ainsley sighed and gingerly took the baby.

He still couldn't believe the change in her. Right after Tira's birth, Ainsley had taken to motherhood with brilliant, easy grace. Now, though, she was awkward and anxious. The problem was no doubt exacerbated by having to pretend she barely knew Tira, and keeping her emotions on a tight leash. The need to play a false role was getting in the way of her natural maternal instincts.

She adjusted her hold, fitting Tira into the crook of her arm. When she glanced at Royal, her face lit up like the most beautiful star in the night sky.

"Now you're getting the hang of it," he said, forcing the words past the emotion tightening his throat. God, he adored her.

"There, now," Victoria said. "She just needed to settle down—"

An earsplitting wail cut her off, and Ainsley all but jumped out of her shoes. Thankfully, she kept a firm hold on her daughter.

"Well, that settles it," she said with a grimace. "Tira hates me."

Royal shook his head. "Hush, daft girl. Just rock her a bit."

She looked dubious, but gently began rocking her daughter from side to side, softly murmuring endearments. Unfortunately, the wails kept building, reaching a crescendo that shredded the serene atmosphere of the park.

"You'd better take her before a constable arrives to arrest us for disturbing the peace," Ainsley said, handing her over to Royal. "Honestly, sometimes I think—" She bit off whatever she was about to say.

"What?" he asked.

She managed a smile. "Nothing. I'm just being silly."

He propped Tira on his shoulder and began patting her back. "Shush, little lass. Papa's got you."

The baby cried for another minute or so but eventually settled into a series of hiccups as she rubbed her tear-streaked face against his coat. Ainsley studied them fiercely, her expression a heartbreaking mix of frustration and longing. Then she turned away to briskly rearrange the blankets in the carriage.

Royal breathed out a quiet sigh. Fate seemed to be conspiring against Ainsley in the cruelest way through her daughter's apparent rejection. Combined with his family's wary attitude toward her, it would be no surprise if she regretted the decision to torch her old life.

It was up to him to fix that.

"Ah, I believe I have deduced the source of little Miss Kendrick's problem," he said. "This lass is in desperate need of a change."

Ainsley was fussing with an oddly bedraggled doll. "I suppose we should return to the house. We're hardly equipped to change her on a park bench, despite your vaunted skills."

"Kade and I will take her," Victoria said. She flicked Ainsley a meaningful glance before smiling at Royal. "I assume you came home from the office to have lunch with us?"

He nodded.

"Well, then there's time for you and Ainsley to have a nice stroll around the park. In any event, luncheon can certainly be pushed back."

"But I'm starving," Kade protested.

"You can have a nice piece of fruit or a glass of milk," Victoria said in a voice brooking no protest.

"Fruit. Ugh," the lad grumbled.

"Thank you, Victoria," Ainsley said. "I'd quite like a walk."

When the women exchanged another knowing glance, Royal lost any doubt that a conspiracy was afoot. So be it, then. As much as he wanted to avoid putting any pressure on Ainsley, it was past time they sorted out their unresolved issues.

"I'll return Tira to her nursemaids," Victoria said, "and

then perhaps Kade and I can look at a new piece of music to pass the time until you return." She smiled at the lad. "Would you like that?"

"Better than eating a moldy old piece of fruit," Kade said, perking up.

"Splendid. Royal, why don't you put Tira back in the carriage so we can be off."

"I think she'd rather be carried." He handed the baby to Kade. "Here, lad, make yourself useful."

His brother took her gingerly. "Gosh, I hope she's not leaking."

Tira screwed up her wee features, as if displeased with her uncle's tepid reception.

"You're all worse than poor Tira," Victoria said, starting to reach for her.

"Victoria, you'll ruin that lovely pelisse," Ainsley protested. She leaned in to sniff her daughter, resting a gentle hand on Tira's little capped head. "That *is* quite appalling, I must say. And if she is, er, leaking, the stain will never come out."

There'd been an unfortunate incident just yesterday when Ainsley picked Tira up before the nursemaid had finished dressing her. Ainsley's expensive gown had suffered dire consequences as a result.

Victoria whipped a baby blanket from the carriage and deftly wrapped it around Tira's sturdy form. "I grew up in a coaching inn and mucked out more than my share of horse stalls. This is a mere bagatelle by contrast."

"I love her," Kade said, gratefully handing her over, "but she smells almost as bad as the twins after a night of carousing."

"Almost? The twins are infinitely worse," Ainsley said, stoutly coming to her baby's defense. "And at least Tira doesn't destroy the furniture."

"Och, give the wee lassie a chance," Royal said in an

exaggerated brogue. "She'll catch up to her uncles in no time."

Ainsley smacked his arm, trying not to laugh. "That's an awful thing to wish on your daughter. Tira Kendrick will be the sweetest and most refined of young ladies, if I have anything to say about it. Not some Highland hellion like your brothers."

Relief eased the knot in his gut. He hated that she was unhappy. It made him feel almost as helpless as that day at Waterloo when he'd lain half-dead in a ditch, unable to fend for himself.

Victoria settled the baby on her shoulder. "Actually, the twins have made progress. They hardly ever destroy furniture these days."

"I'll take your word for it," Ainsley said dryly.

Graeme and Grant, as well as Braden, had yet to arrive in Glasgow for the wedding. By next week, however, the entire family would be assembled under the roof of Kendrick House. How well Ainsley would deal with a houseful of Royal's cheerfully brash brothers—on top of the other stresses in her life—was an open and troubling question.

Ainsley gave Tira a quick kiss on the top of her head. "We won't be long, I promise," she said to Victoria.

"Take all the time you need."

With Kade dragging the carriage behind him, he and Victoria headed for the street.

Royal offered Ainsley his arm. "If you permit, I would be delighted to escort you, my lovely lady."

She dimpled up at him, her smile sweet and rather shy. Since Ainsley was normally the antithesis of shy, it was another indication of how rattled she was. Her vulnerability sent a clear message that he needed to continue to tread carefully.

They strolled down one of the shaded paths, heading toward the opposite end of the park.

"Why are you scowling?" she asked a few moments later. "Is your leg hurting? Do you want to sit down?"

"Ainsley, please don't fuss over my leg. It's fine." Surprisingly, it had been better these last several weeks. Then again, he'd been so busy that he'd barely had time to think about whether his old injury nagged at him.

"I've got to fuss over something, since my daughter won't let me," she said with a rueful smile.

"It's just the teething making her fractious. That's always hard on a baby, you know."

"That's precisely my point. I don't know *anything* about being a mother, because I had to give her up before I learned how to do it."

He tucked her close to his side. "You've been thrown into the deep end of the pond, Ainsley. I have no doubt that you and Tira will soon be inseparable."

She mulled his words in silence for a few moments. "Sometimes I wonder if I made a mistake."

Now they were getting to it. "By coming back to us, you mean?"

"No. By giving her up." Her expression suddenly turned fierce. "I should have found a way to make it work. No matter how hard I tried, I couldn't see it. But I still should have found a way."

"Love, this was the only way to keep both of you safe from Cringlewood. Short of going into exile, I don't see how you could have done anything different." He hesitated, and then made himself say it. "Unless you think you should have married Tira's father."

She shot him a hard glance. "*You* are Tira's father, not that man. I want nothing to do with him."

"And you're sure about that?"

Her irate gaze practically scorched him.

"Fine, then stop questioning your decision," he said.

"Give yourself and your daughter some time, and all will be well. I promise."

"That sounds lovely, but there's still quite a bit of *all* to work out, isn't there?"

"That's why we're having this little chat, from what I was able to deduce."

His comment pulled a small smile to her lips. "It would appear Victoria and I were not as clever as we thought."

"There was no need for a conspiracy. I came home specifically to speak with you today."

"Because you *have* been avoiding me. Admit it."

He waggled a hand. "Maybe a bit, but not because I don't want to be with you."

"Your actions would suggest otherwise."

"And I apologize for giving you that impression. But I'm here now, and I'm happy to spend as much time with you as you like."

"I should hope so, although many fashionable marriages do involve husband and wife barely seeing each other." She shrugged, as if it didn't matter. "If that's what you want, just tell me."

He stopped her and put a finger under her chin, tipping it up. In her fashionable straw hat, tied with pretty violet ribbons that matched her eyes, she looked enchanting. But wariness still lurked in her gaze, along with an intense and wrenching vulnerability she tried to hide.

"I do not want a fashionable marriage, Ainsley," he said. "I want a happy one with you and our daughter."

She searched his features for a few moments before letting out a relieved breath. "Very well, then. Where do you wish to start?"

With what happens in the bedroom. That is, if we even share a bedroom.

"I thought we'd start with our living arrangements," he said. "What are your thoughts on that?"

"I assumed I'd move into Kendrick House. You seem comfortably situated there, and the nursery is already set up and well managed."

"Wouldn't you find it too crowded?"

"I find it very large and comfortable. Besides, once the wedding is over, most of your family will return to Castle Kinglas. Victoria said they all prefer it."

"Victoria, Nick, and Kade will go, but I can safely say that Angus will *not* be leaving as long as Tira is here. Grant will be moving in, since he's going to start working for Logan. And Graeme will at some point as well. Where one twin goes, the other invariably follows."

"Oh, that's . . . that's rather disturbing."

He couldn't resist teasing her. "Let's not forget that Braden will be visiting periodically. Adding in Logan, we could end up with at least four of my brothers, plus Angus, who are living with us at any one time."

Now Ainsley began to look desperate "Royal, it's not that I hate your family—"

"Just some of them?"

"I'm trying to be a good Christian," she said tartly, "but I would like to point out that there is a great deal of weaponry on the walls of your house. If I have to live with Angus *and* the twins, we will soon be re-creating the Battle of Culloden. And I assure you the English will triumph again."

He grinned as he started her walking. "Then it's an excellent thing that I've spent part of this week looking at town houses suitable for us."

She huffed a bit. "Then why didn't you just say so?"

"Because I enjoy teasing you."

"You are an unrepentant wretch."

"Maybe, but I also thought I should ask your opinion before making any final decisions."

"Your alarming depiction of my future has convinced me

that we should move out of Kendrick House as soon as possible." She glanced sideways at him. "I hope you're not offended by that. It's a lovely house, and I'm sure you enjoy living there."

He pulled her closer. "Ainsley, please believe that I want nothing more than for you and Tira to be happy. I will do everything within my power to make that happen."

Her lush mouth slowly curved into a dazzling smile. "I don't care what anyone says about you, Royal Kendrick. You are quite a nice man."

"Your flattery is overwhelming, my lady."

She squeezed his arm. "I don't want you getting a swelled head. One in the family is quite enough."

"Nonsense. You're not in the least conceited. Merely confident." Or at least she had been, until Cringlewood got his hands on her.

"That's not what your grandfather thinks. He called me a *Sassenach* saucebox just the other day."

"Did he? Then I'd better have a little chat with him." Royal understood why Angus didn't trust her, but enough was enough.

"Don't be ridiculous. I can certainly handle the old goat—er, fellow. And that insult at least had a rather nice ring to it."

"You shouldn't have to handle anyone. My family needs to respect you, or else they'll answer to me."

"That's not how respect works, Royal. I have to earn theirs. If, that is, I think it's worth the bother," she said with a dramatic wave. "As long as Victoria and Kade like me, that's all I really care about."

"You know, you actually are a bit of a saucebox."

"Undoubtedly. Now, back to this mysterious town house. Will we be able to afford something suitable?"

"We'll manage."

"Royal, you know I won't be able to depend on help from

my family," she said, turning serious. "And I have very little money of my own, so it's likely I will be a penniless bride."

He didn't care about the money but could sense her embarrassment. And for her sake, he hated how unfair it was.

"It won't be a problem even without your marriage settlements," he said. "But I take it that you have yet to hear from either of your parents."

"I wrote to them shortly after our first discussion, but they have yet to reply. Perhaps it's just not been long enough," she said, sounding a bit anxious.

"I'm sorry to hear that, but in any case, you're not to be concerned about our finances. Logan is increasing my responsibilities and giving me a bigger salary. We should have no trouble finding a suitable place." He paused, feeling a bit awkward. "It won't be Kendrick House or what you're used to, but it won't embarrass you either."

Ainsley had grown up in the lap of luxury, her every material wish fulfilled. He couldn't help but worry she might miss the fripperies and the legions of servants at her beck and call.

She waved a dismissive hand. "It's fine if our accommodations are fairly modest, as long as it's comfortable and Tira is happy."

Royal tried not to look skeptical. Her irritated glance indicated failure on his part.

"If living in luxury mattered," she said, "I would have married Lord Cringlewood, no matter what he'd done to me. Or I could have convinced my parents to accept one of my other suitors. I am still considered a desirable prospect on the marriage mart, even though I cut my eyeteeth long ago."

"I don't doubt that for a moment." He gently bumped her shoulder with his. "Despite your advanced years."

She ignored his teasing. "I could spend my life in the lap

of luxury, but none of that would mean anything if I couldn't be with my daughter. Tira is what matters to me."

Royal's heart sank. Of course, it was always about Tira. He'd hoped for more from Ainsley, but it seemed friendship and shared parenthood would have to suffice.

"I understand perfectly," he said.

She made an exasperated sound. "Clearly you don't, because the *other* person I want to be with is you. That would be glaringly obvious by now if you weren't such a stubborn thickhead."

Irritation got the better of him. "Well, it's not obvious. I'm going to be your husband, and yet I don't have a bloody clue what you actually want from me. Besides providing cover for you to be with your daughter."

"Thickhead," she said again.

She dragged him to a nearby bench. Pushing him down onto the seat, she remained standing, crossing her arms under her breasts.

"I believe I'm in for a scold." Royal didn't really mind at that point. She had the most amazing breasts, especially when she plumped them up like that.

"You deserve one. You clearly think I'm heartless enough to lure you into marriage just to be with my daughter. But I assure you, Royal Kendrick, that there are far easier ways to be with Tira. Kidnapping her, for one. Then I wouldn't have to put up with the Scottish weather *or* your utterly appalling family."

He took her hand and smiled. "No, not heartless. Devious, maybe."

"Don't think you're going to jolly me out of this. You're the one who's been avoiding *me*, not the other way around."

He laced their fingers, feeling like ten times an idiot. "I know."

Her expression softened. "Can you please try to tell me why?"

"Again, I'm not sure what you expect from me."

"As my husband?"

"Yes."

She eyed him. "Well, I expect you to have affection for me. You do still care for me, don't you?"

He turned and kissed the inside of her wrist, just above the edge of her glove. Her skin was as soft as a kitten's. "My feelings have not changed one iota in that regard, love."

Her breath seemed to fracture. "I . . . I was beginning to wonder, so it's nice to have it confirmed. But I expect you're also wondering about what's going to happen in . . ."

"In the bedroom," he finished for her.

Ainsley sank down beside him, still holding his hand. "I wish I knew the answer. It's not that I don't want us to have a normal marriage, with . . . everything that entails. It's just that I don't know if I can. Or at least not right away." She flushed, turning her head away.

But she still held on to his hand

"Ainsley, I will never ask you to do anything that makes you uncomfortable," he said gently. "I just hope that some-day you'll trust me enough—and trust yourself—to see what we can make of this affection we have for each other. We'll take it slowly, I promise."

She looked sideways at him. "You're sure?"

"I am. I just want you to be happy. I want *us* to be happy."

"I do think it would be nice for Tira to have a little brother or sister someday," she said, turning to face him. "Once I figure out this motherhood business."

He had to struggle with his emotions and the enticing image of making babies with her.

"You're a wonderful mother." He leaned in to kiss the tip of her nose. "I have no doubt you'll make a perfectly splendid wife, and I'm honored and grateful that you chose me, lass."

"Royal, you are the only man I ever wish to be intimate with. I might not be able to give you everything right away. But I want to, I really do. Please believe that."

His heart churned with regret and with all that might have been. Ainsley had been hurt in the most fundamental way, and he could never fully make up for that. All he could do was love and protect her, holding fast to patience for as long as necessary. That would be the truest demonstration of his love and loyalty.

"I do believe it," he said, "and I am more than content. As long as you need is how long we'll wait."

For a moment, her gaze was stark with a vulnerability that twisted his heart into knots. Then she unexpectedly scrunched her face up with comical dismay. "Confound it. I wish you weren't so noble and understanding. It makes me feel hideously guilty. And I *hate* feeling guilty."

He laughed. "Then I will do my best to be a selfish blighter at least once a day. More, if necessary."

"I think you'd better. But I *am* truly sorry, my dearest sir. I've made life dreadfully complicated for you. Admit it."

"All complications are most welcome, I assure you."

"You're as unhinged as I am," she said, getting up. She briskly whacked imaginary dirt from her skirts. "So, we're to abandon the family home and set up housekeeping on our own. I suspect that will go over with a resounding thud, especially from Angus."

"I'm hoping it'll encourage the old fellow to go back to Kinglas, where he belongs."

"Live in hope, I always say."

"Really? Because I don't believe I've ever heard you say that. Quite the opposite, in fact."

"I've decided that one pessimist in the family is quite enough," she said with a grandiose wave. "From now on, I will be the sunniest and most optimistic person you know. I cede my crown as resident grump to you."

"Care to place a bet on how long that will last? I give it ten minutes."

She swatted him on the shoulder. "You really are the most irritating man I have *ever* met."

He stood. "Ten seconds. Now, what do I win?"

"The honor of taking me back for lunch. I'm starving."

"Of course you are." He ducked when she tried to hit him again.

Chapter Thirteen

Ainsley felt giddy with relief. For the first time in months, she had a real chance at happiness again, thanks to the extraordinary man who strolled by her side. Behind that sarcastic and sometimes arrogant façade lay a sensitive, thoughtful man who gave her everything she needed, including time and patience. Yet he asked for nothing in return but the chance to love her and be a father to her daughter.

That Royal indeed loved her and wanted her in his bed was no longer in doubt. Ainsley wanted that too, someday, and she would do everything she could to make that someday happen sooner rather than later. Whatever stood between them, she wanted it gone. She wanted to want Royal as much as he wanted her.

"What are you smiling at, lass?" he asked, tucking her close as they crossed the quiet street. There wasn't a carriage or even a cart in sight, yet he guarded her as carefully as if she were the queen.

"It certainly wasn't your description of the service rooms in that town house you viewed this morning," she said. "As scintillating as that was."

He gave her a crooked grin. "I realize you're not very interested in cold rooms and pantries. We'll find a butler to manage that end of things. I don't want you bogged down with boring details if you'd rather not."

"Royal, you do understand I was raised to manage large households, including country manors. I'm quite up to the task of running a small town house."

"It won't be *that* small."

She squeezed his arm. "Whatever it is, I'm sure it'll be fine."

He remained worried she would find it difficult to adjust to a life outside the highest echelons of the *ton*. Though Ainsley was in fact heartily sick of that life, she suspected it might take a little time to convince him of that.

"If it wasn't the anticipation of installing a bang-up-to-the-mark range in your new kitchen, what were you smiling at?" he asked.

"It's going to sound rather silly."

"Love, you're marrying into a family with several exceedingly silly members, not to mention the dogs. You have a long way to go to challenge us."

She laughed. "So true."

"Then confess. If that smile has anything to do with me, I want to make sure I know how to prompt it as often as possible."

When they stopped at the foot of the stone steps that led up to Kendrick House, Ainsley took Royal's hands.

"For the first time in a very long time, I'm truly happy." Her nose started to tickle a bit, which tended to happen when she became emotional. "And it's because of you, Royal. I can never be grateful enough for everything you've done for me and Tira."

He gently extracted his right hand and cupped her cheek. He'd stripped off his gloves back in the park, so she could feel the warmth of his palm, tough with calluses. That hand spoke of strength and hard work, and a man who would do whatever was necessary to provide for his family.

"Ainsley, your happiness is thanks enough." His gaze swept over her face, warming with an appreciation that made her knees go wobbly. "For you and Tira to be happy and safe means everything to me."

If she didn't take a firm grip on her silly self, she'd burst into tears right on the stoop. But the emotions swirling through her—joy, gratitude, and so much more—seemed too big to contain.

"Och, lass," he murmured, his malachite gaze sparking with heat, "if you're not careful, I'll be forced to kiss you right here."

Ainsley was stunned when she giggled. As a rule, she abhorred giggling. And yet here she was, acting like a girl fresh from the schoolroom, engaging in her first innocent flirtation.

It was a marvel.

She placed a hand on his chest. "Mr. Kendrick, are you suggesting that we commit acts of public indecency? Someone might send for the constable to have us arrested."

He covered her hand and pulled her even closer. "It would be worth it, especially if they put us in the same cell."

When he leaned down to kiss her, her eyelids started to flutter shut. But she popped them up in surprise when the door opened behind them.

"Dammit." Royal reluctantly pulled away.

She smothered a chuckle. "Perhaps we can go for another walk around the square after you get home from the warehouse this evening. It should be quite dark and deserted by then."

"Don't tempt me, lass. I don't think you're ready for what I want yet."

She couldn't help responding in a challenging tone. "Maybe I'll surprise you, Mr. Kendrick."

He flashed her a rogue's grin before glancing up to the

open door. His amusement quickly faded when he saw the youngest footman. "What is it, Will?"

William's boyish features were tight with concern. "Ye're both needed inside, sir, my lady."

Ainsley's heart thudded against her ribs. "Is Tira all right?"

"Aye, my lady, she's fine. It's just that ye have a visitor."

"Who is it?" Royal asked as they hurried up the steps.

When William simply gave a grim shake of his head, Ainsley's heart went to her knees. Then, as she saw Victoria standing in the hall, looking disturbed, her heart went straight through the heels of her half-boots.

"This is bad," Ainsley whispered.

Royal helped her off with her pelisse. "Whatever it is, we'll deal with it together."

She looked into his calm gaze and her churning insides steadied a bit. "Promise?"

He took her hands and helped strip off her gloves. "I promise, love. You're not alone anymore."

Victoria came to them. "I'm sorry to surprise you this way, Ainsley, but your mother is here."

"At Kendrick House?" She winced at the shrill note to her voice. "Is my father with her?"

"No." Victoria grimaced. "Kade and I practically smashed into her when we got home. Her carriage was in front of the house, and her footman was just handing her out."

Ainsley had to fight the sudden urge to be sick. "Did she see Tira?"

Victoria gave a grim nod.

"Dammit to hell," Royal ground out. He took off his hat and handed it to the footman, dismissing him.

As William retreated, he threw Ainsley a worried glance, as if he knew exactly why they were all upset. Had everyone in the blasted household figured out she was Tira's mother? If so, it was going to make it almost impossible to keep the secret any longer.

"Was Tira awake? Did my mother get a good look at her?"

"Tira was awake, but I'm not sure Lady Aldridge saw very much. Once I realized who she was, I handed Tira over to Kade and bustled them off to the nursery."

Ainsley pressed her palms over her eyes for a moment, trying to quell her rising panic. "All right. Where is my mother?"

"With Nicholas in the drawing room. I thought it might be a good idea for him to speak with her before you arrived home."

Royal nodded. "You mean you wanted Nick to intimidate her with his stern Highland laird manner. Not a bad plan."

"My mother is not easily intimidated, unfortunately." For her mother to show up like this was a very bad sign. It meant she would try to persuade Ainsley to return to London—or worse.

And if she'd gotten enough of a look at Tira . . .

"I'm so sorry," Victoria said in an unhappy voice. "If I'd known your mother was coming, I would have taken Tira around to the back of the house."

"It's not your fault, Victoria. I had no idea she was coming either. Let me go in and try to find out what she knows."

"I'll come with you," Royal said, starting her toward the drawing room door.

That was a *very* bad idea, for too many reasons to count. "No," she said, holding him back. "It's best if Mamma and I speak alone, at least at first."

Royal made an impatient sound. "I won't have her bullying you, or forcing you to do something you don't want to do."

She mustered what she hoped was a reassuring smile. "You know by now that no one makes me do something I don't want to do, not even my mother."

Or her father, for that matter. But Ainsley was still tremendously grateful that Papa hadn't come along. He could be incredibly stubborn and tended to yell when frustrated. That would have gone down very poorly with Royal.

"Are you sure, dearest?" Victoria asked. "Nicholas can stay with you, or I can come in, if you like."

"Thank you, but my mother is no doubt upset and will not appreciate an audience."

Royal muttered a few curses before escorting her to the door. "All right, but I'm staying right out here. If you need me, just call out."

"Thank you." Although she appreciated his protective instincts, Ainsley was terrified of what her mother might say, and even more terrified that Royal would hear it.

You should have told him the truth right away.

Ainsley squashed that panicked thought. The truth wouldn't change anything, including how she and Royal felt about each other. Or how she felt about Cringlewood.

She squared her shoulders and nodded. Royal opened the door and then stepped back. As she walked by him, he pressed a quick, comforting hand to her shoulder.

His unquestioning support made her wretched with guilt.

Pausing for a moment after closing the door behind her, she worked to settle her tripping heartbeat. Then she adopted her best social smile and crossed the drawing room to join her mother and Lord Arnprior. They were seated opposite each other, the earl cool and imperious in his high-backed wing chair. Mamma looked like she had the fireplace poker up her backside as she perched on the edge of the chaise.

"Ah, Lady Ainsley," Arnprior said, rising. "Your mother and I have been getting reacquainted while we waited for you."

Her mother's expression suggested she'd find a tooth extraction preferable to chatting with the laird—or setting foot in Scotland, for that matter. Her mother loathed the north.

"Thank you, sir." Ainsley bent to press a kiss to her mother's cheek. "I'm sorry, Mamma. If I'd known you'd be arriving today, I would not have gone out. Why didn't you send me a note?"

Her mother allowed the kiss but made no move to touch her or display any sign of affection. "I arrived in the city late last night and did not have time to send a note around."

Ainsley frowned. "Why didn't you have your footman deliver a message to Breadie Manor first thing this morning? I didn't leave the house till after breakfast."

"I thought it best to go directly there, instead. I was surprised to discover you had already gone for the day." Her mother flicked a disapproving glance in Arnprior's direction. "I didn't realize you were spending so much time at Kendrick House, my dear," she said, making it sound like Ainsley was carousing in a pub down in the stews. "It is unfortunate that I had to chase after you."

"We consider Lady Ainsley one of the family, madam," the earl said in a matching tone of aristocratic hauteur. "She is welcome here anytime, day or night."

"How kind," Mamma intoned. "But need I point out—"

"Where are you staying, Mamma?" Ainsley hastily interrupted. "Next time just send a note, and I'll come there right away."

Her mother pressed her lips together for an irritated moment. "I am staying with Lady Montgomery." She glanced at Arnprior. "Her ladyship is Lord Cringlewood's cousin on his mother's side. Our families are exceedingly close."

Damn and blast. They were clearly all lining up against her.

"Oh, that's convenient," Ainsley said lamely.

"Lady Ainsley, would you like me to ring for tea?" Arnprior asked in a kind voice.

"I have already declined refreshments, my lord," Mamma said. "I only wish to speak to my daughter, alone and uninterrupted."

Ainsley flushed at her mother's rude behavior.

That's what you sound like when you're in a snit, my girl.

She made a silent vow to be much nicer from now on. In fact, she would make all sorts of vows to reform her behavior if it meant she and Tira could escape this latest crisis unscathed.

Arnprior pointedly ignored her mother. "Ainsley, would you like some tea?"

Her mother tsked her disapproval, although it wasn't clear whether she objected to his patent disregard of her wishes or to his informal use of Ainsley's name. No doubt both.

Ainsley gave him a grateful smile. "Thank you, sir, but I'll just speak with my mother. I know luncheon is about to be served, so please go ahead without me."

"There's no rush," he said. "And I'll be happy to remain, if you prefer it."

"I would *not* prefer it," Mamma said icily.

Ainsley briefly closed her eyes. Her mother was a high stickler, but she generally had distinguished manners. For her to be acting so out of character with an aristocrat meant she was thoroughly knocked off her pins.

The earl patiently waited for Ainsley to answer his question. Despite how awful this day was turning out to be, she felt enormous gratitude for his kindness. It would seem she had another supporter in the household, after all.

She shook her head. "Thank you, sir, but I'll be fine."

"As you wish. But I will be close by if you need me."

"Along with everyone else," Ainsley said ruefully.

His smile was brief and charming, and then he gave her mother a genial nod. "My lady, I hope to see you again soon."

"I very much doubt that will be the case."

Arnprior threw Ainsley an ironic look before departing the room.

"Really, Mamma, did you have to be so awful? Lord Arnprior was simply trying to be polite."

"I have the headache," her mother announced in a blighting tone.

Ainsley mentally sighed. Mamma was prone to headaches whenever she was upset, which always made things worse. This one was sure to be a whopper.

"I'm sorry you're not feeling well. Are you sure you don't want something to drink? Can I fetch you a headache powder?"

"Oh, Ainsley, stop fussing and do sit down. Staring up at you is making it worse."

"Sorry." Ainsley took the seat Arnprior had just vacated.

Her mother seemed to finally pull in her horns by managing a strained smile. "As I'm sure you can imagine, the last few days have been exceedingly stressful. You know how I hate traveling."

She did look a trifle exhausted, but as lovely and elegant as always. Her mother possessed a slim, straight figure, and had black hair with dramatic white streaks at the temples. Like Ainsley, she had a blue-violet gaze that many considered her best feature, contributing to her fame as a great beauty. Those eyes were striking and unmistakable, a characteristic she now shared with her granddaughter.

Please, God. Don't let her have seen Tira's eyes.

"Did Papa travel with you?" Ainsley asked.

"No, I brought only Biddle."

Biddle was Mamma's longtime dresser and was devoted to her mistress but less than enamored with Ainsley. Biddle made a point of quietly conveying that whenever possible.

"Thank God," her mother added in a bitter tone when Ainsley didn't respond. "Your father is quite distraught over this business, so I felt it best he remain in London given his weak heart. I see now that I was right to insist on that."

Ainsley struggled not to overreact. "It truly wasn't necessary for you to come all this way, Mamma. You could have just replied to my letter."

"You would not have listened. I had no choice but to come here to talk you out of making an inexplicably stupid and selfish decision. Before it is too late, I might add. Leonard's patience will not last forever."

"I don't give a hang about Leonard's bloody patience, Mamma. He *raped* me. Do you actually understand that?"

Her mother flinched. "I beg you to refrain from using such extreme language. It's neither appropriate nor accurate."

"Not when it describes *exactly* what happened?"

Mamma waved a hand. "It was an unfortunate misunderstanding, and for your sake I'm sorry for that. But there is no cause to exaggerate, nor is it helpful in the present situation."

"There was no misunderstanding. I'm not going to marry Cringlewood and that's the end of it."

When her mother studied her with a narrowed, intent gaze, the hairs lifted on the back of Ainsley's neck.

"Even though Leonard is the father of your child?" Mamma asked.

"I . . . I don't know what you're talking about," she managed.

"I am not stupid, child. I saw her. That baby looks exactly like you did."

Ainsley rose and stumbled over to sit beside her mother, grabbing her gloved hand. "You can't tell anyone, Mamma. You *can't.*"

"Of course I cannot tell anyone. It's too late to even acknowledge her." Mamma dragged her hand free, as if repelled by her own daughter's touch. "I should have known when you didn't put up more of a fight about having to spend the winter with that wretched aunt of yours. I should have known something was wrong."

Ainsley forced herself to ignore the hurt of her mother's

rejection. Right now, all that mattered was keeping Tira safe. "No one suspects, though? Not Papa, or anyone else?"

"No, thank God. Your father already feels entirely betrayed by your actions. If he knew about this, it would kill him."

"I've done nothing to betray him or anyone else," Ainsley retorted. "I'm only doing what is right for me and for my daughter. My actions are entirely appropriate under the circumstances."

Her mother's mouth twisted with disapproval. "Appropriate? There is nothing appropriate about allowing your fiancé to get you with child and then refusing to marry him. That is the exact opposite of appropriate."

"I did not *allow* him to do anything. Cringlewood forced himself on me. He's a pig."

"Leonard is a peer of the realm and a distinguished man," her mother flashed. "Yes, he behaved in a manner unbecoming a gentleman, but that does not entitle you to act like a trollop in return."

For several moments, Ainsley felt paralyzed. But she finally stiffened her spine and found her voice. "If that's all you have to say, Mamma, I would ask you to leave now. I refuse to be insulted by you, or anyone else."

Her mother pressed her fingertips hard to her temples before folding her hands in her lap. "I apologize for that uncharitable remark, Ainsley. My fatigue is getting the better of me, but I am simply trying to understand. How could you have done such a foolish thing, especially after discovering you were with child? You should have made the effort to reconcile with Leonard right away. Yes, it might have been awkward, but he would have no wish to embarrass you. Nor would he desire his child to be born a . . ."

"Bastard."

"There is no need to be crude, my dear. You know I do not approve of such language."

"My language is the least of our concerns, Mamma."

Her mother mustered what she probably thought was an encouraging smile. "You're right, of course. And I'm sure we can find a solution to this problem, if you will only be sensible."

"What do you mean by sensible?" she asked, although she already had a fairly good idea.

"You must return to London with me and speak honestly with Leonard. I know he'll be very sorry to hear how dismayed you were by that unfortunate incident, and he will wish to make amends. I'm sure he'll be more than willing to start afresh."

"Oh, that would be big of him."

"Leonard loves you," her mother insisted. "He always has."

"He's got an awful way of showing it."

Mamma sat back with a sigh. "I suppose I should have expected you to be like this. It's my fault, really. Mine and your father's."

"What does that mean?" Ainsley said, startled by her mother's sudden shift.

"I'm afraid we allowed you far too much freedom when it came to decisions about your future. We simply spoiled you, child. It's no wonder you don't understand the consequences of your actions."

"I understand enough to realize I don't deserve a lifetime of mistreatment at Cringlewood's hands."

"That incident was a misunderstanding," her mother stubbornly repeated. "If you would just talk to him, everything would be fine."

"You seriously think he would also be fine about Tira?"

Her mother frowned. "What sort of name is that?"

"It's a fine Scottish name."

Her mother mulled that over for a few moments before answering. "You obviously cannot acknowledge the child as your own, so it doesn't matter. Perhaps it's best at this point not to tell Leonard about her at all. It will cause too many complications for everyone."

"You can be sure I will not be telling him or anyone else in our family about Tira," Ainsley said tartly.

Her mother rewarded her with a smile. "Excellent, my love. I'm so glad you're finally coming to your senses."

Ainsley had never thought her mother lacked a firm grip on reality until now. Still, for Tira's sake, she had to make one last effort to get through to her. "Mamma, would you have married Papa if he had hurt you in that way? Because I truly cannot understand why you would wish me to marry a man who thought he was doing nothing wrong in forcing himself on me."

"Do you truly believe I always desired your father's marital attentions? There was many a night when I heartily wished the man would find his pleasures elsewhere than in my bed. In fact, I sometimes prayed for exactly that." She flashed a bitter smile. "My prayers, unfortunately, were rarely answered."

Ainsley blinked, stunned by that sad, ugly glimpse into her mother's life. True, her parents had never been particularly affectionate, but Mamma and Papa had always seemed content with each other, presenting a united front to the rest of the family.

"Then why didn't you just tell Papa that?" she asked.

Her mother stiffened. "I took vows on my wedding day to honor and obey my husband. That is what a decent and respectful woman does, something you should realize by now."

Ainsley thought of the solemn promise Royal had made her only this morning—a vow to love and protect her and their daughter above all else. Even at the low tide of their friendship, when they could do nothing but snipe at each other, he'd always tried to protect her, even from herself. And he'd done it not for personal gain, but because he was a good, kind man.

It truly was as simple as that.

"I'm so sorry you had to suffer in that way, Mamma," she finally said.

Her mother shrugged. "We all have unpleasant burdens to bear, my dear. I am serene in the knowledge that I have always done my duty to your father and to our family. I expect the same from you. Give up this foolishness and come home. Be what you were intended to be—Marchioness of Cringlewood and a great lady."

Ainsley now realized her mother could never understand. Given what she'd just revealed, Mamma would naturally see her daughter's defiance as a rejection of all the sacrifices she'd made for her family. Indeed, it would be a rejection of everything she believed in most dearly.

"I'm sorry to disappoint you, but no," she said quietly.

"Then you will have betrayed all of us," Mamma snapped. "And for what? For a penniless younger son from a Scottish family no one cares about?"

"As it happens, I care about the Kendricks a great deal. And it's ridiculous to dismiss them as nobodies."

"You will have nothing if you do this, Ainsley. Your father will cut you off without a shilling." Mamma suddenly gave her a canny look. "Does Mr. Kendrick know that?"

"Of course he does, and he doesn't care."

Mamma stared for a few seconds but then pressed a hand to her eyes, suddenly looking quite ill.

"Are you all right?" Ainsley asked, touching her arm.

"Ainsley, the marquess is threatening to bring legal action against you," she said as she lowered her hand. "For breach of promise of marriage. If he follows through, the scandal will be utterly appalling. God knows what it will do to your father, given the weak state of his heart."

For a moment, Ainsley could only gape at her mother. She knew that breaking an engagement was a dreadfully serious business that could potentially damage one's reputation—and financial prospects, if one of the parties was depending on a generous marriage settlement. Since Ainsley's settlement was more than generous, Cringlewood would feel the sting of losing it. Still, he was a *marquess*, for God's sake, and a wealthy one at that.

She also knew that breach of promise suits were notoriously difficult and expensive to prosecute. It had to be nothing more than a stupid, mean-spirited threat on Cringlewood's part.

"The marquess hates scandal as much as you and Papa do," Ainsley said. "I cannot believe he would court it through legal action."

"He hates scandal, but he hates being humiliated and cheated even more. You *must* return home with me, or else he will proceed."

Ainsley shook her head in disbelief. "But why does he care so much?"

"Some days I do wonder," her mother said bitterly. "But the fact remains that you committed yourself to Leonard, and he rightly insists you honor that commitment, as do we. I should not have to tell you how damaging the consequences will be for all of us if you do not."

At this point, Ainsley didn't give a damn about herself or her family. But a court case, with all the attendant publicity, would shine a stark light on her actions over this past year and more. That ugliness would eventually find its way to Tira, exposing her to the world.

In fact, who was to say that her mother wouldn't try to use the knowledge of Tira's existence to force her hand? "Mamma, you cannot tell *anyone* about my child," Ainsley said, trying to steady her quavering voice.

"If you return home with me, there will be no need to do so."

"I can't do that." Ainsley jumped to her feet, battling the urge to race upstairs, snatch her child, and flee with her to safety.

There's no place safe.

Her mother stood. "You leave me no choice but—"

The door flew open. Royal stalked in, going straight to Ainsley.

"Is everything all right?" He curled a supportive arm around her shoulders even as he directed a hard gaze at her mother.

Ainsley's knees quivered with an unholy combination of relief and panic, forcing her to lock them in place. "Yes, thank you. Mamma was just leaving."

"I was doing nothing of the sort. Unless, that is, you are coming with me."

"I will come see you later," Ainsley said. "We can finish our conversation then."

"When, exactly?"

"I . . . I'm not sure. Later."

"That is not acceptable. We need to finish this discussion now." She threw Royal a disdainful glance. "Alone."

"Or, you can finish the discussion with me present. Would you prefer that, Ainsley?" Royal asked.

Ainsley did *not* prefer. Royal would be furious with her for bringing such a horrific scandal down on their heads, one that could threaten Tira. Under the circumstances, Mamma might even be able to convince him that the best way to protect the child would be for Ainsley to return to London and marry Cringlewood, in exchange for promising to keep Tira's existence a secret.

No, Royal would never do that to you.

Still, she needed a plan to hobble her tormentor before he left the gate. If she could do that, there would be no reason for Royal and the Kendricks to be dragged into embarrassing scandal and expensive legal machinations. Royal had forgiven her so much already, but even he had to have his limits.

Ainsley was done with testing men's limits.

"I have no intention of discussing private family matters with you present, Mr. Kendrick," Mamma said, glaring at him. "And take your hands off my daughter."

Royal left his hands where they were. "Then since we have nothing further to discuss, I suggest you take your leave, my lady."

Mortally offended, Mamma snatched up her reticule. "If you were a gentleman, you would encourage my daughter to return home, where she belongs."

"Then it's a good thing I'm not a gentleman."

"You aren't fit to marry her."

His sudden smile was wry. "I am well aware, madam. Fortunately, Ainsley doesn't seem to agree."

"Mamma, *please* go," Ainsley said. "I'll visit you later today, I promise."

For several long seconds, their gazes clashed, her mother clearly reluctant to cede ground.

"May I escort you to your carriage, Lady Aldridge?" Royal asked, holding out a polite but firm hand.

Mamma ignored him. "Do not fail me, Ainsley."

She turned and stalked to the door, where Victoria now hovered. But Mamma brushed past her without saying a word.

"Here, love, sit down," Royal murmured as he guided Ainsley back to the chair. He crouched down in front of her, chafing her hands.

Victoria hurried over. "Does she know about Tira?"

Ainsley nodded, her dismay choking her.

"Do you think she'll tell anyone?" Royal asked in a calm tone.

"Probably," she whispered.

Victoria grimaced. "What do you think we should do?"

Suddenly, Ainsley knew exactly what to do. The answer was so simple it was almost laughable.

She took Royal's hand and met his concerned gaze. "We should get married, of course. This very day."

Chapter Fourteen

Royal glanced at the mantel clock. Most of the servants were already to bed, but Ainsley had yet to reappear. He could only hope she wasn't still locked in combat with Tira, trying to get the wee lassie to sleep.

After the bustle of their arrival at Castle Kinglas late this afternoon, peace had once more descended on the stately old pile—except for the nursery, apparently. Normally, Tira would be fast asleep by now, but the frantic rushing about of the last few days had disrupted her schedule. The fact that Ainsley had insisted on putting her daughter to bed was an added complication. Tira was very particular about her nighttime routine, and any deviation resulted in fussing and tears.

The baby might only be six months old, but she already knew what she wanted. One of those things was Royal or Angus rocking her for a spell whenever she was out of sorts. But Ainsley, now officially Tira's stepmother, had been so anxious to take up her maternal duties that Royal hadn't had the heart to gainsay her, even though he'd anticipated another minor disaster.

Or major, as the case might be, given Ainsley's luck. He'd never seen his feisty *Sassenach* as rattled as she'd been yesterday when forced to confront her mother in Glasgow. The state of her nerves had barely improved since then, even though they were now ensconced at Kinglas.

Even more to the point, Ainsley was now Royal's wife, and safely under his protection and that of the entire Kendrick family. He would do anything to protect her from those who sought to harm or bully her and finally had the right to do so.

My wife.

The truth of it was only just taking hold, and the monumental shift vibrated down to his very bones. That singular moment yesterday in the church, when they'd claimed each other as husband and wife, would be forever engraved on his heart. With Ainsley's small hand clinging to his, her violet gaze turbulent with emotion, Royal had pledged to worship and protect her. He would fulfill that promise until the day he died.

Nothing would ever pull them apart again.

Ainsley was more than a little unnerved by the rapid turn of events, even though their impromptu marriage had been her idea. So unnerved, in fact, that Royal suspected she might be avoiding him tonight—their first night together as husband and wife. After the wedding, Ainsley had returned to Breadie Manor to organize and pack for their trip north. He'd fetched her this morning, and they'd jammed into the Arnprior traveling coach along with Tira, the nursemaid, and an alarming number of bandboxes for a tiring day on the road.

Given the stresses of the last few weeks, he'd been hoping for a quiet evening with his bride, but it would seem she preferred spending time with their daughter. While Tira was not all that keen on her mother's company, Royal was exceedingly keen on spending time with his wife.

Wincing a bit, he stood. His leg was troubling him, which was not unusual after a day on the road. He could think of a few things that would take his mind off the pain, but the most enticing of those was certainly out of the question for the foreseeable future.

He glanced up at the elaborately framed portrait of his parents that hung over the fireplace, which was painted shortly after their marriage. Royal's father was garbed in clan colors, while his mother wore a full-skirted white gown with a Kendrick tartan scarf pinned to her bodice with the family crest. The pose, set against the backdrop of the castle's old tower house, conveyed the power and wealth of the Earl of Arnprior and the beauty of his young wife.

But for all that, something shone through the rather stilted pose—his parents' great love for each other. The artist had captured the pride in the earl's eyes as he gazed down at his countess, her head tilted into his shoulder, as if she would nestle against him. Royal had studied that painting more times than he could count, but tonight it shimmered with fresh energy.

For the first time in a long time, he missed his parents with a yearning that felt almost new.

"It's my wedding night," he said to the silent figures above him. "Yet here I am spending it alone. No wife *or* family to celebrate with." He thought about that for a second, and couldn't help laughing. "And I'm talking to my dead parents."

It was entirely in keeping with the bizarre state of his life. *Whisky it is.*

He headed over to the drinks trolley and splashed some of the rich amber brew into a crystal glass. Settling into the leather chair behind his brother's desk, he cast a negligent glance at the ledgers stacked on the polished wood. Nick had asked him to check a few items having to do with the sale of cattle last month, when he had time. Since Ainsley had either fallen asleep in the nursery or retreated to her bed, Royal definitely had time. Sleep would surely elude him as he imagined his bride slumbering peacefully in the room next to his, clad in nothing but a frivolous nightgown that displayed her ample curves.

Don't think about it, you moron.

As he opened the accounts, he heard a quick footstep on the stone floor in the hall. Royal ignored the leaping of his heart, since it was probably Taffy coming to retrieve the untouched tea tray.

Ainsley peeked her head around the door. "May I come in?"

He pushed back and hurried around the desk. "Of course you can. You need never ask."

"I wasn't sure if you were still awake, but it seemed best to check." She flashed him a wry smile. "After all, tonight is officially our first night together. It would be a poor reflection on my spousal responsibilities if I abandoned the groom without even bidding him good night. You might start looking about for a new wife."

"I *was* beginning to feel quite sorry for myself," he said, returning her smile. "But instead of drawing up advertisements for a new bride, I've been drowning my sorrows in the estate accounts."

"How madcap of you." She glanced at his glass on the desk. "But that's not the only thing you've been drowning your sorrows in, I suspect."

"I thought I should celebrate our marriage with a wee dram, even if it was a celebration of one."

"Oh, Lord, that is an utterly dreary picture. I am an awful wife, aren't I? I should probably sit down and help you draw up that advertisement."

He lifted her hand to his mouth, pressing a quick kiss to her soft skin. "Don't fash yourself, lass. I'm only teasing. I know you want to spend as much time as you can with Tira."

"I certainly got to spend some time with her tonight," she said, stifling a yawn. "She took forever to fall asleep."

"I certainly hope she wasn't crying the entire time."

"Only when we put her down in her crib," she said dryly. "I thought it was me, but she was just as bad with Lucy. So we had to take turns walking with her until she finally dozed off."

Royal frowned. Lucy had been one of Tira's nursemaids from the beginning. "That's odd. Lucy is almost as good with the baby as Angus. I hope Tira's not catching a fever."

It had been a damp, rainy drive north, so even though Tira had been heavily swaddled to keep out the chill, he still couldn't help but worry.

"Lucy suspects she's breaking another tooth."

"But she did let you hold her without crying? That sounds like progress."

This time Ainsley's wide smile was genuine. "She did, although she also got in several good yanks of my hair. I suspect I now have a bald spot."

Royal glanced at her perfectly coiffed head. "For a woman who was just mauled by a fractious baby, you are as elegant as always."

"You say that now, but I looked alarmingly like Angus after he's been standing out in a high wind. I had to ask the maid to redo my hair before I dared venture downstairs."

"You didn't need to fuss on my account, sweetheart." He was eager for the day when he could see Ainsley's shiny black locks tumbling down around her shoulders. Her naked shoulders, preferably.

"My lady's maid was upstairs anyway, since she had to help me change my gown." When he glanced at her dress, she arched her eyebrows with polite sarcasm. "You didn't notice, did you?"

He shrugged. "Sorry. It's a very nice gown."

"You are a sadly typical male, Royal Kendrick. Remind me never to go shopping with you."

It was true that he rarely made note of her attire, primarily because he was too entranced by what was *inside* the gowns to register trivialities like fabric or color. He was always captivated by the swell of her full white breasts over the trim of her bodice, or the lush curve of her delightful backside, showcased by clinging skirts.

"I promise to be vastly more attentive now that we're married," he said. "Every time you change, I will make note of all details, down to the bows on your shoes."

"It won't matter. Here in the hinterlands, I could prance around in a potato sack or a ragged old kilt and no one would take note."

"You know us feckless Highlanders. But I promise to don a new shirt at least twice a week, whether I need to or not. Now, tell me why you had to change. Did Tira have another unfortunate incident?"

Ainsley ruefully nodded. "As usual, her aim is infallible. I wasn't even holding her, yet she still managed to hit my bodice. Without, I might add, getting anything on Lucy. I swear I've become a magnet for baby vomit."

"That is an alarming attribute to discover in one's bride." Royal steered her over to the chaise in front of the fireplace. "However, you have certainly earned a drink."

"Or three," she said as she collapsed in a graceful heap on the cushions. "Although one will likely put me to sleep in short order."

He fetched her a brandy, and joined her on the chaise. "That isn't much of a wedding night celebration for you, either. I'm sorry about that."

After taking a healthy sip, Ainsley let out a satisfied sigh. "Believe me, when I consider what my fate might have been, this seems splendid. I will take a moldy old castle in the Highlands over marriage to Cringlewood any day."

"High praise indeed," Royal said wryly. "But to be serious, I truly regret that we were forced to skulk out of town like a pair of Highland bandits. You deserved better, sweetheart."

She grimaced. "No, you're the one who deserved better.

Forcing your hand was most unfair to you and your family. People are bound to talk about how we rushed into this, and that was exactly what you were trying to avoid."

"You did not force my hand, and you're daft if you think I care about any of that for my sake. I have every confidence Nick and Victoria will manage any gossip."

"I hope they can also manage my mother. After reading my letter this morning, I expect she tore over to Kendrick House in a towering fury."

"Nick is more than a match for Lady Aldridge."

Her gaze slid away, as if she wanted to avoid his eye. "I should have stood my ground and told Mamma myself, but I'm a bit of a coward when it comes to my parents. They can be very determined and more than a little volatile, as you know."

After relieving her of the brandy glass, Royal took her hand, weaving their fingers together. "You are anything but a coward, as the last year has shown. And I don't blame you for not wanting to confront your mother again. The encounter would not have been pleasant, I suspect."

"You can be sure of that," she said quietly.

He decided to voice the concern that had been nagging at him since Lady Aldridge's sudden appearance at Kendrick House. "I wish you had let me speak to your mother, love. I would have been happy to explain that I will always provide for your well-being and protection, regardless of your family's support or lack thereof."

When she started to protest, he gently squeezed her hand. "I would have also made it clear that we expect her silence regarding Tira's parentage. Your mother needs to know that there is nothing to be gained from telling Cringlewood or anyone else the truth about the child."

"I know you only want to help," she said. "But my mother would have seen you as impertinent and interfering, and picked a fight with you."

"That was why I suggested I meet with her alone," he said patiently. "She cannot upset me as she does you, Ainsley."

She withdrew her hand, looking tense and unhappy. "Mamma can be rather awful when she puts her mind to it. I . . . well, such a meeting wouldn't have been good for either of you, Royal."

She surely knew he would never hurt or demean her mother. Was she worried about what her mother would say to him? What could Lady Aldridge possibly reveal about Ainsley that he didn't already know?

"Besides, I explained everything in the letter I sent to Mamma this morning. Now that we're married, there's no point in telling anyone about Tira. And believe me, she'll want to avoid the scandal, especially since the Kendricks have rallied behind me." She cast an embarrassed look down at her lap. "Although that's probably not true. I'm sure your family is quite appalled by our hasty marriage. Even Kade seemed gloomy about it."

"Then you haven't been paying attention, Mrs. Kendrick." He couldn't help but smile at the sound of her new name on his tongue. "Victoria is positively ecstatic that we've finally tied the knot. As for Kade, he was disappointed he didn't get to play at our wedding. He'd been working on a new piece to honor the occasion."

She winced. "We did behave in a rather ramshackle fashion. I cannot imagine what that poor minister thought of me. I was such an emotional wreck."

Royal diplomatically refrained from agreeing with her. "I'm sure you were the prettiest bride the fellow has ever seen."

"I didn't even have time to change into something decent. I looked a perfect fright."

Royal leaned in to kiss the tip of her nose. "You're *perfect*, and don't ever forget it."

Ainsley had been in such a panic that she'd refused to

waste time returning to Breadie Manor for a more suitable gown. Less than three hours after Lady Aldridge stormed out of Kendrick House, Royal and Ainsley had made their vows at the local kirk, with only the family members already in town to witness the event. Although the laxity of Scotland's marriage laws had worked in their favor, a church wedding—no matter how small and rushed—would serve as irrefutable evidence that he and Ainsley were well and truly wed.

"I'm sorry you were denied a proper wedding celebration," he added. "I'd hoped we'd have time to invite some of your friends up from London."

"I don't really have any friends I'd want to invite. If you want to know the truth, I simply don't have many friends. Not true ones, anyway, except for Edie and Alec, and they'd already left town."

The Gilbrides had departed Glasgow a few days ago to return home to Blairgal Castle.

"Not even old schoolgirl friends?" he asked, surprised.

She tilted her head to give him a quizzical smile. "Surely you noticed during your time in London that I didn't have many female friends."

"I assumed none of them could get near you, given the pack of suitors that always surrounded you."

"The reality is considerably less flattering, I'm afraid. I generally wasn't that interested in spending time with other girls my age, since all we ever seemed to talk about were clothes and potential suitors." She shook her head. "I was obviously spending my time with the wrong people. It's no wonder I didn't have many real friends."

"It sounds rather lonely."

"At the time I put it down to boredom with the usual round of social inanities. That's why I liked you so much when we first met. Aside from that poetic, brooding persona of yours, you truly *listened* to me, instead of treating me as a possession to be acquired or a challenge to be won." She flashed him a quick smile. "Even better, I could be rude and you never seemed to mind."

"That's because I was even ruder, a standard requirement for a poetic, brooding persona. Compared to me, you were a rank amateur."

She laughed. "I suppose that's true. I always felt like I could be myself when I was with you."

"That's because we both knew you were never going to marry me. It meant you could say whatever you wanted with little regard for the consequences."

He instantly regretted his blunt words. "Sorry, love. I didn't mean—"

She cut him off with an impatient jerk of the head. "You're not wrong, which was more a reflection on me than it was on you. I used to be a terrible snob. I suppose I still am, so you shouldn't even bother trying to deny it."

They lapsed into a rather awkward silence. Ainsley stared into the fire, a slight frown creasing her brow, while Royal pondered what would happen when they finally retired for the night.

Just ask her what she wants.

"Ainsley—"

"I still cannot believe your middle name is Lancelot," she said, interrupting him. "I was quite stunned to hear it during the marriage ceremony. Who chose it?"

He studied her brittle smile. "Do you really wish to know, or are you simply coming up with idle conversation because you're nervous?"

Her smile went charmingly sideways. "Is it that obvious?"

He tapped a gentle finger to her cheek. "It's perfectly understandable. But remember the promise I made to you in the park?"

"That you'll never push me to do anything I don't want to do?"

"Yes, so there's no need to be nervous, is there?"

"Well, but I would still like to know who came up with such a fanciful name. And since we *are* supposed to be celebrating, I'd like a bit more brandy, if I may."

While he went to replenish her glass, Ainsley wandered over to the wall of windows overlooking the loch. She pressed her hand to a pane and appeared to intently study the night-shrouded landscape.

"So?" she asked when he came to stand beside her.

"My mother named me. She had a romantic soul and loved the old Arthurian tales. I'm sure my exceedingly Scottish father was appalled, but he adored her, so Royal Lancelot Kendrick it was."

"Your older brothers must have teased you about it."

"Logan tried. But after a salutary thrashing from Nick, he desisted."

"Then I will be sure never to call you Lancelot in the earl's presence."

"Or ever."

She smiled and went back to gazing out the window. The uncertain light of a slipper moon traced the edges of the garden shrubs, creating odd and fanciful shapes. The loch was a gigantic inkblot at the base of the wide lawn, the occasional whitecap momentarily glittering into life. On the other side of the water, Highland peaks reached up jagged and black against a starlight sky.

"It's beautiful," she murmured. "Quite my favorite view here at Kinglas."

"Aye, it's grand. But I wasn't aware you had a favorite view. I always thought you loathed everything about this place."

"No, just the inhabitants," she said drolly. "In fact, when we were stuck here last January, I often snuck down to the library to read when the earl was busy elsewhere."

"And when you weren't helping Victoria care for my

stupid, sick brothers. Which, now that I think on it, you shouldn't have been doing since you were pregnant."

"I didn't mind. It was a good distraction from my troubles."

"That's one way to put it." He gently tugged one of the glossy curls framing her face. "I wasn't nearly as careful with you as I should have been, lass. I can't tell you how sorry I am about that."

She turned to face him. When she placed her palms flat on his waistcoat, he covered her hands with his.

"You didn't know I was with child," she said earnestly. "So there's nothing to apologize for."

"But I knew *something* was wrong. I should have done more to help you, instead of letting you slip off to Cairndow all by yourself."

"If there is one person who should never apologize to me, it's you, Royal Kendrick. I owe you *everything*."

"You don't owe me anything, Ainsley. Truly." The *last* thing he wanted from her was the sense that all that bound her to him was obligation.

Gravely, she studied his face. He had the uncomfortable feeling she could read his mind.

"You are a very foolish man if you think that's the only reason I'm here," she said, confirming his suspicions. "I'm here because I want to be with you, not because I have to be with you."

Under her slender fingers, he could feel his heart begin to pound. "Do you think you could be more specific, Mrs. Kendrick?" Emotion had made his voice gruff. "Why are you here right now?"

A teasing smile, blessedly confident, curled up the corners of her lush mouth. "Why, for a good night kiss, of course."

She went up on her toes and pressed a kiss to his lips. It was so sweet and yet so determined that it all but took him out at the knees. He repressed the instinct to drag her into his arms, and instead carefully wrapped his hands around her waist.

He gently pressed close, relishing the soft feel of her luscious lips. For glorious moments, their mouths played with each other, slowly building in intensity. For so long he'd yearned for her kisses, reverently storing in memory the few they'd shared. Now that she was finally secured within his embrace, Royal practically shook with desire, fighting the overwhelming, visceral need to claim his woman. But he could not and would not rush, for her sake and also for his. This was a moment to cherish and remember for as long as he lived.

When he teased along the seam of her lips, silently asking permission to enter, she responded with a breathless chuckle that turned his heart inside out. God, he loved this woman. Ainsley had courage and pride enough to conquer kingdoms, yet she trembled in his arms, so vulnerable and sweet that he wanted to tear down the world and build a fortress to keep her safe.

Gently, he slipped inside and tasted brandy and his wife.

She murmured deep in her throat and wrapped her arms more tightly around his neck, responding with a delicious tease of silky heat. When she drew back a few seconds later, he almost groaned. But then she traced the shape of his mouth with the tip of her tongue, sending fire through his veins, before stealing back inside to torment him with languid, delicate kisses.

For a few moments, he endured it, clamping down on the urge to take. But when she nipped his lower lip, desire blasted through him like a thunderstorm raging across the loch. Royal swept past her ladylike caresses to claim her mouth with all the passion and need he'd locked down and hidden away for long, lonely months.

When Ainsley froze, as if startled, his heart slammed into the wall of his chest. But then she moaned, snuggling even closer. The feel of her full breasts pressing against his waistcoat set him on fire.

Without breaking the kiss, Royal started walking her backward toward the chaise. When she willingly followed his lead, his heart soared. She wasn't afraid of him. She wasn't afraid, period. Because she was Ainsley. If Royal weren't so overcome with need, he'd be dropping to his knees and sending up a thousand prayers of gratitude to all the angels that his beautiful wife was the strongest woman he'd ever met.

You can light a candle later, you lucky bastard.

They were just about to sink down onto the plump cushions of the chaise when the library door flew open and thudded against the wall. Ainsley jerked back, her foot tangling around his boot, and they almost tumbled to the floor as Angus stomped into the room.

"Oh, my God," she gasped as Royal set her upright.

His grandfather scowled at them. "I've been lookin' all over the bloody castle for ye."

Ainsley leveled an accusatory glare at Royal. "You promised your family would leave us alone. You *promised.*"

"I bloody well didn't ask him to come," Royal protested. "Why the hell are you here, Grandda? It's practically the middle of the night."

"Och, it's not that late," Angus replied with a casual wave. "I've been here for at least a half hour, after a nice ride up from Glasgow. And that glad I am to be away from the stinkin' city and back home."

Royal felt like the top of his head was about to fizz up like an exploding squib. "But *why* are you here?"

"I couldna sleep knowin' that the little lassie would be missin' her grandda. So here I am."

"Oh, my God," Ainsley repeated, sounding utterly appalled.

"Do Nick and Victoria know you rode up?" Royal demanded.

Angus hunched his shoulders and gave him a placating smile. "Dinna fash yourself, lad. I left them a grand little note to explain."

"Grandda, this is our *wedding* trip." Never had Royal been closer to throttling Angus than he was at this moment.

"Aye, that's the point. I can watch out for Tira while ye and the missus have a wee bit of private time. Ye'll hardly even know I'm aboot the place."

Ainsley switched her Medusa glare to Angus. "You are so irritating. *I'm* supposed to be looking after my daughter, in case you've forgotten."

"Aye, and ye can bloody well use all the help ye can get," the old man retorted, "especially since the puir wee bairn is feeling poorly. I could tell Tira was off her feed before ye left. It's no wonder I decided to follow ye."

When Angus tapped the side of his nose, trying to look wise, Royal had to hold back a scoff. The excuse sounded like complete bollocks to him.

Ainsley went from irate to anxious in a matter of seconds. "What do you mean poorly? I was with her an hour ago, and she was asleep."

"She's not sleepin' now. That's why I came down to fetch ye." He flashed her a toothy smile. "As ye say, yer her mother. I knew ye'd want to be with her."

Ainsley picked up her skirts and pelted out of the room.

Sighing, Royal followed in her wake, Angus falling into step beside him.

"Is Tira really sick, or was that just an excuse to come to Kinglas?" he asked his grandfather.

Angus shrugged. "Probably just another tooth coming in, but ye never know."

Royal shot him a dirty look. "One of these days, Grandda, I *will* kill you."

Angus snorted. "Laddie, none of ye would know what to do without me, least of all yer new missus. Even for a *Sassenach*, she's bloody hopeless."

Chapter Fifteen

Royal placed his daughter stomach-down on the tartan blanket spread out on the floor of the family parlor. "There you go, little one. Be a good girl for Mamma when she comes down, will you? Papa will get you some nice biscuits to chew on if you promise not to cry or spit up on her."

Tira pushed herself up on her hands and knees and chortled, as if agreeing with him.

"She canna understand a word yer saying, laddie," Angus said with an indulgent smile. "And she'll be doin' whatever she wants, whether her mother wishes it or no."

Royal settled wearily onto the settee. He studied the tea service, set before him on the low, satinwood table, and thought about ringing for something stronger. But since he'd had three cups of coffee this morning and one after lunch, trying to clear his bleary head, it was probably best to stick with tea or else end up with a case of the jitters. Ainsley was already jittery enough for the both of them.

"If she'd stop her fussin' and carryin' on, we might have a little peace," Angus said. "And mayhap a good night's sleep, for once."

"Who? Ainsley or Tira?" Royal poured himself a cup.

His grandfather, seated in his favorite old armchair by the

hearth, snorted. "Tira is a wee angel compared to her high and mightiness, and ye know it."

"What I know is that my wife is doing her best. If you don't stop picking away at her, I will throw you out of Kinglas on your arse. You can walk back to Glasgow for all I care or go stay in one of the crofters' cottages."

His grandfather's whiskers bristled with offended dignity. "I *am* only tryin' to help. But yer wife acts like she's the only one who knows what she's doin' when it comes to Tira. *And* as if she's more rights than the rest of us."

"She does have more rights than the rest of us." Royal leaned forward for emphasis. "Ainsley is Tira's mother. Her *real* mother."

"Mayhap, but a good mother would nae have given her up," Angus stubbornly replied.

The old man had said that more than once. Royal seemed unable to get through to him that the exact opposite was true. For someone like Angus, loyalty to family was everything, and voluntarily giving up a child was impossible to fathom.

"Ainsley gave Tira up to protect her," Royal said, trying to be patient. "It was the right thing to do, given the difficult circumstances."

"More like to protect her own reputation, I reckon. That lass seems fair obsessed with how others think about her."

Royal bit back the reprimand on the tip of his tongue. Only Nick and Victoria knew the details of Ainsley's assault and its aftermath, and she'd begged Royal to keep it that way. Ainsley loathed that others might think her a helpless victim or, even worse, believe that she was somehow irretrievably damaged. Her spirit and dignity had received a grievous wound, and Royal would do whatever was necessary to safeguard her privacy and give her the time she needed to heal.

"Once a woman loses her reputation, it is lost forever,"

Royal said, trying to pick his way through the morass. "And society can be utterly cruel, in those situations."

Angus pulled out a battered white pipe from his vest pocket, along with a tobacco pouch. "I ken yer right, but why didn't the lass marry the babe's father in the first place? Though I'm glad she didn't," he added hastily. "Else we would nae have gotten the little lassie, would we?"

They both glanced at Tira and smiled. The lass rocked back and forth on her haunches, as if just discovering how to do it.

"True," Royal said. "It's hard to imagine how we ever got on without her."

Angus stuffed some tobacco into the bowl and reached for a spill from a brass container next to the fireplace. "She was the savin' of you, lad," he said around puffs as he lit his pipe. "And that's a fact."

Royal didn't much like to think about the days before Tira and how close he'd come to the edge of despair. His daughter *had* saved him—from himself. And it was Ainsley who'd made it all possible.

"If she keeps that up much longer, she'll launch herself right off the blanket," he said as he watched Tira rock with ever greater enthusiasm.

"Aye, she'll be crawlin' soon. She's a pistol, that one. Just like the twins were."

"God, I hope not. She's a handful, but they were little demons."

"Tira's worse now that herself is on the scene. She's got the poor little thing rattlin' about like a fart in a muff."

Royal scowled at his grandfather. "First, that is a disgusting analogy to make about my daughter. Second, I would be grateful if you would refer to my wife as something more respectful than *yer missus*, *herself*, or *her high and mightiness*."

Angus puffed away with great nonchalance, exhaling as much smoke as a chimney in need of repair. "What about *Sassenach*?"

"Try Ainsley, or even Lady Ainsley. Good Lord, even calling her *lass* would be better."

"She dinna like that, either." Angus let out a windy sigh. "I canna expect better from a *Sassenach*. I suppose I can try, though."

Argh. "Grandda, I need you to listen to me."

"Laddie, I always listen to you."

"Angus, I'm serious," he said, finally letting his frustration show.

His grandfather studied him. "Say your piece then, lad."

"Ainsley's decisions might seem almost inexplicable to you, but you need to know that she made them for all the right reasons. As I said, she needed to protect her daughter from Tira's natural father. Believe me, it was imperative to do that."

"That Cringlewood fellow," Angus said.

"Yes."

"Not a good sort, I reckon."

"The very opposite of a good sort. The marquess is a cruel man, and the fact that he's both rich and powerful makes him doubly dangerous. Ainsley's primary goal has always been to keep Tira as far from him as possible."

Angus puffed again with vigor, the smoke wreathing his head in curlicues. "Seems to me the best idea would be to keep *herself* far away from Tira. That old biddy mother of hers caused quite a ruckus because she figured it out. That was a cock-up."

"Yes, things got a bit complicated there, but you'll simply have to trust me. Keeping Ainsley safe from the Marquess of Cringlewood will keep Tira safe, too."

Angus frowned over that for a few moments, then nodded. "Ah, well, anyone named Cringlewood is bound to be a scaly one, so I'm with ye, lad. Ye know that."

"Then you need to be a little more patient with Ainsley, Grandda. She's doing her best with Tira."

"Doing her best is one way to put it. The lass has been that fashed these last few days, trying to manage the bairn."

Tira had been particularly fussy these last few days, suffering through both a new tooth and a case of the sniffles. It was a mild case, to be sure, but enough to send Ainsley into a quiet frenzy, as if something awful might happen if she let Tira out of her sight. His poor wife had spent most of the past two days and nights in the nursery, driving everyone batty, including the nursemaid.

Angus had been the only one with consistent success in getting Tira to calm down and sleep. That fact had done nothing to improve Ainsley's mood, and Royal feared she was on the edge of an emotional explosion.

Unfortunately, Angus was particularly efficient tinder to her spark.

"I repeat, if you could muster a little patience to allow her to sort it out, I would be grateful," Royal said. "Ainsley has had a difficult time of it and needs our support."

"And ye love her, don't ye, lad?" Angus said with a sly wink. "Nay, don't try to deny it. I've read ye well ever since ye were a bairn with a full nappie."

The average schoolroom dunce could probably have deduced that Royal was madly in love with his wife. "I could never pull the wool over your eyes, could I, Grandda?"

"Does the lass ken how you feel about her?"

And therein lay the irony. Yes, she knew Royal was smitten with her, and had been for a long time. But love was different. What he felt for Ainsley was deep and abiding, something that would survive the ending of the world and beyond.

"She knows I care for her," he said, as if it didn't really matter.

When the Louis XIV clock on the sideboard chimed out the hour, Royal frowned. He'd expected Ainsley to join them for tea at least twenty minutes ago. Since she'd hardly touched her lunch—which was highly unusual for her—she must be famished.

"Speaking of yer missus—" Angus started.

"Grandda!" Royal said, exasperated.

His grandfather rolled his eyes. "Fine, then. Speaking of her *ladyship*, will she be gracin' us with her presence for tea?"

Royal hauled himself to his feet. "If you would keep an eye on Tira, I'll go—"

He paused as the door opened and Ainsley hurried in, fussing with her cuffs and tugging them into place. "I'm sorry I'm so late. I closed my eyes for a few minutes and fell asleep. I'm entirely crumpled, but I didn't want to take the time to change and leave you waiting."

Royal glanced at her pale blue muslin dress, which displayed nary a wrinkle. Then again, no dress of Ainsley's would have the temerity to wrinkle without her permission.

"Och, we don't stand on ceremony when it's just us," Angus said in a gruff tone that for him passed as friendly. "If ye came down in yer dressing gown we wouldna care."

Ainsley cast him a wary glance, but quickly shifted her notice to Tira wriggling around on the blanket. "Should she be down on the floor? Isn't it too drafty?"

Royal and Angus both looked at the roaring blaze in the hearth. "It's quite warm in here," Royal said. "She'll be fine."

"But she's just getting over a cold," Ainsley said. "Her nose was still runny this morning."

"Nae, she's just breakin' a tooth, lass," Angus said. "Sometimes that makes them sniffly."

Ainsley scowled. "How can teething make a baby sniffly?"

"Royal was the same when he was a wee bairn. Every time he broke through a tooth he kicked up a grand fuss, just like Tira. Takes after her father, she does."

Ainsley fortunately refrained from pointing out the obvious flaw in that theory.

"And it's a very mild day out, love," Royal added. "There's hardly a breeze off the loch, so no drafts. In fact, I was thinking of opening a window to let in some fresh air."

"Fresh Highland air never hurt anyone," Angus said as he relit his pipe.

"Especially with you puffing away like a dirty chimney," Ainsley said tartly. "I shouldn't wonder if Tira suffers a cough from inhaling your smoke."

Angus shot her a grim look but held his fire. Royal had to give him credit—the old fellow was trying.

"I'll open a window," Royal said. "We could all use a little fresh air."

"Going outside to smoke a pipe seems like an even better idea," Ainsley said. "Then everyone would be happy."

"I'm perfectly happy right here," Angus replied, taking a few extra puffs for good measure. Billows of smoke curled around his head, making him look a little like a demented version of Father Christmas.

Ainsley waved a dramatic hand in front of her face. "I am *certain* that's not good for Tira's lungs."

Royal would have been concerned if Angus was sitting near Tira, but he was a good twenty feet away. Repressing a sigh, he unlatched a casement window and pushed it open. Leaning out, he drew in the clean, heather-scented air. Rather than a quiet stay at Kinglas with his new wife, his wedding trip had been transformed into a state of armed truce. Since there was little chance he could persuade Angus to leave, the sooner they returned to Glasgow the better. Even more to the point, he needed to quickly find a suitable town house for his little family, since separation of the warring parties was growing more critical by the moment.

In the meantime, he supposed he'd better have a chat with

252   *Vanessa Kelly*

Ainsley about managing Angus. Otherwise, there was the risk of coming down to tea one day to discover his new bride had murdered his grandfather with the cake knife.

"Royal, are you all right?"

He turned to see Ainsley peering at him with concern. "I'm fine," he said.

"You don't look fine."

"Just taking a moment to enjoy the peace and quiet of the country," he said dryly.

She gave him a tentative smile. "Yes, I was hoping that we could take a nice, quiet—"

"Royal, can ye fetch me a wee dram while yer up?" Angus barked from across the room.

"Walk," Ainsley finished, shaking her head. She went to join Tira, while Royal crossed to the mahogany sideboard to fetch a glass.

"None of that swill from Glasgow or Edinburgh, mind ye," Angus said. "Fetch me the good stuff."

Royal frowned at the collection of decanters on the polished wood. "Grandda, it's all from Glasgow or Edinburgh. What are you talking about?"

His grandfather pointed the stem of his pipe toward the cabinet below. "Look there."

Royal opened the small door to find several plain, unlabeled bottles. He pulled one out and held it up. The deeply colored amber brew glowed richly in the late afternoon sunlight. "Where did this come from?"

Angus gave him a sly smile and went back to puffing his pipe.

Royal glared at him. "Is this from *our* still? The one Nick ordered shut down months ago?"

Last year, Angus and the twins had secretly run an illegal whisky operation that was tucked away in a small glen on Arnprior lands. Once discovered, it was only by paying a significant fine that Nick had been able to keep Graeme and

Grant—not to mention Angus—out of the hands of the local excise officers.

Angus feigned an expression of offended dignity. "Of course we shut it down."

"Then what the hell is this?" Royal asked, holding up the bottle.

"Just the final batch, I reckon," he said evasively. "And dinna ye be cursing around yer daughter, laddie."

"Oh, that's rich, coming from you."

Angus cursed like a trooper around Tira, and even regular scolds from Victoria couldn't seem to break him of the habit.

Crouched down next to Tira's blanket, Ainsley threw the old fellow a haughty glance. "The family patriarch was running a criminal operation? I suppose I should be shocked, but for some reason I'm not."

Now Angus looked genuinely offended. "It was nae a criminal enterprise, ye daft woman. We always made our own whisky until the bloody *Sassenachs* put their boots on our necks."

"A *fine* example you set for my poor daughter. Defying both the earl *and* the law. It's disgraceful."

"Now, see here, ye blasted—"

"I wouldn't, Grandda," Royal interrupted in a lethal tone. "Ainsley is right. And if there *is* something going on, I want it shut down immediately."

"But—"

"I don't want to hear another word about it," Royal said. "I never wanted to hear about it in the first place, so please spare me any additional palavering."

His grandfather subsided with a grumble. "A lot of fuss and botheration over nothin', if ye ask me."

Royal splashed some whisky into the glass and stalked over to Angus. "Here, enjoy it while you can—before Nick finds it."

"I intend to." Angus took the glass and scowled at Ainsley.

"And ye needn't be givin' me that snooty smirk, young lassie. It's no saint ye are, I ken."

Ainsley's admittedly taunting smile disappeared. "What is *that* supposed to mean?"

"It means nothing." Royal cuffed Angus on the shoulder. "Stop being an idiot, Grandda."

The old man rounded his eyes, trying to look innocent, before retreating behind his glass.

"And instead of picking a fight with Angus," Royal said to his wife, "why don't you enjoy this time with your daughter? She's not crying, for once, which is rather a miracle."

For a moment, Ainsley looked like she might take offense. Then she gave him a charmingly rueful smile. "As always, you have an excellent grasp on the priorities, dear sir."

It wasn't much of an apology, but he'd take it.

Returning to his seat, Royal picked up his cup and swallowed a mouthful of cold, milky tea. It tasted wretched, and for a moment he contemplated pouring himself a large whisky.

"Do you want me to fix you a fresh cup?" Ainsley quietly asked.

He mustered a smile, reminding himself again how difficult this was for her. In the last few weeks, her life had been turned utterly on its head. "It's fine. You play with Tira."

She flashed him a quick smile, then settled down on her knees beside her daughter, who was once more enthusiastically rocking back and forth. When Ainsley leaned on her elbows to look into Tira's face, it pushed her beautifully rounded arse up in the air. It was a delightful view, and for a minute or so Royal allowed himself to contemplate it in blessed peace.

He was only listening with half an ear when Ainsley asked him a question he didn't quite catch.

"Ah, sorry, love," he said. "What was that again?"

She glanced over her shoulder. "I said, I don't think it will be much longer, do you?"

"What won't be much longer?"

She frowned. "Until Tira starts crawling. Royal, are you not listening to me?"

"I ken that something else caught his attention," Angus said with a smirk.

Still peering over her shoulder, Ainsley looked blank for a moment as Royal shot his grandfather a narrow-eyed glare. Then awareness flooded her gaze, and she flushed a bright pink. With commendable dignity, she scooted into a sitting position and neatly tucked her dress around her legs.

"I beg your pardon," she said. "But I do like to be with her, even if sitting on the floor isn't very ladylike."

For a woman notoriously high in the instep, Ainsley had not an ounce of false pride when it came to her daughter. Royal loved that about her. "It's no problem at all, sweetheart. Do just as you like."

"Tira does seem to prefer it when I play with her on the floor, rather than holding her."

"That's because ye cart her about like a sack of turnips," Angus said. "Ye've yet to get the hang of it."

Royal considered dumping the contents of the teapot on his grandfather's head.

"I hold her perfectly well," Ainsley indignantly replied.

Tira startled a bit at her mamma's sharp tone but thankfully didn't start crying.

"Of course you do," Royal said in a soothing tone. "You're very adept with her. Angus is just making a little joke."

"A very little one," she said acidly.

When Angus sneered at her, Royal ground his teeth. Clearly, the exceedingly short-lived truce was over. Not that Ainsley had known there was a truce in the first place, which was part of the problem.

A distraction was needed.

"Oh, look," he said. "I think Tira's nose is running."

At even the slightest suggestion that something might be amiss with her daughter, Ainsley was instantly diverted. She craned over sideways to get a good look at Tira, who had flopped back onto her stomach and was snuffling into the blanket. A moment later, she stiffened and let out a furious sneeze.

"Oh, dear," Ainsley said, "I hope her cold isn't coming back."

"I told ye, the lassie doesna have a cold," Angus said. "Probably just a wee bit of dust up her nose from the blanket."

"And who put her down on a dusty blanket?" she demanded.

Royal plucked a napkin off the tea tray and handed it to her. "I put her on the blanket, and it's not the least bit dusty. Please don't even suggest such a thing to Taffy. She'd have a heart attack."

"I wouldn't think of insulting your housekeeper," Ainsley said as she awkwardly swiped at Tira's nose. Unfortunately, the baby wriggled about like an eel to avoid her mother's ministrations. "She's the only sane person in this place."

"The only sane woman, you mean," Angus muttered.

Royal was spared the need to murder his grandfather by the fact that Ainsley's attention was focused solely on trying to wipe Tira's nose.

"Perhaps you should pick her up and put her on your lap?" Royal finally suggested. "That way you can get a firm grip on her."

"She'll probably start crying if I do that," Ainsley said.

"Babies cry, love. It's on their list of regular duties."

She threw him a wry glance. "I know I need to stop being so skittish about it."

"Practice makes perfect," he said.

She picked Tira up and carefully hoisted her onto her lap, facing forward. Wrapping an arm around her little waist to hold her steady, Ainsley reached around to wipe the bairn's nose. Tira fussed a bit, but then allowed it.

"Well, would ye look at that? Ye might be getting the hang of this motherin' business, after all," Angus said in a tone suggesting the Red Sea had just parted out in the garden.

"Hold still, little one," Ainsley crooned. She leaned forward a bit more, the tip of her tongue between her teeth as she dabbed at her daughter's nose.

Tira chose that moment to finally object, knocking her mother's hand away and then rearing back with all her infant strength. The top of her skull connected solidly with Ainsley's chin.

"Ouch," Ainsley yelped.

They all froze for a subsequent moment of horrified silence before Tira let out a piercing wail. Royal jumped up and hurried to join Ainsley, who now looked on the verge of tears herself.

"Oh, God," she said. "Did I hurt her?"

"I suspect it's the other way around, sweetheart," Royal said. "I'm sure she's fine, but why don't you give her to me?"

Silently, she handed the baby up, then clambered awkwardly to her feet. Royal ran a careful hand over the back of Tira's head. Despite her tears, she didn't flinch, which confirmed his suspicions that most of the damage had been done to Ainsley's poor face.

As he rocked her, Tira quickly started to calm down.

"She's fine," he assured his clearly distressed wife.

"Aye, the lass has got a hard head," Angus said. "Just like her mother."

"Shut up, Angus," Royal said. He strode over to his

grandfather. "Here, make yourself useful. Take her while I fix Ainsley a cup of tea."

After handing the baby off, he returned to his wife.

"Are you sure she's all right?" she asked.

"Positive," he said, gently taking her chin so he could inspect her face. "I'm more worried about you."

"I must say, it hurt like the devil," she confessed.

"Did you bite your tongue?"

"I did."

"I wish I could kiss it and make it better."

As he'd hoped, that won him a rueful smile. "I'm sure you do, but I think a cup of tea is what I need right now."

"Or a wee dram?"

"That would probably burn too much. Just tea with lots of milk and sugar, please."

He steered her to the chaise and fixed her tea while Angus bounced Tira on his lap, trying to distract her. Unfortunately, the bairn was still a bit fussy and was soon gnawing on her fingers. That was a sure sign that her gums were sore.

After he handed her a cup, Ainsley put it down without taking a sip and eyed Tira. "If I didn't hurt her, why is she still fussing? Do you think we should send for the doctor?"

"It's the teething, lass," Angus said. "Don't fash yourself. No need for a sawbones."

"I'm not fashing myself, I'm simply—"

She broke off in consternation when the old man dipped a finger in his whisky glass and then flicked off the droplets. When he stuck his finger in Tira's mouth and started massaging her little gums, Ainsley shot to her feet.

"What in heaven's name are you doing?" she all but shrieked.

"Och, don't blast our ears off, ye daft woman," Angus said. "I'm massaging her gums, dinna ye ken?"

Ainsley practically levitated off the floor with outrage. "With whisky? You're giving my daughter *whisky*?"

"It was just to clean my finger," Angus protested. "Not to get her drunk. Besides, she likes the taste."

That seemed to be the case, as Tira gnawed on her grandfather's finger with evident relief.

Royal took Ainsley's hand and tried to tug her back down on the chaise. She resisted.

"A taste of whisky won't harm her, love," he said. "I remember my mother doing that with Braden, and I'm sure with the twins, as well."

"Aye, that she did," Angus said. "Works like a charm."

"But . . . but they're boys," Ainsley exclaimed, clearly revolted. "Tira is a girl."

Angus rolled his eyes. "That makes no bloody sense. But it doesna surprise me, coming from ye."

"I don't have to make sense to you, you grubby old goat," Ainsley snapped. "I'm her mother."

"Aye, and a goat would be a—"

"Angus, enough," Royal ordered. He stood and took Ainsley's hand. "Please sit down and try to relax. I promise you Tira is fine."

She snatched her fingers from his loose hold. "Why do you always have to take his side? It's *incredibly* annoying."

"I don't always take his side." Royal was incredulous at how quickly the situation was spinning out of control. "But, to be fair, you did just call him an old goat, which isn't very nice."

The flash of hurt in her gaze told him that he'd just firmly inserted his own foot into his mouth.

"Men. You always stick together," she said in a low, quivering voice. She then rushed from the room, slamming the door behind her.

Royal pressed a hard palm to his forehead, like his head

was about to explode. He'd cocked that up as thoroughly as one possibly could.

"Dicked in the nob, that one is," Angus said in a pious tone. "Let's hope it skips a generation."

"Ainsley is right," he snapped. "Sometimes you *are* a grubby old goat."

He plucked Tira from the old man's arms and stalked after his wife.

Chapter Sixteen

Her horse trotted beside the stream that tumbled its way through the brushy glen and down to the loch. Ainsley gave the dainty beauty her head, since there was not a remote possibility of getting lost. The trail was clearly used on a regular basis and led straight back to the castle.

At the moment, though, getting lost seemed rather a good idea.

She closed her weary eyes against a hot wave of shame. What a ninny she'd been to act like a tragedy queen. If her husband didn't cast her off after yet another episode of stupid family drama, it would be a miracle.

Ainsley's eyes flew open when a grouse exploded from the underbrush with a squawk, spooking her horse. She corrected her seat and encouraged the animal forward with a bit of leg pressure. Within seconds, the mare settled back into a steady trot.

"Sorry, old girl." She patted the animal's neck. "I'll send myself into the stream if I'm not careful."

The stable master had been reluctant to let Ainsley ride out without a groom, skeptical of both her abilities and state of mind. She couldn't blame poor Brody, since she'd rushed into the stables like an escapee from Bedlam, demanding he saddle a mount for her.

After she'd stormed away from that ridiculous scene in the drawing room, she'd gone straight to her bedroom, where she'd struggled into her riding boots and yanked a pelisse out of the tallboy. Grabbing the first pair of gloves that came to hand—kid dinner gloves, for God's sake—she'd pelted down the back stairs and slipped out through the gardens to the stables. She had to avoid Royal, who would seek her out to either gently scold or even more gently appease her. The man had the patience of a saint. Sometimes it tempted her to dump a teapot over his head simply to make him lose his sangfroid.

She deserved that he lose his temper with her. Perhaps if he did, she could stop feeling so guilty, and finally come to terms with the overwhelming sense of failure that was her daily companion.

Once clear of the castle gatehouse, she'd sprung the horse into a gallop. For a few glorious minutes, the rush of speed had blasted away the fatigue, the fear, and the frustration that kept her awake, night after bloody night.

But even the speed and the bracing Highland air couldn't keep the emotions at bay. As soon as she'd slowed to a canter her demons had all come rushing back. Fear that she was failing as a mother, fear that her secrets would be discovered, and fear that the entire edifice of her fragile, spun-glass life would come crashing down around her ears.

And then there was the awful sense of shame that she was utterly failing as a wife. Bad enough that she'd ruined her own life; she couldn't ruin Royal's, too. She was driving a wedge between him and much of his family, especially his grandfather, so it was no wonder most of the Kendricks disliked her. Most days, she didn't like herself very much either.

"It's my punishment for all those years I was a terrible snob," she said to the mare as they plodded by the stream. "Fate has a way of throwing one's mistakes in one's face, doesn't it?"

Her biggest challenge was Angus. Ainsley could almost hear the gods laughing over that. But as a Kendrick wife, she was now stuck with the old goat. She knew she had to find a way to make it work, since Royal and Tira loved him, and he loved them back with equal devotion.

"If it came down to it," she said, "they'd probably pick Angus over me, and I'm not sure I could blame them. Although I *am* a great deal prettier, so there's that in my favor."

The horse snorted and flicked her ears, as if amused by Ainsley's nonsense.

If she wasn't so bloody tired, she might be amused herself. It had perhaps not been the best idea to spend the last two nights on a cot in the nursery. Everyone had thought she was silly, and they were probably right. Tira was fine. She was always fine, whether her mother was with her or not.

You should have spent those nights with Royal. Then you would have slept.

To be snuggled against his strong, sheltering body in a lovely warm bed . . . she wanted that so much. She wanted to be with him, but the very idea of conjugal relations frightened the wits out of her too.

"Face it, you're a confounded mess," she said as she nudged the mare toward a large outcropping of rocks.

The animal whickered, as if to comment.

"I'm glad someone around here agrees with me."

And, yes, she was muttering to herself. It was an old habit she'd picked up as a young girl who'd spent a great deal of time alone in the schoolroom, reading books or working on puzzles. The habit always helped sort things out when she was confused or worried, or just plain lonely.

She used one of the flat-topped rocks to assist her dismount, and then tied the mare to a sturdy bush before looking for a comfortable place to sit. A springy cushion of moss and grass on the slope of the stream did the trick, since it was a sheltered spot in the full warmth of the sun. Ainsley wrapped her skirts around her legs and settled onto moss that was surprisingly thick and almost as well padded as a cushion.

Sighing, she turned her face up to the gentle September sun. The quiet of the place settled over her, broken only by an occasional splash of the water and the call of a passing eagle. The water was quite low this time of year, meandering by her on its way to the loch. According to Royal, it ran fast and high in the spring, gorged with snowmelt off the Highland peaks. He'd delivered quite a lecture about the dangers of the stream, giving her strict orders to stay well back on the bank and to never go wading without him. He'd then promised to take her fishing at some point, although apparently now was not the best season to do so.

The poor man had been so earnest that Ainsley had refrained from telling him she'd rather eat haggis than splash about in icy cold water, much less go fishing, which required the handling of slimy worms and other nasty things.

But today, the stream was like a genial, self-effacing neighbor, the sort who tipped his hat with a smile and never made a fuss. And the vista before her was so dramatically beautiful, the craggy Highland peaks topped with a diamond-bright blue sky and some powder-puff clouds. If she were a different sort of person, she might have pulled off her boots and gone wading. Perhaps she and Tira could do that someday, when Royal was there to hold their daughter's chubby little hands and keep her safe. Ainsley couldn't help but smile at the image of a laughing toddler with dark, tumbled curls and a violet gaze, watched over by loving parents who had not a care in the world but for their child.

Ainsley finally gave in to the fatigue dragging at her bones and stretched out on the mossy bank. Her maid would scold to see her lying on the ground, but the rippling stream sounded like a lullaby and the sun was so warm on her face. She'd just close her eyes for a few moments and . . .

She jerked awake at the sound of a galloping horse, the ground vibrating beneath her with the pounding of hooves.

When she heard a muffled shout, Ainsley stumbled clumsily to her feet in time to see a fast-approaching rider.

And to see her husband then sail over his stallion's head and hit the ground with a horrifying thud.

"Royal," she shrieked.

Ainsley pelted around the rocks, tripping over her skirts as she ran along the trail to reach him. Royal lay flat on his back, his gaze wide and blank. Was he even breathing? Her fear was now sheer panic.

"Oh, God," she gasped, dropping to her knees. Tears flooded her eyes, making it almost impossible to see.

Impatiently, she swiped them away and pressed a hand to his chest. "Oh, God," she blurted again. "Royal, can you hear me? Please be alive!"

When he sucked in a huge breath under her hand, she almost collapsed with relief.

"It hurts too much to be dead," he managed in a tight voice.

"I thought you'd killed yourself." She kept patting him on the chest, as if that would help, but she felt too dazed and shaky to think rationally.

Please, please don't be injured.

He lay there for what seemed forever, staring straight up at the sky. His face was ghostly pale.

"I thought the same about you," he finally replied. "When I saw you lying on the ground."

When he turned his head to look at her, she realized that he was furious, his gaze glittering and sharp-edged, like shards of green glass.

"Why would you think that?" she asked.

"Because you were lying flat out on the ground like a corpse?"

"I was just taking a little nap."

"On the ground? By the blasted river?"

She couldn't help bristling at his tone. "What's wrong with that?"

"Everything," he snapped. "And how the devil was I supposed to know you were napping? You're hardly the sort of person to lounge about in the dirt. Hell and damnation, Ainsley, I thought your horse had thrown you."

"Royal, I'm truly sorry I gave you that impression, but did you not notice that my horse was tied to that bush? That would hardly be the case if she'd thrown me."

He blinked a few times, then went back to glaring at her. "Why the hell did you ride off without a groom? I told you *never* to come down to the river by yourself. It's too dangerous."

By the time he finished, he was all but shouting. Under normal circumstances, she'd have shouted right back, but Royal's fury obviously sprang from fear. And not just the garden-variety fear, either.

"I'm sorry I frightened you," she said contritely. "But as you can see, I'm absolutely fine. My horse is fine, the river is fine—we're all fine."

"That's not the point," he ground out. "You shouldn't be racketing about Arnprior lands by yourself. Anything could happen."

"Really? Are there cutthroat brigands lurking about the glen that you failed to apprise me of? Or pirates sailing up from the loch?"

"Ainsley—"

She patted him again. "Dearest, I'm perfectly well. You, however, took a ghastly fall. Do you think you can get up now?"

He blew out a frustrated sigh. "I should make the attempt. But this is not the end of the discussion, I assure you."

"You can scold me to your heart's content when we get back to the castle." She peered at his big stallion, now calmly grazing several yards away. He looked fine, too, thank goodness.

Royal had gone back to glaring at the sky, which was an improvement on glaring at her. But his complexion was positively bleached, and sweat beaded on his forehead.

"Can you stand if I help you?" she asked.

"I don't know."

Alarm again spiked in her chest. Years ago, she'd seen a man brutally thrown from a horse. He'd been paralyzed from the waist down as a result. "Can you move your limbs?"

"That is not the problem," he gritted out as he pushed himself into a sitting position.

Ainsley shifted back to give him room. "Then what is?"

"My leg bore the brunt of the fall."

Her heart sank. "Your bad leg."

"Of course my bad leg," he barked.

"I *can* hear you," she said, trying not to flinch. "You needn't shout."

Royal grimaced. "Sorry. But the damn thing feels like it's on fire."

Blast. This was all her fault. "I feel wretched about that, but can you try to get on your horse? Else I must go back to Kinglas to fetch help."

"God, no. I won't lie here like an idiot while you're forced to ride home by yourself."

Ainsley tactfully refrained from pointing out that she'd had no trouble riding out here and would have no trouble riding back.

"Then let me help you up," she said, scrambling to her feet.

Her husband shot her an irritated glance but took her hand. It was a sure sign he needed assistance, since he hated appearing like an invalid.

Ainsley planted her feet but still staggered a bit as Royal awkwardly hauled himself to his feet with her help. She slipped under his arm to provide better support. "Don't be afraid to lean on me. As you may have noticed, I'm not a frail miss."

He didn't answer, obviously too busy grinding his teeth in pain and trying to find his balance.

When he was finally steady on his feet, Royal glanced at

his horse. "I hope poor Demetrius didn't lame himself because of me."

"He looks uninjured," she said. "Grazing his head off, in fact."

"No thanks to me, fool that I am."

"Royal, none of this is your fault. It's *my* fault for acting like a spoiled child. Well, Angus was awful too."

"We can apportion blame once we get back to Kinglas. *If*, that is, I can actually manage to get on my horse, and *if* Demetrius didn't lame himself."

"If he did, you can ride my horse and I'll walk Demetrius back to the castle. It's not that far."

"You are *not* walking back to the castle."

She gave up trying to reason with him. "Can you stand on your own while I fetch Demetrius?"

When he gave her a curt nod, she cautiously withdrew her support. But he staggered, so she grabbed his arm.

"I'm fine," he said. "Please just get the blasted horse."

Repressing a sigh, she went to fetch the horse. Although Demetrius was a massive animal, he had beautiful manners. He patiently waited while she ran a quick hand over his flanks and checked his legs for obvious injuries. Finding none, she took the reins and led him to his master.

"He seems quite fit," she said.

"Thank God for that, at least."

Royal still looked dreadful. His complexion remained ashen and perspiration trickled down his temples, despite the cool breeze off the river. His normally clear eyes were hazed with pain, and she could only hope he didn't keel over before she got him home.

"Royal, I'm so sorry you hurt yourself because of me."

"I'm sure I'll be fine, Ainsley. Stop worrying."

His stubborn refusal to even acknowledge that he needed help stirred her irritation. "You're not fine. I'm sending for the surgeon as soon as we get home."

"We'll see."

"Royal, this is not—"

"Would you please just help me check Demetrius? I'm not riding him until I'm sure he's uninjured."

"Your horse is *not* injured."

"I need to check."

Ainsley mentally gave her husband a good shake before taking his arm, supporting him as he limped his way around the horse. He ran his hands carefully over the animal's legs and examined the hooves. By the time he finished, he truly looked ready to keel over.

"I believe he's safe to ride," he said. "If you could just hold his head while I get myself into the saddle."

"I can boost you up."

"Ainsley, you're a big girl, but you're not *that* big."

"There's no need to be insulting. I'm simply trying to help," she retorted, then immediately felt horrible for snapping at him. "Sorry."

"Don't be. Just hold Demetrius, will you?"

Silently, she went to the stallion's head and took hold of the bridle. Royal managed to hoist himself into the saddle, swearing under his breath the entire time, while Demetrius stamped and flicked his ears to signal his displeasure with the awkward process. Ainsley firmly held him, telling him what a good boy he was, and rubbed his nose until he settled down.

"Are you all right?" she asked her husband.

He hunched forward along the horse's neck, trying to catch his breath. "Yes, although that just about killed me."

She wanted to cry with frustration and anxiety as she came around to touch his knee. "Royal, I am so, so sorry. This never would have happened but for my idiotic behavior."

He sat up straight, his malachite gaze narrowing to infuriated slits. "For Christ's sake, Ainsley, would you please stop apologizing? It was I who failed *you*. Again. In fact, I seem completely incapable of giving you what you need to be happy, no matter how hard I try. *I'm* the one with the problem, not you, so please stop trying to pretend otherwise."

She gaped up at him, too stunned to muster a sensible reply. "I, ah . . . I'm not sure how to respond to that, except to say I don't think it's true."

"You don't need to say or do anything but get on your blasted horse so we can put this episode behind us and return home. My lady," he added in a commendably sarcastic tone for a man driven with pain.

Silently, Ainsley went to fetch the mare, pondering that she had a great deal of ground to recover with her much put upon husband.

Chapter Seventeen

Ainsley hurried down the staircase from the nursery floor and turned into the east wing. With the exception of the earl and countess, the family was situated in this wing of Kinglas, although most of the bedrooms were currently deserted. Braden's room, next to Royal's, had been hastily converted into a bedroom for Ainsley. Since Braden spent most of his time at university in Edinburgh, that arrangement made the most sense.

Or it would have made sense, if she and Royal enjoyed a conventional marriage. As it was, having her husband so close was more than enough to keep her awake at nights. She didn't know what ruffled her more—her anxiety over conjugal relations or the almost overwhelming desire to initiate such relations. The confusing mix of emotions had obviously turned her into a melodramatic ninny, so she could hardly blame her husband for finally snapping.

Time to make it up to him, my girl.

Ainsley almost skidded to a halt when she saw her nemesis parked in a straight-backed chair outside of Royal's bedroom, one of his scruffy dogs stretched out at his feet.

Hell and damnation.

She hadn't seen Angus since she and Royal returned to

Kinglas late this afternoon. The old curmudgeon had pitched a fit when he laid eyes on his grandson. The castle's redoubtable housekeeper, thank God, had intervened with her usual brusque efficiency, but it had been quite the chore getting Royal up to his bedroom.

By the time Royal, with the help of a brawny footman, finally staggered upstairs to his bed, he looked close to collapse. Ainsley and Angus had hovered about him like a pair of old biddies until Mrs. Taffy had finally ordered them from the room.

She and Angus had parted ways in the hall with a silent understanding to avoid each other whenever possible. So far, she'd managed that by staying with Tira and having her dinner sent up to the nursery. Unfortunately, her luck had finally run out.

Squaring her shoulders, Ainsley marched down to confront the results of her bad decisions.

The truth was it was time to stop acting like a spoiled child, pitching Royal into the middle of one conflict after another. Besides, if she kept forcing him to choose between her and various members of his family, he might someday pick them over her. And the idea of losing her husband's regard was too painful to bear.

You love him, you jinglebrains, so start acting like you do.

Staggered by the simple clarity of the revelation, she almost tripped over her own feet.

She *loved* Royal. It wasn't just the gratitude, admiration, and affection she'd felt for him in the past. She loved him the way a woman loved a man, with all the messy, glorious bits that went along with it. It had taken her much too long to finally realize how lucky she was that she did.

After gloomily regarding his disgusting but thankfully unlit pipe, Angus glanced up with a scowl. "Yer lookin' buffled-headed *Sassenach*. What's amiss?"

She stopped in front of him, crossing her arms. "You mean besides the fact that your grandson took a terrible fall, and that you and I are the stubborn donkeys who caused it to happen?"

He regarded her modest peace offering with suspicion. Even the dog—probably Tina, although they all looked alike—seemed suspicious, warily sniffing the toe of her shoe before resuming a slumberous pose.

The old man's scowl became slightly less wrinkly and he gave her a nod. "Aye, besides that. Problems with the wee lassie, mayhap?"

"Believe it or not, Tira let me rock her to sleep tonight. She went down with nary a peep."

"Likely worn out by all the commotion today. Poor bairn was probably too tired to kick up a fuss, even with ye."

Ainsley counted to five before she answered. "No doubt."

Surprisingly, Angus flashed her a grin. "Nae, I wasna tryin' to insult ye. But ye must admit the two of ye have had a rocky start."

She settled into the scroll-backed antique chair on the opposite side of the hall, wincing at the hardness of the seat. Much of the furniture at Kinglas was ancient and uncomfortable. She'd come to the conclusion that romantic old castles were generally more appealing in fairy tales than in real life.

"I'm feeling quite confident that the situation will be much improved from now on," she replied in a bracing tone.

Angus looked dubious.

"Is the surgeon still with Royal?" she asked, glancing at the bedroom door.

"Gone well-nigh a half hour. Taffy and Brody are applyin' ointment to the bruisin' and gettin' the lad set up for a wee rest. That old sawbones tried to dose him with laudanum, but

Royal wouldna take it. He hates it, ye ken. Says it makes him feel out of his head."

"Oh, blast. I wanted to see Mr. Dillon before he left. What did he say? Does . . . does he think there will be any permanent injury?"

Angus waved his pipe dismissively. "His hip took most of the fall, and he's got a crackin' bruise or two but no broken bones. Strained his muscles, but Brody's liniment will set that to right."

Deeply relieved, Ainsley pressed a hand to her lips for a moment. "Thank God. When I saw him go flying like that—"

She couldn't continue.

Angus studied her with a thoughtful gaze. "I was that surprised to hear he took a tumble. That boy sits a horse better than anyone here, even with his game leg. Do ye ken what happened?"

She grimaced. "He got distracted because he thought *I'd* taken a tumble."

"That sounds daft. Why would he think that?"

"I'd found a nice, sheltered spot by the stream, farther up the glen." She gave him a rueful smile. "I'd lain down for a bit and ended up falling asleep. When Royal saw me on the ground, he assumed the worst."

Angus thoughtfully sucked on the stem of his unlit pipe. "Where did ye take yer snooze?"

"A few miles up the stream, just before the bend in the road takes you toward the woods. There's a group of large rocks on the riverbank."

Angus grimaced. "Ah, that explains it."

She waited, but the old man had lapsed into a brown study.

"Explains what?" she prompted.

"Why the lad got so rattled."

"Since I am not a mind reader, I would be grateful if you explained it to me."

He warily eyed her.

"Angus," she said, forcing patience, "surely you realize by now that I very much care for Royal. I would never knowingly hurt him."

"It's the unknowin' bit that worries me."

"Since you can't get rid of me, you must learn to trust me, sir. Please understand that I have every intention of taking care of Royal as best I can, just as he takes care of me."

"Royal wants to take care of everyone. That's who he is."

She gave him a rueful smile. "Why do you think I asked him to marry me?"

"And a good day that was for ye, lassie."

"I do know that."

"If ye have a brain in yer head, ye do."

"Angus—"

"Ye ken his nickname, do ye?"

She frowned at the seeming non sequitur. "No."

"It's Loyal Royal."

Ainsley couldn't hold back another smile. "It certainly fits."

"And dinna tell him I told ye, neither," the old man added. "He says it makes him sound like a chub or a jolter-head."

She had no idea what those things were but she did know that Royal, underneath his occasionally brash demeanor, was genuinely modest. He didn't give a hang if anyone thought poorly of him. But try to pay him a compliment? He'd sooner snap your nose off than say thank you for it.

"There's nothing worse than a nickname that rhymes," she said. "My brothers used to call me Painsley Ainsley."

Angus laughed. "Sounds right, lassie."

"I won't ask you which part I'm right about. Now, will you please tell me what happened down at the river? Apparently, Royal was upset about that particular spot?"

The old man's expression quickly shuttered.

"I won't tell him you told me, if that's what you're worried about," she said. "But I do think it would help me to know."

Angus seemed to wage an internal debate for a few moments before he waggled his head, making him look a bit like one of his mop-headed dogs. "Ye ken that Victoria is Nick's second wife?"

"I was aware that his lordship was widowed some years ago."

"And ye ken that he and his first lady had a son?"

She blinked. "Royal has never mentioned that." Nor had anyone else, including Victoria, which was surprising.

"Aye, we don't talk about it much."

When Angus shifted restlessly in his chair, the dog scrambled up and put a head on her master's knee. Absently, the old man stroked her, more to comfort himself than the dog, Ainsley suspected.

"What happened?" she asked softly. "Was it an illness?"

"That would have been easier to bear."

"An accident, then."

"Cam was only four." He paused for a moment, as if seeking strength to continue. "He drowned in the stream, in that same spot ye were today. That's why Royal reacted so poorly. It's the memories, ye see. They still run strong for all of us."

Ainsley had to swallow a few times before she could answer. "I . . . that's horrible. I'm so sorry. For his lordship, for all of you."

"It all but killed puir Nick. His wife died a few years prior, ye ken, so little Cam was everything to him." He shook his head. "It almost killed the lot of us, to tell ye the truth."

The old man looked so quietly heartbroken she was tempted to wrap her arms around his scrawny shoulders. But that would only embarrass him, she suspected.

"Was Royal there when it happened?"

"All the lads were, except Nick. They were fishin', and

Cam slipped and fell into the water. By the time Logan got to him, it was too late."

Ainsley frowned. "But the water seems quite sluggish there."

"Now, but in the spring, it's a torrent that can drag ye down before ye have a chance to catch yer breath."

No wonder her husband had been so emphatic about her staying clear of the water. "Did Royal go in after the boy too?"

"Nae, not after Cam. He had to go in after Kade."

"Kade fell in too?" she asked, aghast.

"The boy tried to rescue Cam, but the water was too strong and he almost drowned too. Royal got to him in time, but it was a near thing."

She briefly pressed a hand to her eyes to hold back the tears. "Oh, God, I cannot imagine what a nightmare that was."

"Ye dinna want to, lass."

She lowered her hand. "I'm assuming the poor child's death had something to do with the estrangement between Lord Arnprior and Logan."

Angus nodded. "He blamed Logan for Cam's death. Nick would have killed him that day, so mad with grief he was. But Royal stopped him and convinced Logan to leave Kinglas for a spell, for Nick's sake."

Emotion gripped her throat. "It always comes down to Royal, doesn't it? He tries to save everyone, no matter the cost to himself."

Her husband was truly the most selfless, big-hearted person she'd ever met. What in God's name had she ever done to deserve the love of such a man?

"Aye," replied Angus. "He even followed Nick off to war to watch over him. Royal was afraid the laird would throw himself in front of a French bullet so he could be with his little boy again."

"But I doubt his lordship would ever do anything like that. He's so devoted to his family."

"That he is, but he was so torn up with grief back then. Royal insisted on joinin' the Black Watch, too, and then *he* was the one who caught a bullet for his troubles," Angus added bitterly. "Abandoned and left to die in a ditch, like a wounded animal. If Nick hadn't found him when he did—"

Angus clamped his mouth. Tina whined and nudged his hand with her wet nose.

"Abandoned?" Ainsley asked.

The old man's demeanor became rather brusque as he gave Tina a quick pat. "I've said too much. Ye'll nae be draggin' any more family secrets out of me, lassie."

"It's hardly a secret that Royal was wounded in battle," she said, frustrated. "And in case you've forgotten, *I'm* family now too."

He stubbornly shook his head. "Royal will nae thank me for tellin' war stories to his bride. He hates even talkin' about it, which ye ken very well. Makes him feel less of a man."

"That's ridiculous. I've never met a finer, stronger man."

"Don't tell me, tell him."

"I intend to, but that doesn't mean you can't finish the story."

"He'll tell ye himself in his own time. Ye just need to be patient."

"That is not one of my virtues, as you might have noticed," she said tartly. "And may I just state that your family has a ridiculous number of secrets. It's incredibly annoying."

Angus stuck his pipe between his lips. "What's the old saying ye *Sassenachs* like so much?" he mumbled around the stem. "Something about the pot callin' the kettle black."

She let out a grudging chuckle, even though her heart ached over the suffering of Royal and his family. It now made perfect sense that he'd be so alert to her various moods, that he'd be so patient with her. Royal recognized her pain because he was intimately acquainted with wrenching emotion himself.

"Point taken," she said. "But—"

The bedroom door opened and Taffy bustled forth with a bundle of clothing in her arms.

Ainsley jumped to her feet. "Is Royal feeling better? I'm sorry I missed the surgeon when I was upstairs with Tira."

The housekeeper's gaunt features eased into a smile. "Dinna fash yerself, my lady. Mr. Royal is resting more easily, though he's still in a bit of pain. Not that he'll complain about it, mind ye."

"Stoic, the lad is," said Angus. "Never wants to cause a fuss."

"Unlike some people in this household," Taffy said, narrowing her gaze on the old man.

The housekeeper, who'd been with the family for decades, was the only person at Kinglas who could boss Angus with any success. Ainsley had her own theories about why that was so, and had quizzed Royal during her first stay at Kinglas. Looking vaguely appalled, he had abruptly replied that it was best to leave some questions unexplored. His answer had confirmed her suspicions.

It was really rather sweet when one didn't think about it too much.

"Ye canna be talkin' about me," Angus protested. "I'm as meek and mild as a pudding sleeve in a pulpit."

"I have no idea what that means," Ainsley said, "but I suspect it's not true."

"It means a parson," Taffy explained. "And we'll no be mistakin' Mr. MacDonald for one of them."

"Quite the opposite, I would think," Ainsley said.

Taffy let out a little snort, and Angus bristled. "Now see here, *Sassenach*—"

Ainsley held up a quick hand. "I'm teasing, my dear sir. And since I'm just as responsible for Royal's predicament, Taffy may as well scold me, too. We've both been perfectly dreadful. I'm astonished my husband didn't toss us out the window days ago."

"Mr. Royal loves ye both," Taffy said, "so there's no need to be fightin' for his attention."

Ainsley scrunched her face in acknowledgment of that truth. "I suppose that's exactly what we've been doing. Goodness, we're worse than Tira."

Angus shot Taffy a scowl. "I dinna need ye to tell me the lad loves us."

"Then stop kickin' up a fuss and help the puir man."

"That's why I came back to Kinglas in the first place, ye daft woman. To help with Tira."

"Oh, is that what ye call it?"

As entertaining as it was to watch Angus get his well-earned comeuppance, Ainsley was increasingly impatient to see her husband. "You've been a *great* help, Angus, and if you could check on Tira right now, that would be lovely. I'll go in and see Royal."

"But I thought I'd go see the lad now," Angus said. "He'll no be easy until he sees me, I ken."

Taffy shook her head. "Mr. Royal needs a rest, not visitors."

"I'm no visitor. I'm his bloody grandfather."

The housekeeper responded by dumping the pile of clothes into the old man's arms. "Ye'll oblige me by taking Mr. Royal's dirty things down to the laundry. He landed in a mud puddle when he tumbled off that great beast of his."

"Do you think I might be able to go in?" Ainsley asked. "I promise I won't stay long."

Taffy smiled at her. "Of course, my lady. I ken he'll be happy to see *ye.*"

"Why does *she* get to see the lad and I don't?" Angus demanded.

Taffy rolled her eyes. "Because she's his wife, ye daft old man. Now please be off with those things and take that scruffy dog with ye. I won't have her muckin' up my clean floors."

"It wouldna make a difference if I did mind," Angus grumbled.

"Angus, I'll come find you and tell you how Royal is, if you check on Tira," Ainsley said.

The old man gave her a tentative smile. "I'd appreciate that, lass."

"You have my word."

He clicked his tongue at his dog and headed off down the hall. Ainsley turned back to find Taffy shrewdly regarding her.

"What?" she asked.

"Have ye made yer peace with each other, then?"

Ainsley waggled a hand. "More like a truce for Royal's sake, I imagine."

"Mr. MacDonald is an old fool, but he means well, ye ken. And he'd do anything for Mr. Royal. We all would."

"As would I."

Taffy studied her a bit too long before nodding. "As ye say, my lady. Now, Brody is just makin' Mr. Royal more comfortable. But the poor man is a bit . . ."

"Grumpy?"

"He's always such when his leg troubles him. He hates to give in to it."

"I promise not to fash him."

Taffy flashed a brief smile. "And ye'll no be keepin' him up too late?"

"I promise."

After bobbing a quick curtsy, the housekeeper went off down the corridor. Ainsley slowly walked to the bedroom door. For some silly reason, her heart was thudding like a hammer against her ribs.

It's because you love him, you nitwit.

That simple revelation made her vulnerable, which was not a feeling she much enjoyed.

Taking a deep breath for courage, she knocked on her husband's door.

Chapter Eighteen

The door swung open to reveal the castle's stable master. Brody's sharply arched eyebrows always gave him a vaguely astonished appearance, and now they twitched even higher. He cast a wary look over his shoulder in response to Ainsley's intrusion into the male sanctum.

"Who is it, Brody?" came her husband's gruff voice from inside the room.

"It's yer lady, sir. Do ye wish to see her?"

"Of course he wishes to see me." Ainsley ignored Royal's low-pitched curse as she pushed by Brody and marched in. "I am Mr. Royal's beloved wife, after all."

Sighing, the stable master closed the door and followed her.

She stopped several feet from the bed to dart a quick glance around. Since this was the first time she'd ever been in her husband's bedroom—a marital oversight of epic proportions—she felt curious and slightly awkward.

The wing housing the family bedrooms, built during the Restoration, displayed that era's taste for ornate decoration. The paneled walls were beautifully carved, and there was a truly gorgeous mantel topping the old stone fireplace. What furniture there was—Royal seemed to prefer a more austere style—came from a later period. Joining the sturdy oak chest and a battered press cupboard were a plain leather armchair with a matching footstool and small bedside table with a lamp. It was spare and to the point, like the man himself.

The only exception was the enormous, old-fashioned bed in the French style. Its four posts were beautifully scrolled and polished to a high gleam. They reached almost to the ceiling, supporting a massive wooden canopy that featured elaborate carvings of crowns and stags. From the beautiful old wood hung gold and burgundy drapes that matched the coverlet on a mattress wide enough to house half of Marie Antoinette's court.

It was ridiculously grand, and not at all the sort of bed one would imagine for a brusque, scowling ex-soldier with not the least bit of patience for frills and furbelows, much less lounging about. Somehow, though, Royal's dark, masculine good looks and his hard-edged arrogance seemed perfectly suited to a setting that harkened back to the dramatic glories of days gone by. There was a sense about her husband that he belonged in a time mistily shrouded in tales of romance and adventure, a time when a man fought to defend his lady and his land, and to uphold the honor of his clan.

"I'm not really in the mood for visitors, Ainsley," he said. "In fact, I'm not in the mood to see anyone for a good long time."

Ainsley pointed to the simple gold band on her ring finger. "This says otherwise. I'm not a visitor, I'm your better half."

Apologizing again would only prompt another display of temper and surely lead to her losing her temper as well. She needed to prove that, all evidence to the contrary, she was a mature woman, perfectly capable of taking care of her husband, her daughter, and his annoying old grandfather if necessary.

"That's debatable," Royal muttered.

Ainsley cupped a hand to her ear. "I'm sorry, what was that?"

"I said you shouldn't be in here. I'm not properly dressed."

She pressed a dramatic hand to her bosom. "Yes, and I'm not sure my delicate sensibilities can withstand the shock of seeing you attired in your nightshirt. Brody, would you toddle off next door and ask my maid to fetch my smelling salts? If I faint, Mr. Royal is in no condition to catch me. As he so delicately pointed out this afternoon, I'm *rather* a big girl."

"I did not say that," Royal indignantly replied.

"Still, it's best to be prepared, don't you think?" She heaved a gusty sigh. "Run along now, Brody. I don't know how much longer I can hang on."

"Ah . . . mayhap ye best sit down?" Brody said, looking alarmed.

"Good God, man. She's pulling your leg," Royal scoffed.

The stable master mustered a weak smile. "Sorry, my lady."

"No apology necessary, I assure you. People often mistake my intention." She gave Royal her sweetest smile. "My dear husband suffers from the same unfortunate inability to understand me. It's quite tragic, although a common affliction of the married state, I'm told."

The dear husband rolled his eyes. "Maybe it's because you don't make your intentions clear."

She pretended to consider that, and then shook her head. "No, it's certainly you."

"Brody, I feel in need of liquid courage," Royal said. "Please fetch me a glass and the bottle from my dresser, and then you can go. Apparently, my *dear wife* has come to nurse me."

"I'm happy to do whatever I can, of course," she said. "Although I hear that Brody has done a bang-up job."

The stable master cut her an uncertain look as he went to fetch the requested items.

"I'm actually serious this time, Brody," Ainsley said. "Taffy told me that you did a splendid job fixing Mr. Royal's leg."

Brody flashed her a shy smile. "Thank ye, my lady. I've got a wee bit of experience, since I've been patching up Kendricks for many a year."

"And much better than that old sawbones," Royal grumbled. "All he did was maul me about."

"Nae, sir, Mr. Dillon is a fine surgeon," Brody said. "I ken he's got the measure of that leg of yers."

"I'm glad someone does," Royal said.

Ainsley wandered closer to the bed. "Is it very bad?"

He hesitated.

"The truth, please," she coaxed.

"If you insist on knowing the truth, it hurts like the devil."

"Royal, I don't want you hiding how you feel from me. I'm your wife, and I have a right to know what troubles you." For good measure, she wagged a finger at him.

His mouth twitched.

Ah. Finally, a glimpse of sunshine.

"Yes, my lady," he said.

When Brody carried over a tray holding the requested decanter and glass, Ainsley took it and placed it on the bedside table, shifting the oil lamp to make room. The fading dusk threw shadows under the canopy and deepened the hollows of Royal's cheekbones. Her heart clenched at the weariness and pain hazing his green eyes.

"Are you finished with your ministrations?" she asked Brody.

"Aye, my lady, although Mr. Royal could use a wee bit more liniment massaged into his leg. Helps to keep it from seizing up."

Ainsley nodded at the small bottle on the table. "Is that it?"

"Aye."

"Very well. I'll take care of that."

For a few moments, both men sported similarly incredulous expressions. Then Royal's mouth flattened into a disapproving line. "You'll do no such thing."

"I'm perfectly capable of putting liniment on an injury, Royal."

"Not this injury."

Ainsley turned her back on him. "That will be all, Brody. I'll ring if we need help."

The older man's smile was wry. "Ye'll do just fine. Have Taffy fetch me if ye need anything else."

"Brody, I don't want Lady Ainsley—"

"I'll be checkin' on ye later, sir. Good night, my lady." With a respectful nod, Brody quickly retreated from the field.

Clearly taken aback by his henchman's refusal to cooperate, Royal muttered under his breath. He stretched out a long arm past Ainsley and grabbed the decanter. After splashing a generous measure into the cut crystal glass, he tossed it back in one swallow.

Without flinching, which made her wince.

"Does that actually help?" she asked.

When he splashed another measure into the glass, she had to swallow a protest. The poor man was in pain and didn't need a scold. Likely, he'd haul himself off the bed and toss her from the room, injury or no. Ainsley sensed that today's unfortunate events had finally breached his self-control, bringing his impressive willpower crashing down. Her husband was dangerously on edge.

Though she could never be afraid of him, triggering another verbal outburst would not benefit either his health or their marriage.

"It certainly doesn't hurt," he said, tossing back his drink.

She glanced at a small medicinal bottle next to the liniment. "Are those laudanum drops? Might they not be more effective for the pain?"

"Undoubtedly, but they also make my head feel like wet wool."

"Whisky obviously doesn't have the same effect."

The only time she'd ever drunk too much whisky was the night before she'd asked Royal to marry her. She'd awakened the next morning with an aching head and a stomach as sour as an old lemon. It had taken three cups of strong coffee before she'd been able to think again.

"Not like the drops," he said. "If you'd ever taken them, you'd know exactly what I mean."

"I have taken them."

A quick frown of concern replaced his surly expression. "Why?"

Her skin crawled at the thought of even mentioning that awful time. But she'd just told him she wanted nothing but honesty from him. Could she offer him anything less in return?

"After Cringlewood assaulted me, I had trouble sleeping. I thought it would help."

He sucked in a breath. Several seconds elapsed before he replied. "Did it?"

"I think a brain that feels like wet wool is a very apt description."

True, the drops had made her sleep, but they'd also given her nightmares. And while awake, she'd felt apart from herself in a dreadful, detached sort of way.

"I felt like I couldn't think, or make any decisions," she added. "And I needed to think."

Royal reached over and briefly squeezed her hand. "I'm sorry, Ainsley. I didn't mean to bring up bad memories."

She shrugged. "But they're always lurking, aren't they? I'm not sure it makes sense to pretend otherwise."

"Still, I shouldn't have snapped—"

"Oh, do stop apologizing," she said, echoing his words from earlier in the day. "I'm the one who's at fault here. My idiotic tantrum compelled you to come dashing to my rescue."

He scratched his bristled chin. "It wasn't much of a rescue."

She had to repress a smile. "Sadly true. I was forced to rescue *you*, which must have been quite the blow to your masculine ego."

He narrowed his eyes in warning.

Consistent with her fatal tendency to ignore warnings, Ainsley flashed him a little smirk. "Especially with you being a war hero and whatnot. You have a reputation to uphold."

His laugh was grudging. "Especially the whatnot."

"I don't see why men should get to do all the rescuing, anyway. It's not fair, when you think about it."

"Nonsense. It's our job to rescue children, puppies, and damsels in distress, especially from fire-breathing dragons or marauding pirates. Didn't anyone ever teach you that?"

"I must have missed that lesson." She propped her hands on her hips. "But do I really look like a damsel in distress?"

"At the moment, you look rather like a hectoring wife."

"And you, sir, look like a bad-tempered husband."

When she kicked off her shoes and started to clamber up on the high mattress, Royal went as stiff as a hitching post. Then he snatched the coverlet and sheets up under his arms, as if to safeguard his virtue.

"Ainsley, what the hell are you doing?"

"I should think it obvious even to a man all but insensible from drink."

"I've barely had a drop!"

She sat tailor-style next to his legs, trying not to jostle him. The bed was so wide that she could choose to put considerable space between them, but she had an almost desperate need to be close. More than anything, she wanted to snuggle up and kiss the grumps from his stern mouth.

Sadly, he seemed disinclined to accept her affection. In fact, he was all but glowering at her.

"I'm not going to have my way with you, if that's what you're worried about," she said. "So you needn't bristle like your outraged maiden aunt."

"I don't have a maiden aunt."

She tapped her forehead. "I will file that for future reference."

He sighed. "Ainsley, you should not be in here, much less sitting on my bed. It's not proper."

"Royal, I'm your lawfully wedded wife. It's quite shocking that I hadn't yet seen your room until now." She glanced up at the expansive canopy with its elegant draperies. "And this bed is perfectly splendid. It does give a girl some interesting ideas, if you know what I mean."

A surprising flush bronzed his cheekbones. Although she was simply trying to tease him into a better mood, she had to admit he looked altogether enticing with his broad shoulders showcased by the fine linen nightshirt, and a nice sliver of chest exposed by the gap of his collar. She'd never really seen a man's naked torso before, and her fingers itched to play with the dark hair that dusted his brawny muscles.

Still, she had no intention of throwing herself at him, knowing her nerves would likely get the better of her. The idea of cuddling with him, however, was enormously appealing. She suspected they both needed comforting—if only he was willing to receive as well as give.

Her husband cleared his throat. "I suggest you get those ideas right out of your head. I'm in no condition for any sort of . . ." He paused. "I'm not sure what you're proposing, come to think of it."

"I'm only trying to tease you out of the sullens, my dear sir. You've had an exceedingly trying day, and I'm truly sorry for that."

"I thought no more apologies?"

"There's no need for you to apologize to me, certainly. You've been an absolute saint since the day I reappeared on the doorstep of Kendrick House. But I do wish you would let me abase myself at your feet, especially now that I'm sitting right next to them. I've been an awful pill, Royal. How you continue to bear me is the question."

His gaze warmed. "It's not your fault, love. You've been under a great deal of strain."

She waggled a hand. "The strain is partly my fault. Angus is responsible for the other part."

"I suspect he wouldn't agree."

"You'd be wrong about that. Your grandfather and I had a little chat, and we owned up to responsibility for our bad behavior."

Royal's eyebrows shot up. "You did?"

She nodded.

He settled back onto the plump cushions propped behind him. "Did you get him drunk first?"

"Believe it or not, we simply talked. In fact, we had barely insulted each other even after twenty minutes of conversation."

"Amazing. I hope I won't have to keep falling off my horse to enforce the truce."

Ainsley laughed. "I will certainly keep you apprised. But I do think Angus and I have come to an understanding."

He looked dubious. "So, what did you two talk about, aside from mutual guilt?"

"You."

"As I feared," he said, reaching for his glass. "I hope he didn't tell you any outlandish stories."

"That's for next time."

"Something to look forward to, then."

She ignored his sarcasm and rested her hand on his blanket-swaddled foot. How did one even approach such a terrible subject? But it had to be done if they were ever to have the marriage she longed for. Royal needed to know she truly wished to ease the pain that plagued him, both in body and mind.

"What is it, Ainsley?" he quietly asked.

"Angus told me about your little nephew."

Even through the layers of bedclothes, she felt his body go tense.

"If I'd known, I never would have chosen that spot." She gently rubbed his foot, trying to convey her sadness for him.

Royal's strong features fell into brooding lines. "I've been by that place a hundred times since it happened. I won't say it's not still painful, but it was stupid of me to overreact the way I did."

"Of course, it will always hold tragic memories for you. Then to see me sprawled in the grass, it's no wonder you thought the worst."

"You weren't sprawled. You were flat on your back, straight as a board with your hands tucked up under your chin." He gave his head a little shake, as if trying to clear the painful memory. "In fact, you looked like a . . ."

"A corpse? I'm sure, because I tend to sleep like that. It can be very disconcerting for hapless bystanders. There was a maid in my father's household who refused to come into my room to light the fire in the morning. She said I gave her the frights." She tapped his foot. "So, forewarned is forearmed, husband."

He gave her a faint smile. "Thank you, wife."

For a few charged seconds, they held each other's gazes. Then Ainsley looked away, her newly discovered feelings making her shy. She wanted to tell him but lacked the courage to face it head on, at least for now.

Besides, he probably wouldn't believe her. *Hello, I've just discovered that I'm madly in love with you.* It sounded ridiculous, even to her ears.

"What did Angus tell you about Cam?" Royal finally asked.

She met his somber gaze. "He told me what happened at the river that day, and how it tore your family apart. He also said you saved Kade, and that you, more than anyone, helped Lord Arnprior and the family through that terrible period."

He waved an irritated hand. "I'm no hero, Ainsley. We were all just hanging on by our fingernails."

"Angus certainly seems to think you're a hero."

"Och, he's a silly old man." His brogue was low and rough.

"He's a silly old man who loves you and is worried about you. I hope you'll let him apologize tomorrow. He was quite downcast when you wouldn't let him in the room."

"He gets fashed whenever my leg is bothering me. It's not good for him."

"Do you know what I think?"

"I'm sure I will momentarily."

"Behave, Royal Kendrick, or you'll be sorry." She jabbed his good leg. "What I think is that you don't like people fussing over you. It doesn't fit with your image as a mighty Highlander who can wrestle a wild boar to the ground and hold off a ruthless band of brigands, all whilst playing the bagpipes."

"That's ridiculous. I never learned to play the bagpipes."

"Don't try to distract me with humor. You hate it when people try to help you. Admit it."

"I admit nothing," he said firmly. "What other whiskers did Angus tell you about me?"

"He told me a little bit about Waterloo." She went back to gently rubbing his foot. "He said you'd been abandoned on the battlefield. I'm not entirely sure what he meant by that, but it sounded absolutely horrific."

Her husband growled. "I am going to throttle that old man as soon as I'm out of this bed."

"Why shouldn't he tell me what happened? I'm your wife."

"In name only," came the terse reply.

She had to swallow a few times before she could answer. "That was not very nice, you know."

He grimaced as he rubbed a hand over his face. "Sorry, lass. I'm a thorough brute. You're my wife in every way that matters, and I'm that proud to be your husband."

His obvious sincerity eased the tight feeling in her chest. "Then why won't you tell me what happened at Waterloo?"

"It's not fit for a woman like you to hear."

She crossed her arms over her chest. "You think I'm too sheltered? Well, I'm not."

Not anymore.

"It's not fit for *any* woman to hear. It's too ugly."

"I've lived through ugly, Royal. It no longer frightens me."

"I know you have. But war is a different kind of hell, and I don't want you touched by it. You've been through enough, love. You shouldn't have to carry that burden, too."

"But—"

"Angus should have held his tongue."

"He didn't tell me very much. He said it was your story to share."

He mirrored her posture by crossing his arms over his chest. For a moment, she was distracted by the widening gap of his nightshirt, exposing more of his impressive chest.

"That's right," he said. "*My* story."

"To *share*. With your *wife*."

His gorgeous green eyes flickered with irritation, but she held her ground—or her piece of the mattress, so to speak.

"It would be good for you to talk about it," she said.

"Why?"

She searched for the right words. His wartime experiences were so much a part of who he was, and yet he refused to talk about them. She understood why, but the cost of carrying so much pain, all alone, was a heavy one.

"For months, no one but my mother and then Aunt Margaret knew I'd been assaulted," she said. "My mother certainly didn't wish to talk about it, and my aunt would grow too distressed. So I had to lug it around inside, like a great, iron chain that grew heavier by the day. So heavy that I could hardly bear it."

He made a distressed sound deep in his throat and reached for her.

Ainsley held him off, needing to finish. "When I came back to Glasgow and was finally able to talk to you and Victoria about it . . . well, the chain began to unravel, link by link, and I felt like I could breathe again. I didn't have to carry the weight of that horrible truth alone anymore."

He took the hand she'd clenched over her breastbone and pried it open. When he leaned over and kissed the middle of her palm, Ainsley had to blink back sudden tears.

"I'm so glad you told me, love," he said gruffly. "But you don't have to worry about me. I can breathe just fine, thanks to you and Tira."

"Maybe, but you still carry a very grim burden from the war. I can see it, and your family can certainly see it too. That's why they worry, especially when you withdraw from them. It's almost like you don't want them to come near you."

Abruptly, Royal leaned back into the pillows, adopting

the sardonic expression he wore like a suit of armor. It clearly said *do not trespass*.

"What nonsense," he said. "You make me sound like a caricature of an inane poet, shutting myself in my room to pen gloomy poems and drink myself into oblivion. In case you haven't noticed, I'm much too busy working and taking care of my family for that sort of idiotic behavior."

He finished his little speech by grasping the whisky bottle. But Ainsley plucked it out of his hand and put it back on the nightstand.

"I'm sure that's all true," she said, "but look what happened today. You're positively beating yourself up because you think you somehow failed me."

"Because I *did* fail you," he growled.

"That's a demented way to think, and it's the product of the shame you seem to feel about your injury."

He flinched but quickly recovered. "I have no idea what you're talking about."

She barely refrained from rolling her eyes. "You think what happened to you makes you weak, like you are not a whole man because of it. You can't bear to ask for help because you believe people—including your family—will think less of you. That *I* will think less of you."

His gaze darted off, narrowing on the fire. He studied it with a ferocity that conveyed an inner battle raging in his soul. She could only pray it would tip in her favor.

The seconds passed, marked by the quiet tick of the mantel clock and the hiss of coals in the grate. Dismay hollowed her stomach at the lengthening silence and the shuttered expression on his face. She'd pushed Royal, wanting him to open up and share the hidden parts of his life, as she'd shared her deepest secrets with him. But perhaps some wounds ran too bloody and deep for that.

And perhaps some words, no matter how honest or true, were too bitter and ugly to ever be said.

"Royal, I'm—"

"I was left for dead on the battlefield for hours," he interrupted in an oddly flat voice. "Overnight, in fact. A soldier rolled me into a ditch and left me there."

Her stomach lurched into her throat.

Maybe he's right. Maybe I'm not strong enough to hear this.

But she had to be strong for him. For them both. "They didn't check to see if you were alive?"

He gave a credibly nonchalant shrug. "It was utter chaos when I went down. I'd been lucky until then. My arm had been winged in the mess at Quatre Bras a few days before, but I was still relatively untouched. After we marched to Waterloo and took up our position, we faced heavy artillery fire and direct attacks from the French troops. I was wounded during one of those later cavalry attacks."

"How did it happen?" she softly asked.

"I caught a lance in the thigh." His mouth twisted in a travesty of a smile. "Didn't even see the French lancer coming at me. I was caught outside the square, you see, hacking and slashing away like an idiot. Fighting like the wild Highlander that I was, as you would say."

Her heart ached for him. "I'm sure you were simply trying to survive in desperate circumstances."

His nod was somber. "You have the right of it, lass. It was carnage. We were all just trying to stay alive, including the French."

"But how could your men just leave you there, wounded like that? You weren't unconscious, were you?"

"Not at that point, no. A British infantryman shot the soldier who lanced me, and then pulled me back into the square. A couple of fellows tried to get me to the back of

the line, but we were overrun by a regiment of Cuirassiers."
He grimaced. "And when I say overrun, I mean overrun."

"By horses?" she asked, horrified.

"Yes. One trampled my wounded thigh. What were the
odds of that?"

Words utterly failed her. Her imagination failed her too,
mostly because she couldn't bear the thought of him in such
horrific straits. For several terrifying moments, Ainsley
couldn't catch her breath.

"Sweetheart," Royal said, gently cupping her cheek. "It's
all right. I'm here, and I'm well."

"I know. I . . . it's just that I'm so terribly sorry you had
to endure such a horror."

"Are you sure you wish to hear the rest?"

She stiffened her spine, mentally and physically. "If you
could live through it, then I can certainly hear about it."

He nodded and withdrew his hand. She missed his
warmth, but sensed that he needed to retreat a bit to finish
the tale.

"Needless to say, the pain from the encounter with that
bloody big horse put me right out. When I awoke, I found
myself halfway under a hedge, with no idea how I'd gotten
there. My regiment was well gone, taking part in the final
advance against the French army, as I later learned. I managed to crawl a few feet, but all I could see were dead
bodies, both horses and men. And I was so weak at that point
I could scarcely move. Night was falling and I had no idea
which direction to go in, anyway."

Ainsley swallowed against a sudden rush of tears. "You
must have felt so terribly alone there in the dark." After her
assault, she *hated* being alone in the dark.

"I wasn't alone for long," he said dryly. "Nightfall was
when the scavengers came out."

"You mean people who rob the bodies of dead soldiers?"

"It's a time-honored tradition amongst soldiers of both sides, unfortunately."

Anger seared like a hot poker in her chest. She wanted to kill anyone who'd hurt Royal—or would ever try to hurt him again.

"And you were obviously robbed," she said.

Royal nodded. "The man thought I was dead, so he was quite surprised when I grabbed hold of his coat and asked for water."

"Did he give you any?"

"Hardly. He coshed me on the head, riffled my pockets, and then rolled me into a ditch."

When she gaped at him, too sickened to muster even a sympathetic word, he shrugged again, as if it didn't matter.

"I . . . I don't know what to say," Ainsley finally stammered.

"There's nothing to say, love. It's war. That's what men do."

"Awful men. But not you," she protested. "Or Lord Arnprior. Neither you nor any of your brothers would act like that."

"I hope not. But war is a desperate, dirty business. It brings out the best and the worst in men, and you never know for certain what you're capable of until the moment is upon you. You never know if you're going to survive. That's the worst part. The not knowing."

She grabbed his hand, desperate for his touch. "But you *did* survive."

"Thanks to Nick. He defied orders and spent the whole night searching for me. He finally found me in that damned ditch, half-drowned and nearly dead. And I was in bad shape for weeks after that." He shook his head. "Sometimes I wonder how—or even why—I survived when so many didn't. There's no making sense of it."

She lurched up onto her knees and crawled to the head of the bed.

Royal peered at her with a concerned frown. "Ainsley?"

She grabbed him by the shoulders and shook him. "You survived for me, you stupid man, for me and for Tira. And don't you ever, *ever* forget it."

And then, too upset to care that she hated to cry, Ainsley collapsed into his arms and burst into tears.

Chapter Nineteen

Royal cradled his wife as she sobbed in his arms. Desperately, he rummaged through his brain for the words that might console her. He'd never seen Ainsley cry with such abandon, not even when she'd given up Tira that fateful day in Cairndow. Her courage back then had filled him with awe. But if she'd cried then as she was crying now, he would not have been able to turn his back and walk away from her.

He never should have abandoned her, no matter how right the decision had seemed at the time. But the past was a country they could never revisit. Now, they could only go forward. Despite their shared legacy of pain, they could try to create a better life, a good life as husband and wife.

Nothing and no one would ever take Ainsley away from him again.

He stroked her silky black hair, breathing in the faint scents of lavender and mint that drifted up like a whisper of magic. "Hush, love. You mustn't cry so, or you'll make yourself ill."

She half sobbed something into his nightshirt, her body plastered against him. Ainsley was a delicious armful and he was aware of every bit of it, especially the lush breasts that pressed into him when she gulped in air. His leg was killing him, he'd just told her about the worst day of his life, and she was a distraught mess in his arms, yet he still wanted to tip the lass onto her back and kiss her until she trembled for other reasons besides grief.

Get your mind out of the gutter, you idiot.

Ainsley needed comforting now, not a husband slaking his lust, even though that lust had grown to monumental proportions.

He focused on her muffled words. "What did you say, sweetheart? I couldn't hear you."

She was trying hard to contain herself, swallowing her broken sobs. Royal stroked a hand down her back, simply waiting for her to settle.

After a minute or so, she flattened her hands on his chest and pushed into a sitting position. The blue lace ribbon of her formerly impeccable coiffure had come undone, sending most of her hair down in a bedraggled tumble. Her cheeks were flushed, her eyes were swollen, and her nose had turned a rather bright shade of pink. She'd be utterly appalled if she caught a glimpse of herself, thanks to her fierce need to control how others saw her.

To Royal, Ainsley had never looked more beautiful. Every emotion shimmered right on the surface, raw, honest, and vulnerable. She was not a woman who liked being vulnerable, so the fact that she could be that way with him felt like a precious gift.

She pushed her hair out of her eyes and swiped a sleeve across her nose as she gave a hearty sniff. Royal found her lack of self-consciousness utterly charming.

"I said, I never get sick," she replied in a husky voice. "You're the one who's sick, and here I am acting like a hysterical female. I am utterly mortified by it. You should just shoot me and put us both out of our misery."

He snagged a soft cloth from the bedside table and gently

dried her damp cheeks. "You've nothing to be ashamed of, Ainsley. It's an ugly tale. It was wrong of me to tell you."

She suffered his ministrations, even though he could tell she wanted to take the cloth and dry her cheeks herself. Ainsley was a stubborn, independent lass and he loved her all the more for it.

"I asked you to tell me, as you might recall," she said. "In fact, I insisted on it."

"That's no excuse. You've suffered enough in your life. You don't need to hear my gruesome old war stories."

"Yes, I do," she said, giving his shoulder a little shove. "And I'm glad you told me. Since you know everything horrible that's happened to me, it's only fair that I know everything miserable that's befallen you."

"Ainsley, I don't want you touched by that sort of horror. It's my job to protect you from such things, not expose you to them."

Irritation sparkled off the damp tips of her eyelashes. "Royal, I want your help and support, but you don't have to tiptoe around me like I'm some frail miss who could shatter at the first sign of trouble. I'm perfectly c . . . capable of taking care of myself."

He smiled at her little hiccup. "That is most apparent and undeniable."

"Although you are certainly free to spoil me, on occasion. I haven't been spoiled in some time, and I think I'm due for it."

"I would be happy to spoil you and take care of you. But, alas, today illustrated all too clearly that I've been mucking that up. In fact, I clearly need *you* to take care of *me*."

That won him a reluctant smile. "What a shocking reversal of the natural order."

"So shocking that I may find myself going into a complete decline. Then who would spoil you?"

Her smile faded. Perhaps she was remembering how very

sick he was when they first met. His declining health had been no joke then.

"I know how difficult it was for you to tell me about what happened to you," she said. "I'm dreadfully sorry I fell apart. I promise I won't do so again."

"I thought we both agreed that you needn't keep apologizing to me?"

"Only if you stop blaming yourself for failing me. Or failing at anything, for that matter." She again poked him in the shoulder, but more gently this time. "You are never to think of yourself as anything but strong, Royal Kendrick. For you to have survived all those horrors and to still be the man you are . . . well, you quite put me to shame. Honestly, I'm a selfish lout compared to you."

He smoothed her bedraggled curls away from her face. "You were the one who saved me, don't forget."

She frowned. "Your brother saved you."

"Yes, Nick pulled me out of that ditch and kept me alive. Mostly from sheer stubbornness—and by threatening every physician in the army if they gave up on me."

"That sounds like your brother."

He took her hand, lacing their fingers together. "But you saved me too, Ainsley. I was dying. And while my body fought back, trying to get strong again, my . . . spirit was withering. I just couldn't seem to get over what had happened on that battlefield. And I don't know how much longer I could have held on before I just gave up."

"I would *kill* the people who hurt you, if I could," she said fiercely. "They'd end up in that damn ditch with a bullet in their backs, if I had my way."

He bit back a smile at her threat. "Not necessary, love, because everything changed the moment I first saw you. I remembered what it was like to be alive again—truly alive."

Ainsley appeared almost stricken by his confession.

"Royal, have you forgotten how horrible I was to you? I was an absolute witch."

"I've not forgotten one moment. But even when it all went wrong, it didn't matter. I knew you were in the world. Because of that, life seemed worth living again."

She briefly pressed her hands to her eyes. "What an awful thing to say to me, you brute."

He laughed at her unexpected response. "Why?"

"Because you're going to make me cry again. I *hate* that. It's so messy and emotional. And my nose gets red, which I also hate."

"I'd say that messy and emotional just about sums up our relationship, doesn't it?"

She let out a watery laugh. "Very true. But I've never been responsible for someone else's life before. It's rather terrifying."

"Now you're responsible for two lives, mine and Tira's. I'm afraid you're stuck with us."

"You were both doing perfectly well without me. All I've done is complicate things."

He uncurled her fingers and rested her palm against his chest. "Any complication is a small price to pay for having you in our lives, I assure you."

She blushed. "I can scarcely believe that, but thank you."

When her warm fingers curled into the thin fabric of his nightshirt, his heart skipped a few beats. It took every ounce of willpower not to lean forward and tease a kiss from her luscious lips—her red nose notwithstanding. In fact, he was tempted to kiss that too, since it was so adorably vulnerable.

Kissing his wife was the last thing he should do, considering how emotional she was. He prayed that her gaze wouldn't drop down to his lap. If it did, she couldn't fail to see the erection that had pushed up the covers.

Bloody hell, man. Get control of yourself.

But his body refused to obey, and her gaze *did* wander down to his lap—and stuck there.

"Sorry about that," he said with a sigh.

She lifted an ironic eyebrow, even though her cheeks had turned a shade that matched her nose. "You must be feeling better."

"No, it's you. I could be three-quarters dead and I would probably still react the same way."

Their gazes locked and they both froze, as if trapped in amber. Her breath caught nervously in her throat, but he swore her violet gaze shimmered with longing. It was the most awkward and intensely arousing moment of Royal's life.

"You'd better go," he forced himself to say.

She jerked, as if coming out of a trance, and then glanced at the bedside table. "But I promised Brody I'd massage some liniment into your leg."

The image of Ainsley's slim hands rubbing his thigh almost undid him. If she didn't leave the room at once, he expected he'd explode. And *that* would be the final, humiliating end to an already trying day.

"That won't be necessary," he said.

She eyed him with a degree of uncertainty. "Brody seemed to think it was necessary."

"Brody is an old woman. I'll just have another whisky, and everything will be fine."

"You'll have no more whisky."

She scrambled sideways as he reached for the glass on the side table. Royal grabbed it, twisting to keep it out of her reach. His thigh muscles immediately went into spasm.

"Dammit," he gasped, almost dropping the glass.

"Now look what you've done." Ainsley snatched the crystal tumbler from his hand.

He was too busy trying not to pass out from the pain to

answer. Ainsley placed the glass out of his reach and pressed him back into the pillows.

"Lie back and catch your breath before you expire from your own stupidity," she said.

Despite her tart words, her hands were gentle as she brushed the damp hair off his forehead. She murmured soothing, nonsensical words under her breath—the same as she did for Tira when she thought no one was listening—while blotting the sweat from his face and neck with one of the small towels from the night table. When she started massaging his temples, his nausea began to fade.

After a minute or two, his eyes drifted closed. He sank into a velvety dark, lulled by the heat and gentle crackle of the fire. Her hands were better than whisky and better than any laudanum he'd ever forced himself to drink. If she kept it up, he just might be able to sleep.

"Better?" she whispered after a few minutes.

He pushed his head into her hand and murmured his approval.

"Good. Because I'm going to put some liniment on that leg right now."

Royal opened his eyes to see Ainsley hoisting her skirts and then caught a glimpse of her pretty ankles and calves as she scrambled up onto the bed. The tops of her breasts merrily jiggled over the confines of her bodice as she scooted over to him.

God, she was truly going to kill him.

"Hand me the bottle, will you?" she asked.

Royal found himself clutching the covers around his chest like an outraged maiden aunt. "No."

As she pulled the bedclothes away from his leg, wadding them to the side, she glanced up at him with a frown. "Are you worried I'll hurt you? I promise to be very careful."

"The only thing I'm worried about is how I'll control my reaction if you start touching me."

She briefly eyed his erection, once more tenting the sheets. "That thing? I suppose we'll just have to ignore it, won't we?"

"Easy for you to say."

"If I can pay it no mind, then I'm sure you can too," she said, sounding a bit like a stern schoolmistress.

Perversely, Royal found that image even more arousing.

"Besides," she added, "massaging in the liniment probably won't feel very nice, so I suspect that will take care of the problem."

He made one last effort. "The scar is gruesome."

"Royal, I am not hen-hearted," she scoffed. "Now give me the bottle."

When she held out an imperious hand, he sighed and handed it over.

She folded the sheet over twice, deftly obscuring his embarrassing erection. Of course, that also left him lying with only his nightshirt between them.

"Can you lift up the hem of your garment?" she murmured. "I don't want to hurt you."

He shifted as he reached down, wincing at the stab of pain. Carefully, he exposed his mangled thigh.

Her harsh intake of breath conveyed her shock at the appalling brute of a scar high up on his leg—one the width of a hand. The skin was puckered over the damaged muscle, white in some places and faded purple and red in others. The doctors had stitched and braced him as best they could, but the combination of the lance and the trampling had turned his leg into a horror. The bones had eventually knit, although not perfectly, and the flesh had pulled together into the ghastly scar. It had taken months, the wound opening twice in the process and resulting in even more stitches.

Finally, though, the muscles had bulked up and were

growing stronger every day. But it would never be less than a vile sight, and he couldn't help flushing with embarrassment under her gaze.

"This was a mistake," he said, reaching for the hem of the nightshirt.

Ainsley swatted his hand away. "Don't be an idiot. I had to see it sooner or later, didn't I? We will start sleeping together at some point."

"Ah . . ." he said, sounding exactly like an idiot.

"And since that is the case, let's take this opportunity to get used to each other. Practice, as it were."

Her gaze held a complex mix of emotions. He saw sadness there, along with more than a bit of nerves. But mostly he saw determination, a need to rise to whatever challenge this represented for her. And if she needed this, how could he say no?

He gave her a rueful grin, trying to lighten the moment. "When you put it like that, how can I possibly refuse?"

She flashed him a quick, relieved smile. "You know, you're really *much* smarter than people give you credit for."

He had to laugh outright.

But his amusement died when she uncorked the liniment bottle and carefully tipped the viscous liquid into her hand. "Ready?" she asked.

He nodded, unable to utter a word but nearly undone by the thought of her hands finally touching his body.

When she placed her soft hand on his thigh, tentatively rubbing the liniment into his skin, Royal swallowed a groan. He squeezed his eyelids together to shut out the sight of what she was doing to him. He *would* control himself. He'd die rather than frighten her, even though he all but shook with the need to drag her up to his mouth for a devouring kiss.

Thankfully, the burgeoning pain as she massaged the tight thigh muscles did enforce a necessary discipline. Sweat prickled along his hairline as she worked to ease the spasm.

"Are you all right?" she asked.

He gave a terse nod without opening his eyes.

For the next few minutes, he was caught between heaven and hell. As the liniment heated under her surprisingly assured touch, odors of cloves and menthol teased his nostrils, and his skin began to tingle with the familiar warmth of Brody's potion. As she worked his thigh with increasingly firm strokes, the spasm finally began to ease, and he relaxed into the pillows.

"Better?" she quietly asked. "Shall I continue?"

He dragged open his eyelids. She regarded him earnestly, her complexion flushed from her efforts. The light from the bedside table cast a warm glow on her creamy breasts. Kneeling as she was and leaning slightly forward, her position allowed him to see straight down to the shadowy edge of her nipples, a dusky tease that he felt deep in his groin.

She was so lovely it all but stopped his heart.

"You don't have to," he gritted out.

Her tiny snort was both feminine and knowing. "Close your eyes, Royal. Just relax."

He *should* tell her to go, especially for her sake. But when she started up again, her long, sensual strokes pulled a moan from his lips even as his eyelids shuttered once more.

With every touch of her fingers, desire added fuel to the fire in his belly. Her touch soothed yet tortured, one moment lulling him to sleep, the next stoking his lust. It was the most delicious, frustrating experience of his entire life, and all she was doing was massaging his damn leg.

The leg that had not felt so good in a very long time. His wife was a bloody miracle worker.

When her hand suddenly slipped down to the inside of his thigh, tantalizing close to his straining cock, his eyes shot open.

"Ainsley, what the hell are you doing?"

Their gazes locked. Royal suspected his eyes were bugging

out of his skull, but hers had turned a dark, velvety blue, slumberous and enticing.

"I'm touching you," she said, rather breathless. "And I think I'm going to kiss you, too."

Too stunned to respond, he simply stared at his beautiful wife as she planted her hands on his shoulders and proceeded to do just that.

Royal's brawny shoulders stiffened under her fingertips as she pressed a trembling kiss to his lips. She caught the faint tang of whisky and felt the stern set to his wonderful mouth. When that mouth held its unwavering line, Ainsley's heart pounded like Thor's hammer.

Had she misread him?

His body's reaction, barely concealed by the sheets, suggested she hadn't. But what did she truly know about a man's wants and needs? Perhaps it was an unexpected physical reaction he couldn't control. Perhaps he was just as stunned by what was happening between them as she was.

Or her bizarre timing could be putting him off. She was supposed to be nursing the poor man, not seducing him. Given his level of pain, it was a miracle he could even have a sensible conversation, much less return her clumsy advances.

But with her husband stretched out under her hands, all her difficult, surging emotions had crested into an irresistible tide. Feeling that tough, masculine body respond to her touch, hearing the deep groan rumble quietly in his throat, she'd simply given in to the impulse she'd been fighting for so long.

Tentatively, she kissed first one corner of his mouth and then the other. Still, though, he refused to yield, stiff as a plank of oak beneath her. She obviously *had* made a mistake and had no idea how to get out of it other than to slink from the bed and scurry to her bedroom as fast as her weak knees could carry her.

Squeezing her eyes shut against a rush of shame, she started to retreat but didn't get very far. Royal's hand shot up to wrap around her neck, keeping her face only inches away from his. She reluctantly opened her eyes, fearing disapproval in his gaze.

His cheekbones were glazed with a dark flush, and his pupils were huge, making his eyes look more black than green.

"Sweetheart, exactly what is happening here?" he asked in a low, rough voice.

His breath, warm and whisky-scented, brushed her cheek with an invisible caress.

"I . . . I'm kissing you," she stammered. "Is that all right?"

"I don't know. Is it all right?"

"What does that mean?"

He reached up with his other hand to gently tap her nose. "It means I don't want you doing anything you're not comfortable with."

Heat rushed to her cheeks. "I must be very bad at this, because I do wish to kiss you, Royal. I'm sorry if I'm making a hash of things."

He ran a featherlight finger along the top of her upper lip, making her shiver with pleasure.

"Love, you're doing it perfectly," he said. "I can barely keep my hands off you."

She felt shaky with relief. "Then why are you?"

"Because I don't want you to do this because you feel sorry for me."

"Royal, is that truly what you think is happening here?"

He gave a casual shrug, as if it didn't matter. "You wouldn't be the first woman to bed me out of pity."

Ainsley had to repress the impulse to whack some sense

into him. "Are Highlanders always this dense? I am *not* doing this out of pity. And may I just add that I insist on being the only woman who sleeps with you from now on. If you have any notion of sneaking off to consort with a local barmaid or anyone else, you can simply forget it. I won't put up with it, Mr. Kendrick. I'd murder you first."

With a vague feeling of surprise, Ainsley realized that might not be an exaggeration.

His big hand gently cupped her head. "I have no intention of touching any woman but you, Mrs. Kendrick, not ever," he said in a smoky voice that made her muscles go weak.

It was a good thing she was already sitting on the bed.

She mustered a chippy tone. "Then what, pray heaven, is the problem? I wish to be with you, and you wish to be with me."

"Because I don't want to rush you, love. You've had a difficult day—"

"Rush me, by all means."

He tilted a skeptical brow, but his other hand moved to cuddle her waist. And she could feel the evidence of his impressive erection nudging her thigh.

Snuggling closer, she slipped her fingers into the gap of his nightshirt to caress his bare skin. His harsh intake of breath was immensely gratifying.

"What happened to you was horrible, and I won't pretend it didn't affect me," she said.

In fact, she'd almost burst into tears when she'd first seen his awful scar. But there was nothing weak or damaged about Royal Kendrick. He was a beautiful, hard warrior who'd overcome challenges that would have put most men in the grave.

"But your injury doesn't make me feel sorry for you. It's a part of who you are, Royal. And who you are is the best man I've ever known. You're my husband, and I want to be with you."

"That makes me exceedingly happy," he said in a gruff voice.

"Although it's sadly evident that I don't know what I'm doing when it comes to the marriage bed," she said ruefully. "I'd like very much to please you, though. Perhaps you could show me how."

His mouth curled into a smile so seductive that it made her insides quiver. "I'd be happy to. But first I'd like to please you."

"Oh? That sounds rather nice."

"So, let's start with kissing again, shall we?"

He took her hands and placed them around his neck. "But I want you to tell me if I'm going too fast," he added, "or if I'm doing something you don't like. I'll stop right away."

She nodded, too nervous to reply. They were *finally* going to be together as man and wife. It was wonderful and terrifying at the same time.

He bent his head so they were eye to eye. "Do you trust me, Ainsley?"

She snorted. "Of course, you booby. More than anyone in the world."

"Then everything will be just fine."

His expression was so tender and loving that her fluttering insides began to settle. Of course it would be all right. This was Royal. If she couldn't open herself to him, then she would remain forever closed off from her emotions, always afraid. She didn't want to be that woman anymore. She wanted to be free—free to both give and to accept love.

"Yes?" her husband said quietly.

"Yes." She stretched up to press her lips to his.

He cradled her close as he returned her kiss. The tips of her nipples rubbed against his chest, and heat coursed through her veins. Her stays suddenly felt so tight.

Embarrassed by her body's reaction, she repressed the shocking urge to wriggle against him.

Royal's chuckle vibrated against her lips.

Ainsley pulled back. "What's so funny?"

"You." His heavy-lidded eyes gleamed with sensual heat. "You're allowed to move. In fact, I would encourage it."

She sighed. "I told you I wasn't very good at this."

"My darling, you are splendid. Besides, we're just practicing, remember? We're finding out what feels good."

When he gently turned her head and kissed the most sensitive part of her neck, Ainsley shivered.

"And what feels even better," he whispered, working his way across to her mouth.

Feeling quite a bit better, she shifted closer, almost toppling into his lap.

Royal slipped an arm around her shoulders. "You need to get more comfortable, love."

Before she could reply, he tipped her back into the cushions piled at the head of the bed, and arranged her snugly against him. Slightly disconcerted by her sudden change in posture, Ainsley blinked up at him.

Royal toyed with the curls falling down around her cheeks. "I've been thinking."

"Yes?" she whispered.

"I'd like to start by kissing your pretty little feet and then working my way up to the top."

She gave this intriguing suggestion the attention it deserved. "I think I'd prefer that you start at the top and work your way down," she said after a moment.

His smile transformed into a grin so boyish and happy it made her want to laugh.

"In fact," she said, suddenly feeling quite bold, "let me help you get started."

When she started on the buttons at the top of her bodice, Royal's gaze narrowed on her hands. "Be my guest."

Since there were only three buttons, she didn't do much more than expose the lace and ribbons that trimmed her shift. But from the expression on Royal's face, it was like she'd stripped off her clothing and was prancing naked about the room.

When he leaned down to kiss her, the hungry swipe of his tongue stole her breath. His mouth was silky and hot, and his kiss so possessive that her body vibrated with an arousal that had her trembling in his arms.

When he eventually pulled back, Ainsley had to struggle to clear her muddled brain.

"For so long, I couldn't even kiss you." His brogue was deep and husky. "To have you in my arms and to be able to touch you is heaven. Right now, I don't need anything else."

For a long moment, emotion threatened to overwhelm her. "Really? Because I want a great deal more out of you," she finally replied in a wobbly voice. "I didn't just marry you for your sterling intellect."

"Such a shocking confession, my lady."

He leaned down to flick a tongue between her lips, and before she could kiss him back, his mouth drifted down to her neck. He kissed his way lower, leisurely building her arousal. Ainsley closed her eyes and concentrated on the sensations sparking to life in her body. A spike of heat flared in her belly, and a delicious ache began to gather between her thighs.

She knew her body, and she knew what it was capable of—had once been capable of. To know she could still respond to a man's touch—her husband's touch—flooded her with unspoken gratitude.

Royal's hand moved to her bodice. "These fripperies are almost too pretty to take off. So much ribbon and lace."

His hand traced along the top of her stays, his calloused fingertips making her shiver. When one finger dipped down to touch her nipple, she bit her lip to hold back a groan.

He glanced up. "Do you like that?"

She nodded, too breathless and shy to reply.

"Splendid. You are, however, rather laced up."

She grimaced. "Drat. They're back-lacing stays. Silly of me to forget that."

As wonderful as his attentions were, and as much as she wanted them, Ainsley wasn't sure she was ready to strip off her gown and allow Royal to unlace her stays. But considering how far she'd gone, it seemed silly to develop such qualms now.

She tried to struggle up into a sitting position. "Here, let me—"

Royal gently pushed her back down. "No need. Just relax."

"I'm trussed up like a Christmas goose. It won't be easy to get to the good bits."

"Never fear, I'll get to all of them in good time. There's no need to rush into anything." He kissed the tip of her nose. "We're practicing, remember?"

As usual, he knew what she was feeling without her having to say a word. "And what are you practicing at the moment?"

"How to undress my wife without embarrassing her."

"I suppose it's silly of me to be so shy about it."

He kissed her eyebrow, then wandered down over her cheek, slowly making his way to her mouth. His tongue traced the seam of her lips, exerting a gentle, provocative pressure. Ainsley clung to him. Within moments, she was once more trembling in his arms.

"Still feeling shy?" he asked.

"Me, shy?" She sounded breathless. "You must be joking."

"Good. Then let's practice some more."

He hooked two fingers into the top of her stays. They were laced quite snuggly, but with several firm tugs on the quilted fabric and some wriggling on her part, Royal was able to slip a hand inside her shift and ease her breasts up over the top of her undergarments. It took some doing, since her curves were generous, but her husband didn't seem to mind.

Neither did she. His warm, caressing hands felt utterly delightful.

"There you are, my beauties," he murmured when her breasts finally eased free. "You were certainly worth the wait."

Ainsley couldn't help but giggle.

He gave her a lazy smile. "Do I amuse you, Mrs. Kendrick?"

"You're talking to my bosom, Mr. Kendrick."

"I told you once that I wanted to build a monument to your breasts. Now that I've actually seen them, I'm going to begin construction immediately."

"Perhaps not *quite* immediately."

"Perhaps not," he said with a deep chuckle.

He curled a hand around her breast, cupping it. "You're so damn pretty, Ainsley. I can hardly believe I'm finally touching you."

"I love you touching me," she whispered.

When he scraped a gentle thumb across her nipple, Ainsley caught her breath. As he played with the rigid tip, gently flicking it, she couldn't hold back a whimper. Pleasure arced from that tight point to the gathering arousal in her sex.

"Och, that's lovely," Royal growled.

He slid his palm back and forth over the tip. Ainsley arched her back, pushing her body into his hand, silently begging for more.

With a husky laugh that sounded close to a groan, he complied. For deliciously agonizing minutes, he played with her breasts, sending her into a daze of sensual pleasure. When he wrapped his fingertips around her nipple and gently twisted, Ainsley all but levitated.

"Royal," she gasped, "you're driving me insane."

"But you want more, don't you?"

"Yes, you booby. Do something!" She froze, mortified. "Oh, God, I sound like an idiot."

His only reply was a knowing smile before his head came down to her breast.

Ainsley gasped when he took her nipple into his mouth. It was a thrilling sensation, and she'd never felt anything like it. For long, luxurious minutes, he went from one breast to the other, nipping, tasting—and slowly driving her into sensual frenzy. Her breasts felt heavy and full, and her nipples ached, deliciously tormented by his hungry mouth.

She curled her fingers into his thick, silky hair, holding him close. She squirmed beneath him, still wanting, still needing more.

He finally drew back with a gentle, lingering pull. His gaze glittered with passion, making her lightheaded. It was almost terrifying to feel so much and know that she'd also roused him to such heady desire.

Despite his devouring gaze, his mouth lifted in one of his lovely, tender smiles. "I'll give you whatever you need, sweetheart. Just tell me if it's all right to touch you."

"You've been touching me quite a lot, in case you've failed to notice," she hoarsely replied.

His hand drifted down to rest low on her belly. "Down there, I mean."

Ainsley sucked in a breath. Her breasts, still damp from his attentions, quivered. He'd worked her into such a state that she barely knew what to do with herself.

Actually, she did. "If you don't touch me, I'll be forced to do the job myself."

Then she clapped a hand over her mouth. What an appalling thing to say to one's husband, especially during their first time together.

Royal choked out a startled laugh.

"What is so blasted funny?" she asked.

"You're a bossy little thing, aren't you?"

She sighed. "May I remind you yet again that I'm not very good at this sort of thing?"

"Nonsense. You're splendid at this sort of thing, though I must admit that I would *quite* enjoy watching you pleasure yourself."

"Royal Kendrick!"

"Another time, perhaps?"

She grabbed the collar of his nightshirt. "If you don't get on with it, I can safely promise that there won't be another time."

When he laughed again, Ainsley contemplated boxing his ears. Fortunately, he pressed a firm hand between her thighs, right on the perfect spot. Even through the bunched fabric of her garments, it felt wonderful. When his fingers shifted, gently rubbing her, she didn't even try to hold back a moan.

"My beauty," he murmured. "Does that feel nice?"

She curled a hand around his neck and drew his face down to hers. "*Very* nice."

Then she took his mouth, pouring all her pent-up emotions into the kiss.

Royal quickly took control, feeding her desire with kisses that robbed her of all coherent thought. He seduced her with deep glides of his tongue, tasting her with urgent passion. All the while, his hand stroked her through the fine linen of her shift. As the fabric grew damp, tiny contractions began in her womb, building toward her climax.

Ainsley arched her hips, pushing into his hand, seeking the burst of heat and light that would bring her relief. She hovered close to the brink, but then Royal gentled his movements, stoking her frustration as well as her desire.

Feeling more than a bit desperate now, she wrapped both hands around his neck and thrust her tongue deep into his mouth. With a frantic whimper, she pressed close, seeking both shelter and pleasure within his strong embrace.

"That's my beautiful girl." His mouth devoured her with a hunger that made her shiver.

Seeking release, Ainsley rubbed her breasts against his brawny chest and felt his erection jerk in response. She squeezed her thighs together, trapping his hand. For a wild moment, she wished his hard length was parting her damp folds and filling her up until she came apart in his arms.

When Royal finally released her from the soul-stealing kiss, he loomed over her, his eyes glittering like the green lights that lit up the northern night sky. His whisky-scented breath washed over her in hot, short bursts, and his features were tight with masculine need.

"God, lass, you're so bloody gorgeous. And your body . . ."

He cupped her breast, feeling the voluptuous weight before rubbing his palm over her aching, stiff nipple. Ainsley cried out as her climax danced just out of reach.

"Please, Royal," she gasped. "Please don't stop. I need you to touch me everywhere."

"I need that too, more than I need to breathe."

Then, *finally*, he slipped his hand under her skirts. His blunt fingertips gently parted her, finding the tight bud slick with her arousal. When he flicked it, a bolt of fire shot through her, and she couldn't hold back a strangled cry of need.

"Let yourself go, my love," he crooned. "I promise to keep you safe."

Held securely in his firm embrace, Ainsley did just that. When he spread her legs, exposing her fully to his touch, she shut her eyes and let sensation—and Royal—rule her body. His fingers danced over her sex and teased the sensitive opening of her body, building pleasure in a relentless wave. Her mind turned soft and dark, as if wrapped in plush velvet.

Clumsily, Ainsley reached for him, vaguely needing to pleasure him, too.

Royal pressed her back into the mattress. "Let me take care of you," he whispered.

She didn't have the strength or the will to resist.

His heat surrounded her, his body brawny and hard. Everywhere he touched, fire raced through her veins to burn deep in her core. All the while, he poured out his love for her in tender, arousing words, telling her how beautiful she was, how strong she was, and how he adored her.

Finally, it was all too much. Her body, heart, and soul needed release.

She dragged open her eyelids and met his searing gaze.

"Look at yourself, Ainsley," he rasped. "Look at how magnificent you are."

She glanced down at her body, disheveled and half-naked, her clothes twisted around her. Her breasts were full and pink from his attentions, and her legs had fallen open, pliant and weak from his touch. But it was the sight of his hand on her sex that truly gave her a jolt. He cupped her gently but possessively, claiming her in a way that was shocking yet utterly erotic.

He smiled down at her. "My brave lass, I am the luckiest bastard on the planet to hold such beauty and heart in my arms."

For a moment, she blinked back tears. Then he did something with his fingers that drew a cry from her lips. His hands slicked over her tight bud, circling and teasing, quickly driving her into a sensual frenzy.

"Royal," she gasped.

"Yes, now. Let go, my love."

One final stroke from him and she tumbled. She squeezed her eyes shut, letting the joy explode throughout her body.

For once, she didn't hold back. For once, she let herself feel *everything*, knowing she was safe and secure in his arms.

Eventually, her shudders subsided. Royal kissed her damp forehead and smoothed back her hair with such tenderness that she had to stifle a sniffle or two. Ainsley settled into his arms, trying to catch her breath and find herself after the release that had swept through her like a summer storm.

Yes, she'd felt desire before, but nothing like this. Her husband's touch had sparked a fire that had all but consumed her.

It was earth-shattering—and thoroughly disconcerting.

She closed her eyes, trying to calm herself. Royal tucked her close, cradling her with the protectiveness that was second nature to him. There was nowhere safer than in her husband's arms, despite what her old, damaged self was trying to tell her.

Even so, she couldn't hold back a few sniffles. Gratitude, vulnerability, and love were all mixed in one confusing, glorious mess, and she'd need more than a few minutes to sort it out. She'd probably need a lifetime—a lifetime with Royal, she hoped.

He caressed her shoulders, his touch warm and gentle. She felt him shift a bit, and his mouth brushed the top of her ear.

"All right, love?" he murmured.

She rubbed her face against the soft linen of his nightshirt, drying her tears and feeling more than slightly embarrassed by her overwrought reaction. The last thing her poor husband needed was a hysterical wife who came apart at the seams whenever he touched her.

"I'm very well, thank you," she said, mustering a smile. "Although I'm acting rather like a foolish chit, aren't I? I suspect I've ruined your shirt."

His malachite gaze glittered with banked passion, but his

smile was tender and so loving that it threatened to bring more tears to her eyes.

Stop being a watering pot.

"You can ruin all my shirts, especially if it gets you into my bed." He passed a thumb over her cheek, catching a stray tear. "But you're sure I didn't hurt you or upset you in any way?"

"You mean you couldn't tell? I would think it quite obvious what just happened to me."

He flashed a rather smug grin. "Yes, I was aware of that part of the business, but I'm not used to you crying. You hardly ever cry. Twice in one night is disconcerting, to say the least."

Ainsley patted his chest. "Just like a man. Runs at the first sight of tears."

He pulled her closer. "Do I look like I'm running?"

The evidence of his arousal was still apparent. "Thankfully, no," she said with a choked laugh.

"Good." His smile faded as he tipped up her chin. "But tell me why you're crying."

"It's nothing to worry about, dearest. I was simply a little overwhelmed by the emotion of the moment. You have to admit it's something of a milestone—for both of us."

He tenderly cupped her cheek. "One I am most happy to have achieved with you, my dearest heart."

She couldn't resist wriggling against him and had to suppress a smile of glee when he sucked in a breath.

"It's only a partial milestone," she said, "given the state you're in."

He kissed the tip of her nose. "I don't mind in the least. I simply want you to be happy and enjoy yourself."

"But I want you to be happy, too."

"I am happy, Ainsley. With you in my arms, I could wish for nothing more."

Again, she lifted a brow. "Really?"

"Well, obviously I could wish for something more, but I'm willing to wait."

"I'm not. I want us to be happy together."

He lowered his head to study her face. "I'm assuming that *happy together* is not some vague euphemism?"

"You really are a bit dense at times. I'm talking about sex."

When he continued to regard her with a degree of skepticism, Ainsley decided it was time for a little challenge—and before her nerves *did* get the better of her. "If, that is, you're up to it."

He laughed. "Is that a dare? Because it's one I'm perfectly capable of meeting."

"Good, because—oh, drat. Would that hurt your leg? Maybe we'd better not. You might strain it."

"Wife, I'm more than capable of having sex with you without using my leg."

"Truly?"

"Let me show you."

Without any further ado, he wrapped his hands around her waist and picked her up, depositing her with easy strength onto his lap.

"Goodness," she said, feeling a little breathless.

"There, see?" he said with a wicked smile as he arranged her to fully straddle his hips. "I think this will be the perfect position for both of us." His questing fingers went to her stays, which were twisted sideways, half exposing her. "This doesn't look very comfortable—"

When a thunderous knock sounded against the door, Ainsley squawked and almost tumbled backward.

Royal grabbed her arms and steadied her. "Easy, lass."

She pressed a hand to her pounding heart. "Who *is* that?" she gasped.

"Likely just one of the servants checking on me. I'll—"

"Laddie boy, are ye all right in there?" yelled Angus.

"Dammit to hell," Royal muttered. Then he raised his voice. "I'm fine. Go away."

"I'll no be doin' that until I check on that leg of yers. I'm comin' in whether ye will it or no."

Ainsley yelped and rolled sideways, trying to clear the bed before the old man charged into the room. When her knee connected with some part of Royal's body, he let out a strangled cry as she scrambled down to the floor. Desperately, she yanked her stays over her breasts and pulled her bodice back into place. Then she popped up to look at her husband, terrified that she'd hurt him.

He was curled forward in a ball, his face a rictus of agony.

"Oh, my God, did I hurt your leg?" she blurted out. "Royal, I'm so sorry."

Angus barreled up to the bed. "What the hell is goin' on in here?" He scowled at Ainsley. "What did ye do to him, ye daft girl?"

Still in a crouch, Ainsley struggled to pull her tangled skirts over her legs. "I . . . I don't know. I think I might have done something to his leg when I, um, got off the bed."

Angus looked blank for a moment before peering down at his grandson. A slight smirk lifted the corners of his mouth. "I dinna think it's his leg ye hurt."

Her terror abated a jot.

"Are you sure?"

Cautiously getting up, she got a good look at Royal. He'd uncurled a bit, but his face had gone a ghostly white and his hands were down between his legs, covering . . .

"Oh, dear," she said, mortified.

"Aye, now that's a sad end to the evenin'," Angus said, clearly trying not to laugh.

Ainsley glared at him. "It's *your* fault." She reached across the bed to pull the sheets up over her poor husband. "Here, Royal, let me help you."

"That's not the kind of help he needs, lass," Angus said.

"I would be exceedingly grateful if you would both just get the hell out of here," Royal said from between clenched teeth.

Ainsley's stomach took a miserable twist. "Royal, I—"

"Please, Ainsley, just *go*," he snapped.

Feeling like an utter fool, she resisted blurting out yet another apology and fled the room.

Chapter Twenty

Royal ducked his head against a gust of wind as he crossed the garden square. The weather in Glasgow had finally turned, the lingering warmth of summer fading into the cool mists of autumn. Soon enough snow would fall in the Highlands, enveloping Kinglas in the wintery blanket that cut it off from the outside world for days at a time. Royal had never found it isolating, due to his boisterous family and the small but vibrant community that made up life on the large estate.

But his wife was not designed for life in a remote Scottish glen, as their disastrous wedding trip had starkly illustrated. Better that they establish themselves in town, with only occasional visits to Kinglas. Glasgow was not the cheeriest of cities in the colder months, but there would be parties and assemblies over the holiday season, and visits with the Gilbrides and other friends to cheer up his long-suffering bride.

Not that she'd complained about her time at Kinglas, at least not lately. But if Ainsley had to spend any more time rattling around that drafty old pile, he feared she might succumb to her pent-up frustration and toss him into the frigid waters of the loch. It was a punishment he'd surely earned by making a cock-up of everything, including his wife's sweetly awkward attempts to seduce him.

His blood still ran hot every time he thought about that episode. Royal had never seen anything more beautiful as his wife's lush body, or felt more alive than when he'd brought her to a shivering climax in his arms. Ainsley in ecstasy was glorious, and he'd made a silent vow to spend the rest of his life repeating the experience.

Unfortunately, with a little help from his demented grandfather, life had decided to throw a spanner in the works. Getting thoroughly kneed in the bollocks had sent everything sliding sideways. Royal wasn't proud of himself for losing his temper, but he *was* only human. For the second time that day, he'd been injured and humiliated by his wife, however inadvertently. The direct shot to the family jewels had finally tipped him over the edge.

Now, he and his wife were right back where they'd started—unable to have a sensible conversation that didn't involve at least one misunderstanding, and still struggling to make their cobbled-together family work.

He slowed to a halt in the middle of the path, gazing absently at Kendrick House on the opposite side of the square. This marriage business was proving to be trickier than he'd expected, and he'd never expected easy.

When two little boys pelted by him on the path, shrieking at the top of their lungs, Royal jerked so hard that his hat toppled off. As always when startled by loud noises, his heart leapt forward like a frightened stag. It was a lingering effect from the battlefield that he loathed with a passion. Some days, he wondered if he would ever be the man he used to be—a *whole* man, not one with a mangled leg or a moody temperament that disconcerted even those who loved him most.

"Sorry, sir," yelled one of the boys over his shoulder. "Our dog slipped her lead."

Royal gave a wave and watched them race after a little black terrier in fast pursuit of an even faster squirrel. He couldn't help smiling at their innocent glee. They reminded him of the twins at that age, miniature hellions constantly in trouble and yet as good-natured as any lad one could hope to meet.

Despite the family's later travails, Royal had enjoyed a happy childhood. Roaming the hills around Castle Kinglas with his brothers, protected by loving, intelligent parents, had been close to idyllic. That is, until all the terrible deaths had started, battering them like a bloody great ram. For a time, the future had seemed poisoned.

But change had finally come to Kinglas, as change always must. It had brought them Victoria, who'd swept away sorrow like a housewife cleans out a musty closet, bringing light and air where they were needed most.

And then Ainsley had exploded into his life, dragging him up and out of the oubliette he'd built in his mind. She'd given him hope, she'd given him a daughter, and she'd given him a chance at a happy, normal life. He'd almost forgotten what such a life was like. But he remembered it now, and he was going to fight for it—for Ainsley, for Tira, and for himself.

Retrieving his hat from the dirt, he brushed it off and clapped it back on. Striding out of the square, he mentally ticked off his blessings. He had a family who loved him, a daughter he cherished, and a wife he adored. And if his wife didn't adore him back, well, he was working on that part of the plan.

He limped up the steps of Kendrick House and knocked on the door rather than searching for his key.

"Good day, sir," Will said as he opened the door. He took Royal's hat. "Did ye have a good visit with Dr. Baker?"

Thanks to Angus, it was common knowledge in the Glasgow household that Royal had taken a bad fall. Nick, alarmed as always by any sign of physical ailment in his siblings, had insisted on a specialist, as had Ainsley. Royal had resisted for several days until Victoria finally begged him to put the rest of them out of their misery.

"Nicholas and Ainsley will simply pester you until you agree," she'd said at breakfast yesterday.

Logan, reading the local gazette, had lowered the paper to eye him. "Better do it, old man. If you don't, I'll have to sling you over my shoulder and carry you there myself."

"Try it and see what happens," Royal had snorted.

"I know we're fussbudgets," Victoria had said with a placating smile. "But it's because we care about you, my dear. We can't help but worry."

"Not me," Logan had said, winking at him. "I'm just sick of hearing Nick and Ainsley whinge about it. It's 'Royal this' and 'Royal that.' You'd think you were on your damn deathbed, instead of just limping about like some Byronic idiot in order to gain our sympathy."

Since he couldn't deny their logic, Royal had finally submitted to a lengthy and painful examination by Dr. Baker this morning. The truth was, the effects of his tumble had lingered, although he'd cut out his tongue before admitting it.

Stripping off his gloves, he handed them to the footman. "I'm fit as a fiddle."

"Grand news, sir. Her ladyship and Mr. MacDonald will be that relieved to hear it, I ken."

"No doubt."

In fact, his wife and his grandfather would be receiving a heavily censored report. Although Baker had detected no lasting damage, he'd delivered a stern lecture on the need to rest and to ease back on his leg exercises. Royal had piously agreed while crossing his fingers behind his back. He had no intention of giving up on the exercises, since they were all that had ever helped to rebuild his strength. He now needed his strength more than ever.

"I take it that my brother and his wife got off in good order this morning?" he asked.

"Aye, sir. Lord and Lady Arnprior set off soon after ye left for the doctor's."

Nick and Victoria, along with Kade, had decided to return to Kinglas. As much as the family enjoyed one another's company, Kendrick House was a little too crowded with most of them in residence, and the twins were expected home to Glasgow in a few days. Fortunately, both Nick and Victoria preferred Kinglas, and Kade went wherever they went. Royal would miss his little brother, but the lad was best left under their watchful and loving care.

"Is Lady Ainsley at home?" he asked Will.

"Yes, sir. Her ladyship is in the study."

His brother's study was Ainsley's preferred retreat at Kendrick House, but Royal intended to change that. With a little luck and with as much courting as was required, he planned to make his bedroom her favorite spot from now on.

Of course, the ideal venue for seduction was not a house with his brothers and grandfather knocking about. So Royal hoped to have an appropriate town house rented for his little family within the next few weeks. In her own establishment, Ainsley could relax, and he could give her the privacy she needed to feel comfortable again.

When he opened the study door, he found Ainsley tucked into one of the needlepointed armchairs by the fireplace. She glanced up from her book with a relieved smile.

"I was getting worried," she said, rising to greet him. "You were gone for rather a long time."

He limped over and took her hands, bending slightly to press a lingering kiss on her soft lips. She hesitated, as if surprised, then gently returned his pressure. When he tried to deepen the kiss, she gave an embarrassed little chuckle and pulled away.

"Goodness," she said. "Whatever was that for?"

"I missed you. I wanted you to know that."

She gave him a wry smile. "Then mission accomplished, although you've only been away for a few hours. Certainly not long enough to miss me."

"You just said you were worried by my absence. That certainly sounds long enough for us to miss each other." He gently tugged on a silky tendril of hair curving down her neck, enjoying the light scent of her perfume.

"I was worried about your leg, silly." She adroitly sidled away to the drinks trolley to fetch a glass. "And anxious about what the doctor had to say."

He noted her reluctance to meet his gaze. Ainsley had never been shy with him until that shattering encounter when she'd climaxed in his arms—before kneeing him in the balls. Since then, she'd swung between fussing over him as much as she did Tira, and skittering away at the first sign of romance on his part. Clearly, their initial sexual encounter had rattled her more deeply than he'd thought.

Or maybe she'd started to regret marrying him. He couldn't blame her for that, since the road to domestic bliss had so far been fraught with peril.

At least she's stuck with you, old son. It's not like she can divorce you or seek an annulment.

Not surprisingly, that fact was hardly one to lift the spirits. He wanted Ainsley to love him as much as he loved her, even if that made him sound like a pompous fool.

"Is that for me?" he asked as she poured whisky into a crystal tumbler.

"Just a small one to take off the chill. Now, why don't you sit down by that cozy fire and tell me about your visit with the doctor."

She obviously felt the need to coddle him a bit. If that made her happy, then coddling it would be.

"Do you need a lap blanket?" she asked, handing him the glass.

Not that much coddling. "Sweetheart, I'm not in my dotage yet."

She gave him a soothing smile that suggested she would soon be conjuring up warm glasses of milk.

He hated milk.

"Of course not," she said. "But we don't want you getting chilled. Your muscles will seize up."

"If they do, you can always massage them."

She blushed and shook her head. Still, he couldn't help noticing the little grin that lifted the corners of her mouth.

Progress.

Ainsley settled into the opposite armchair. "Well, what *did* Dr. Baker have to say about your leg? Nothing bad, I hope."

"Just the opposite. I'm in fine trim. No need to worry about anything."

"Royal Kendrick, that is a load of old bollocks, and you know it."

The whisky went down the wrong pipe, bringing on a fit of coughs. When he recovered, Royal eyed his wife's indignant expression. "Is that your expert opinion, my lady?"

"I refuse to believe that any doctor would say you were in *fine trim.* Your limp is still quite bad, and the bruises are only now beginning to fade."

"How do you know about my bruises? Have you been spying on me when I was getting undressed?"

"Don't be ridiculous. I never spy."

"That's too bad," he said with genuine regret.

"I have people spy *for* me, of course."

He had to laugh. "Angus."

"Much to my surprise, he's turned into an excellent co-conspirator."

"I've noticed."

Although grateful that Angus and Ainsley had sworn a truce, that welcome state of affairs was mostly dictated by their worries about his health. It meant they fashed themselves to a ridiculous degree, consulting in loud whispers when they thought he wasn't listening. Mostly he ignored them, but a few times he'd been forced to speak sternly when they'd tried to push some ghastly potion on him or smear him with yet another foul-smelling ointment from the local chemist.

"I know you hate it when we fuss," she said, "but someone has to take care of you."

"I'm perfectly capable of taking care of myself. You and Angus can confine your impulses to play nurse to Tira."

"We do, in fact, argue about Tira on a regular basis. But Angus and I are in complete agreement that you need to take better care of yourself. Most importantly, you need to get more rest."

He rubbed his chin. "I can think of one thing that would help with that."

"Splendid."

"If my wife were to join me in bed, I'd be sure to get plenty of rest. More rest than you could shake a stick at. So to speak," he added, waggling his eyebrows.

Ainsley cast an exasperated glance to the heavens. "I refuse to dignify that wretched joke with so much as an embarrassed chuckle. Besides, such an arrangement would not be restful. Quite the opposite, I believe. *And* you could hurt yourself again."

"Well, to be fair, *I* didn't actually hurt myself."

Her shoulders went up around her ears.

"But most of that episode was exceedingly pleasant, as I recall," he hastily added. "For both of us."

"I *hurt* you, Royal. Have you forgotten that?"

So that was the reason for her skittishness—at least part of it. She was still upset that she'd injured him.

"Love, you must stop worrying so much. Dr. Baker was quite clear that there would be no lasting damage at all."

"Did he prescribe any treatment?"

"He simply said I was not to overtax myself for a week or so."

"Thank goodness," she said with a relieved smile. "You took a hackney home from the doctor's office, I presume? It's much too long a walk."

He mentally crossed his fingers. "Much too long. Oh, Baker did say that massage would assist in healing the injury. To stimulate the muscles and increase circulation of the blood, I believe."

"Are you sure?" she asked in a dubious tone. "I wouldn't want to, um, aggravate anything."

As far as he was concerned, she could aggravate anything she wanted. "Absolutely. But it would be very helpful for the healing process, apparently."

"I suppose that makes sense." She brightened, obviously warming to the idea. "It did seem to help before, didn't it?"

"So much so that I would be grateful for another—"

The door swung open and Angus stomped in, carrying a stack of mail. Royal had to clamp down on his impulse to leap across the room and throttle him. The old fellow had an infallible knack for intruding at the worst possible moment.

"Ah, here ye be," said Angus, inspecting him with a concerned eye. "What did that old sawbones have to say? Is all well?"

"Dr. Baker feels there is no lasting damage," Ainsley jumped in before Royal could reply. "But he's to rest for at least a week and not strain himself."

Angus shook his head. "That canna be right. The limp seems fair nasty to me."

"We're going to try massage again," she said. "The doctor said that will be helpful."

"Aye, that makes sense. Brody sent down a new ointment

for Royal to try. Mutton fat, mustard paste, and camphor, rubbed three times a day into the bruises. Works like a charm, Brody said."

Ainsley wrinkled her nose. "That sounds quite awful."

"He won't be smellin' of roses, I grant ye, but if Brody—"

"I don't give a hang what Brody says," Royal interrupted. "I am not rubbing blasted mutton fat on my thigh. And may I remind you both that I am actually in the room? You needn't act as if I'm invisible or deaf."

"Sorry," Ainsley said with an apologetic smile.

"Of course we ken yer in the room," Angus said. "Do we look like a pair of jinglebrains?"

"You might not want me to answer that," Royal said.

"Now, see here, laddie—"

"No, Grandda, you see here. I am perfectly fine, *and* perfectly capable of looking after myself."

"Not with rushin' home like ye were. Canna be good for yer leg, all that stompin' about."

Hell. "Who told you I was rushing home?"

"Young Willie. I asked him to keep an eye out for ye. He saw ye come home just now, cuttin' through the park instead of takin' a hackney."

"Splendid. A network of spies tracking my every move," Royal said, trying to ignore his wife's huff of outrage. "This is getting to be ridiculous."

"Well, at least now we have the truth instead of an out-and-out fib," Ainsley retorted.

He waggled a hand. "I didn't really fib, my love."

Her violet eyes narrowed to irritated slits. "You just failed to tell the truth."

"A small omission. So as not to worry you."

Her answering scowl suggested that a massage—with or without mutton fat—was out of the question for the foreseeable future.

"I think we've discussed my leg quite enough for one day," Royal said. "Now, would someone please tell me how Tira is feeling? She was still sleeping when I left this morning. Have the sniffles improved?"

"Och, the wee lass is as right as rain," Angus said. "It's the teethin', that's all."

Ainsley shook her head. "The poor dear has *not* improved, in fact. I'm convinced it's another cold."

"Yer daft, woman. She's no more got a cold than I do."

Naturally, that launched a fractious debate about Tira, who Royal was convinced was fine. But at least Ainsley's ire was now directed at Angus instead of at him.

"Why don't you give me the mail to sort while you two insult each other," he said to Angus.

His grandfather handed over the small stack, not pausing for breath as he lectured Ainsley on the finer points of drooling babies. She, in turn, rolled her eyes and reminded Angus that *she* was Tira's mother, and that a mother could always tell when her child was sick.

Despite the loud discussion, Royal couldn't help smiling. His wife never backed down, which meant she was a perfect match for the Kendricks, whether she realized it yet or not.

He quickly shuffled through the mail, putting aside business correspondence for Nick or Logan. There was a note from Graeme, confirming that he would be returning to Glasgow in a few days, as well as a lengthy missive from Braden, which he would read later. There was also a letter from Grant to Angus and a few invitations to parties and assemblies.

At the bottom of the pile was a rare letter for Ainsley.

Estranged as she was from her family and most of her friends, his wife received little correspondence. It infuriated him whenever he thought of how quickly she'd been abandoned by those who claimed to love her. Ainsley put on a brave front, doing her best to ignore both slights and nasty gossip that filtered up from London. It mattered not that she was entirely innocent of any wrongdoing. In the eyes of the world, Ainsley was a jilt and a fool, giving up wealth, position, and status to marry a penniless, crippled Scotsman.

But the letter Royal held in his hand appeared to be from her mother, the one person who could have helped her after the rape and yet had refused to do so. And while one could always hope that Lady Aldridge was regretting the callous rejection of her only daughter, he found it hard to believe.

For a moment, he debated withholding the missive from Ainsley, hating to distress her or, worse, send her into a panic. But his wife was no fragile miss and wouldn't thank him for treating her as if she was. Nor did he have the right to control her in so high-handed a fashion. That's what Cringlewood had tried to do, and Royal was determined she never feel such a loss of power over her own life again.

When Ainsley happened to glance over at him, she frowned, turning her back on Angus. "Royal, is something wrong?"

"This appears to be a letter from your mother," he replied.

She stared blankly for a moment before a hectic flush reddened her pale complexion. "Oh, well, that's a surprise. I wasn't expecting to hear from anyone in my family."

"Best throw it in the fire, lass," Angus said. "That mother of yers is a right—"

"That's enough, Grandda." Royal leaned forward and took Ainsley's hand. It trembled slightly. "I can read it for you, sweetheart, if you'd rather."

She mustered a lopsided smile and took the small, folded packet from him. "I'm not such a faint-heart that I need my husband to read my mail. It might be about my father, you know. He's not been well, and Mamma did promise to write if he took a turn for the worse."

Royal nodded before glancing at Angus, who looked ready to leap out of his chair and snatch the paper from her grip. "Grandda, would you mind getting me another whisky?

My leg is a bit twitchy, and I'd prefer not to get up right at the moment."

Properly diverted, the old fellow trotted off to the drinks trolley. "Aye, lad. Don't fash yerself. I'll fetch it for ye."

When Angus returned with drinks for both of them, Royal handed him the letter from Grant. His grandfather settled into his chair to read it, while Royal pretended to peruse the missive from Braden. In truth, though, he watched Ainsley, who was worrying her lower lip as she read. He couldn't fail to notice that the bright blush of a few minutes ago was draining from her cheeks, leaving her pale as chalk.

"Ainsley, is something wrong?" he asked.

She jumped in her seat. "Um, what?"

"Did your mother say something to upset you?"

Her gaze appeared fastened on him, but Royal got the distinct impression that whatever she was seeing, it wasn't him. The hairs on the back of his neck prickled.

"Ainsley, something is wrong, isn't it?" he asked.

"No," she whispered.

"Are ye sure, lass?" Angus asked. "Yer lookin' fair hipped, ye are."

Her gaze darted nervously between them. Then she drew in a breath and dredged up an entirely artificial smile. "My mother simply wished to pass along some news about the family. My brother's wife is with child, and Mamma thought I should know, since it's unlikely that my brother or his wife will write to inform me that such is the case."

"Nincompoops," Angus said in a disgusted tone.

"Indeed." Ainsley briskly folded up the letter and rose to her feet. "If you'll excuse me, I must write a reply, then check on Tira. I'll see you both at dinner."

Royal pushed himself up. "Ainsley, wait just a moment."

But she was already halfway out the door.

Angus stared after her, tapping a thoughtful finger on his

chin. "I do believe something's amiss with your lady. She lit out of here like a pack of hellhounds was snappin' at her arse."

"Just one hellhound, I think," Royal said in a grim tone. "And I have a good idea of who it is."

Chapter Twenty-One

She'd forgotten about the Scottish marriage laws.

All these weeks, Ainsley had thought she and Tira were finally safe from discovery, from scandal, and, most importantly, from Cringlewood. She'd convinced herself they'd pulled it off, and that she and Royal would finally have the chance to create the life they both longed for.

How naïve she'd been.

Clutching her candle, Ainsley snuck down the quiet hallway toward Royal's bedroom. She'd heard him pass by her door five minutes ago, recognizing the quiet but unmistakable hitch in his tread. He'd hesitated outside her door for several long seconds, while she'd waited with bated breath, half wishing he'd barge in and demand an explanation for her odd behavior this afternoon. But he didn't, of course. Royal never demanded or pushed, though sometimes she thought it might be better if he did. If he forced her to tell him the truth, she imagined that somehow she'd be absolved of the consequences of her own stupid behavior.

"Almost like going to confession," she muttered. "And I'm not even a Catholic."

But no one could absolve her of her sins or fix the mess

she'd created. She needed to think, and then she needed to act. And she had to do it in a way that didn't make her husband even more suspicious than he already was.

Sinking into one of the chairs in the corridor, Ainsley put her candle down on the small table next to it. She covered her face and sucked in slow, steady breaths, trying to quell the panic that had threatened to overcome her after reading her mother's letter.

Royal had known something was wrong, and she'd had to exert every ounce of willpower against the urge to run into his arms and tell him everything. But if he ever found out how foolish she'd been, both with her own safety and with Tira's, he'd never forgive her. In fact, he just might decide to make use of those liberal Scottish marriage laws to be rid of an exceedingly troublesome wife. So far, she'd brought nothing but trouble to the Kendrick family, and she might bring down a great deal more if she didn't find a way to protect *all* of them, especially Tira, from the potential mayhem thundering their way.

Ainsley knew what she had to do, even though the idea made her cringe with guilt. As far as she could tell, it was the only thing that could potentially protect her from Cringlewood's threats. Divorce was all but impossible in England, but not in Scotland, as her mother had triumphantly pointed out in her letter.

The fact that Cringlewood still wished to marry her was something Ainsley had never thought remotely possible. Her former fiancé was a proud, arrogant man, and should have been mortally offended to be thrown over in favor of an untitled and relatively impecunious Scotsman. Once she married Royal, it should have been inconceivable for the marquess to want anything to do with her again.

Yet according to her mother, he did. If anything, Leonard was more terrifyingly obsessed than ever, although Ainsley wasn't sure if he had the leverage needed to fully bend her to his will. Mamma, unfortunately, had been frustratingly vague about what she'd actually told Leonard about Ainsley's circumstances, and what he intended to do about it.

"My lady, are ye all right?"

She jerked upright, almost knocking over her candle. William stood a few feet away, gazing at her with consternation.

"Do ye wish me to fetch Mr. Royal?" he asked when she gaped at him like a booby.

She mustered a bracing smile. "Indeed no. I'm perfectly fine."

William looked even more concerned. "Or I can fetch yer maid if ye'd like, my lady."

Sighing, Ainsley picked up the candle and rose. "Thank you, but that won't be necessary."

The footman flicked a gaze over her figure, his eyes widening with alarm. Even in the dim light of the hallway, she could see the poor fellow blush, no doubt unused to a lady wandering around the hall in a frilly wrapper and nightcap. Ainsley had always thought of herself as a rather dignified person, but her recent behavior would suggest otherwise.

"Are you on your way to Mr. Royal's room to help him get ready for bed?" she asked, trying to regain control of the situation.

William's cheeks blazed an even deeper red. "Aye, ma'am. I usually pulls his boots off for him at the end of the night."

"I'll help Mr. Royal tonight, William. You may retire."

He seemed flummoxed. Like all the servants in the household, he was aware that she and Royal did not share a bed.

"Um, but Mr. Royal—"

She shooed him. "Good night, William."

"Yes, my lady. Good night, my lady."

The footman scurried off, likely to share a juicy bit of gossip about Mr. Royal's wife preparing to storm her husband's bedroom to pull off his boots. It all felt suddenly rather ridiculous.

But it's what you want, isn't it?

She did want it, desperately. But not like this. Not when it felt like a lie.

But a necessary lie. You're protecting him, and Tira, too.

Ainsley marched down the hall. She could spend all night dithering, but there *was* only one course of action—to make her marriage a real one. It was the only way she could protect the Kendrick family, whether Royal ultimately approved of her tactics or not.

So make him approve.

Ainsley tapped on his door.

"Enter."

She slipped inside and put her candle on the chest of drawers.

Royal was comfortably ensconced in a claw-footed armchair by the fireplace, apparently deep in a book. Clad only in breeches and a flowing white shirt, with his long, booted legs propped against the firedogs, he looked more a rugged Highlander than a respectable Glasgow businessman.

"Ah, Will," he said without glancing up. "I was beginning to think you'd forgotten me."

"I dismissed William for the evening."

Royal carefully marked his place and put the book aside. Then he glanced over, his gaze tracking from the tips of her feathered mules to the top of her frilly nightcap. By the end of his perusal, his dark eyebrows were all but touching his hairline.

"Is this a social call?" he finally asked. "Or is there a matter you need to discuss that couldn't wait until morning?"

Ainsley realized she hadn't thought of a way to open up

what was sure to be an awkward discussion. As she searched for an answer that sounded at least somewhat reasonable, her gaze snagged on the decanter on the table next to his chair.

"Cannot a wife visit her husband's bedroom for a small brandy before bedtime?" she brightly asked.

When Royal's mouth dropped open, she had to repress the impulse to groan. The poor man must think her entirely demented. One moment she was pushing him away, and the next she was charging into his bedroom like a brazen hussy.

She almost fainted with relief when his glance slid over her once more, and a slow smile replaced his befuddled look.

"Indeed a wife can," he said, rising to his feet. "But I'm afraid this husband only has whisky to offer. Do you want me to ring for Will to bring brandy?"

"Whisky is fine. Besides, I've already shocked the poor fellow enough for one evening. He looked ready to swoon when I ran into him in the hall."

"I can imagine, especially with you dressed in such delightful dishabille."

"I'm sure I looked ridiculous, wandering around the halls like Ophelia or one of the Kendrick family ghosts."

"We don't have ghosts. And ridiculous is not how I would describe your appearance, my love."

She blushed at the heat in his gaze, but then remembered why she'd come to his room in the first place.

"Oh? And how would you describe me?" She mentally cringed at her squeaky voice.

Once, she'd been very good at flirtation, but the travails of her life had destroyed the innocent fun of it.

Royal pretended to give the question serious thought, although his mouth twitched with amusement. "*Charmingly delectable* would best describe it. I've never seen you in a nightcap before. It makes you look . . ."

Ainsley sighed. She hadn't really thought through her attire, either. A beribboned nightcap and a wrapper with a ridiculous amount of silk, ribbon, and lace was not an ensemble calculated to turn a man's mind to seduction, especially not a man like Royal. Yards of frilly nonsense would strike him as expensive foolishness.

"Rather like a bag of laundry exploded when I walked by, I expect," she said.

He closed the distance between them and planted a kiss on the tip of her nose. "You look incredibly sweet. Almost like an angel escaped from heaven, bent on a spot of mischief. With me."

She had to smile at his nonsense. "Be careful what you wish for, Mr. Kendrick. You just might get it."

"Then I will be sure to wish very hard, Mrs. Kendrick," he murmured as he handed her to the chair.

She sank down, happy for the chance to perhaps settle her wayward heartbeat.

When he poured out a measure of whisky for her, Ainsley lifted an eyebrow at the small amount.

He lifted one in return. "Need a spot of liquid courage, do we?"

"Is it that obvious?"

"You hid your nerves very well, but your mother's letter rattled you."

Royal poured her an extra splash. After retrieving his own glass, he then propped his broad shoulders against the mantelpiece and commenced studying her with a thoughtful frown.

Ainsley had to admit he appeared rather intimidating as he loomed over her with his brooding demeanor, tall and impossibly brawny. But even if he did look like a Highland brigand, he could never frighten her. She knew his heart, and it held more generosity and love than a woman like her had any right to expect.

She gave him what she hoped was a serene smile before taking a fortifying sip of whisky.

Royal continued to study her, obviously waiting her out. But when it came to keeping secrets, she was equally adept.

Finally, he let out a small sigh. "I don't wish to pry, love—"

"Oh, of course you do. You're a terrible busybody. All the Kendricks are."

He flashed a quick grin. "True, but we always have everyone's best interests at heart, including yours. Especially yours."

"I do know that, and I'm grateful."

"But?"

"But . . . nothing. My mother caught me up on our family's affairs, and that's all."

"That's all?" he echoed, more than slightly incredulous.

She simply shrugged.

"Even Angus could tell you were distressed," he said, "and he's about as sensitive as a stag in rut."

Ainsley practically choked on her drink. "Thank you for putting that appalling image in my brain."

"Made to underline my point."

He took the glass from her hand and plunked it down on the table. Then he grasped her chin and tilted it up. Ainsley thought about bristling, but then reminded herself that she was here to seduce, not to argue. And his gaze was so warm and understanding, his smile so tender, that any ire faded away. It was hard to bristle when a man loved you so much and constantly put your needs ahead of his own.

Since he was also as sharp as the point of a javelin, she'd best parcel out at least a bit of the truth or he might get too suspicious.

"Very well," she admitted. "I *was* upset."

He briefly cupped her cheek before dragging over a padded ottoman from beside the hearth. Placing it in front of her, he settled onto it, wincing a bit as he stretched out his leg.

"Won't you tell me about it?" he quietly asked.

She nodded. "Her letter was quite cold. I'm not used to that from her. Mamma always doted on me."

"Both your parents did, as I recall."

"They did," she said, feeling a bit wistful. "I was the baby of the family and the only girl. So, it makes sense, I suppose."

"Not to mention you are beautiful, funny, and sweet."

She widened her eyes at him. "Royal Lancelot Kendrick, you should not tell such plumpers. I was *never* sweet."

He leaned in and pressed a soft kiss to her mouth. He lingered for a few moments, letting his tongue slip a fraction between her lips. As soon as she started to respond, he pulled back, his gaze smoky with desire.

"One can be tart and sweet at the same time," he said.

"You make me sound like a cherry pie."

"An exceedingly apt analogy, pet. But getting back to that letter—"

She slid a slow, teasing tongue over her upper lip, hoping to distract him. "Perhaps you might like another sample, just to check."

When he gently traced the outline of her lip, Ainsley's heart gave a hard thump.

"I will make a note so as not to lose my place," he said. "But first tell me more about your mamma's letter."

She sighed. "Oh, very well. As I mentioned, she informed me of my sister-in-law's pregnancy, but also said that I was not to expect further updates, especially not from my brother. Or from either of my brothers or their families, in fact. According to Mamma, they're all mortified and disgusted by my selfish behavior."

"Your brothers sound like a pair of stupid prats, if you ask me."

"You're sadly correct in that assessment."

"Then why does their disapproval trouble you? As far as I'm concerned, they're beneath your notice."

"Perhaps, but my sisters-in-law are quite nice, and I do hate the idea of never seeing any of my nieces and nephews again."

Royal frowned. "Even your family must eventually become reconciled to our marriage. At that point, you can try reestablishing relations."

"It doesn't matter," she said, forcing a smile. "I have all the family I need. I don't think I could manage both mine and the Kendricks, to tell you the truth."

"Of course it matters," he replied. "I know how much this hurts you, Ainsley, and I'm deeply sorry for it."

He was right. Her family's rejection had been a dagger blow to the heart. Even though she'd known it would be the likely outcome, such a comprehensive break was still shocking. Only by acceding to their demands could she possibly return to their good favor. That she could never do, for a hundred reasons starting with the man sitting before her.

"Would you like Nick to write to your parents?" he added. "A letter from the Earl of Arnprior might help, especially if he employs his most imperious, high-stickler manner. Your parents would like that—a message from one snob to another, as it were."

"God, no! He can't ever write to them, and neither can you."

When Royal's eyebrows shot up, she mentally cursed her blunder. But it would be fatal if *any* of the Kendricks communicated with her parents. Then the whole sordid mess would surely come out, and Royal, along with the rest of his family, would likely toss her out onto the street.

"I mean, it's very nice of you to offer," she amended, trying to smile, "but I'm convinced it would do no good, and might only make matters worse."

When his gaze narrowed suspiciously, Ainsley felt heat creeping into her face.

"What aren't you telling me?" he asked.

"Nothing!"

He made a frustrated sound under his breath. "Ainsley, I truly wish you would trust me. I cannot help you unless you do."

"Of course I trust you, Royal. With everything, including Tira."

Well, everything but the whole truth, which made her feel like a vile worm. But complete honesty at this point would only benefit Cringlewood.

He drew back and crossed his arms over his chest. "You certainly have an odd way of showing it."

That stung. "*You* kept your secrets, as I recall. I had to push to get you to share them."

"And as I recall, share I did."

She'd walked right into that one.

Better find a way to walk out of it.

"Royal, it's just that . . ."

"Yes?"

Ainsley could sense him retreating even further, and she hated that. Hated feeling like there were still so many obstacles between them. Maybe it wouldn't be so awful to tell him part of it. After all, it was a simple statement of fact, and one he'd probably thought about already.

She looked down and began fiddling with her wedding ring. "It's just that it's embarrassing to discuss."

Royal covered her hand with his, stilling her fidgets. "More embarrassing than Angus walking in on us while we were having sex?"

She glanced up with a rueful smile. "We weren't actually having relations at that precise moment."

"Close enough."

"This is a different kind of embarrassing."

He held her gaze, steadfastly waiting her out. This time it worked.

"It's the Scottish marriage laws," she said reluctantly. "They're quite different from England's."

"Yes, everyone knows that, but what does that—" He clamped his mouth shut.

"I know. It's awful," she said, taking in his disgusted expression. "I didn't wish to trouble you with it."

"They want us to divorce," he said in a flat tone.

She nodded.

"On what grounds?"

"Divorce on grounds of desertion takes too long, apparently. So, Mother thinks adultery is the most expedient choice."

Anger sparked in his gaze. "Are they truly mad enough to think I would ever betray you like that?"

She twirled a finger. "It would be the other way around."

"You're supposed to betray me?"

"As Mamma so kindly pointed out, under those conditions the process only takes six weeks." She hated even saying the ugly, hurtful words. "And you would no doubt be so disgusted with me that you would file for divorce without any more prompting."

"What about the scandal? Do they not realize how it would affect your reputation?"

"I suppose they think the scandal will fade over time," she said evasively. "My family is rich, after all."

When he fell silent, Ainsley had to resist the temptation to fidget again.

"And where does Tira enter into this?" he finally asked.

"She doesn't, at least if Mamma has her way. The Kendricks could keep her, with no one the wiser."

Ainsley couldn't bring herself to meet Royal's gaze. All she could do was stare at their interlaced hands and listen to the thud of her heart.

"Just one more question," he said.

Ainsley mentally braced herself. She'd already revealed too much. More would surely be fatal.

When she glanced up, her stomach pitched sideways. He looked furious enough to leap onto a horse and ride pell-mell to London to confront her parents in person.

"Yes?" she whispered.

"Does *anyone* in your family even know you? Does your mother really think you would divorce me and abandon your daughter? They're idiots if they think you would ever leave Tira again."

The sickening twist of tension in her gut started to unspool. While her family might not understand her, Royal did. He always did.

"In all fairness, only Mamma knows about Tira. But, yes, I take your point."

"And why the hell would you expose yourself to that kind of scandal? I may not be a prime catch on the marriage mart, but my family is respectable and well regarded. Divorce makes no sense at all."

It made more sense than one would think, when one knew all the particulars.

"Maybe my parents heard about the twins," she said, trying to make a joke of it.

He simply scowled at her.

Ainsley sighed. "That's why I didn't wish to tell you. It's quite awful."

"Your whole family is both crazed *and* awful." His expression softened as he studied her. "I understand why you didn't want to tell me, but I'm glad you did. Thank you."

The tension unspooled ever more, and she felt like she could breathe again. "You're welcome. And thank you for understanding."

He cupped her chin again. "I will always understand, love. Or at least give it my best effort. I promise."

What had she ever done to deserve him? The guilt was surely going to kill her.

"Thank you," she managed.

"You're welcome. But if you had no intention of telling me all this, why did you come to my room in the first place?"

Finally, the perfect opening.

She slipped her hands to his chest, curling her fingers in the soft linen of his shirt. "I came for this, silly man." Stretching up, she feathered a kiss across his lips. "I came for you."

Chapter Twenty-Two

If not for her nerves, Ainsley might have laughed at the stunned look on her husband's face. As it was, her stomach was doing handsprings. She couldn't decide whether kissing Royal was delicious or nerve-racking.

Of course, it was a combination of both, with the scales weighted in favor of delicious. So delicious, in fact, she'd best kiss him again.

When she moved closer, he grasped her shoulders and held her back.

"Hang on, lass," he said, his brogue growing thick. "Are you saying what I think you're saying?"

She sighed. Seducing her husband was turning out to be surprisingly hard work. "Do I really have to explain it?"

Amusement warred with heat in his gaze. "Just to be on the safe side."

"What does that mean?"

"Ainsley, I'm about one minute away from flinging you onto that bed and having my wicked way with you, preferably all night. I simply want to be sure we're on the same page about this. If not, tell me now."

She loved him for being so careful with her, but the time

for caution was past. Grabbing his side whiskers, she tugged his head down until they were nose to nose.

"Ouch," he said.

"Don't be such a baby. I'm not hurting you in the least."

"I'll have you know I'm very sensitive to pain. Ask anyone."

"Ha. You're the most stoic person I've ever met. Insanely so."

"You're too kind, madam. Now, why are you tugging so fiercely on my whiskers?"

"Because I want you to listen to me and truly understand what I'm saying."

His gaze softened. "Love, I always listen to you."

"You do, but sometimes you don't hear what I'm saying. You hear what you think I'm saying."

"Now you've lost me."

"Then let me explain in terms you might understand. It's midnight, everyone else is in bed, and I've snuck into your room dressed only in my nightclothes."

"There wasn't much sneaking. Barging in would be more accurate."

"Stop quibbling," she said, tugging again on his whiskers.

The laugh lines deepened around his eyes. "My apologies, wife. So, you're saying that you crept into my bedroom because you want me to seduce you?"

"No, because *I* want to seduce *you*."

His lips curled up in a slow smile. "Even better. I'm quite fond of nubile young women trying to seduce me, especially when I'm married to them."

"As I mentioned in our last encounter of this nature, there are to be no more nubile young women but me. Not ever. Are we agreed?"

"Love, you're almost more nubile than I can manage. Any more and I'd likely perish on the spot."

"Dear me, is that a compliment? If so, it's a rather obscure one."

"Then allow me to show you exactly what I'm thinking."

He stroked her neck, brushing aside the triple layers of lace flowing down from her collar. "Good God. How am I to find you under all this fabric? It's worse than a dandy's cravat."

Ainsley was too busy shivering at the play of his fingers over her collarbone to giggle. He reached for the ribbon that tied shut the top of her wrapper, tugging on it and slowly slipping it free of its knot.

"I'm sure you'll manage just fine," she said in a breathless voice.

His hand stilled. "Are you still seducing me, or is it now the other way around?"

Exasperated, she batted his hand away. "Royal, I'm beginning to think you don't want me in your bed after all."

He took her hand and pressed it over his heart. Underneath the fine weave of his shirt, she could feel its hard thump.

"Ainsley, you are my heart," he said. "I want you so much I can hardly breathe."

"Then why are you acting like a virgin on her—or his—wedding night?"

"Because this is turning out to be our wedding night—our real wedding night. So, yes, I'm a little nervous."

She stretched up and kissed his cheek, her tongue slipping out to taste his faintly salty, bristled skin.

"Don't be," she whispered as she kissed her way along the slashing line of his jaw. "I promise to be gentle."

She felt the husky rumble of his laugh as she caressed his chest. But then he curled his fingers around her shoulders, pushing her back a few inches.

"Now what?" she yelped.

"You've been avoiding me for the last several days, so why now?"

Drat the man. He was much too perceptive for his own good.

"I'm tired of this halfway between sort of marriage," she

replied. That, at least, was the truth. "And I think you are as well."

"I will take whatever you can give me, Ainsley. But you know I want more." He rolled his lips inward, as if struggling to keep in the words. "I want everything."

"So do I. I . . . I love you, Royal." Her words echoed the stuttering of her heart. "And I want to be with you, as a woman wants to be with the man she loves."

His hands tightened on her shoulders. "You love me?"

"I know it seems rather sudden, but it's been coming on for quite some time." She gave him a weak smile, feeling foolish. "Rather like a case of the sniffles that doesn't seem to want to go away, no matter what you do."

A grin, dazzling in its intensity, transformed his solemn expression into one of joy. "I have been waiting for those words for a very long time, my lady."

He stood and pulled Ainsley to her feet.

"You've been waiting for me to make a stupid joke about sniffles and loving you?"

Royal swept her into his arms with a dramatic flourish. "It was the perfect thing to say. You're generally most truthful when you're insulting me."

"Oh, dear," she said. "I am the worst wife in Scotland. Probably England, too."

He plopped her on the edge of the bed, then leaned down and planted his hands on either side of her thighs.

"You're the perfect bride for me, my angel."

She rested her hands on his shoulders. "Truly?"

"I am yours, Ainsley. Now and forevermore."

His quiet declaration made her throat go tight. All she could muster was a misty smile.

"Now," he said. "May we commence with the mutual seduction?"

"Yes, please."

When he started to untie her wrapper, Ainsley brushed his hands away. "Let me do it."

She pulled her legs onto the bed and rolled up into a kneeling position. Her heart was pounding so hard it made her lightheaded, but she didn't care. Despite the ugly images that still lurked in the darkest corners of her mind, she wanted this. She wanted Royal with a need that made her insides tremble.

And she wanted to please him. She wanted him to burn with a fire that could only be quenched in her.

A smile lingered on his lips, but Royal's gaze was intent and smoky. "Need help?" he asked as she fumbled with the laces of her dressing gown.

"I'm quite capable of undressing myself," she said, trying to sound pert.

Unfortunately, her wrapper sported an unreasonable number of laces and ties, each apparently determined to tangle itself into a Gordian knot.

Her husband rubbed a hand over his mouth, obviously trying not to laugh.

"I do hope I'm not boring you," she said.

"That would be impossible. But while you're divesting yourself of that very charming garment, I might as well get undressed too."

Ainsley realized she'd never seen her husband entirely naked. "That makes perfect sense. Carry on."

His eyes twinkled. "Logistically, it will facilitate the process."

"Oh, blast." She'd managed to utterly snarl the delicate ribbons that secured the waist of her robe.

Royal sat down to pull off his boots. "Do you want me to cut the ribbons for you?"

"God, no. Do you have any idea how much this outfit cost?"

He yanked off one boot and went to work on the other.

"Here's a thought. Why not just pull the damn thing over your head?"

Ainsley gave another fruitless tug on the hopelessly tangled ribbons. "I suppose that makes sense."

"Or, you could just leave everything on." He waggled his eyebrows. "I'm sure I could manage."

"Don't be silly. You'd likely get caught in the ribbons and strangle yourself."

"Then over the head it is. Here, I'll show you."

He stood, and in one swift movement dragged his shirt over his head. "Now, doesn't that look easy?"

Her tart reply died on her tongue. All she could do was stare at her husband, now clad only in breeches.

Firelight slid lovingly over his wide shoulders, making his skin glow like gold. His chest, broad and muscular, was dusted with black hair that narrowed down to his trim waist. Royal's impressive physique was hard and utterly masculine, yet imbued with a grace that reminded her of ancient Greek statues. Not the ones of the gods, though, which were almost inhumanly beautiful. Royal was a warrior, lean and battle-scarred. Just looking at him made her heart pound with anticipation.

Especially when she saw the impressive erection tenting his snug-fitting breeches.

Obviously comfortable with his semi-naked, aroused state, her husband slowly raised his eyebrows in a silent dare.

Well.

Two could play at that game.

She bunched up her wrapper and dragged it over her head. There was quite a lot of it—yards, in fact—so it took a while. By the time she wrestled free, she was cursing under her breath while Royal was laughing.

"You needn't be so smug. Men have it easy when it comes to getting dressed—or undressed."

"You've never tied a cravat," he said, coming to join her.

She went to work on yet another set of stupid laces at the top of her nightgown. Royal covered her hands.

"Leave it," he said in a gruff tone.

"But you said—"

"I like the way you look in this, Ainsley."

From the heavy-lidded gleam in his eyes—and the state of his breeches—he clearly did.

"I'm glad, because it was *frightfully* expensive," she joked.

He played with the lace trimming on her bodice. "It was worth every shilling."

Made of the finest mull, the fabric whispered over her body. Delicate as a butterfly's wing, it barely concealed the dusk of her nipples or the dark nest of hair at the top of her thighs.

Royal cupped her breasts, rubbing his thumbs across her nipples. Instantly, they pulled into stiff little points.

"I'm hoping you'll wear this or something like it every night for the rest of our lives," he said as he continued to play with her.

Ainsley bit her lip to hold back a moan. "I'll do my best to comply, dear sir."

He smiled and drew the fabric tight across her breasts. Her nipples proudly jutted out, begging for his touch.

When Royal leaned in to suck one into his mouth, Ainsley let her eyes drift shut. Pleasure rose in the dark. As he gave her a gentle nip, she moaned and grabbed his shoulders, relishing the feel of his naked skin under her fingertips. He clamped his hand around her waist, holding her steady as he lavished attention on her breasts through the gauzy fabric.

As he teased her into a sensual frenzy, Ainsley's hands began to wander, tracing across his shoulders and down his brawny arms. His body radiated heat, the skin smooth over muscles dense with strength. She stroked her hands over his chest, playing with the coarse, masculine hair before following the trail down to the top of his breeches.

When her hand brushed against his erection, Royal growled and sucked her nipple deep into his mouth. Ainsley cried out and arched against him.

With a final nip that she felt deep in her core, Royal pulled away. Dazedly, she opened her eyes to see him stripping off his breeches. His linen smalls did nothing to obscure the large erection straining to break free of its confinement.

It was an impressive, if rather intimidating sight.

Ainsley couldn't help pressing a hand to her bedraggled bodice. "My goodness."

He gave her a rather sheepish smile. "Sorry. I'll keep these on for now, if it makes you feel better."

"There's really no hiding it, I'm afraid."

He hesitated. "We can slow down, if you like."

"I'm perfectly fine. Besides, I suspect you'll be hurting yourself if we don't take care of that."

His laugh was rueful.

Ainsley pulled down the bedclothes and slipped under the sheets. "Come to bed, Royal. For once, let me take care of you."

A look of intense yearning crossed his features as he joined her. He took her face between his palms and feathered a kiss across her lips. "I truly don't know what I ever did to deserve you."

Her eyes prickled. "It might have something to do with the fact that you're the nicest man in the world."

"That sounds rather boring."

She scooted over to make room. "There's nothing boring about you, as I believe you're about to show me."

Royal settled them in a comfortable cocoon of bed linens and blankets, tucking her securely against him. "Before I show you anything, I must ask you a question."

She let out a mock groan.

He turned on his side, looking serious as he traced a fingertip down the length of her nose. "I'm just wondering how you want to do this."

"Sorry?"

"Which position will be most comfortable for you?"

She blinked, disconcerted. "Oh. Well, I don't know, actually. What do you think?"

He propped an arm behind his head. For a moment, his bulging muscles and the dark feathering of hair in his armpit distracted her. She had to resist a silly impulse to tickle him.

"There are a number of positions that might suffice," he said, sounding rather professorial. "But for our first time, I suggest either you on top, or you underneath me, face-to-face. I am, however, open to suggestion. Whatever you prefer, love."

She frowned. "I suppose either would be fine. Although . . ."

"Yes?" he gently asked as she hesitated.

Her anxiety flared, but Ainsley forced herself to ignore it. She understood why he was asking the question. As usual, Royal was taking gentle care of her.

"Actually, I would prefer that I not have my back to you," she said.

He frowned. "Of course not. Not for our first time—" He broke off, his mouth suddenly a taut line. The spark of anger in his gaze told Ainsley that he'd understood.

That's how Cringlewood had assaulted her. When he'd hit her, the force of the blow had spun her around, sending her stumbling against a chaise. The marquess had then pushed her face down into the cushions and violated her.

She knocked about in her head, trying to find the words to lighten the moment, but they eluded her.

Royal studied her for a moment before nodding. "Definitely you on top, then."

Ainsley gave him a tentative smile. "You'd like that?"

"It's one of my favorite positions. Even better, you get to be in charge. I can be your helpless love slave while you do all the work."

Relief had her laughing. Thank God she'd found a man who understood her so well, and who realized how much she loathed being an object of pity.

He wrapped his hands around her waist and lifted, helping her to straddle his hips. His erection nudged between her legs, sending a lovely jolt of sensation to her core.

"There is one stipulation to engaging in this position," he said.

Ainsley wriggled, getting more comfortable. A gratifying moan rumbled from her husband's throat.

"And that is?"

"You are not to go leaping or rolling off, as you did last time," he said with mock sternness. "I don't care if Angus and his entire pack of hounds come storming into the room. No more misplaced knees to the most delicate parts of my anatomy."

Ainsley rocked a bit, enjoying the press of his erection against her aroused sex. "I promise. But I must point out that your anatomy currently feels anything but delicate."

"No," he rasped. "You've made me as hard as a standing stone."

She started to chuckle at the silly description, but her amusement faded when Royal began kneading her breasts. He urged her to rock against him while he played with her tight nipples, and they pleasured each other for long, luxurious minutes. Soon Ainsley was shaking, poised on the verge of release.

"I don't think I can wait much longer," she gasped as she leaned forward to rub her breasts against the hard musculature of his chest.

"Nor I," Royal growled. "Up on your knees, sweetheart."

Since her legs were shaking, she was forced to brace her

hands on his shoulders to push up. He slid a hand between them and unlaced his smalls, freeing his erection.

Ainsley glanced down, awestruck and slightly intimidated by the size of him.

Royal wrapped a hand around his shaft and pushed the tip against her sex, gently rubbing through her slick heat. She moaned, curling her fingers into his shoulders as the first spasms rippled out from her womb.

"Ready, love?" His voice was deep and rasping.

She nodded, rather astonished at how ready she was. Yes, she was nervous, and yes, she feared it would hurt. But she was done with being afraid. And as for the pain . . . well, that would eventually fade. And it was a small price to pay to make Royal happy.

"Look at me, bonny lass," he rumbled.

They locked gazes as the head of his erection slipped into her tight entrance.

"If it hurts, tell me and I'll stop."

She clamped her hands on his cheeks and leaned over him. "If you stop, I'll kill you."

He choked out a laugh before moving his hands to her hips, holding her steady as he pushed farther into her.

Ainsley mentally braced against the pain. He was thick and incredibly hard, parting her in a slow, relentless slide. For a few seconds, she struggled to catch her breath. Her slick channel clamped around him, throbbing, as her body adapted to Royal inside of her.

And there was no pain. There was only him.

Amazed, she stared down at him. Royal stared back. His pupils were huge, and his cheekbones were flushed with heat. She could almost believe he'd been drugged.

"All right?" he gritted out.

She nodded.

"Can you say it?"

Ainsley took a deep breath and flexed her hips. Royal's eyelids fluttered as he let out a groan.

"Better than all right," she whispered, leaning down to kiss him.

He curled his hands around the back of her head, exploring her mouth with a thorough, determined passion. Then he gave a small thrust, and it was Ainsley's turn to moan.

He pressed into her in a series of long, gliding strokes, his strong body lifting her with each thrust. She rocked to meet him, surprised by how easy and natural it felt. For so long she'd been afraid of this. But in Royal's arms, with him buried deep inside her, she felt only incredible happiness.

She leaned over him, wriggling to increase the contact between their bodies. He clamped his hands around her waist, holding her still.

"What are you doing?" she yelped. "That felt wonderful."

"I want you to feel even more wonderful. Sit up, love. Put your hands behind you and lean back."

Frustrated by the interruption, she grumbled, which made him chuckle. But when she shifted, following his murmured guidance, she understood. The new position opened her up even more, and he slid in another inch. Now, it felt like he was touching the deepest part of her.

"Good Lord," she whispered.

His smile was wicked. "You should always listen to your husband, Mrs. Kendrick."

"I will take it under advisement, Mr. Kendrick."

When he started thrusting again, she arched her back with a moan. Royal wedged a hand between their bodies, and his fingertips found her throbbing bud.

"Oh, oh," she gasped as fire shot through her.

He stroked her inside and out, his body hot and hard beneath her. Desperately, Ainsley rocked against him, straining for the release that danced just out of reach.

"That's it, my beautiful lass. You're almost there."

His hands roamed over her curves, tangling in the fabric of her nightgown. His erection touched her deep inside, in her most intimate part, and yet there was still a barrier between them. Suddenly, Ainsley knew she wanted that gone, too. She wanted nothing between them but their bodies, their hearts, and their love.

She batted Royal's hands away before grabbing the hem of her nightgown and whipping it over her head. She tossed it to the floor, then boldly met his gaze.

For a moment, he looked stunned. Then his hands came back to her body, settling on her hipbones with careful reverence.

"You are the most beautiful thing I've ever seen," he whispered in a voice choked with emotion.

"Take off your smalls," she ordered.

His grimace was slight. "I don't think you want—"

"I don't care about your scar, Royal. I don't want anything between us."

He gave a tight nod.

She lifted up, breathing a small sigh of regret as he slipped out of her. She'd been *so* close, and it had been better than anything she'd ever felt. But it didn't matter. She needed all of him.

Carefully, he helped her shift onto her back. He stripped off his smalls, dropped them to the floor, and then turned to her, magnificently naked. She stroked her fingers over his scarred thigh, trailing her hand up to his twitching erection.

"My beautiful warrior," she whispered.

He took her hand and pressed it flat over his heart. "Your warrior, my darling. I will always protect you."

She smiled mistily up at him. "I know."

Then she opened her arms, silently encouraging him to come to her.

Royal eased between her spread legs, slowly parting her flesh and slipping deep inside. As he started to move,

Ainsley wrapped herself around him, burrowing her face into his neck, wanting to hold him forever.

His strokes came long and hard, his thick length rubbing her with delicious friction. Once more her passion spiraled, building to even greater heights. Now that there were no barriers between them, nothing to keep them apart, joy shimmered like the most beautiful star, close enough to touch.

When Ainsley's body trembled on the edge of climax, Royal slid a hand beneath her bottom and tilted her up. He stroked one more time, going impossibly deep.

She clutched his broad shoulders, crying out. Fire raced through her veins, dissolving the last stubborn shards of ice that had gripped her soul for so long. In Royal's arms, she felt free again. She felt loved.

She felt safe.

With a loud groan, her husband poured his release into her body. Ainsley clung to him through the aftermath, making a silent vow to love and protect him to the very ends of the earth.

With a shuddering sigh, Royal rolled onto his side, taking her with him. Ainsley ended up in an inelegant sprawl on his chest, but she was too exhausted and happy to care.

After a minute or so, he craned up, inspecting her with a gaze that still shimmered with heat, but now also held more than a hint of concern.

"All right, lass?"

She propped her chin on his chest. "Never better."

His let his head fall back with a quiet sigh of relief. "I'm glad."

They lay quietly for a time, listening to the hiss of the fire and letting the peace of the moment settle around them.

"Royal," she finally whispered.

"Hmm?"

"Thank you for loving me."

A big hand moved to caress her bottom. "Och, lass, you're easy to love."

"No, I'm not. I'm a difficult, annoying person with far too many secrets."

Again, his head came up, a tiny frown marking his brow. "There's nothing between us now, though, is there?"

She forced a smile. "Apparently not, from the looks of things."

His gaze softened with understanding, and he once more stroked a hand over her bottom. "I love you, Ainsley. I will always love you, no matter what."

She nestled closer and silently prayed it would be so.

Chapter Twenty-Three

Ainsley tried to stifle a yawn.

"My lady, would you prefer to do the accounts later?" Henderson asked.

She gave him a sheepish smile. "No, I'm fine. But perhaps a cup of coffee wouldn't be amiss."

"Excellent idea, madam," the butler replied.

After giving instructions to a footman, Henderson rejoined her at the desk in the small office off the service rooms. "Cook will brew up a fresh pot."

"Thank you. I was up rather late with Tira, so I suppose that's why I can't stop yawning."

It was a bold-faced lie, and Henderson knew it. Tira was an excellent sleeper—unlike her father, who'd kept Ainsley awake *very* late for the last three nights in a row.

Not that she had any objections. Royal was a sensual, playful, and occasionally dominating lover, yet incredibly kind and careful. Under his skillful touch, the barriers between them had fallen until they were finally husband and wife in every way that mattered.

Life was now quite perfect, or at least it would be if not for the threat of action by the blasted Marquess of Cringlewood. Though it had been four days since Mamma's letter, she'd yet to hear a peep from her former fiancé. Perhaps it was all hogwash anyway, and Mamma had just been making a last-ditch effort to scare her into compliance.

There was little point in upsetting Royal and the rest of the family with half-baked legal threats and potential scandals that more than likely would never materialize.

But you should have told him anyway.

"My lady, are you all right?" Henderson asked in a concerned voice a few moments later.

Ainsley jerked, and a blot of ink from her quill dropped onto the ledger. "Oh, dear, how clumsy of me."

The butler swiftly sprinkled some sand on the ink and blotted it up. "Easily remedied, madam."

"I suppose I need that coffee, after all," she said as the footman came in with a tray.

"I can finish the accounts if you like," Henderson said as he poured her a cup.

"No, I promised Lady Arnprior I would take care of them. I know you're a bit short-staffed at the moment, without a housekeeper."

Ainsley fortified herself with the coffee, and then with the butler's efficient help quickly finished the household accounts and started on the menus for the following week.

"I understand that Mr. Royal is quite fond of scallops," she said. "Perhaps if Cook can find fresh ones at the—"

"Beg pardon, Mr. Henderson," William said, sticking his head into the room. "There's a visitor for Lady Ainsley. I told him my lady wasn't at home today, but he insisted." The footman grimaced. "Strongly insisted."

Ainsley never took callers unless either Royal or Logan was in the house. Her husband had suggested the tactic to prevent surprises from unwelcome visitors. At the time, she'd thought it an overreaction. Now she felt a shiver of apprehension.

"Who is it, Will?"

"Lord Cringlewood, my lady. I tried to turn him away, but he insisted that ye'd want to see him."

For a few awful seconds, black dots swarmed across her vision and the breath stuck in her lungs. She clutched the edge of the desk. How could Cringlewood be in Glasgow? Had Mamma known he was already traveling to Scotland when she'd dispatched her letter? To withhold that information seemed too great a betrayal, even given her mother's level of anger.

"Do you wish me to see the marquess off the premises?" Henderson asked. "William and I will be happy to do so."

Ainsley was surprised by the hard expression in the older man's normally kind eyes. Clearly, Royal had apprised him of the magnitude of the potential danger from the marquess.

"Aye, my lady," added William, looking pugnacious. "I'll fetch one of the other lads and we'll make short work of it, dinna ye fear."

Her anxiety abated a jot, knowing that the staff would protect her. Still . . .

She jumped to her feet. "Where's Tira?"

Henderson stood too. "In the nursery, napping. One of the nursemaids is with her."

Ainsley leaned against the back of her chair in relief.

Think. What do I do next?

"Should we send for Mr. Royal?" Henderson asked.

Her heart clutched at the idea of Royal meeting Cringlewood. For a moment, she was overcome with the enormity of the secrets she'd been holding back from him. Part of her was tempted to flee, to snatch her sleeping child from the nursery and disappear through the back door, running as far as she could to escape the danger hurtling toward her.

"Madam, what are your wishes?" Henderson said in a quietly urgent tone.

Her wishes.

What she wished for was a life without fear. To be honest with herself and with her husband, no matter the consequences. She wanted to stop being so bloody afraid, both for herself and for Tira.

It was time to confront the monster, once and for all.

"Where is Lord Cringlewood now?"

"I put him in the antechamber off the hall, my lady," William said.

"Is he alone?"

"Aye."

"Leave him there for now and send someone for Mr. Royal. He should still be at his offices at this time of day. But don't send one of the other footmen," she added. "I want you all to remain here. In fact, have one go up to guard the nursery. I also want someone watching the servants' entrance and the back of the house."

She was probably being overcautious, but if her nemesis had come all the way to Glasgow, God only knew what he would do—especially if her mother had finally told him about Tira.

Neither Henderson nor the footman blinked at her odd instructions.

"Aye, my lady, I'll take care of it," said William before dashing out.

"I'm going up to the drawing room," Ainsley said. "Please bring his lordship to me in five minutes."

"You don't wish to wait for Mr. Royal?" Henderson asked, clearly worried.

Indeed, she was tempted to wait. But before Royal arrived, she needed to know exactly what Cringlewood intended to hold over her head. "As long as you and William are nearby, I'll come to no harm."

The butler didn't look happy, but he nodded and held the door for her.

Surprised at how calm she felt after her initial panic, Ainsley made her way to the formal drawing room. But after catching a glance of herself in the pier glass over the fireplace, she grimaced.

Not so calm, after all.

She pinched some color into her dead-white cheeks and blinked several times to clear her anxious gaze. Then she straightened her collar and turned her back to the fireplace, taking comfort in the coal fire that seeped heat into her chilled bones.

When the door opened, Ainsley called on all the arrogance of her upbringing to face the brute who'd shredded the fabric of her life. If she couldn't stare down the devil for herself, she could and would do it for her daughter.

"Lord Cringlewood, my lady," Henderson announced in a blighting tone.

The marquess threw the butler an amused glance as he strolled into the room. "You seem to have a servant problem, my dear. I was forced to wait in that dreary room for an appalling amount of time, and your butler's manner leaves much to be desired."

Henderson ignored him. "Shall I leave the door open, my lady?"

Ainsley forced a smile. "That won't be necessary, Henderson."

"William and I will be just outside if you need us, madam."

"Thank you."

Though the thought of being alone with Cringlewood was deeply disturbing, she had no wish to expose her situation in front of the servants. Still, she couldn't help breathing a sigh of relief when Henderson left the door fractionally ajar.

The person she truly needed was her husband, although she felt sick at the thought of how Royal would react to what was about to unfold.

Can't be helped, old girl.

The Marquess of Cringlewood was a handsome man, although not as brawny as Royal or the other Kendrick men. Lean and fit, he was both an accomplished horseman and fencer. His wheat-colored hair was arranged in the latest style, and his classically aristocratic features and sky-blue eyes held a trace of arrogant amusement. As always, he was dressed in the height of fashion, as spotless as if he'd just left the careful ministrations of his valet.

Then again, he probably had. Her former fiancé never traveled anywhere without a large complement of servants and massive amounts of baggage.

Gracefully, he flipped open his snuffbox and took a leisurely sniff. After he put it away, he lifted a golden brow in an ironic arch.

"Nothing to say, my dear girl? Are we simply going to stare at each other, daggers drawn? Perhaps you could at least offer some refreshments. After all, I've come such a long way to throw myself at your lovely little feet."

He punctuated his nonsense with the smile that had charmed so many young women and their matchmaking mammas. But it had never charmed her, she now realized.

"You won't be staying long enough to take refreshments," she coolly replied.

He let out a gentle sigh, his smile turning rueful. Really, it was too bad he'd never taken up amateur theatricals.

"May I at least sit down, so we can converse like civilized people?"

"Civilized people don't go around assaulting defenseless women, but suit yourself." She waved a hand at the chaise opposite the fireplace.

A scowl briefly surfaced, but he smoothly recovered and sat. Cautiously, Ainsley perched on the edge of a straight-backed chair several feet away from him.

"Ainsley, as I explained previously," he said, "I didn't

assault you. At the time, you could hardly blame me for thinking you were quite as willing as I was."

Her outraged gasp had him holding up a hand. "But as I said, it was clearly a misunderstanding, which I regret. I'm eager to clear it up and leave this whole ugly business in the past, where it belongs."

"And as I told you at the time, it was no misunderstanding," she said through clenched teeth. "You knew very well I wasn't willing. You took me without my consent."

When he let out a snort of derision, her fingers itched to snatch up the vase of mums at her elbow and throw it at his head. Instead, she adopted her coldest manner.

"And I insist that you call me Lady Ainsley, or even better, Mrs. Kendrick."

His gaze went flinty. "I am just about out of patience, my dear. It's time for you to stop this nonsense and come home."

She folded her hands in her lap. "I am home."

He waved a dismissive hand. "Where is Mr. Kendrick, by the by?"

"At his offices. Unlike you, he works for a living."

He simply laughed. "My poor girl, reduced to the wife of a tradesman. No wonder your long-suffering parents are so upset."

"They'll get over it."

"No, they won't," he said, his voice hard. "I'll see to that."

His malicious expression pushed bile up into her throat. Still, she began to feel cautiously confident. He'd yet to mention Tira, which suggested Mamma had kept that ultimate leverage to herself, after all.

"Now we get to the point," she said. "How, exactly, are you threatening my parents?"

He studied her for a moment before pasting on another charming smile. "Ainsley, my love, surely you can see that—"

"I am not your love. I was *never* your love. I was only

ever a possession to you. Well, I'm afraid you must give up any pretensions to a prior claim. I will not be divorcing my husband. It's entirely absurd to think that I would."

He stared at her, incredulous. "If you're telling me that you have affection for the fellow, I refuse to believe it. End this farce now, and come back to the life you were born to lead. I'll give you whatever you want, I promise."

"I want nothing of yours." She lifted her chin. "And I have much more than mere affection for my husband. He's the finest man I've ever met, and I'm honored to be his wife."

The marquess leapt to his feet, moving toward her with surprising speed. Ainsley was barely able to scramble up and put the chair between them before he reached her.

"You are *mine*, Ainsley," he snarled. "You've been mine for years, whether you knew it or not. And *no one* takes away what's mine."

His vicious expression and the ugly tone of his voice turned her blood to ice. In that moment, she believed he might kill her. Every muscle in her body urged flight. But she'd done that once before, and trouble had arrived on her doorstep anyway. It was time to end the madness once and for all.

"You do not own me, my lord. I am free to make my own decisions with my future. And my future will never include you."

Though his complexion remained a mottled, angry red, he regained a measure of control. "You're making a grievous mistake, my girl. If you wish to avoid the ruination of your family, I suggest you do as your mother suggested. I will be happy to set you up in a quiet house in the country for the requisite time. Or a town house in Edinburgh, if you prefer." He suddenly laughed. "I could visit you, in fact. That would certainly make the charge of adultery convincing to the courts."

She shook her head in anger and disbelief. "Aside from the fact that I will never allow you to touch me again, have you gone entirely mad? The scandal would be enormous, and would reflect on you and *your* family as well as mine. Why would you wish that? To put *all* of us through that?"

"As I said, what's mine is mine. Until I say it isn't."

"You mean this is simply about your pride? That cannot possibly be true."

She studied his cold expression, trying to figure it out. Yes, Cringlewood was an incredibly proud, arrogant man who was used to getting whatever he wanted, but something was off. Revenge for embarrassing him was one thing, but this was . . .

"Something else is at work here," she said.

When his gaze darted away for a moment, understanding hit her like an earthquake.

"Ah, it's about the money, isn't it? You want the settlements." Yet that didn't make sense either. "Why? You're already rich as Midas."

The sudden blaze of hatred in his eyes had her retreating back to the fireplace.

"Not anymore, you stupid girl," he said as he stalked after her. "Thanks to you."

She contemplated grabbing the fireplace poker and braining him. But surely not even he would be foolish enough to attack her, with the butler and a footman just outside the door. Still, she hastily moved and put another chair between them.

"Then I don't understand," she said. "I have nothing to do with how rich you are."

"You think not, Ainsley? You were to bring a large fortune to our union. Based on that and on prior discussions with your father, I made certain investments. Some of them were quite . . . forward-thinking."

Now she understood. "Risky, you mean."

"There is no profit without risk. Unfortunately, I was ill advised on two of them—one a mining venture, the other founding a bank." His features pulled tight. "Sadly, both went bankrupt."

"How unfortunate. But surely you could find another heiress happy to marry you and pull you out of the River Tick."

He tilted his head to study her. "Would you like to know how much I owe to my creditors?"

"Not really."

He told her anyway. The figure was beyond staggering.

"Since the vast majority of my estates are entailed, I have very few options," he said. "You are one of the richest heiresses in England, and I need both the money and land you will bring to our marriage. The money and the land *promised* to me." He flashed a wolfish smile. "Your dear papa has offered to enhance the settlements if you agree to come home, like the good girl I know you are."

"Blackmail. You're blackmailing my parents."

"Call it what you will. But be assured that any scandal from your divorce would be well worth it." He took another step forward. "You and your family owe me this, Ainsley. And I will collect, no matter what."

As badly as she felt for her parents, she was heartsick that they would offer her as a war prize. "Not from me, you won't. There is nothing you can do that will—"

When he snatched the chair and threw it aside, Ainsley jumped back. Her foot caught the edge of a claw-footed table, causing her to stumble. The marquess was on her in an instant, grabbing her by the neck of her gown and slamming her shoulder into the mantelpiece. For a moment, she was too stunned to utter a sound.

"Nothing?" he snarled, inches away from her face. "I think you'll soon find how wrong you are."

She flinched at the sour smell of his breath. For a few,

horrible moments, black swarmed at the edges of her vision. Ainsley fought it back, terrified and infuriated by the feel of his body against hers.

"Let me go," she ground out. "Or I swear I'll kill you."

Cringlewood's mouth split into a nasty grin. But it froze on his face a moment later at the sound of a pistol cocked behind him.

"Best do as she says, ye *Sassenach* prick, or I'll blow yer bloody brains out," said Angus.

Chapter Twenty-Four

Ainsley had never been happier to see her former nemesis.

"Let her go," the old man snarled when the marquess didn't move.

"You should do as he says," Ainsley managed in a hoarse voice. "He *will* shoot you."

"Aye, that I will, lass, and I'll enjoy it, too."

The marquess cast a glare over his shoulder but finally released her and took a step back. She staggered a bit, her legs shaky with relief.

"Here, sit ye down," Angus said, coming over to guide her to the chaise. He kept the pistol trained on Cringlewood every moment.

"Are ye all right, lass?" he murmured.

Ainsley nodded. "Yes, I'm fine."

She wasn't, but she refused to give Cringlewood the satisfaction of seeing how badly his violence had frightened her.

Angus jerked his head toward the door. "Do ye want me to have the bastard thrown out?"

Henderson and William loomed in the doorway, ready to do just that.

"I wouldn't, if I were you," the marquess said to Ainsley.

"I have a few other things to say that might influence your decision."

"Shut yer mouth," Angus growled. "Ye'll no be telling the lass what to do, ye bloody ponce."

Unbelievably, Cringlewood began to look amused. "Ainsley, who is this pattern-card of gentility, might I ask?"

Ainsley glared at him. "This is my grandfather-in-law, Mr. MacDonald."

"Oh, my poor dear. How far you have fallen. I have obviously arrived in the nick of time to save you from complete degradation."

Angus smiled and extended his arm as if preparing to fire. For a stunned moment, Ainsley thought he was actually going to do it.

Royal suddenly appeared, shoving his way between Henderson and William. "Grandda, put down the pistol."

"The bloody bastard threatened the lassie," Angus protested as his grandson stalked over to him.

Royal flicked a killing glance in Cringlewood's direction, but then looked back at Angus and held out his hand. "I'll deal with him."

With an aggrieved sigh, Angus handed over the pistol. Royal uncocked it and placed it on the table before hunkering down in front of Ainsley. He took her hands and began chafing them.

"Are you all right, sweetheart?"

He was hatless, his hair whipped into a tangle and his color high, as if he'd run all the way from his offices. Even though his gaze shimmered with concern for her, there was a lethal calm about him that boded ill for Cringlewood, who, of course, would be too arrogant to realize it.

The marquess might be a powerful aristocrat, but Royal was a Highland warrior. He would do anything and everything to protect his family and his wife.

"Yes," she said.

"Did he hurt you?"

Her shoulder ached a bit, but she shook her head.

"Only because I stopped him," Angus said. "Bastard had his hand on her neck when I came in."

Royal slowly rose to his feet. "Did he now?" he said, his brogue growing thick. "Then I suppose that pistol will be of use, after all."

Cringlewood extracted his snuffbox and helped himself to a pinch. "Best not to do anything until you've heard what I have to say about your wife."

"I'm not interested in a damn thing you have to say."

"Oh, I think you will be. What I'm about to tell you could have a marked effect on the entire Kendrick family."

Ainsley touched her husband's arm. "Perhaps we'd best hear him out."

Royal glanced down at her, his gaze troubled. "You don't have to do this, love."

"We need to know everything, Royal."

Now that her fate was upon her, calm had once more descended. No matter how bad it was, there would be no more questions or secrets. There was relief in that, at least for now.

Reluctantly, her husband nodded. "Agreed, but there's no need for you to stay. I have a few things to discuss with his lordship that I'd rather do in private."

Ainsley practically shot up from the chaise. "No!"

Royal blinked.

"I appreciate that you want to protect me," she said. "But I'm not afraid of him."

"She's afraid for you to hear the truth, though," the marquess said as he snapped shut his snuffbox and stowed it away.

Ainsley tried to ignore him, focusing on her husband. "Could we please do this without an audience?"

The marquess let out a soft laugh that made her want to shove him off a very high cliff.

Royal drew Angus aside and quietly issued some terse orders. Although his grandfather objected, Royal steered him from the room and firmly closed the door. Then he urged Ainsley to return to the chaise, standing behind her and resting a comforting hand on her shoulder.

"All right," he said to Cringlewood. "Say your piece quickly and then get the hell out of my house before I throttle you."

The marquess sized Royal up with a faint smile. Ainsley recognized that canny expression—he was looking for a chink in her husband's armor.

"I take it that Ainsley failed to admit how she was more than willing to have relations with me," the marquess finally said.

She again shot to her feet. "That's a lie."

Royal gently pressed her back down. "Cringlewood, I'm on a very short leash. If you value your life, never again refer to the outrage you perpetrated on my wife."

The marquess looked briefly disconcerted, but then shrugged. "Fine. I have advised Ainsley that she must end this ridiculous marriage and return to London. It is in everyone's best interest that she do so."

"Don't be an idiot," Royal snapped. "That's in no one's interest but yours."

"You're wrong, Kendrick, because I will sue her family and your family for breach of contract. My lawyers tell me I have an excellent case. And given the size of the marriage settlements previously agreed upon, I assure you I intend to pursue very large judgments. Then there's the scandal, of course. Extremely embarrassing for everyone."

Royal's hands tightened on her shoulders. "Marriage settlements?"

"Oh, didn't she tell you? The contracts for our marriage were negotiated, witnessed by lawyers, and signed before Ainsley foolishly broke our engagement."

Ainsley had to struggle to hold back the rising tide of

panic. She twisted in her seat to look at her husband, who was clearly taken about by Cringlewood's declaration.

"It . . . things might be a bit more complicated than I originally suggested," she stammered.

He stared down at her. "The contracts were actually signed?"

"I'm afraid so," she weakly replied.

His reaction was understandable. Marriage contracts were legally binding documents, almost as binding as the marriage ceremony itself. Once the papers were signed, some couples didn't even wait for the wedding day to consummate their relationship, seeing themselves as already bound. The marquess had certainly made that assumption, even though Ainsley had not.

Breaking such a negotiated settlement made one vulnerable to a breach of contract lawsuit. In the eyes of the law—and of the polite world—Ainsley and her family would be perceived as the guilty party, deserving of whatever legal and social sanctions were imposed on them.

Breach of promise suits, while rare, could be ruinous.

"Why didn't you tell me the contracts had been signed?" Royal asked her. Frustration seethed beneath the quiet tone of his voice.

"I thought it unlikely . . . I hoped he would never do something this insane," she said. "Especially not once you and I were married."

Her husband clamped his lips together and shot an angry look at the marquess.

"So you see, Kendrick," Cringlewood said with a smirk, "I can and will make your lives a misery, if you do not comply. But there is a simple solution. Ainsley departs this house today, and in six weeks one of you sues the other for adultery. Given that your marriage is obviously a sham, it should be an easy decision to make."

"Our marriage is not a sham," Ainsley snapped. "It's a true marriage in every way, I assure you."

Out of the corner of her eye, she saw Royal flinch. When she glanced up at him, his gaze flicked away from her.

Her heart sank.

"You cannot be serious," Cringlewood said.

"She's completely serious. Legal and true in every sense." Royal gave the marquess a taunting smile.

The marquess clearly had to struggle for a moment before he could continue. "Ah, yes, but then there are those pesky little contracts."

"I don't care if she signed the damn Magna Carta," Royal growled. "Ainsley is not yours, and she never will be yours."

"In any case, my daughter certainly is," the marquess said with malicious triumph. "It's Tira, I believe, such an ugly, Scottish name. I'll have to change that, certainly."

Ainsley didn't remember moving but she found herself on her feet and standing only inches away from Cringlewood, her hands balled into fists.

"You'll never lay a hand on her," she ground out. "I'll deny everything."

"Too late, my dear," he said. "Your dear mamma already told me the entire truth. You will divorce Kendrick and return to me, or I'll take your daughter from you and you'll never see her again."

"That will never happen," Royal said. "Tira stays with the Kendrick family, no matter what."

Tira stays.

Ainsley's heart shriveled at the possible meaning of those words. But how could she blame him? Her daughter's safety must always come first, even if it meant . . .

"And what if I agree to your demands?" she asked. "Would you leave Tira alone?"

Royal's hand closed around her arm. "Ainsley, stop!"

She shook him off and kept her attention on the villain in front of her. "Well?"

The marquess gave her that famously winning smile again. It made her want to vomit.

"I'm sure I could be persuaded to leave her here in Scotland," he said. "And if you become the biddable wife I know you could be, I might even let you visit her now and again. If you were very good, that is."

Royal stepped around her and grabbed the marquess by the cravat, lifting him onto his toes. Cringlewood's eyes went wide with shock and he started to struggle. Royal shoved him hard against the bookcase behind him, tightening his other hand around his throat.

"If you ever come near my wife or daughter again, I'll kill you," he said in a voice as cold as a Highland winter gale. "On my mother's soul, I'll end you."

"And if he doesn't, I will," said Logan, striding into the room.

Royal glanced over his shoulder. "It's about bloody time you showed up."

"Took the kitchen boy a while to track me down," Logan said. "What do you want me to do with the bastard?"

"Just get him out of here," he said, shoving Cringlewood away.

The marquess staggered, coughing. "That was a fatal mistake, Kendrick," he hoarsely managed.

Logan clamped a massive hand on Cringlewood's shoulder and propelled him toward the door. "Let's have a little chat about mistakes on the way out, shall we? Then we'll see who's made one."

"Get your blasted hands off me." Cringlewood shot Ainsley a look of pure hatred as Logan pushed him toward the door.

After a quick, troubled glance in their direction, Logan hurried out too. In the ensuing silence, Ainsley could hear Royal's fractured breathing as he struggled to control his anger.

"Royal, I'm so sorry," she said.

"For God's sake, Ainsley, why didn't you tell me about those blasted marriage contracts?"

"I . . . I was afraid."

"Afraid that I wouldn't marry you if I knew the truth?"

She nodded, even as she struggled not to burst into tears. "Would it have made a difference to you?"

"*No*." He sucked in a breath, making a visible effort to calm himself. "I don't know, but if you'd told me, I could have planned for it. As it is . . ."

"I'm sorry," she miserably whispered.

"Consummating our marriage . . . was that because of this?"

She flinched, even though she'd been expecting the question. "In part, but I still wanted to be with you. Still want to be with you."

He closed his eyes, looking so weary and frustrated it broke her heart. "Ainsley, when are you ever going to learn to trust me?"

She had to fight back tears. "I do trust you. I love you."

"You've got an odd way of showing it," he said in a bitter echo of his words from the other night.

When he headed for the door with a noticeable limp, her heart clenched even harder. Had he hurt himself when he shoved Cringlewood against the bookcase?

"Where are you going?"

"I have to speak to Logan, and then I'll consult with the family's lawyer about how to handle this before it spins completely out of control."

"Do you want me to come with you?"

"No, I want you to stay right here," he said, throwing her a frustrated glance. "And for once, try to stay the hell out of trouble."

Chapter Twenty-Five

"He'll never forgive me," Ainsley said. "Not this time."

She plunked her reticule down on the park bench. The dratted thing was heavy, since it concealed a small pistol she'd acquired before leaving England. Royal would have a heart spasm if he ever discovered she sometimes carried a weapon, but experience had taught her to be prepared for the worst.

"Och, don't be daft," Angus scoffed. "Ye just caught him by surprise, and in front of the Sassenach prick, too. Royal was a wee bit embarrassed, that's all."

She stared gloomily at the children playing on the other side of the garden square. "He barely spoke two words at dinner last night, and then he and Logan went off together for hours. I'm not sure when he even went to bed."

Actually, she was quite sure, although she would choke before admitting that she'd waited up for him. If he would have given her the chance, Ainsley could have adequately explained the reasons for her secretive behavior and how much she regretted it. Unfortunately, her hopes in that regard had gone unanswered, as Royal's firm tread had passed by her bedroom door last night without hesitation.

Unfortunately, she hadn't been able to work up the nerve

to go after him. He'd obviously reached his own conclusions and needed no explanations from her.

"The lads are workin' on a plan to deal with the legalities," Angus said. "It's tricky, ye ken. But they'll figure it out, especially once Nick arrives in town. He'll deal with Lord Fathead, never ye fear."

"Angus, Lord Fat—er, Lord Cringlewood is anything but stupid. Ruthless, conniving, and without principle, but certainly far from stupid."

"He's a jolter-head if he thinks he can take on the Kendricks and come away with his skin intact. Everythin' will be as right as a trivet in no time. I promise."

"I very much doubt that."

"Here, stop bein' such a gloomy guts and take hold of Tira. I can tell she's wantin' her mamma."

Ainsley arched her eyebrows at that bit of nonsense. Tira was thoroughly swaddled in a soft cashmere shawl, happily snoring away in her grandfather's arms. Still, the gesture was a measure of the old fellow's concern for her, and Ainsley was touched.

She gently pulled the shawl back from her daughter's face. Tira's cheeks were sweetly flushed with sleep. Her mouth was a rosebud oval, emitting snores so adorable that Ainsley could hardly breathe. The possibility that she might lose her again wrapped a horrid vise around her chest.

"I don't want to wake her," she whispered.

Angus rolled his eyes and plopped Tira onto her lap. "Ye could run the Kiplingcotes Derby through this bloody square with no fear. Tira's a grand sleeper, now that she's gotten used to ye."

Ainsley settled the comforting bundle within her arms. Her daughter snuffled a bit against the ruffles of her pelisse, then nestled closer with a little yawn. Her eyelids fluttered for only a moment before the baby snores resumed.

"Told ye," Angus said. "She kens who ye are now, like I said she would."

"You never said that. You called me utterly hopeless on more than one occasion."

"Aye. I can be wrong—on the rare occasion."

"I must engrave this moment in my memory. Angus MacDonald admits he was wrong about me."

"I wasn't wrong about the Ainsley ye was. I was wrong about the Ainsley ye are."

"That's a rather murky distinction."

"Makes perfect sense to me. Now, just sit ye quietly and let the lads worry about Lord Sneaksby. We'll kill the bloody *Sassenach* bastard before we let him hurt ye or Tira."

Since she'd nursed murderous thoughts herself, she couldn't scold Angus for actually voicing them.

"The marquess is an influential man, even given his current money problems. He could make our lives exceedingly hellish."

"We're used to the English tryin' to get the best of us, lass. The Kendricks can handle one poncy marquess."

"Yes, but—"

He put a firm hand on her arm. "Ainsley, I ken yer worried, but ye'd best let Royal take care of this. It's his job to protect ye and Tira."

"But I want to protect him, too." She was terrified of Cringlewood's vengeful nature, and dreaded what he could do to Royal.

"Ye've got the rest of yer life to protect him. For now, just let Royal and the lads do what they do."

The fact that she had little standing under the law, and was almost entirely dependent on Royal and the family to protect her, was a frustrating state of affairs.

"If you say so, Grandda. But it's hard to sit and do nothing."

"Ye be takin' Tira and yer old grandda for a spot of fresh

air—and trustin' Royal. I know it goes against the grain, but he won't fail ye."

She carefully shifted Tira and turned to smile at him. "I know, and thank you for spending time with me. I know it's mostly about Tira, but I still appreciate it."

"Fah. Did ye not just call me Grandda?"

Ainsley mentally blinked. "I believe I did."

"There ye go, then. Now, just sit and enjoy the fine day while ye have the chance. The weather will be turnin' soon enough."

"That's a happy thought."

"Yer the one who married a Highlander and moved to Scotland."

"What was I thinking?" she joked.

They sat in companionable silence until they heard raised voices behind them. Angus looked around.

"Who's young Will talkin' to?" he asked.

Hoisting Tira onto her shoulder, Ainsley stood and peered toward the street that fronted Kendrick House. Royal had made it clear that she was not to venture outside without an escort, not even for Tira's daily airing in the little square. Ainsley had felt rather silly about the whole thing, with an undoubtedly armed Angus by her side, and the brawny William only yards away. The whole staff of Kendrick House was close by too.

Still, it was good to be prudent, ergo the pistol in her reticule.

"I'm not sure." She studied William and the man in a greatcoat. "There's a carriage right there. Maybe the man is asking for directions."

"Doesna look like a polite conversation to me."

When Angus unbuttoned his coat, Ainsley caught a glimpse of the pistol shoved into the waistband of his breeches.

"You and the wee lassie wait here."

"Maybe we should just go back to the house instead."

"Nae, that carriage is too close for my comfort. Stay here."

"Angus . . . oh, blast," she muttered.

With his usual spryness, the old fellow hurried across the lawn to confront the man. "Here now," he called out. "What is it ye be needin' from—"

Without hesitation, the greatcoated man spun around and drilled Angus in the chin. Ainsley let out a strangled shriek as the old man dropped to his knees. William leapt forward to attack, but another stranger appeared from behind the coach. He smashed the butt of a flintlock into William's skull. The footman collapsed onto the grass like he'd been shot.

Horrified, Ainsley backed away, clutching Tira to her chest. The attackers were between her and Kendrick House, and she couldn't depend on any of the servants looking out the window and rushing to help. She could scream, but even then it was unlikely that aid would arrive in time.

She pivoted and scurried toward the opposite side of the park. If she could make one of the other streets, she could slip into one of the back alleys running behind the houses and—

Ainsley skidded to a halt when *another* man in a great-coat dashed toward her across the lawn. Where had *he* come from?

Tira, finally jolted awake, let out a wail. Ainsley hoisted her higher on her shoulder and turned back toward Kendrick House. But when she tried to dart around the men who'd attacked Angus and William, her leather boots slipped on the grass. Tira, her cries rising in volume, shot up a hand and grabbed the edge of Ainsley's poke bonnet, yanking it down over her eyes.

"Give it up, missus," came a low growl. "There ain't no way you're getting away from us."

Ainsley pushed her bonnet from her eyes to see the man

who'd cut off her escape to the side streets. Despite his rough speech, he was dressed in a well-tailored greatcoat and a beaver hat. He looked more like a prosperous shopkeeper than a thug, except for the pistol that was half-concealed by his coat.

"What do you want?" she demanded. Her daughter squirmed, and it was all Ainsley could do to keep hold of her.

"Lord Cringlewood sent us to fetch the brat." The man grinned, revealing a mouthful of broken teeth. "Looks like you can't manage her anyway, missus, so you might as well hand her over."

Ainsley took a step back. "I'll kill you if you touch my daughter."

The man scoffed. "We ain't gonna hurt the kid, but we have our orders. We're to bring her, no matter what."

She cast a wild glance around. The other two men, both hulking brutes, stood only a few feet away and blocked her path. William was still flat-out on the grass, while Angus was struggling to get up.

Think.

"Hand her over, missus," snapped the man with the gun. "We ain't got all day."

Ainsley squeezed her eyes shut for a moment, praying for strength. Then she met the man's gaze with her own challenge. "You're taking her to his lordship now?"

"Aye."

"Then I'm coming too."

He nodded. "Cringlewood thought you might say that. Come along with you, then."

When the man reached to take her arm, she jerked away. "Don't touch me."

He shrugged, briefly flashing his pistol. "Suit yourself. But get a move on it, if you know what's good for you."

They started off toward the carriage, which had moved toward them.

"My husband will go to the magistrate. You won't get away with this," she said.

"His lordship ain't worried about that. She's his kid, isn't she?"

"But you're kidnapping me."

"I ain't. You're comin' of your own free will. Now shut your damn mouth, else I'll shut it for you."

Ainsley clamped her lips shut and concentrated on putting one foot in front of the other. Tira cuddled against her, now quietly sobbing into the lace trim of her pelisse.

"Hush, darling," she whispered. "Mamma won't leave you, no matter what. No one will ever take you away from me again."

At this point, that was all that mattered.

They'd almost reached the carriage when Angus finally managed to stagger toward them. "Stop, ye bastards," he shouted.

"He ain't no threat," said one of the men. "We got his pistol."

The brute beside her cocked his own pistol, even though the old man was unarmed.

"Angus, stop," she called out. "Think of Tira. She might get hurt."

He stumbled to a halt, his bloodied features pulled tight with anguish.

"They're going to take her either way," she said to him. "So I'm going with her."

"Lass, you canna do this," he choked out. "Ye'll make it harder for Royal to get the wee one back."

"I'm sorry, Angus. But I will not be separated from her ever again."

Her captor jabbed her in the shoulder. "Get in the bloody coach."

She looked Angus straight in the eye. The old man was in tears. "Tell Royal I love him."

"Lass—"

"Angus, go home, now."

She turned and climbed into the carriage that would take her to the man about to ruin her life.

Again.

"It's my fault." Royal braced himself as the town coach swung hard around a corner. "I never should have left the house."

"The marquess would have gotten his hands on Tira sooner or later," Logan said from the opposite bench. "The law would have seen to that."

Angus, seated next to Logan, scowled. "To hell with the law. We'll take care of the English bastards ourselves."

In the dim light of the carriage lamps, the old fellow's bruised and swollen features looked gruesome.

"Are you sure you're up to this?" Royal asked.

The side of his grandfather's mouth that wasn't swollen lifted in an attempt at a ferocious smile. "Dinna fash yerself, lad. I'm fine."

"You're not fine. You were almost—" He clamped his mouth shut against the rage and fear that threatened to swamp him.

Angus divined his thoughts. "That *Sassenach* codpiece has no reason to hurt our lasses. He's got what he wants. For now."

"He doesn't give a hang about Tira, but he *will* punish Ainsley." It was driving him mad just thinking about it.

"It's been less than two hours," Logan said. "Your wife is

a smart, capable woman. She can take care of herself and Tira until we rescue them."

Royal would lay waste to Cringlewood's entire life and kill him, if necessary. But without Ainsley and Tira, *his* life would be a hollow shell. No matter what he had to do, he would get them back.

"Logan's right," Angus said. "Your lady is a canny one. And she'll know we're coming for her."

Royal hoped so, but her last words to Angus had suggested exactly the opposite. He wouldn't blame her for doubting his loyalty. Yesterday, he'd been angry and critical when he should have been reassuring her. Ainsley knew Cringlewood better than anyone, and she knew what he was capable of doing. Every action she took—even the lies she told—was to protect herself and Tira.

But Royal's pride had been wounded by what he saw as her lack of faith in him. So he'd cut her off, leaving her alone and vulnerable when she needed him the most.

As usual, Logan also deduced what he was thinking. "Stop beating yourself up. We'll get them back, and then we'll get you all out of town. We have a plan, so let's just stick to it and get the job done."

Royal managed a smile. "Have I told you lately how happy I am that you're back in Scotland?"

"We're Clan Kendrick, lad," Angus said. "We dinna give up on each other, and we never back down from a fight."

"True, Grandda," Logan said, "but I share Royal's concerns about you. You got quite the knock on the head."

"Och, I've had worse. And I want my own piece of that bastard."

"Cringlewood is mine," Royal said. "No one touches him but me."

Angus bristled before Logan shut him down. "Grandda, from what you told us, there will be plenty of heads to knock about. Just do what Royal tells you, all right?"

The old man harrumphed. "I dinna ken about this plan of yers. Seems a mite risky."

"You're not the one taking the risk," Royal said.

"Exactly my point," Angus said. "That leg of yers isn't up to it."

"I just need to buy us the time for Logan and the other men to get into the house. It shouldn't take long, if everything goes well."

"And everything always goes so well in this family, ye ken," Angus retorted.

"We don't have a choice," Royal said. "If Cringlewood gets them out of Scotland, it'll be almost impossible to get Tira back."

And that meant he would never get Ainsley back. She would never leave her daughter again.

"I'd feel better if Nick were here," Angus said. "His bloody lordship would have to pay heed to the Earl of Arnprior."

"We'd all feel better if Nick were here," Royal said. "But he should be in town tomorrow, so he can take care of the cleanup."

Logan peered out the window. "We're close enough, I think. Best signal the coachman."

After Royal thumped on the roof of the carriage, it slowed to a stop. Logan opened the door and jumped down to the side of the deserted road. Royal followed more carefully—he couldn't afford to aggravate his bad leg, with everything that was at stake.

"Angus isn't wrong," Logan quietly said. "That leg of yours could be our undoing."

"I'll manage. I have to. They'd never let me keep a pistol, for one thing. And we also need a gambit that gives you enough time to get into the house and take control."

His older brother sighed. "Aye, well, I suppose a half-baked plan is better than no plan at all, given the lack of time."

When Royal and Logan returned from their offices,

they'd found the household in chaos. William was barely conscious and Angus was staggering about, raging and bloody. The several minutes it had taken to get a clear measure of the situation had been the longest of Royal's life. If not for Logan holding him back, he would have charged out of the house like a maniac, tearing Glasgow apart in a fruitless effort to find Ainsley and Tira.

Fortunately, Henderson had recalled that Ainsley's mother had stayed with a cousin, Lady Montgomery, in her manor house just on the outskirts of town. Logan had saddled a horse and ridden there, sneaking through the gardens and peering into windows until he spotted Ainsley in one of the drawing rooms. She appeared unharmed. As Cringlewood and two of his men were also present, Logan had little choice but to return to Kendrick House with the news.

That delay, as nerve-racking as it was, had given Royal the time needed to put a plan in place.

Henderson hurried over from the second carriage, now pulled up behind them. The butler had been included in their foray because he was friendly with Lady Montgomery's butler and housekeeper. Royal thought his presence—along with four well-armed Kendrick footmen and grooms— should be enough to give Logan the support he needed in both convincing Lady Montgomery's servants to stand down and neutralizing Cringlewood's hired thugs.

"All right, let's do this," Logan said as he extracted a pistol from his greatcoat pocket. He pulled Royal into a brief hug. "Good luck, lad. Be careful, and be safe."

"You too," Royal gruffly replied.

The small band of men climbed over the short wall between the manor house gardens and the road, then disappeared into the evening gloom. With a nod to the coachman, Royal climbed back in and braced himself as the vehicle rattled forward. The second carriage would remain where it was, out of sight but close enough for a nimble retreat.

A few minutes later, the coach turned into a gravel drive and wheeled up to the front portico of the manor house.

"Ready, laddie?" Angus asked.

Royal leaned forward and gripped his shoulder. "Thank you, Grandda. Whatever happens, I know I can depend on you to keep Ainsley and Tira safe."

"Ye'll be doin' that, son. Never fear."

"I know, but if anything happens to me, I want you to take care of them. Ainsley will be . . . vulnerable without me."

A flash of anxiety darted across his grandfather's face. "Then don't let anything happen to ye, or I'll paddle yer bum. Yer not too old for me to do that, ye ken."

Royal smiled. "All right, Grandda. Just follow my lead and don't do anything stupid."

"Now, when do I ever do anything stupid?"

Royal was spared the need to reply when the door opened. He stepped down, Angus right behind him.

They gazed up at the imposing mansion, where many of the windows were dark. Royal had suspected that Lady Montgomery was currently not in residence. Cringlewood's cousin was a respectable, well-regarded woman who would never participate in something as heinous as a kidnapping. Her absence meant that the household would likely be running a skeleton staff.

Of course, it also meant there was no voice of reason to serve as a check on Cringlewood's obsessive behavior. He would no doubt be bordering on the irrational by now, and would respond aggressively to any attempts to take Ainsley away from him.

Royal was counting on that.

The black double doors swung open before they knocked.

"May I ask who ye be callin' for?" a footman cautiously asked.

"Royal and Angus Kendrick, here to see Lord Cringlewood," Royal said.

"Aye, sir. I'll just—"

"Let them in, you barmy fool," barked a rough voice.

The footman gave Royal a slight, apologetic grimace as he stepped aside. He was a local man, obviously, and a possible ally.

They stepped into a tiled reception hall, decorated with elegant plasterwork in shades of blue and cream. A spiral staircase with elaborate ironwork curled up from the right side of the hall to the upper floors.

"Is her ladyship at home?" Royal murmured as he handed the footman his hat.

"That she is not, sir," the young man grimly replied.

"Stop your jawin' and get over here," ordered a massively built man at the bottom of the staircase.

The fellow had a smashed-in nose and a pugilist's ears, a former boxer—most likely. But despite his rough appearance, he carried himself well and dressed with a certain amount of style. He was obviously not a common street thug.

Another man stood next to him, however, looking very much like a street thug. He held a flintlock pistol, which did nothing to dispel that impression.

"His lordship is expectin' you," said the well-tailored man.

"Told ye the bastard would want to see ye," Angus murmured. "He wants to rub it in yer face."

Royal moved to the staircase, his grandfather close on his heels.

"Who are you?" he asked.

The man obviously in charge sneered at Royal, revealing an execrable set of teeth. "Don't matter who I am, but you can call me Mr. Smith."

"How original," Royal said.

"Ain't it just. Now, open your coats. Both of you."

Royal complied, as did Angus.

Smith's eyebrows shot up when he saw what Royal had

strapped to his waist. "A short sword? What the hell do you think you're gonna do with that?"

"Kill your master."

Smith shook his head. "Bloody Highlanders, stupid as the day is long. No wonder we beat your arses at Culloden."

"Ye won't be beatin' us this time, ye *Sassenach* scrub," Angus said.

"Hand it over." Smith jerked his head at his compatriot. "Search them for other weapons."

Royal unstrapped the blade, and then submitted to an exceedingly rough search, which certainly didn't help the pain radiating down his leg. The thug then did the same to Angus, removing the pistol from the waistband of the old man's breeches.

"Yer the bully boy who gave me the topper, aren't ye?" Angus asked in a conversational tone.

"And a good one, from the looks of your ugly mug," the brute smirked.

"Then I'll be blowin' your brains out before the night is over, I ken," Angus said, rubbing his hands as if anticipating a treat.

Grandda did tend to overplay things, but the thug actually looked a little disconcerted by the cheerful threat.

Smith led the way up the staircase, with the other man following behind, his pistol leveled at their backs. Royal strained to hear sounds from other parts of the house but heard nothing but their own footsteps. He couldn't decide whether that was a good or bad thing.

As they followed Smith down a corridor, Royal sized him up. The man truly was massive, as was his companion. Royal wasn't worried about handling Cringlewood, and he could probably take on Smith, too. But if the other thug stayed in the room, he and Angus would have their hands full. If Logan was delayed, events could swiftly go south.

They stopped outside a door and Smith shot Royal a

warning glance. "Try anything funny, and your missus will suffer for it. I'll see to that myself, if his lordship don't."

Royal's fury, barely under control, flared to life. "Touch my wife and you're a dead man."

"If not for my orders, I'd be doin' more than touchin' her."

"She's a prime article, that one," said the other man with obvious regret.

Royal was torn between a burning desire to rip their heads off and relief that Ainsley was unharmed.

Angus shook his head. "Yer both dead now, lads. Best start saying yer prayers."

"Shut up, you old fool," Smith growled. He rapped on the door, then opened it and shoved them through.

"Remember what I said," he warned.

Royal cast a swift glance around. When he saw Ainsley, huddled in an armchair by the fireplace, clutching her reticule, his heartbeat stuttered. She was still clad in her pelisse and gloves, but her bonnet had disappeared. Her hair had tumbled down from its pins, as if someone had manhandled her.

She dropped her reticule and shot out of her chair with a startled cry. "Royal, my God!"

They met halfway across the room. He swept her into a tight embrace, half lifting her off the floor. She threw her arms around his neck and burrowed close, clinging to him like moss to a tree.

"Royal, I'm sorry. I'm so, so sorry," she choked out.

As relief flooded through his body, his muscles relaxed and his mind started to fully clear, now that he knew she was safe.

He checked her broken litany of apologies. "Hush, love. No more apologies, remember?"

She half swallowed a sob and nodded. But she maintained a deathlike grip on his shoulders.

"He didn't hurt you?" he asked.

"I'm fine, and so is Tira."

"Where is she?"

"Upstairs with a maid. And a guard."

"That's enough, Ainsley," came a haughty voice from behind them. "Not another word. And step away from Kendrick immediately."

Royal turned, still holding Ainsley in a loose embrace. The soldier in him was already taking over, walling off his emotions and helping him to focus on the enemy and the battle ahead.

The marquess stood on the other side of the formally appointed drawing room, looking as if he'd just dropped in for afternoon tea. He gently swung a quizzing glass in one hand. His demeanor was almost languid, as if bored by the scene playing out in front of him.

But his expression gave the lie to that. It was frozen in lines of utter hatred.

"I said, step away, Ainsley," he repeated. "I allowed your good-byes to your erstwhile husband, but that's over now. Do not make the mistake of disobeying me."

She responded with a suggestion that turned Cringlewood's face a bright red. It had Royal mentally blinking that she knew such language.

"Not a particularly helpful suggestion, love," he murmured.

"Sorry," she whispered, "but I've been holding that back for the last two hours. It simply had to come out."

God, he loved her.

The marquess took a hasty step forward. "Ainsley, I order you—"

"You're a bloody idiot, Cringlewood," Royal interrupted. "You kidnapped my wife and my daughter. Step away from this now, or face the consequences."

"Really? What might those be?"

"My brother, Lord Arnprior, will be taking legal action against both you and your men. You attacked my grandfather and abducted a woman and her child at gunpoint. You can't possibly hope to get away with that."

"Nonsense. Tira is my daughter, and her mother voluntarily chose to come rather than be separated from her child. Nothing illegal about any of that."

"You coerced me," Ainsley said. "You left me with no choice."

"You came of your own free will, which I expect you to make clear to Kendrick and then we'll be done with it. My intention is to leave for England tomorrow, taking my daughter with me. If I do so, however, you will never see Tira again. The choice is up to you."

"You'll never separate me from her," Ainsley exclaimed. "No matter what."

Cringlewood flashed a malicious smile. "Then the choice is made. In that case, we will remain in residence here for the obligatory six weeks, and then you can sue your husband for divorce. So, say good-bye to him now, Ainsley. It's the last you'll see of him for some time—possibly forever."

She turned a white, anguished face up to Royal. "Can he really do that? Can he really keep me away from Tira if I don't do what he wants? I can't bear to lose her, not again."

"No one will take her away from us, I promise," Royal replied.

"Kendrick, you are as big a fool as I thought." The marquess glanced at Smith. "Get them out of here, and make sure it hurts."

"I wouldn't, if I were you," Royal said. "The Kendricks have friends in high places. Lady Arnprior, in particular, has a great deal of influence."

The flicker in Cringlewood's gaze told Royal he'd scored a hit. The marquess obviously knew of Victoria's close connection to the royal family.

A moment later, however, he shrugged it off. "I also have connections in high places, Kendrick. And, in case you've forgotten, the law is on my side. Tira is my daughter, not yours."

Ainsley breathed out a tiny, heartbreaking whimper.

"There's another way to handle this," Royal said. "One that doesn't involve dragging in various members of the royal family, which I'm sure would be unpleasant for everyone."

Cringlewood's mouth twitched with displeasure. "I'm losing my patience, Kendrick."

"I challenge you to a duel, right now."

The man's eyebrows shot up. "Pistols? You must be joking."

"No, swords."

"He brung this along." The thug held up Royal's short sword.

The marquess stared at it for a moment, then laughed. "Madness, even for a Scotsman. Why would I bother dueling with you when I have everything I want?"

Royal let go of Ainsley and stepped in front of her. "Because if you don't, I'll hound you to the ends of the earth and destroy your life. My family will destroy your family, and by the time we're through, there will be nothing left of your ridiculous name but bitterness and ashes. And," he said, taking another step forward, "you will never lay hands on my wife again. My wife, never yours."

The marquess glared at him, his complexion mottled with rage as he wavered in silence.

"Ah, you're a coward," Royal said. "But we already know that."

"What do ye expect from a *Sassenach*?" Angus said with a dramatic sigh.

"Give Kendrick back his sword," Cringlewood snapped to Smith's henchman. "And go fetch mine from my luggage. My valet will know where it is."

"What are you doing?" Ainsley hissed, yanking on Royal's sleeve. "Cringlewood is an accomplished fencer, and he doesn't have a bad leg."

"I'm better, even with the limp," he whispered back.

"But he trained with the best Italian masters. He's incredibly good."

"I trained on the battlefield. I'm better."

"But—"

He turned and dropped a quick kiss to the tip of her nose, as he always did when he wished to comfort her. "Love, I know what I'm doing. Please trust me."

She breathed out a funny little growl. "I do, you impossible man. Do you trust me?"

"With my life."

"You should listen to her, Kendrick," the marquess said as he struggled out of his tight-fitting tailcoat. "She knows I'm lethal with the blade."

"You're a braggart, too, I see," Royal said.

He glanced at Angus, who stood near the door under Smith's guard. The old man gave a tiny shake of the head. Royal mentally cursed, since his grandfather had yet to hear any indication from downstairs of their impending rescue.

They waited in fraught silence until the thug returned, carrying a highly ornamented scabbard.

"I suggest you prepare," Cringlewood said as he rolled back his ridiculously frilled cuffs.

Royal turned to his wife. "Please return to your chair, love."

She grimaced. "But I have—"

"Now, Ainsley."

She muttered another earthy curse and stomped back to her chair. She grabbed her reticule and plopped down on the seat, glaring at him.

"That's my girl," Royal said, unable to repress a smile.

The lethal hum of a blade swishing through air had him turning around. Predictably, Cringlewood was warming up with a series of extravagant flourishes and parries, no doubt hoping to frighten him. Royal thought he looked like a bloody ponce, but there was no doubt the man was skilled. The duel would be far from a stroll in the park.

Royal stripped off his coat and rolled up his sleeves.

After Smith directed the other thug to push the chaise and a few chairs out of the way, the combatants moved to the center of the room.

"Good luck, lad," Angus called.

"You'll need it, with that leg of yours," Cringlewood said with a sneer.

Royal brought up his sword. "En garde."

They engaged with a hiss of Sheffield steel, blade sliding on blade. Royal immediately lunged, using the strength in his arm and wrist to push hard, forcing the marquess to fall back. The man recovered with a skillful parry, holding his own against Royal's risky, full-on attack.

His leg wouldn't hold up for long. He had to take Cringlewood out quickly or hope Logan would appear in time to save them.

Even though Royal kept up a fierce pace, Cringlewood was as skilled as he'd boasted. He parried with dexterity, escaping the lethal slide of Royal's blade again and again as their boots alternately pounded with a lunge or slid when they disengaged.

The minutes stretched in a dangerous and swift thrust and parry of steel. Royal's focus narrowed to the tip of the blades and the reach of Cringlewood's arm. The chance of death didn't matter. All that mattered was saving his wife and daughter. If he had to die, so be it.

He blinked sweat from his eyes and saw an opening. Disengaging, he passed his blade under Cringlewood's point and slashed through the man's right sleeve. The marquess cursed and fell back, allowing Royal a few precious moments to catch his breath.

Smith leveled his pistol at Royal, obviously preparing to defend his master if necessary.

"Here, now," barked Angus, turning on the man. "Ye'll not be—"

A thundering crash and a shout from somewhere in the house froze them all in their tracks.

"What the hell was that?" the other thug yelped.

Royal wiped his brow on his sleeve. "You'll see. Best give it up now, Cringlewood."

"One of you, go see what's going on," the marquess ordered.

Smith jerked his head at his henchman, who lumbered out the door. Angus smiled at Royal and casually reached for the top of his boot.

"It's done, Cringlewood," Royal said. "Those are my men. They'll be up here momentarily."

"Too late for you, unfortunately," the marquess snarled.

Cringlewood lunged, and the point of his blade flashed dangerously close to Royal's shoulder, forcing him to twist violently to the side. His thigh muscles cramped, and blazing pain shot up his leg. He stumbled, falling heavily against the chaise.

The marquess let out a breathless laugh and pressed forward, his eyes blazing with triumph. Royal dragged his blade up, trying to block him, but he was exposed. He was . . .

Boom.

Gunshot echoed off the walls.

The marquess jerked, and dropped his blade. He swayed as a red stain bloomed in his shoulder, spreading rapidly.

With a snarl, Smith turned and pointed his weapon at Ainsley. "You bitch!"

But a moment later, Smith let out a startled yell. He staggered forward a few steps before crashing heavily to the floor. The handle of a knife stuck out from his back at a wicked angle, having been neatly slid under his ribs. Smith gurgled and thrashed for a few moments, then lay still.

"You killed him," Cringlewood gasped.

"Aye, looks like it." Angus stooped to retrieve his blade.

Cringlewood's gaze filmed over with shock and astonishment. The color drained from his face as the bloodstain spread from his shoulder down to his chest.

"I suggest you sit down," Royal said as he kicked Cringlewood's sword out of the way.

The marquess staggered around to stare at Ainsley, who was standing by her chair.

"You . . . you shot me," he croaked.

She finally lowered the small pistol. "And I would do it again," she said in a voice that barely trembled at all. "No one hurts the man I love."

"Good for ye, lass," Angus said. "That's a nice little popper ye have there. Where did ye find it?"

"I had it stowed in my reticule. They never thought to search it."

"You goddamn whore," Cringlewood choked out.

Royal grabbed the marquess by the back of his shirt. "That's enough out of you," he said, shoving him onto the chaise.

Cringlewood yelped and collapsed into a half swoon.

Ainsley rushed across the room and threw herself into Royal's arms. "Are you all right?"

He held on as tightly as he could, breathing in the sweet scent of her hair. "I'm fine, my love, thanks to you. You truly saved the damn day."

"As usual." Then she pulled back to anxiously inspect him, and a sob caught in her throat. "I thought he was going to kill you."

"Nay, lass, Royal would have gotten the better of him in the end," Angus said. "Although yer intervention was most timely," he added when Royal stared at him with disbelief.

"Tira's upstairs under guard," Ainsley said. "We need to get up there."

"I've got her," said Logan, striding through the door with a cashmere-swaddled bundle. "All is well."

With a cry, Ainsley hurried over to him, and Logan carefully placed Tira in her arms.

"She slept through the whole thing," he said, "even when I tossed the guard into the wall. The wee lass is a grand sleeper, she is."

"What took you so long?" Royal asked his brother.

"Sorry. Just a spot of trouble in the kitchen with one of the guards, but it's all sorted now."

Ainsley nestled the baby against her chest. "Can we go now, please?" she asked Royal.

"Yes." He nudged Cringlewood with his boot. "Wake up, you idiot."

The marquess roused long enough to glare up at him. "I'll see you hang for this, Kendrick."

"If you ever come near my wife or daughter again, I will slit your throat. I'd gladly hang to protect them, Cringlewood. Don't forget that."

"Royal, time to get a move on," Logan said.

As he passed Smith's body, Royal threw Angus a glance. "Good work, but it's unfortunate you had to kill him."

His grandfather shrugged. "Didn't want to take any chances with the bastard."

"True, but it's thrown a spanner in the works," Logan said as he led them down the hall. "It'll be harder to hush this up with a dead body lying about."

"Och, Nick will handle it," Angus said, not sounding particularly bothered.

When Royal put an arm around Ainsley to guide her down the stairs, she gave him a worried glance. "What's going to happen now? The marquess is sure to send for the magistrate and anyone else he can think of."

"Just watch your step, sweetheart. We didn't go through all this trouble to see you pitch headfirst down the stairs."

"Wretch," she said with a reluctant smile. "*You're* the one who needs to be careful. You hurt your leg, didn't you?"

"It doesn't feel particularly good at the moment, but I'll recover."

"Don't *ever* scare me like that again, Mr. Kendrick."

"I might say the same to you, Mrs. Kendrick."

Henderson was standing by the front door, next to Lady Montgomery's footman.

"Everything all right, Henderson?" Logan asked.

"Yes, sir. The rest of the villains are tied up and locked in the pantry, and I've explained the situation to the butler and the housekeeper. Needless to say, they are extremely perturbed by Lord Cringlewood's gross abuse of Lady Montgomery's hospitality."

"That's one way of putting it," Logan said wryly.

Royal nodded to the footman. "Lord Cringlewood will need a surgeon, and with some urgency. You might want to inform her ladyship's butler."

"But not too quickly," Angus added.

"We don't need another dead body on our hands, Grandda," Royal said.

"I'll take care of it, sir," the footman weakly responded.

Royal escorted Ainsley out to the waiting carriage. Angus climbed in first, then turned to take the baby.

"Henderson can go with you," Logan said. "I'll round up the others and meet you back at the house."

Ainsley put a hand on Logan's arm. "Thank you, sir. I don't know how I'll ever repay you."

He briefly enfolded her in his massive embrace. "Just make that brother of mine happy. That'll be thanks enough."

"I'll do my best," she said with a teary little sniff. "Although I'm clearly a terrible wife."

"Don't be daft." Royal picked her up by the waist and plopped her onto the carriage step. "In with you, now."

Once she was inside, he hauled himself up and settled next to her with a quiet groan.

"Are you sure you're all right?" she asked, twisting to get a good look at him.

His leg was killing him, but he didn't give a tinker's damn. "I've never been better."

"You're lying," she fussed. "We need to get you to a doctor."

He put an arm around her shoulder. "Hush, love. I've got you and Tira back, and that's all that matters. Everything else can wait."

Angus, who'd drawn back Tira's shawl for a quick inspection, gave a satisfied nod. "Aye, and ye both seem fine, thank the good Lord." Then he sniffed. "Although I'm thinkin' the wee one might need a change. She's smellin' a bit ripe."

Ainsley let out a watery laugh. "I didn't have a chance to change her, what with the kidnapping and dueling and such."

"God, Ainsley," Royal said, hugging her close. "I'm so sorry I put you through that. Can you ever forgive me?"

"I'm the one who should be apologizing," she said, her voice muffled against his coat. "I should have told you the truth long ago."

"You did nothing wrong. You were trying to protect your daughter and yourself in the best way you knew how. I was simply too pigheaded to see it."

"Maybe just a little bit," she said. "But I didn't wish to criticize."

"He gets that trait from the Kendrick side of the family," Angus said with a twinkle. "Thick as planks, the lot of them."

"Thank you, Grandda," Royal said dryly.

Then he tipped up Ainsley's chin, drinking in the love he saw in her beautiful violet gaze. "But despite how thick I am, I want you to know that you never have to be afraid again. I will always put you and Tira first, and I will always protect you."

She blinked a few times before leveling him with her dazzling smile, one that lit up every corner of his world.

"My loyal Royal," she whispered. "And I will always protect you, I promise."

"I'm counting on it, lass," he whispered back.

Angus elbowed Henderson, who was pretending to be deaf in his best butler fashion. "Best avert yer eyes, man. The canoodlin' is about to commence."

Chapter Twenty-Six

Dawn fast approached. Their luggage had been stowed, and the deckhands were loading the last of the cargo and provisions onto the ship. Now all Royal had to do was say good-bye to his family and to Scotland.

The Kendrick clan huddled in the fitful light cast by lamps and torches on the pier. Kade, trying hard to be an adult, wiped his eyes on his sleeve and gave Royal a tremulous smile.

"You'll take good care of Grandda, won't you?" the boy asked. "He'll miss us all very much, and he's worried about the Kinglas estate business. He told me he's afraid Nick won't know what to do without him."

Standing behind them, Nick managed to turn his laugh into a cough.

"Of course he'll miss everyone, especially you," Royal said. "But Angus will be busy helping with Tira. Ainsley and I would be lost without him."

Even Kade looked dubious at that assertion. "Truly?"

"Truly. He's helping Ainsley get the baby settled as we speak."

Angus had turned into a wreck at the thought of leaving his family, including his beloved dogs. He'd all but broken down while saying good-bye to Kade, who'd struggled valiantly to hold back tears. The twins had started sniffling, and Victoria looked positively shattered. After the stresses of the last few days, it wasn't a scene Royal or Nick felt equipped to manage.

Fortunately, Ainsley had taken the situation in hand. With a dramatic start, she'd announced that Tira had sneezed, and that she feared a cold coming on. Angus had been instantly diverted, bustling over to inspect his darling, held safely in her mamma's arms. He and Ainsley held a quick discussion and decided to get the baby belowdecks and out of the wind. Grandda had then bustled back to say good-bye to Nick and Logan, clapping them on the back and telling them not to make a cock-up without him. He'd then briskly herded Ainsley and Tira on board the ship with a cheery wave good-bye.

Once more, Royal's splendid wife had averted a crisis.

Kade gave him a wobbly smile. "Tira *is* his favorite. As long as he's got her to look after, he'll be fine."

Royal pulled his little brother in for a hug. "No, you will always be Grandda's favorite," he murmured. "And mine, too. Don't ever forget it."

Kade fiercely hugged him back. "I'm so happy you finally got what you deserved, Royal. You're the best person I know."

"Thank you." He could barely choke out the reply.

He forced himself to let go, and ruffled his little brother's hair. "Look after the others for me. I'll expect reports from home on a regular basis."

Kade nodded. "With every ship."

Royal turned to the twins and to Braden. All three lads were clearly struggling with their emotions. They were tall, strapping young men, but in so many ways still youngsters. He knew they were taking this rushed good-bye very hard.

Sending up a silent prayer of thanks that his brothers had

managed to reach Glasgow before he and Ainsley departed, Royal put an arm around each of the twins and pulled them close.

"Take care of each other, lads," he said gruffly. "And at least try to stay out of trouble."

"We hardly get into trouble anymore." Grant, who'd always been the quieter and more studious twin, looked very serious. "But we'll try even harder. We promise."

"I know. And I'm proud of you both."

"I'm sorry we've been away so much," said Graeme. "If we'd known you were in trouble, we would have returned home immediately."

Of all his brothers, Royal worried most about Graeme. The young man had a restless spirit and an unerring knack for trouble. Still, he had a grand, loving heart and Royal knew the rest of the family would look out for him.

"You have your own life now," Royal said. "Just write to me and let me know what you're up to."

"Logan said we could visit you in the spring," Grant said, cheering up. "We'll go to Halifax with him when he sails in April, and we'll stay for at least six months."

"That will be jolly fun," said Graeme.

"Splendid. Ainsley will be, er, thrilled when I tell her." The idea of the twins let loose in the colonies was appalling.

"I'm sure she'll be delighted," said Victoria with a twinkle.

Braden stepped forward and grasped Royal's shoulder. "Don't worry, Royal. I'll look after the twins."

"But we're older than you—" Graeme started to protest. Grant elbowed him to silence.

Royal had to stifle a smile. Although Braden was the second youngest Kendrick, his bespectacled brother had a gravity and maturity well beyond his years. Everyone in the family took his advice, even Nick.

"Just concentrate on those medical studies of yours," Royal said. "When you get a chance, let me know how you get on."

Braden gave him a tight nod and a quick hug before stepping back to join Kade, protectively resting his hands on his little brother's shoulders.

Royal moved to embrace his sister-in-law. "And you take care of yourself, you grand, beautiful lass. I'll miss you ordering me about."

She let out a laugh that sounded more like a sob, and then gave him a little shake. "Take care of that family of yours, and take care of yourself, too. I won't be happy if I hear from Angus or Ainsley that you're working too hard."

He smiled into her sky-blue eyes. "Thank you, Victoria. Thank you for saving the most stubborn, annoying group of men in Scotland. We were all quite lost until you came into our lives."

"Amen," Nick said softly.

"Drat," Victoria said. "Stop making me cry, Royal Kendrick. You'll give me a headache."

"Yes, your highness," he teased.

"Say good-bye to your brother, and then be off, you dreadful boy." She gave him a little shove in Nick's direction.

This was the hardest leave-taking of all. In so many ways, Nick had always been more father than brother. He'd taught Royal all the things a man should know, and loved him with a fierce, unquestioning devotion. Nick had quite literally saved his life. He was the best man Royal had ever known.

"I'm sorry I'm leaving you with such a mess," he said, clasping Nick's arm.

His brother snorted. "Logan and I can handle Cringlewood and any other little matters that might arise."

Little matters like a dead body in Lady Montgomery's drawing room. Angus was facing a potential murder charge, Royal had taken part in a thoroughly illegal duel, Ainsley had shot a British peer, and they could all very well be charged with abducting that peer's child. Along with Angus, they'd spent the last three days hiding out at a small country inn near the River Clyde until one of Logan's merchant vessels was ready to sail. Nick had already put it about that they'd fled to France. Along with Victoria, he'd also begun exerting considerable legal and social pressure to manage the fraught situation.

Still, there was no doubt it would take months and possibly years to resolve, and much depended on convincing Cringlewood to stand down. Until that happened, who knew when they would see Scotland or England again?

But if anyone could get them home, Nick could.

In the meantime, there were certainly worse things than starting a new life in a new land with the woman you loved and the child of your heart. It was an unfortunate necessity that Angus was also forced to leave his home, but he was growing reconciled to it. As long as he had Tira and a purpose in life—a good part of which constituted bossing Ainsley about—the old fellow should be just fine.

Royal waggled a hand. "Still, we both know it won't be easy. And here I am, running off and leaving you to manage everything. It's not fair, is it?"

His brother took him by the shoulders. "Listen to me, Royal. I am incredibly proud of you. I've always been proud of you. I want you to be well, and I want you to be happy. No one, and I mean no one, has worked harder for happiness or deserves it more. Do you understand me?"

Unable to speak past the boulder clogging his throat, Royal nodded.

Nick pulled him close. "I'm going to miss you, little brother," he said in a hoarse whisper. "More than you can possibly know."

They held on until Logan placed a firm hand on Royal's

shoulder. "I'm sorry, lad, but it's time to go or you'll miss the tide."

Royal was grateful for the intervention. Nick looked entirely gutted, and both Victoria and Kade were now openly crying. Royal felt like his heart was cracking wide open.

Logan extracted a small packet from inside his coat and handed it to him. "Some letters for my son. Give the lad a grand hug for me when you see him, and tell him that Papa will be home in the springtime."

His words had a remarkable effect, freezing the entire family into an astounded tableau.

"You have a son?" Nick finally asked.

Logan scratched the bristles on his cheek. "Oh, I say, did I forget to mention that I have a little boy?"

"Apparently so," Victoria said wryly.

"It just slipped your mind, I suppose," Nick said in a decidedly frosty voice.

"Zeus!" Kade waved his arms. "I have a nephew? What's his name? How old is he?"

Everyone started gabbing at once, although Nick's annoyed tones could be heard over the others.

Logan glanced over his shoulder, his eyes twinkling, and gave Royal a little jerk of the head.

With a salute of thanks to his outrageous but wonderful brother for the distraction, Royal turned and boarded the ship. The gangway was quickly pulled back and seamen began scurrying to and fro, pulling lines and shouting instructions. Royal stood by the rail as the vessel began to slowly drift away from the dock. Logan and Nick were still arguing, Braden was trying to intervene, and the twins were clearly enjoying the verbal debate.

Kade, however, had turned and walked to the end of the pier, his earnest gaze fastened on Royal. Victoria joined him and slipped an arm around the lad's shoulders. As the ship pulled into the channel leading to the firth, they both raised their hands in farewell.

Royal swallowed his tears and waved back.

A brisk click of heels on the deck sounded behind him before Ainsley slipped her hand through the crook of his arm.

"Goodness," she said, peering back at the docks. "You Kendricks certainly are an emotional lot."

He smiled down at her. "Highlanders like to do everything with a certain dramatic flair."

"I've noticed. What are your brothers arguing about? I can hear them shouting even out here."

"As I was getting ready to board, Logan casually mentioned that he had a son. The announcement had the desired effect."

"Jolly good of him to do that for you. By the way, I just shared the same distraction with your grandfather. He was getting entirely too emotional thinking about Kade and the dogs."

Royal had told Ainsley about his brother's secret a few days ago, although he'd sworn her to silence until their departure. "How did he take it?"

"He was too astonished to say a word for a full six minutes. I timed it."

He laughed. "Perhaps we can come up with other shocking announcements when necessary."

"It could be the one way to preserve our sanity. The notion of being cooped up with Angus for several weeks is rather daunting."

He pulled her close as the sails unfurled and the ship moved farther away from shore. "Oh, I'm sure we can think of other ways to entertain ourselves."

"You shock me, dear sir."

"I hope so, dear madam."

She flashed a grin before snuggling into his arms to keep watch with him. The figures on the pier receded into the distance until finally disappearing in the haze of the early morning fog over the water.

Still, Royal couldn't bring himself to go below deck. He needed this last taste of Scotland. He needed the rugged cliffs where Loch Long, the loch he'd grown up on, emptied into the River Clyde. He needed the early snows that glinted off the high peaks in the distance, the peaks he'd climbed as a youth with his brothers. He needed the gannets and the cormorants wheeling overhead, and the comical puffins burrowing in the cliffs. Even the seals came to bid him farewell, flashing by the ship and heading for the heart of the firth.

Royal needed to engrave those images in his heart for the months or years to come. Ainsley seemed to understand, keeping silent watch with him as his beloved homeland slipped away.

Finally, she stirred. "I know you'll miss it terribly, and I'm truly sorry about that."

"We'll be back someday."

"I hope so. It'll be quite the challenge to make that possible, even for your brother."

"True, but don't forget he's got a secret weapon."

She lifted an enquiring eyebrow.

"Victoria," he said. "My sister-in-law will storm Carlton House, if she has to. The Prince Regent won't stand a chance once she starts giving him a piece of her mind."

"But Victoria has never even met her father, has she?"

"She won't let that stand in her way."

Her eyes briefly crinkled with laughter. "Still, I think it will take some time and doing."

"Yes," he admitted. "In the meantime, we're off on a grand adventure, are we not? Think of all the fun we're going to have—you, me, Tira, and Angus. We can go sledding and ice skating in the winter, and Logan said we might even see a moose."

"That sounds utterly dreadful." She shook her head. "Nova Scotia, of all places. I used to hate setting foot outside of London, and now I'm off to the colonies."

He hooked an arm around her neck and pulled her in for a lingering kiss. "You'll conquer the colonials, just like you conquered the Scots, love."

"God knows I tried." Then she placed her hands on his chest and turned serious. "But it doesn't matter where we go as long as we're all together. Thank you, my dearest love, for giving my life back to me."

"Ainsley, you did that when you had the courage to come back to us. You rescued yourself. And in doing so, you rescued me and Tira, too."

"I love you, Royal Kendrick," she said in a gruff little voice.

"I love you, Ainsley Kendrick."

He bent to kiss her again, but stopped when the wind from the stiffening breeze snatched the hat right off her head and whipped it out over the water.

"Drat," she sighed. "That was a new hat, too."

"I'll buy you a better one when we get to Halifax."

"Yes, I'm sure they'll have *all* the latest fashions," she said wryly.

With a laugh, Royal took her arm and steered her toward their cabin. The sun rose at their backs, transforming the water into a sparkling mirror that lit up their way to the future.